To My

Beloved Richie

To My

Beloved Richie

Rebekah Tyne McKamie

Settings Publishing
Calhan, CO

Painting for Cover Art by Niki Wyneken. Used by permission. Copyright © 2017.

Cover Design by Settings Publishing. Copyright © 2017.

Scripture taken from the New King James Version®. Copyright © 1982 by Thomas Nelson. Used by Permission. All rights reserved.

Settings Publishing

ISBN: 978-0-692-88744-8

Settings Publishing and the "S" logo are trademarks of Settings Publishing.

Printed in the United States of America.

for Momma

"As far as the east is from the west, So far has
He removed our transgressions from us."

Psalms 103:12

"Darian!" A familiar lament. "Please hurry, buddy. We're going to be late for Sunday school again."

"I'm sorry, Mommy." I experience these three words in the form of a still, quiet voice. No further excuses.

The tiny boy appears at the top of the stairs in a perfect suit with a clip-on tie. In one hand, he carries a Bible on which his name is embossed in gold. With the other, he uses the handrail to guide him in case his glasses fail.

We'll be late for church. So late. But he needn't apologize. My anxieties are overcome at the sound of Darian's voice.

I hold the seven-year-old's hand because the driveway is slick from last night's unexpected snowfall.

"Happy Birthday, sweetheart." I offer gently. He looks up at me and does not respond. The radiant innocence of his smile speaks instead.

My husband is waiting with quiet impatience in a weathered, but reliable, white vehicle. So is Robbie, whose hair is parted to the side, just how he hates it, and Mia, who is yawning in her purple dress. Robbie frowns and exits the vehicle to allow his little brother to sit atop the booster in the middle of the back seat.

"He always does this," the twelve-year-old's complaint materializes in the air as a wisp of white steam.

"He always looks nice for church," I defend, looking up into my son's mossy green eyes. I gesture for him to enter the car after his brother.

I hurry around to the passenger seat to escape the cold on my bare calves and encounter eyebrows of inquisitive frustration on my husband's face.

"It's his birthday," I respond so the chattering, crammed-in children cannot hear. My husband rolls his eyes and sighs before he smiles and puts the car into drive.

When we arrive at church, I send Mia into her classroom while Robbie waves as he jogs to his. My husband, Darian, and I enter a class full of first graders and a flustered woman from the information desk attempting to round them up.

"I'm so sorry, Ruth," I plead. She nods forgivingly and exits the classroom.

Darian seeks Olivia, his favorite cousin. My husband finds the dry erase markers, and I find the coloring sheets.

"Aunt Paige, can I pass them out today?" Olivia yells from the far corner.

"If you promise not to chase boys today."

"I promise." She giggles.

When my better half prompts, the children are seated. Olivia hands each child a copied sheet of paper. Upon each sheet is a simple cartoon of a man who appears to be glowing. He is sitting at a table with two other men. A woman is sitting at the glowing man's feet. I am silent as my husband tells the familiar story in six- and seven-year-old terms.

"The woman was a sinner. She cried and washed Jesus's feet with her tears and her hair and kissed them. The men didn't understand why Jesus had let such a sinner wash His feet. But those men hadn't even given Jesus water for His feet. This woman loved Jesus so much that she used her own tears."

"Ew! Why would someone want to wash someone else's feet?" The beautiful blonde-haired and caramel-skinned Olivia is infamous for talking out of turn. We often joke that she has a preacher's kid complex already budding.

"Well, back then, people's feet got very dirty because they wore sandals and walked everywhere. When someone would invite guests to their house, they would give them water and have a servant wash their feet. But when this woman washed Jesus's feet, it wasn't just to clean them. It was a symbol that she loved Him and wanted to serve Him completely." My husband chooses this moment to wink at me from the front of the classroom.

"Well, those men were angry. What did Jesus do? Was He mean too?" Olivia again.

"He forgave her sins," says the handsome teacher. "He told her to go in peace because her faith had saved her."

When it is time to pass out the snack, I announce that it is Darian's birthday and that we will have mini-cupcakes to celebrate. Darian assists me in making sure each of his classmates has a cupcake perfectly centered on his or her napkin. It seems he has forgotten about himself, as usual, so I put one in his place. He then takes his seat and folds his hands with the rest of the children.

"God is great, God is good, and we thank Him for our food. Amen!" The chorus of young voices eagerly ends the prayer to consume the special treats they have received. But Darian sits quietly with his head down. I drop to a crouch at his side.

"What's the matter?" I whisper.

"Can I have one too?" The innocence of his tone severs my heart. I have forgotten that Darian is so conscious of his blood sugar.

"Of course, Buddy. The cupcakes are for *your* birthday. So today, you can have one."

He looks up at me and smiles, procuring a tiny speck of icing with his finger and carefully placing it onto his tongue.

During the car ride home, we hear all about Mia's fifth-grade version of the same story we had taught. Same passage, just much more in-depth, as our Senior Pastor desires of the fellowship. Robbie sees it necessary to remind his sister of this, which she ignores. Darian sits smiling, looking out the window at the falling snow. He is still elated that he got to eat a real cupcake—icing, sprinkles, and all.

As we enter the house, Robbie hurries to his room to finish some homework. Mia gathers painting materials and sits at the dining room table with Darian.

"Newspaper," I remind her gently.

"Oops, almost forgot." She finds the classifieds in the stack that her Daddy hasn't picked up yet. He is sitting in his chair, reading the front page. I go upstairs to finish wrapping Darian's wished for train set.

When I return to the corner of the couch closest to my husband's chair, he clears his throat and nods at the children sitting ten feet away at the table.

"Don't look, Darian," Mia says, attempting to cover her painting with one arm and complete it with the other. Darian elongates his neck to see what his eyes won't allow him either way. When Mia looks up, they both giggle. My husband and I share in admiration of our children—the impossible blessings. Then we look at each other, still in awe at God's hand all these years.

"You're looking like an old man over here, Boss. No one reads the Sunday paper anymore. You need some glasses?" He wears a tattered t-shirt and begins squinting to see the tiny words on the newspaper he's holding.

"So, does that make you my old lady, then?" My husband shoots me a mischievous grin and a wink.

After dinner, I clear the table as my family sits, awaiting the inevitable. I bring out the cake, and my husband runs upstairs for Darian's presents. When he returns, he shuts off the lights, and the candles illuminate my little boy's sweet face. The blond hair of unknown origin. The green eyes of unquestionable source. He closes his eyes, and it takes him two breaths to blow out the seven candles.

"Is the cake sugar-free?" Mia whines.

"I'm sorry," Darian's head drops.

"Don't make him feel bad, Mia. It isn't his fault." Robbie is as protective as he is bull-headed. Just like his dad.

Robbie's defense shows Mia her flaw. "It's okay. It's still yummy."

Darian loves the train we bought him, and Mia proudly hands him a painting of a little boy with big glasses riding an elephant. As expected from my daughter, the painting could easily be mistaken for that of a young professional. Darian is reminded of something when he sees it.

"Mommy, I made you a picture!" He hops out of his seat and runs to the coffee table, where his now-dry painting has been transported. He runs and gives it to me with a smile.

"It's us at my birthday party!"

In a mess of a little boy's painting, there is still remarkable detail, and he's included everyone that had been at his party yesterday. His grandfathers. Uncle. Cousins. And, of course, his auburn-haired sister and frowning preteen brother. Copper the cat. And a precious little boy in glasses sandwiched between his parents. They are all recognizable, the blobs of paint—all, that is, except for one man off to the side. This unknown man has yellow hair and red eyes. He is frowning bigger than the preteen boy.

"Who is this?" Though I'm not sure I actually want to know.

He frowns. I worry. "The phone man. From out the window." His eyes will not meet mine for a moment. And then, as if he has forgotten the picture altogether, he smiles at me once again.

"Robbie, please clear the table. Darian, why don't you go upstairs and set up your train?"

"Okay, Mommy."

"I'll help!" My little girl is oblivious to all the bad in the world.

"You don't think. . ." My husband inquires as he examines the anomaly in the painting.

"You know his imagination," I offer, remaining safely in my denial. Neither of us is willing to acknowledge the unpainted elephant in the room.

My children have been sweetly dreaming for over an hour. I lie awake next to my sleeping husband and convince myself that I am staring at the ceiling in peace. A customary tear falls that I barely invite. Then I hear a sound. The cat, demanding entrance into the back door, I suppose. I descend the stairs that divide the living and dining rooms.

I see the orange cat cross the bottom step with a leap of my heart. A flash of cold air crosses with him as I hear the sliding door quietly meet its closure.

I search for comfort. My frantic heart tries to remember a door opening in the hall before I got out of bed upstairs. To replicate the normalcy that would be a twelve-year-old walking about in the night. Perhaps a thirsty child. No such memory. I freeze in my spot, halfway down and halfway up the stairs.

Summon my great protector from our bed? No. I'll be heard, and the children might awaken. I remember the baseball bat that was left carelessly near the bottom of the stairs. My bare left foot moves one more step toward the cold wooden floor below.

But he has beaten me to the bottom of the stairs. I hear what must be boots against that hard floor. My mind is in shock and can only consider the mud that will need to be cleaned up. I hate myself for having illuminated the hall before heading downstairs. I have no cover of darkness.

I want to be ignorant to who or what may be prowling just a few steps from my sight. But my memory will not allow it. It is him. He has found me. I want to see my son downstairs. Or a random criminal that will strike me down and steal my worldly possessions. But I see what my heart has truly feared. He turns to face me as he reaches the bottom of the stairs.

"Hey, Paige." The tenor voice is filled with charm. The blond hair is wild. He has taken no care to dress in black to conceal his intrusion from the night. Except, that is, for the same black combat boots I fearfully remember. He is removing his tattered coat as if arriving home. His eyes are wide and bloodshot.

"Jake." The name escapes my lips only to precede the inaudible hiccup.

"You were hard to find. I didn't expect the name change." He hangs his coat next to my husband's on the rack, through a stumble. I have no need to smell the alcohol, but my nose catches it, regardless.

"What are you doing here?" My whispered words become frantic.

"Come sit with me, baby. Your man is asleep, right?" He collapses onto my husband's beloved chair and taps his thigh twice with one hand.

"My *husband* is not your concern. Get out of my house, Jake." The courage is not my own.

"Watch how you talk to me." His words are slurred, and he points at me with sudden and abrupt anger I'd almost forgotten. I am startled at his tone and worry about his volume and precious ears above. I falter and glance up the stairs. He sees.

"Mmmm, how many?" He is intrigued. I descend to the bottom stair so that perhaps he will lower his voice in response.

"How many what?" I try ignorance and fail.

"I saw one peek out the window at me yesterday during that party you were having. Bet you'd do anything to protect them, huh? But you remember what I said, don't you?" He rises and walks far too close to me, yet he is still five feet away. When I see his eyes, I do the math. He's thirty-seven now, but his eyes have aged far beyond that.

"We're already calling the police in the morning because of your phone calls. But if you don't leave now, I will call them tonight." I speak with level-headed clarity as I move toward the baseball bat that is now in my sight. He sees this too.

I hear the unmistakable clicks before my eyes return to him.

"That won't be necessary, baby."

I suppose the weapon is a revolver when the click reminds me of my husband's favorite firearm. I have replayed this scenario in my mind a thousand times and hope that the bullet will come soon and that he will exit just as quickly.

Lord, preserve my children's lives.

"Mommy?" A voice that would otherwise soothe has chilled my blood to a halt. I see my youngest son's tiny frame against the light of the hall upstairs. My heart pounds violently in my ears as I see Jake's gaze quickly shift to the stairs.

"Jake, please," I hear the quivering uncertainty of my own voice, "Darian, why aren't you in bed?" Though it comes in just an earnest squeak, I have never been so angry with my youngest child. Never Darian.

"Darian," The man is looking into my fear-filled eyes. "Darian?" He glances again at my son.

"Jake, just go. I'll forget you were ever here. I'm begging you." My tears have escaped the stronghold of my broken soul.

"You beg from your knees." Jake's tears flow, but the weapon in his shaking hand is set on my face as I lower my body to the ground.

I am sobbing—something Darian has not seen me do. I know his life will be changed as a result of watching his mother die just feet from him. Something I protected my children from their whole lives. Something I know I deserve but have always hoped to the contrary.

I hear Darian's sniffles. I know he is stunned upon the stairs. I am crying. Jake is crying. Yet, there is a painful silence in what I perceive to be my last moments. Helplessly kneeling on the cold floor, I watch the tears fall on a muddy boot print. And with some supernatural compassion, I remember a promise I made what seems like a lifetime ago. With courage that fights against every tensed muscle in my body, I fulfill that promise, though it is literally the last thing I'll ever do. I release a shaking and insecure peep of a voice. I know that any voice will suffice if I can only conjure the words.

"Jake. . .I forgive you." And with more confidence and less of a squeak, I say it again past the pistol, into the cold eyes. "I *forgive* you, Jake. For whatever happens tonight and everything that happened before. I am giving up my right to be angry with you. And I'm *sorry* for ever hurting you. I'm so sorry, Jake."

"Shut up," he says, shaking. His teeth are gritted, and tears released over dark circles and pale, tattered skin.

I whisper with sobbing compassion. "My *God,* Jake, you must be in *so* much pain, and I know a lot of that is my fault." I clear my throat and come back to confidence. "But I hope you can somehow, *someday* forgive me too because neither of us deserves it. But Jesus died for us and forgave us anyway. The least we can do is give one another. . .*grace*."

Jake lowers the weapon. I am relieved. He is in tears, and my heart shatters for him—for pain I never considered was his to bear. His tears are sorrowful, then suddenly bitter. And then unsettling laughter joins his twisted thoughts. I hear the disturbed blond man inhale hastily in preparation for words.

"He should have been *mine!*" The tormented tone precedes a weapon that moves quickly to his left, up the stairs. I have only the time to scream some incomprehensible word just before I become deaf at the gunshot.

I rise to run to my son, who has crumpled at the top of the stairs. No fear in all my imagining. Never such defeat. Until fire penetrates my back and I am falling backward down the stairs. I feel it all as I tumble down. And yet, I am numb.

I am at the foot of the stairs, and my vision is darkening as I see the gun turn into the mouth of a tortured man. I am aware of all the world as I close my eyes. My ears are falling away as I hear, at a deafened distance, the shouts, the gunshots, the frantic footsteps. And then I am only aware of the darkness I thought I'd hidden long ago.

Part 1

The Affliction

"Look on my affliction and my pain, And forgive all my sins."

Psalms 25:18

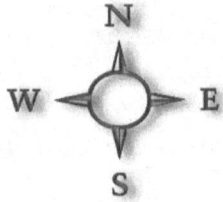

I awaken to quiet. A warm and musty silence. I open my eyes, and I'm surprised by my surroundings. I'm curled up in a wooded shadow, back against a tree. I have been crying in bitterness, as I often do. Dreaming, I suppose.

A log lay gently across a shallow trench to my right. I take joy in the simplicity. The log is old, and there is evidence of a long life that ended with this elegant display. I hope my funeral someday is graced with such a story of triumphant simplicity. But perhaps I am dead now, and that funeral will happen prematurely.

My ears awaken, and I hear a creek nearby. I wipe away tears and try to listen for its direction. To my left is a tree in its prime, choking a sapling with its strength. I don't know why, but this image disturbs me.

It is midmorning, and the fading dew still enables a comforting fragrance. A beam of light escapes into the shaded woods, illuminating a mist, or dust. I cannot tell which. Either one is equally mysterious. Equally alluring.

Chapter 1

Typical

I was fifteen. Especially aware of my youth that day. I gazed into a mirror at my vast and alluring emeralds of eyes. Freckles that might have reflected my youth were combated by high cheekbones and a gentle but slender jawline, soft skin, and lips that were just pouty enough.

The world seemed mine to manipulate as I placed the ribbons in my hair. They decorated the bright ginger locks that flowed freely from the ponytail atop my head, my hair relenting only at the small of my back. I smiled at the image in the mirror before brushing my teeth, which never needed the aid of braces. They all told me I was beautiful. That day, I believed them.

I almost lost the homecoming high as I saw the tarnished compass on the bathroom counter. Out of place in any setting, really. I placed the burden of a compass in my purse that day, hiding it from sight, unable to bear it but unwilling to part with it. Nevertheless, I refused to be reminded that my beauty and excitement were a thin mask for the secrets beneath those overcast eyes.

I paraded down the stairs in a skirt my father silently disapproved of. But he had no control over the chosen cheer squad uniform or any other part of me—nor did he try to. A boy wearing a football jersey met me at the door just before we were expected to arrive at the homecoming bonfire.

Aaron was handsome, with eyes that hid in the night. He was charming and respectful to my father. We said goodbye in our counterfeit innocence and bounced to the beat-up old car, of which I didn't care to know the make and model.

As I cheered, he walked around the bonfire in the superficial glory of a teenaged quarterback. We talked with people we liked to label as "friends," and someone began passing around a bottle. My lips were tainted by many passes, and after a while, I stopped feeling the searing sensation in my esophagus that reminded me of my delinquency.

She was blurry at best, but I saw the beautiful Pacific Islander with thick curls. She approached with a friend on each side of her. Deidre had a look of determination on her face, and Emma and Marley were distraught that their pack leader had led them in my direction. Emma had loose dark curls and stark blue eyes. Marley was the third brunette, with short flat hair and simple eyes and mind. But it wasn't their names that came to mind first.

Christians. I cursed in twice as many necessary syllables in my foggy mind.

"Are you seriously *drunk*? Do you have any idea what God thinks of what you're doing? You never know when you'll step into eternity. If you did it today, you'd go to hell, just so you know. Typical cheerleader, huh?" Deidre used her haughty laughter to egg on her friends.

Even severely inebriated, the words stung me. It was a bit late, I thought, to be told that God hated me. I didn't respond except by searching the field with my eyes for Aaron. He arrived at my side and kissed me with drunken fervor in front of the girls.

"She's totally gonna end up pregnant." Marley's IQ was about half mine on a clever day for her. But hopelessness is of the spirit, not the mind. She walked away from the situation, mostly for her own comfort.

"Too bad your God didn't give you a brain!" Aaron laughed with me at the juvenile comment I yelled after Marley. I was indeed a juvenile, not seeking greater things as those self-important Christian girls did.

"I don't know why I bother reaching out. Look at her. All that beauty and brains just wasted on *nothing*." Deidre rolled her eyes and walked off with a heart-wrenching level of confidence in her wrathful and unforgiving God. Good for her. Who would want to be in Heaven if it is filled with people like Dee Martin? Emma remained. In all the focus I could find amid the alcohol, I braced myself against further ridicule. They assumed I was hardened. But I was simply done trying to please anyone but myself. I was all I could count on. Yet even a mirror was my greatest foe.

"I saw a teacher walking around pretending to be a student, trying to catch people with contraband. I'd make it disappear or be careful. I'm not judging. I just. . .you could get expelled, Paige. I heard you're up for valedictorian in a couple years. Please consider that." Emma's pleading tone was laced with genuine kindness. But she chose the wrong order in which to speak out.

She was merely warning me. But since I was all I thought I'd ever be, and since I could clearly see she was much more, I hated her. So, when I was passed the vodka at that opportune moment, I gave her the cruelest of words in the presence of the most popular students in school. I told her she was right. I should get rid of the "contraband." And I poured the remainder of the bottle on her—down the front of what I hoped wasn't an expensive top.

She stood in silence and allowed the attack. She was scorned then by a dozen drunken voices. And she simply looked down into my eyes with compassion. My laughter ceased, though no one heard. With one gigantic streaking tear, Emma nodded graciously—only to me—just before she backed away.

It hurt. Of *course*, it hurt. Everything hurt. Emma had never harmed anyone. Ever. We were friends in younger days. The pain was practically physical, and I knew I couldn't pretend my way out of it. I left the bonfire with Aaron and removed my heart from the circumstances the only way I knew how.

Aaron thought I loved him. He pointed to me after he scored the winning touchdown the following afternoon. He thought we were living some teenage American dream, whatever his perception of that was. He was not the first to think it. I cheered innocently to the rejoicing crowd that day. My soul cried out in emptiness.

I wore a tiny black dress and red heels to the homecoming dance. Aaron's hands wandered all evening. I received again, in that tiny car, my drug of choice. But after the numb, there was always more pain. I somehow forgot that each time.

I arrived back at my quiet house to both relief and regret. My father was asleep. I ignored the pain and responded to the numb I thought I'd achieved with a familiar ritual. I got on my hands and knees in another drunken fog and scrubbed the kitchen floor until it sparkled. Obsessive, some might have thought. But if I died the following day, I wanted my father at least to be able to say his daughter served him.

I climbed the stairs to my room when the hours had begun again and buried my face in my pillow. My father didn't awaken to the pungent cleaner on the kitchen floor. And he never heard the sobs.

There is only peace. An easy tranquility that people chase after all their lives and dread leaving when they find it. And I hate the peace. It mocks my pain. Another tear falls, and I rise in search of a distant stream my ears only hear in an echo.

I attempt to awaken, but there is only darkness. I panic that I feel each of my limbs with great pain, but they will not move at my command. My eyelids refuse to part ways. I scream into the darkness with every molecule of strength and passion. But the sound is lost in my own mind. It only manifests as a methodic beeping that increases in frequency each time I cry out. I become weary and give in to the darkness to regain my strength.

Chapter 2

Him

I fashioned my lifeless orange locks into a French braid on Monday morning. Some days I felt full of life. That Monday, I trudged downstairs, hating every step my scrawny legs descended. Aaron was at the door with a rose. I hated the rose and its beauty. I hated the fragrance and myself for wanting the privilege of its joy. I smiled at Aaron. I hated him too, for admiring only what he saw.

My father told me to have a good day at school. But what was a good day? What could fill the void in my soul? The void my father would have me fill with good grades and a successful career. Good grades, I gave him with ease. But why was that all he asked? The middle-aged man was oblivious to how shamefully I tried to fill the void. He accepted the lie that was an immaculate house as the true character of his only child. His pale green eyes couldn't see the bars he constructed by allowing me those wings.

I exited my first-period class, and a dangerously handsome senior was waiting for me. His dirtied platinum locks were intentionally unruly and grown below his chin. His blue eyes were cold but magnificent. This second-year senior had a reputation. He left for weeks at a time for suspensions. He had destroyed the reputations of many a naive girl. The thought of this should have turned me away. But once Jake Stone's eyes were trained on me, I was in ecstasy.

"Paige, right? I saw you at the bonfire." One of his thumbs curled to catch the edge of his front pocket.

"You and several hundred other people." I turned my eyes away after the bold sarcasm, but my feet stayed planted two feet from him.

I was the only sophomore varsity cheerleader. A status from which I drew no pride, except that which attracted unsuspecting boys. This senior was different. He intended to woo me without my prior manipulation.

"I didn't see them. I saw *you*." He unabashedly moved his hand to my face and tucked a wandering hair behind my ear. My eyes closed in approval, but I pulled my head away.

"I have a boyfriend," I said to the gum-infested carpet of my high school. I was intrigued by the combat boots adorning his feet. Therefore, the declaration was less of a defense than a challenge.

"I know. Like I said, I saw you." I panicked, remembering booze and kisses and shame. But there was a rugged sort of charm about this boy that was already starting to win me over much faster than the single rose in my locker. The argument with it was just powerful enough to make me think. "You don't know what you're missing."

He accepted my challenge by removing my phone from my back pocket and inputting his number. Then he invited me to use the number with a whisper that rasped against my ear. As his final gesture, he slowly placed my phone back in my snug jeans as he walked away.

He had me addicted. A girl with any sense would have treated him like the disease he was for the remainder of his high school career, however long that could have been. A girl with any standards would have had her quarterback boyfriend beat the snot out of him for touching me. A girl with any class would have reported the eighteen-year-old senior for sexual harassment. But I was worthless. Nothing. I had no class, no standards. Except that I wouldn't dare miss out on an opportunity.

I saw Aaron walking toward me after school. I handed him back his rose with a note attached.

It's over. I'm sorry. I don't deserve you.

Aaron called me that Monday night, begging me for another chance. But he never had a chance to begin with. I turned sixteen on Friday. After a few days of text messages, I spent the evening in a filthy motel room between two sheets with a blond senior by the name of Jake Stone. I only wanted to test the waters of wild. But Jake told me I was *his*, which I didn't quite understand at the time. Still, I was thrilled at the arrangement. With Jake, the pain was duller. The void, less noticeable. And yet I cried again, into a pillow that could not hear.

I take in the tranquility of the woods as I set my feet beneath me. The lingering dew smells sweeter. My pain is slightly dulled when I am standing on my own. The ache in my soul is deeper and farther from the front of my mind.

I remember now being told to stay by the stream. But the water that trickles in the distance no longer concerns me. I need not return to it to bask in the humid darkness of these woods. I don't feel as alive, but I am yet renewed. I see a shimmer in the opposite direction of the unseen rushing water.

The glisten is small, and I assume it is most likely something attached to a person. Another human life might be comforting. I look once more at the beam of light with the promise of a flowing stream. Then I turn and move my feet in the direction of a tiny glimmer that promises nothing but a cooler, darker wood. What is the use of water when my skin can be cooled beneath the dark trees?

I am calm and still, even in knowing my legs might have failed me. The irritating beep continues but slows. I am soothed by the darkness. The cold. I reject the muffled voices as a figment of truth in the dark world I've chosen.

Chapter 3

Fog

"I don't know, Jake. Isn't this a little dangerous?" He was unmoved by the subtle plea.

"That makes it even better." The eighteen-year-old boy was pleased to celebrate New Year's Day. He planned to do so with the tiny yellow pill in his hand. "Come on, baby. You won't even care in a minute, trust me."

I trusted him. I trusted him with my life, as I had for months by then. He protected my name and my pride, though usually by keeping them tarnished. He kept me from anyone else. I was flattered. I was afraid. I thought I was in love. I trusted him still as he placed the pill on his tongue and then kissed me to transfer it. The pill was bitter as it began to dissolve in my mouth. I regretted the decision to trust and swallow the pill.

He paused for a moment to put a second pill in his mouth. He took it with a swig of beer and then handed me the can to wash down my own pill. Vomit itself would be a far better drink than beer. Jake drank it often. I pretended not to care about the way it tasted within his kisses.

"Is this safe?" I asked as I was blinking, attempting to bring my pink bedside lamp into focus.

My question was ignored.

I hated and loved the overwhelming fog that came over me. I heard my father thundering up the stairs, though I knew he was an hour away at his beloved cabin. I had to cover my ears for the sound. I realized I may have been hearing my pounding heart, especially as Jake Stone put his arms around me. I didn't know why the light from my bedside lamp danced on the ceiling so. But Jake stopped my wondering.

That night, I experienced some version of paradise. Nothing changed, but I saw a place with no pain. A place where my father stayed in town for holidays because my mother never left. A place where he looked at me instead of giving me a blank check. Numbness usually worked for a time, but that was pure bliss and painlessness. The light was dancing. My heart was pounding.

I lost time. Jake was on my bedroom floor doing pushups in a puddle of sweat. I wondered how long I had been staring at my own troubled face in the mirror on my vanity. I was sitting on my bed in an old cheer uniform. I stood and began to laugh and jump on my bed like a child, propelled by some unknown force to keep moving. My heart started to pound out of control, bringing me to my knees in breathlessness and dizziness. It took Jake a moment to notice I was ailing.

"What did you give me?" I asked after he lifted me effortlessly onto my bed and handed me a bottle of water. I suddenly remembered running downstairs and retrieving it about an hour before.

"Would you quit asking that?" Jake was annoyed and out of breath from incessant pushups. He was often short with me.

"I'm sorry. I don't feel right. I need to throw up." I bolted for my private bathroom and fulfilled my prediction in the toilet. Jake rushed in after me and placed his hand on my neck. I caught only a flicker of his panic-stricken face. He lunged past me and turned on the faucet. My eyes focused again in just enough time to see that he had only engaged the right handle.

"Cold," I barely murmured before falling in a heap onto the tile floor.

I couldn't will my limbs to move. Arms bearing superhuman strength nearly tossed my limp form into the cold tub. I watched helplessly as the son of a nurse tore apart my medicine cabinet and produced two, much safer, bitter white pills. I nearly choked as water was poured into my parted lips.

"Swallow, damn it!" I heard in an echo as I felt myself drift away.

I awoke in the same position, shivering violently, ice-cold water pouring repeatedly over the back of my cheer uniform. The goosebumps stung against the unforgiving fabric.

"Paige! There you are! You scared the daylights out of me! I told you not to run up and down the stairs so many times. You were at a hundred and five." I had never seen such fear in his eyes. I was grateful for the hero I saw in him. Perhaps he had saved me out of love.

"One-oh-five? Wow." I was dazed but understood why I felt so sick. "I told you it was dangerous."

"But it was worth it, right? That was crazy."

"Yeah, I guess." My memory of probably a couple hours was patchy. I remembered why I was given the pill in the first place. My euphoria, I decided, was not worth nearly dying for. What cruel irony. I longed for death but couldn't find its justification.

Crueler still was the light that filled my bedroom, revealing to me the headache with the morning. My fatigue and nausea adhered me to my pillow when panic should have entered, knowing my father would be home soon. I was alone, but evidence of delinquency littered my normally immaculate room. I chose to drift back into painless sleep and clean up later.

Asleep, or at least mostly, I basked in the comfort of the sunlight and the tingle of what seemed to be fingers gently meddling the entire waist length of my crimson hair.

"Jake?" I asked groggily.

My eyes couldn't accept the light to open them. But I perceived the gentle comfort as my imagination when there was no answer. Even imagined, it was a better paradise. And I drifted away, almost hearing with tainted ears whispered words I didn't understand.

"Lord in Heaven, bring my Sweet Pea home."

I stop to assess my position in the woods. I know I have been walking aimlessly for too long, when even as I turn back, I see only darkness. No sign of the flicker of light I had followed. No sound of trickling water.

I smell musty leaves about me and a few crunch under my feet. I am puzzled, perceiving that the warm light near the stream had been from summer. When did I arrive in autumn? I shiver with cold.

I am lost. The incessant beeping quickens as I turn in every direction. I panic. I look for a sign. I see darkness. I listen for a stream. I hear the deafening beep.

Chapter 4

Cold

I was bitter with cold as I passed the block of buildings in ten-degree weather. A diner. A police station. A gigantic church building behind an empty parking lot. I rushed into my school after the mile walk, angry that everyone in that church was so warm. Jake told me he'd pick me up but decided to sleep in instead. I was late for school. Another source of self-loathing against my type A nature.

When I arrived at my locker, I met a cruel coincidence. It was Daniel. Tall and lanky. He wore a letter jacket that I knew to cover a basketball he'd tattooed on his arm with my encouragement and a fake ID. Daniel was Aaron's best friend. That day, we were late together.

"Hey." Daniel only momentarily raised his eyes to meet mine. I glanced at him in response and knew he was going to speak again. "Look, Paige. I want you to know that I get it. I get you dumping me for Aaron. I also get you dumping Aaron. Nothing lasts forever. But for *Jake Stone?* You deserve better."

I laughed once. Within the laughter, there was pain. If only he knew how little I truly deserved. How badly I wanted to feel like I was on his level. I laughed to conceal the sob over the cheer uniform Jake disliked, so I didn't try out for basketball season. Oh, to have a friend to stick up for me, like Daniel did for Aaron. I laughed to think that Aaron thought I ended it because of anything *he* did or didn't do. What I would have given for a ride to school in that car where I robbed his innocence.

"I know I'm going to sound like a teacher or something. But that dude is really bad. I just don't want you to get—" Daniel's voice stopped suddenly, and I heard the door close to my left with a gust of frigid air.

"What the hell do you have to say to my girl, jockstrap?" A voice I loved. A tone I hated.

His wild blond waves advanced quickly to the boy in the letter jacket. I pressed my back helplessly against the locker I'd quickly closed. Jake's face was two inches from Daniel's.

"Jake, it's okay, baby. He—" Jake's icy eyes turned coldly to mine.

"You stay out of this," he said with a finger in my face before turning back to Daniel.

The basketball star stood his ground for a moment to speak. "Nothing, man. Not like she'd listen anyway."

Daniel closed his locker and glanced at the shock in my face before turning away with remorse. Dan was sweet. But he was a coward. For a single moment, as I watched him walk away, I was smug with my choice for a better lover and protector than he and Aaron and all the others combined.

Suddenly, my thoughts were made to scatter. A strong hand pressed fiercely into my chest, slamming me into the locker. I felt a twinge of pain in my back from the locking mechanism he disregarded, and my vision blurred briefly from the blow to my head.

"Ow, Jake! What the heck?" I stood firm, rubbing the back of my head. My eyes met an inferno of a gaze. I was filled with a fear that had been rare in my life and looked at my pink snow boots. His black combat boots. I mumbled, "I didn't say a word to him, I swear."

I purpose myself to forget the panic. I have been running in circles for a sign of something. Some life. Some hope. I stop again in some damp leaves. I close my eyes and breathe.

I make a mistake. Eyes still closed, I take a step. The step is into a hole a foot deep. My foot slips against the damp leaves, and my ankle bends unnaturally with an unsettling snap. I cry out once, and I hit the ground with a thud. In the dim woods, I strain to see my ankle as I touch it.

I remember that my ankles are weak. A preteen's ankles. I am touching the glittery shoe of girlhood. I see that my fingernails are an electric pink. My only rebellion within my innocent sadness.

I hear a stick break in the distance. I try to stand, but my ankle does not allow it. I hear another or my frightened imagination. I am a girl. Injured and helpless and lost in the dark woods. Alone. Or not alone enough.

Chapter 5

Rosebud

Stupid. So stupid. He had commemorated that opinion with a sick bluish-purple nose and eye that remained weeks later, unable to be covered with mere makeup. If only I wasn't so stupid like he'd said.

I had forgotten to go to the drug store to buy the precious commodity Jake and I relied upon for peace of mind. I wanted to start the school year ahead and completed a summer project that would earn me an extra graduation credit instead. Regardless of the reason, I forgot, and he was angry. He caused my nose to bleed and then disregarded the risk he'd been angry about. Surely, I'd hoped, one irresponsible afternoon wouldn't count against my perfect record.

I'd been left with lies to tell where the makeup failed during this first week of my junior year. My mind was preoccupied as I prepared to leave school for the day, headed for the familiar drug store. Aaron and Daniel's sympathetic eyes were on me. If only they knew it was *my* fault Jake made me look that way.

I closed my locker and took a moment to pull out my tarnished old compass. The one engraved with *"To My beloved Richie."* I was in search of direction, and it was always the only source of definitive hope. North was always north. I opened it and closed it twice and then looked out the nearby door to see a familiar figure waving. He was there, at my one place of safety and solace.

He *looked* nontoxic. He didn't resemble the monster that inflicted anger on my once beautiful face. He didn't look like a guy who was no longer a student because they told him he couldn't attempt his senior year a third time. He gestured to me, intrigued by my barely-to-code shorts and tank top. I had to go to him. I hadn't the choice or the strength of will to do otherwise. He'd broken all that.

"Hey, babe. My mom is working the night shift. We can grab some food and then head to my place," Jake spoke quickly, and I was sure to hear every word, even on the crowded walkway. He always refused to repeat himself. The last time I asked had earned me a sprained wrist. Luckily that time, as was almost always the case, his intentions were predictable and clear—to awaken the harlot with a meal she didn't have to cook. But that time, the harlot was feeling woozy, and food didn't appeal to me.

"I can't, Jake." I tried a smile and a little laugh to throw him off. I turned and headed toward the parking lot.

"Oh." Jake's face came closer to mine. "Homework more important than me again?"

I looked into his eyes. Kind at the moment. Calm and tranquil. A rare occurrence. I assessed and determined he might be receptive to the actual truth. My eyes betrayed me and welled up with tears.

"No, it's not homework. I. . .I'm a few days late. My. . .cycle."

He was confused at first, and I watched his wild eyes look back and forth at mine. I hoped he could read them. I couldn't say more in the crowded parking lot. I knew he'd read correctly when his slight smile relaxed, and his face lost some color.

"Oh. . ." He was serious in tone, but not angry. I had been hoping for that reaction.

"I was on my way to the store for a test." When I spoke, I saw some anger mounting in him. Any strong emotion manifested into anger. I tried to stifle it, remembering a time when he'd put out a cigarette on my thigh in quiet anger. "It's my fault. I was stupid and forgot. Please don't be angry. I'm so sorry."

I watched him slow to a simmer, glad to catch him in public and in the correct mood.

"Well, let me give you a ride. We'll take the test at my place."

We rode in silence to the drug store. I ran inside for the fateful treasure. While inside, the cashier looked at me with compassion. The middle-aged woman was intelligent, so I always avoided her eyes that hid behind coke bottle lenses. She worked the shift that fell just after school every day. She watched me buy contraceptives for years with various young men. More recently, she had moved a brace for a sprained wrist across that glass scanner. Painkillers, bandages, and creams for countless bumps, bruises, and burns. This one, I considered to be the worst purchase of all. We were alone in the store. She was the only employee. I was the only customer.

"Sweetheart, I'm not allowed to do this. But this one's on me." The kind eyes behind the glasses showed true compassion as she de-magnetized the box and handed it back to me.

"Thanks." I put the item in my purse and began my exit.

"Wait. Honey, there's lots of fish in the sea. And there's a God who loves you. Who has better for you than a young man who won't even come in the store with you to help fix all the things he's broken." I looked at the kind woman and then out the glass wall at Jake, who was smoking a cigarette impatiently in the driver's seat of his car.

I was touched that she cared. But amused at her words.

"Well, he's the best I can do. 'God' should know that." I thanked her again and left.

It's not that I didn't believe in God. I'd stood at the edge of the ocean and looked for the other side. I'd seen the way a rose's petals un-swirled elegantly from what once was a bud without consequence. I'd sat in the woods, far from civilization, and stared up at the unobstructed stars, wondering if I could count them all if given the time. It makes much more sense that someone spoke those perfections into existence rather than accepting that they were one big cosmic accident. *I* was the cosmic accident.

Why would the Creator who swirled the rose and poured the expanse of the ocean care about the meaningless crimson hair on my head after creating the stars in that great darkness? Why would I think that love was any more than Jake's smoky breath or a hundred-dollar bill from my father? It would have been nice. But I'd seen the evil the world could access. It was all the darkness in my heart could ever seek to know.

I pondered that in another silent drive to Jake's house. The house had two bedrooms and two bathrooms. One suite for him, the other for his mother on the other end of the house. Jake never met his father, and his mother worked two jobs to keep the tiny house. She was never home to know the things I surrendered in her son's room. I knew I wasn't the first. I didn't pretend to deserve someone's first and full affections. Pictures of naked women and dark bands adorned Jake's walls, yellowed with smoke stains.

Normally, the racket of one of those bands was blasting as I allowed Jake to numb me for a moment. Then he would smoke a cigarette, contributing to the wreaking of the house. A beer would usually follow. That afternoon, there was no music or beer or smoking. We were two scared teenagers sitting on the edge of a bed, staring at a plastic stick.

When the result came, we both continued to stare. I suddenly found it impossible to keep the tears at bay.

"The line is really faint. Is that still a positive?" Jake was searching for confirmation of his blatant denial.

"That's what the box says." I hated to cry in his presence and wiped the tears away with my hands, storing up the rest.

"Are you sure it's mine?" Jake accused.

"Are you kidding me? We've been together a *year*. I don't cheat, you jerk." I regretted the words even before they escaped into the musty air of his bedroom.

"Watch what you say to me." I heard as I was vigorously rubbing the stinging sensation from my cheek.

"Sorry, baby. This is my fault, okay? I'll take care of it."

"What, like get rid of it? Like hell, you will. If it's mine, *I* get to say what you do. We keep him. Get an apartment or something."

"Really?" A weight was lifted.

"Yeah, whatever. A kid needs a father around to keep him in line." Jake's demeanor changed from the boy who slapped me moments before.

We lay on Jake's bed talking about the change that would come in our lives. He told me it was stupid, but I told Jake I'd like to call the baby Darian.

I am crying now, terrified. It may be a reality that I will never find my way back. Die here in the woods, without view of light or stream. I cower in the fetal position against a nearby tree. I am crying like the barely pubescent girl I am. I am startled by a voice, nearly forgetting my injured ankle. Nearly.

"Hello." An innocent and friendly voice.

I look up, straining my eyes in the darkness. And then she is in clear view, which I can't explain. Stark blonde hair is pulled into a neat ponytail on the back of her head. Not a day older than myself, yet dressed like a grown woman. She wears three-inch designer heels, a blazer, and an eggplant button-up shirt. Dark-wash jeans. No attire for a walk in the woods. She is standing in front of me, then comes to my level and sits so I can see her kind but solemn caramel eyes.

"Hi. . ." I am more confused than startled.

I wonder if I am correctly oriented. The beep is more distant as the girl sits in her fancy clothes. She seems heedless of the effect of the damp forest floor.

"You're lost, I think. I can help you if you're lost. I came to meet you where you are." I notice her timbre seems younger than even her freckled face. I begin to recognize her. Or at least her likeness.

"Maureen? Why are you here? This is impossible." My thoughts spin and twist. Dream? Memory? Reality? Some combination thereof?

"I have to leave for now. But I'll come back, I promise." She rises and walks away, not looking back, from my darkness.

Chapter 6

Hate

I sat through my school days thinking only of the baby that would come. No one knew. But there was no one to care, either. I imagined they wouldn't care until they saw I had a basketball beneath my shirt, which would have given them plenty to imagine. I imagined, too. I imagined Darian as the opposite of his temper-laden father. He was good, regardless of the hand he was dealt.

I was barely seventeen, but I was in love with my unborn child. The hope of valedictorian had slipped from my grasp, but still, I'd been bound for college. Yet suddenly, I was looking forward to motherhood. I carried him a total of two months before I began to truly see what motherhood could be like.

Jake had a part-time job flipping hamburgers. I had no job to speak of. No driver's license. Every day, I became warier, more fearful of Jake's temper. I hadn't told my father about my situation. I hadn't seen a doctor.

My heart was moving. I felt as though I'd aged ten years since the lines showed up on that test. I began to see Jake for who he was. He was terrible. He was everything I didn't want my own son to be. I'd lost touch with the part of me that loved Jake. And yet, I didn't know how to escape him.

Had Darian been conceived by Aaron, I might not have been in such turmoil. If it had been Jeff, my heart would not have been moving. Josh or even Stephen would have made acceptable fathers. But Jake was the worst choice of them all as the father of my son. Jake was every fear that a mother would rather die than see her child endure.

I was that girl who apologized just to keep herself from injury. I was that girl who defended a man who cared only about himself. I didn't want to be that girl anymore. I wanted to be Darian's mother. I *was* Darian's mother in my eyes. I no longer needed to be numbed by anything his father or any other man could offer me. I'd found a purpose. One innocent truth in my life. Darian. Therefore, I resolved to rid myself of Jake, even if it killed me.

We were sitting in my living room just before my father was due home. I sat with my back to the front window, the stairs to my left. Jake sat across from me. My father suspected that I wasn't as clumsy as I'd mumbled lies about in the past year. We weren't close then, but he would have protected his own flesh and blood from harm had he been present.

"Jake," I started, but didn't look into his eyes. I thought quickly, hoping I could get my point across with the same haste.

"What's the matter, baby?" He responded, urging me to continue.

"I need to break up with you." When I finally looked into his eyes, they read sorrow. I was crushed, but stood by my decision.

"You can't do that to me. You're all I've got, you know that. And we're having a kid." He begged me. I knew my next words would destroy him.

"*I'm* having a kid." When I conveyed with my own eyes all I'd learned from his cold ones, his true sadness shifted in a familiar direction, as I'd predicted. He stood and pointed down at me angrily.

"That kid is mine. *You* are mine, remember?"

"I don't *belong* to you!" I stood to face him, as I'd never done. I knew my fear was building in the several inches of height difference.

"Wanna bet?" His nostrils flared. His thin upper lip quivered. I knew I was about to experience true terror but had no time to prepare or even run.

He gathered my hair in one swift movement. Just as quickly, I was falling on my tailbone as he yanked me off my feet. My mind strayed a moment to defend itself. I was astonished my hair was long enough for him to wrap around his hand twice. I fought him. I kicked my heels against the hardwood in an attempt to stand while desperately trying to reclaim my hair from his hands. But my neck stretched. I was being dragged.

I barely heard some angry murmurings about where he was dragging me. I didn't believe he could or would until the corner of each stair radiated in my spine. I held tight to my hair at my scalp to soften the stress and scrambled with my heels, but the pain was still excruciating. I was screaming, to no reward. I was horrified, but no one heard. I only knew I reached the top when he lifted me off the carpet to throw me against the wall in the hallway—hands at my throat.

"Tell me again how you don't *belong* to me." I was in pain already, everywhere, and barely able to see him as he tightened his grip on my neck.

I tried to plead with him to stop, but I couldn't speak. My head was throbbing, and with his immense strength, he lifted my feet off the ground, stressing my throat further. My legs began to flail on their own.

Air. Please, God, I need air.

With strength my heart materialized from somewhere, I extended my legs at his stomach, which forced him to loosen the grip of his hands. I immediately attempted an escape toward the stairs.

I didn't see him come behind me, but again, he pulled me to my back by my hair. He lifted me so that I was looking into his eyes, but I struggled to free myself from the hands that bruised my shoulders and slammed me into the wall again— the hands with a nauseating amount of red hair that remained tangled upon them.

Tears of terror were flowing, but a part of me surfaced that I'd never shown Jake. I spat in his eyes and screamed into his face with a voice he couldn't permanently silence.

"Go to hell! I *hate* you!" The words were barely discernible within the scream, but they somehow translated.

I felt his soul shift in a dilemma. He took to an awkward calm within a dramatic situation. His grip on my shoulders loosened a bit, and he pressed his forehead against mine, almost sensuously. Longingly. Sadly. I pushed him away and rubbed my shoulders, crying bitterly. I leaned against the wall, running my hands over my hair, which smeared some blood onto my fingertips. Normally, when this type of moment occurred, he realized what he'd done and apologized to me, begging me not to quit on him. He'd tell me he didn't mean to hurt me. I dreaded the worst of those moments that day, knowing I had to stand my ground against him, as I'd never attempted before.

I ran my fingertips across my belly, fearing again for the safety of my child. It ached a bit from the journey up the stairs. In my heart, I spoke.

Just hold on, Darian. I'll take care of you.

Jake didn't hear my heart; I'd never let him near enough. But the sight of my worry was what lit fire to Jake's temper once again.

"What did you say?" His voice was boiling, horrifying.

"Go to hell, Jake. I'm done with you." For Darian, I stood firm against the fear. I turned to the stairs to make my exit.

"Then I'm done with you too." It seemed too easy. I knew he had far more fight in him. That troubled me greatly.

Before the trouble led me to react, two hands landed violently on my back with enough force to jar me from my feet and into the air. I only heard myself scream as I watched the middle stair draw dangerously close. I extended my arms too late and fell into deep darkness.

I am calling out into the darkness for the girl I recognized only a little. In her place is an overwhelming sense of dread. In a panic, my heart, my very flesh, urges me to rise and run from the footsteps I hear approaching through the leaves. But my ankle, one bit of bone that failed me, continues its treason.

I attempt to calm my spirit. To convince my survival instinct that the footsteps bring hope and assistance in my pain. The footsteps stop suddenly in front of me. My eyelids are unnaturally tight against the panicked eyes beneath.

"You lost? You hurt?" The deep and labored voice matches the aroma of cigarettes that emit from the man I refuse to see. The voice that haunts me, though I don't remember the reason for my dread.

Chapter 7

Choice

I regretted waking up immediately. I moaned with pain I couldn't quite pinpoint, which woke up my father, who was in an uncomfortable-looking chair at my side. He called for the nurse to hopefully sedate me into painlessness once again. The nurse, instead, sent for a doctor to speak to me.

The doctor was a pretty Latina, proud of the white coat she wore. She was young for a doctor but walked with confidence. She introduced herself as Dr. Moreno with the proper accent. No matter her confidence or heritage, her words stung me. Maimed me. I don't know how she managed to say them so gently.

"You're barely seventeen, Paige." Simple words for the purpose, but they served it nonetheless.

"I know." A tear escaped for the pain as I looked away from the doctor.

I heard her rustling some papers the nurse had handed her as she entered. She breathed in and hesitated for a moment. When the words finally came, they were remorseful.

"A broken wrist, three cracked ribs, head trauma, abrasions on your neck, scalp, and all over. Evidence of past injuries less severe but numerous. Your father gave us consent to sedate you and run exams and tests. There was quite a bit to document. Including a ten-week-old fetus that is clinging to life."

My father seemed contrite like he'd already heard everything, including about the baby. I replied accordingly, "I'm sorry."

The doctor was annoyed at the interruption, but my dad answered me. "They said you were in shock, so you wouldn't remember. But that baby is all you asked about all the way here until they put you out. I wish you'd told me, Paige. What. . .what happened at the house today?"

"Jake," I whispered.

"*Jake* did this? I knew this boyfriend was bad news, but I had no idea he was capable of—"

"I broke up with him. It was stupid. I had no right. It's his baby." This was said through and then destroyed by my own brainwashed tears.

The nurse in the room and my father hushed me, attempting to share in a pain they could never know. The young doctor was upset but kept her head.

"Let's talk about this fetus. There's evidence. . ." She lost her composure for a moment, then cleared her throat, banishing her own emotion. "There's evidence of a blunt object, perhaps a boot, striking your abdomen repeatedly. Probably after you were out cold. You're fortunate not to have organ damage. But your placenta is barely formed, and it's not looking so good. There's a chance the baby could make it, but there are a lot of issues it could have if it does make it to term. In the world of obstetrics, we consider this a situation that can't have a positive outcome, you understand? The decision is yours, but I recommend we terminate."

There was silence in the room, except my sobs.

My father spoke. "Why don't we talk for a minute and decide?"

"We never talk about anything, *Paul*." My heartless remark echoed within him.

The forty-year-old man was crushed with a familiar look of defeat on his face. Deep inside, I begged him to challenge me. To tell me what to do. There was a constant sadness in his green eyes from being betrayed by my mother—the only woman he ever loved. But I hated him for betraying *me*. I had anything I asked for handed to me from my successful accountant father. I had a nice roof over my head, and I was lacking nothing. Yet, I was lacking everything. How dare the man with graying hair delve into my life suddenly and want to discuss my own unborn child with me. How *dare* he?

"Umm—" I began and then cleared my throat, casting away tears so I could focus.

I was in love with the child inside me. He was all I cared about. Everything pure and innocent. All that was ever beautiful in my life. But I was far from deserving of any of those virtues. How could I bring him into the world knowing who his father was? Constantly fearing for our lives. I was in *love* with my Darian. And so I let him go, to preserve his innocence forever.

"Okay." With a word, I surrendered my best hope of redemption.

The stranger helps me to my feet. To a secluded hunting cabin a hundred yards in the wrong direction. I go with him, as my vulnerability leaves me no choice.

He lights a fire. He feeds me a single biscuit, so dry I nearly gag. He wraps my ankle in silence. I thank him. He helps me feel comfortable and trusting. He helps me relax, even after he loads a shotgun and places it on the table, pointing at me.

And then, without notice or provocation, he destroys my innocence.

He takes what he was after without shame. He muffles my screams and pleading within a cruel hand that has just fed me. I stare down the barrel of a weapon with desperate tears, hating that what strength I may have had to fight is compromised by a broken ankle. Every part of me is in anguish. Every joy replaced with darkness.

I am twelve. I am naïve. I am terrified. He convinces me that if I shower in the cabin's cold water, as he forces me to do, no one will ever know or believe that he has hurt me. That if I wash away everything, I will become the harlot who asked him to violate me.

He watches me dress and then gives me a compass and a dimming flashlight. The compass is heavy for such a simple purpose. The face is inset in brass with a lid that makes a tiny clicking sound as I open and close it. The brass is engraved with "To My beloved Richie." Beloved. That sickens me. How could he be beloved? Regardless, the compass with mahogany edges is beautiful, and is my last hope to survive.

My violator tells me that my father's cabin is one mile northeast along the stream I will encounter. I look at my broken ankle, now three times its regular size, and realize that I am required to walk this distance. Alone. As the sun goes down. I must even leave behind a glittery shoe that wouldn't fit anymore if I tried.

The October air is already cruel through my thin denim jacket as I stand at the entrance to the cabin that changed me. I look into the face I could never allow myself to forget.

"You better get going." A voice I hate. A door that slams. A hopelessness that hangs like a stench in the air at dusk.

Why hadn't I stayed at the stream like my father said? I would be back at his warm cabin. I would be innocent still in every way.

Instead, I hobble into the darkness and feel a stranger's putrid breath on my skin, though he is no longer near me. I hear the distant crackle of a fire—a once-beloved sound I now despise. I allow the tears to flow because I know they will probably be my last. But still, I am determined to find my father. So that he does not have to lose his daughter after my mother left him just weeks ago.

Chapter 8

Direction

After the police officer took my statement and left, they came in and told me other medical information I was too woozy to really comprehend. Then I was alone in the room but aware of every eye that peered through the glass door as they passed. I focused on a single object I was glad they didn't take into evidence. *"To My beloved Richie,"* I read for the ten-thousandth time. I opened and closed the old compass and fought the tears. I never felt as empty as I did that day, having allowed my hope to be ripped from my womb.

I hated Jake more than I ever loved him. I hated my father for ignoring every cry for his instruction. But I couldn't blame either of them for my transgressions. I could only blame my own darkness and rebellion. That's what walked further into the woods that day. And that's the part of me capable of ending my own child's life.

I'd kept the compass those five years to help me find my way. Yet somehow, it had only led me further and further from any light or happiness. I had some morbid relief, knowing that the whole world could finally see the state my spirit had been in for years. A nurse entered the room and took my vitals. I told her I wanted to take a walk. *Off a cliff*, I specified in my heart. She gave me permission, but with a promise of soreness from the "procedure" and my extensive injuries.

The soreness where my child had been served as a welcome punishment, I suppose. Everyone else, if they spoke at all, told me that I'd "done the right thing." And though it was because he was gone, it meant I was alive, if nothing else. I opened the compass and began to walk northeast. My only constant in life was that compass. Its consistency was some measure of comfort. What was north was north. What was south would always be south. In that kind of indisputable truth, I could trust. I had faith in an object that supplied certainty, even if it was acquired with great anguish.

Desperate for hope, I barely laughed at the irony of where the compass led me. The Mercy Main Hospital Chapel.

I'd spent much of my life mercilessly making fun of Christians. Those people who spent pointless hours of their weekends praising their Creator. The "mighty Creator" who let my mother care so little for me that she divorced my father on my birthday. They worshipped the "Savior" who allowed my innocence to be stolen by some man trying to "save" me. The "just" Spirit who watched me fall in love, get pregnant, and be pushed down the stairs by another of His creations. As far as I could tell, He was just like every other man I'd ever known in any sense of the word. If He accepted me at all, it would have been fleeting. I only hoped His wrath was just as quick.

I read the Ten Commandments to the left of the open chapel door and knew I'd broken each one in just a few years. I was seventeen. Yet, I was positive most fifty-year-olds had yet to endure the pain I had in my life. I hated even my own life expectancy. Death would be better, or maybe it was just the only place lower than where I was. So, when I turned to the silliest, most irrational thing I could find, it was an improvement. I entered that tiny, dark, and empty hospital chapel and agonizingly lowered myself into a cushioned pew.

The room was dim, with two sections of pews and an aisle between them that led to the flicker of candles up at the altar. A worn and wooden cross was elevated upon the wall. It was simple and lackluster by sight. And yet, I was puzzled by what could not be seen.

Why, in one empty room in great physical pain, did I feel this eerie comfort? My soul quieted. How could mere peace be so powerful? How was I so overwhelmed yet so unmistakably at ease? I could nearly take and drink the calm in the room. I longed to feel its splendor overtake me. To allow the smile that almost crossed my lips. But I deserved no such thing.

I allowed the murmur of the hospital hall behind me to fade behind my eyelids before I sensed a presence enter the room. I'd experienced enough of them to know that it was a male person that quietly sat in the pew behind me. I perceived a sort of quiet tension amid the peace of the room—as a blissfully playing child might experience at the sound of their name to complete a chore. I dreaded that he was about to speak into my most pleasant experience in years. But in my defeated heap, I allowed the intrusion.

"God loves you more than you can ever imagine." The voice was warm. Warmer than my father's when I was a child. The voice didn't ask for anything, but gave the most beautiful report I'd ever heard. The voice moved me to tears because I'd lost control over every aspect of my life. Why not this one?

"So I've heard. No offense, but that's crazy." I said it abruptly, but my tears revealed something else to the stranger.

"Why are you in a chapel if it's crazy?" I was suddenly glad the voice, most likely a middle-aged man, had continued. And with a hinted joviality of all things. I realized then he was probably a priest of some kind. Probably a celibate. Some perspective he had of how God felt about *me*.

"Sort of a last resort. It seems safer than the rest of the world." I spoke the truth with pain and bitterness and tears.

"As long as He's *some* resort." At this, I turned to see the face of my encourager. I saw something I didn't expect. He was a bit shocked at the state of my battered face but didn't shy away as all the doctors and nurses had done. The compassion in his eyes simply deepened. He was in a blue plaid shirt and jeans on a stout frame. Cowboy boots. A worn-out cowboy hat in his hand. From that, he had hat hair, grayed from what once was probably brown. A full beard on a round face. Light brown eyes so kind I wanted them to envelop me.

Another voice called to him from the hall, "Grandpa!"

A young boy of about five bounced in, rambling about the new cast on his left arm. The kind man replied gently to the beautiful curly-haired boy, asking him to go to his mother in the hall. He told the boy he was talking to his friend and would be out shortly. I had assumed the man was a virgin priest, complete with collar and naivety. What I saw was a grandfather with hard-earned wrinkles. Who was this man?

"Are you a doctor?" Wary of all strange men, probably for the rest of my days, I made sure that I was safe.

At the prospect, the man released a hearty, rustic laugh that filled the little chapel a moment. No matter what the laugh meant, it earned my eternal trust.

"More of a teacher." The same, gentle, weathered smile.

I nodded, not fully understanding his meaning. I expected he would try to teach me some life lesson. I expected he would ruin my only peace in years with his human voice. Instead, he allowed the silence. The peace. And simply accompanied me in it for a full ten minutes. I'd heard about angels. Messengers sent from God adorning human flesh to accomplish a purpose. For most of those minutes where his comforting presence acted as balm, I assumed I'd met an angel of God. That chapel seemed to exist in a bubble or a fog—in a dream. Nothing seemed impossible there.

He only spoke, and we were only transported back to reality when the same little boy called his grandfather again.

"It was wonderful to meet you. But please do not let it be the last time. If you ever want to feel safe again once they discharge you, I know where you can find some more comfortable pews." He stood and procured his wallet from his back pocket, fiddling with it. He lowered his voice to a friendly whisper, "We call them chairs."

At this, the man smiled and handed me a business card, then quickly exited the room before my eyes trained themselves to read in the dim light.

Robert Henley
Senior Pastor
Grace Community Church

I was bewildered. The church logo on the card was the same as the one on the gigantic building I passed twice a day going to and from my high school. I knew it to be the second largest church in our city. I knew many students from my school who went there, including Dee, Emma, and Marley. The man I spoke to was not an angel but a flesh-and-blood, well-respected man in the city. And yet, he took more than a moment for me. His words were few, but they seemed to ignite something in me. They begged the thought—what if God really does have the capacity to know me?

I experience the eerie sounds a girl dreads in the woods at night, and yet I'm unshaken. No force or beast on earth could further mutilate my spirit. The flashlight batteries run low. I set the bearing on the compass on the word of a wicked man. And then I hear gentle footsteps approaching.

"I told you I'd be back." The same too-young voice. The same familiar countenance.

"I needed you in there! Why did you leave me?" I scream this at her.

"I can't change what happened. I think you know that." She puts her arm around me to help me walk. Her touch is gentle, but she is stronger than she appears.

"Just go! I have to do this alone." I desperately long for her help but will only accept it if she is willing to fight for it.

"You have never been alone. I can't heal you. But I can help you get to the source."

I know now I'm dreaming from the way words jumble into unease.

"I'm so cold. I hurt so bad. I don't know if I'll make it."

"You can make it. You've already made it."

The encouragement from the compassionate blonde helps me push through the darkness, the cold, the pain. The methodic beep returns.

Chapter 9

Fear

I missed him unrelentingly. I mourned him alone in that hospital room. I cried only when alone. My procedure's pain wouldn't last, they said. I tried to tell my soul the same, but it was steadfast in grief. I first thought that sleep would allay the tears. Then I dreamed in nightmares. A screaming baby tossed into the ocean. Or Jake driving off with him in a car I could never find. Horrified and heartbroken, I cried, night after night. Worse than my previous pillow tears of self-hatred and pain. Fiery tears that burned but did not refine. They couldn't cleanse my eyes of the images I'd never see. Hands I'd never hold. A heart I'd never know to beat. I was in agony. But the "healers" tittered around, helping to heal my broken body. Oblivious to how desperately I missed my Darian.

After a week in the hospital, I stayed home an additional week to rest my body and catch up on homework. During the week, I began to feel, yet again, the stir in my heart that made me break up with Jake. I was somehow prompted to call a counselor at my school, who was able to include me in the graduation ceremony in May, an entire year early.

I was determined to leave the God-forsaken school filled with boys and evil as soon as I could. Despite the test scores and advanced courses and projects that earned me extra credits, I had to take a full schedule the semester that followed, when I'd planned to slack off. But I was done slacking off. Done sleeping around to make myself feel okay. Or feel at all. If I was going to overdo something, it might as well help me escape what didn't work.

I concluded the phone call and looked into my closet. My outfit had been taken into evidence that fated day when I invited Jake to my home. It echoed the other pieces in my wardrobe. Miniskirts and mini-dresses. Low-cut and/or midriff revealing tops. Things that accentuated everything that made boys turn their heads. I no longer wished to receive that type of attention. I emptied my closet of everything but modest necklines and pants and skirts that extended below my knees. The freckles not on my face were no longer anyone's business. I'd only ever considered intrigue and lust in my wardrobe choices. This showed as I stared into a closet that was then all but empty.

Oddly, my primary motivation for emptying my closet into a black plastic bag was not to avert the eyes of boys. I planned to stop into the church I'd pass walking home and knew a low-cut top would have likely gotten me thrown out. I had to know that peace again, as I found in that chapel. I dressed for that peace and my return to school in a long skirt and a designer hoodie that hid every freckle and bruise on my battered body. The sleeves were wide enough to cover the cast I was doomed to wear on my wrist for a few more weeks.

I found some odd sense of freedom in something I *wouldn't* give up for the sake of modesty—my collection of about fifty pairs of flip-flops. I wore the terrible fashion piece through four seasons in those days. Something about having nearly naked feet gave me comfort. I had control in the grip my toes needed to retain them. I owned some enticing heels and my pink snow boots, but mostly I was devoted to those flip-flops.

My heart moved again before I allowed myself to pretend to sleep for the evening. I realized it had been months since I shined the kitchen floor. Jake required so much of my time that my grades had slipped a little, and the house had been a mess. So had who I was before being pushed down the stairs, if I was anyone at all. To remind myself, I remembered the smell of pine cleaner. And though it was painful with my yet unhealed body, I felt a wave beginning—a momentum I couldn't control or understand—in the mere shining of a kitchen floor.

At school, I started to see the other students through a new set of eyes. They squeezed drama from every ordinary situation. They were all desperate for love and acceptance. I was them just weeks before. But when one has seen what I had seen in that amount of time, perspective changes. They all stared at the fading bruises on my face and whispered as I walked past in the halls. My year-long rapport with Jake had alienated me forever from anyone I once called my friend. They all knew who I was and what happened to me, no doubt.

But I was alone in a world that would never accept me. My only relief was when the last bell of the day allowed me to walk off campus.

I mounted the burden of my backpack on me and placed my enormous denim purse on my shoulder as before. But as never before, I strolled the half-mile toward the church, wondering what the inside of the dull brick building looked like. My heart was all nerves and all excitement as I hoped for a fraction of the peace I felt in the hospital chapel.

Suddenly, just blocks from the peace, I heard a familiar vehicle that caused my skin to brace itself for turmoil. Jake drove what he called a "classic." A rusted, beat-up old Camaro. The sound and smell of its lack of maintenance or restoration were unmistakable. Therefore, I was sure that it was following me. *He* was following me. I tried to ignore him.

"Is it true?" Jake shouted out the window.

"Go away, or I will call the police," I boldly said what the hospital social worker advised me to say, should I encounter him. The investigation was still in the works. My own home had been a crime scene for the time I was in the hospital. They'd arrested Jake but let him out on bail after he lied his way through an interrogation. Claiming his innocence, even his absence, during the assault.

"So, it *is* true. You killed my kid." Jake was shouting too loudly for my comfort. Though at any volume, the words were salt on the wound.

I cringed but remained silent as I quickened my pace. The church was in sight.

"You had no right." I heard the anger rising in his voice and tried not to panic as I remembered the fear of being dragged up a flight of stairs by my hair. He was in a car. I was on foot. Knowing the danger, I was only moved along by that fear.

I was defenseless as I passed buildings, wondering if I should enter one for safety. But even the police station I passed did not appeal to me. My destination was set.

He revved his engine as if reading my mind. I reached the edge of the church parking lot, and my fight-or-flight response resulted in a full sprint that was excruciating on my still-sore midsection. I saw the nearing of pillars made of block. A balcony hanging over a wall of glass doors beckoned me. Somehow, I got a sense that if I was to run from Jake in any direction, this was the only one that could redeem me.

The car thundered after me, but to my relief, it stalled and he had to leave it at the back of the lot. The door of the church opened as I approached, and I was met outside the door by a familiar face. A calm and gentle presence, powerful enough to stop us both, though we'd been at a full run. While Jake began his verbal assault, I stood next to Pastor Henley and faced Jake with courage.

His anger flowed visibly into the chilled mid-October air. "You had no right! It was mine! *You* were mine! Don't think this pansy preacher man is gonna stop me from teaching you a lesson."

I found a new resolve even in catching my breath from a hundred-meter dash. "No, *you* had no right." I said it loudly but stayed calm, taking a hint from the man of God who was now standing guard in front of me. "You think *I* killed the baby? *You* did! Don't ever come near me again, Jake. I mean it."

"You listen close, you worthless tramp. If you ever find some blind half-wit to knock you up, I'll kill *his* kid too. Got that?" Jake spat on the ground in front of me, then backed up. I gasped in the panic of worry I might have had for any future children. But then I cast the worry away, knowing it wasn't likely I'd have them anyway.

"Got it. Loud and clear, kid." Pastor Henley said this as a police cruiser pulled up, lights and siren blaring.

It sounded like a shouting match, but it didn't last long. The police officer got the message and arrested Jake immediately for domestic violence after seeing he was a suspect in my assault. Especially after Jake uttered some remark about his regret over not hitting me with his car. The officer instructed me to make a statement at their office when my father could accompany me, then Jake was handcuffed and removed from my presence in the cruiser.

I was afraid for my life and my future. No handcuffs could change that. But I entered the church with its pastor, and my anxiety was replaced with immediate awe. Half a dozen people who saw me run across the parking lot were attempting not to stare. But I barely noticed them. My attention is on the awareness that all the beauty on earth had been gathered into one place—in the form of an enormous foyer.

To my left was an information desk in a corner behind two curved staircases. The staircases ascended high in the room, but no part of either level was out of my view. There were numerous tables and sitting areas on both levels of the foyer. I realized my feet were cold upon the expertly waxed, colored concrete floor. I must have lost my flip-flops while running. Ahead of me, at the foyer's end, there was a glass wall where I could see that a stage was dimly lit in the distance. The sanctuary. Unworthy and terrified of that room, my attention returned to the foyer.

I never ever wanted to leave. The powerful peace of the hospital chapel was but an altar candle against the sunlight next to the peace that overpowered me there. I looked straight up to an enormous skylight made of frosted glass, allowing every flicker of light from the outdoors to trickle down into glory. The smile that almost came that day sitting in that pew overtook me without my consent as my eyes closed for what I wished was an eternity.

"Is it okay if I stay here until my dad gets off work? I don't want to be a bother. I'm just a little shaken up. I probably don't deserve to be here, so I won't stay long." My mouth was barely mobile enough to speak to the pastor by my side.

"I am so glad to see your face again. I know I gave you my card, but I never introduced myself before. I'm Robert Henley." The Senior Pastor reached out and shook my hand as though I was an equal. He *recognized* me.

"Paige Ellis."

"Well, Miss Ellis. If you feel safe here, I would love for you to stay as long as you need. I don't deserve to be here either, but God lets me hang around anyway." I was confused. How could a pastor not deserve to be in his own church?

Even more perplexing was that he heard and understood every word that Jake said to me and every word I again relayed to the officer. The terrible things I'd done. But he left that scene outside in the dusting snow that captured it. As if nothing mattered after those doors had been breached.

I was given a tour of the church. Pastor Robert showed me several tables where I could do homework, a small shop where they sold books, and a coffee cart outside it for anyone who was thirsty. He told me the praise band was about to practice for that night's service, and I could listen if I'd like. He told me that if I wanted to talk to someone, he would find someone who was available.

I feared that if Pastor Robert knew all the commandments I'd broken, he wouldn't have been so quick to meet my needs. But I also felt as though I was home. And that home was a palace with thirty-foot ceilings and two staircases that curved and met on a landing high above my vision. A place that was open. Everyone looked me in the eye and greeted me, looking past the cast on my wrist. The fading bruises on my face only gave them reason for compassion, not judgment.

I found a table to occupy just after my barefoot tour. It was in the corner of the foyer before a door took it into a hall of offices and classrooms. It was about twenty feet from the information desk, which had a high counter that circled a cove, probably designed just for that purpose. Pastor Robert brought me my flip-flops, which had been collected from the parking lot by a maintenance man. I thanked him and put the shoes on. Then I opened my backpack and completed my Trigonometry homework. Trigonometry had me at risk for not graduating early, but the day I met the foyer at Grace Community Church, it didn't seem so hard.

I looked up when the shimmer of the sun that had conquered the brief October snow bounced against the glass of a door as it opened. This was an insignificant refraction of light I'd seen thousands of times in my life. But the peace there made even the opening of a door new to me. I watched at a distance as Pastor Robert greeted a blonde woman in her late twenties at the door.

The woman stood at five feet ten inches with the three-inch designer heels she adorned—a couple inches taller than Pastor Robert. She wore an eggplant-colored blouse that day with a black blazer. She carried an enormous designer handbag on one arm. All of this with perfect dark-wash jeans. She walked with confidence and direction. I immediately thought she was the most put together woman I'd ever seen. Like she had stepped out of a fashion magazine for young professionals. Her blonde locks were pulled back from her pale face into a ponytail, large iron-made curls bouncing gracefully with her every movement.

"I'm sorry it took so long. Lane had an appointment, and I couldn't get free. But I'm here. What can I do?" The woman was eager to be helpful. I suddenly saw the power of a "Senior Pastor." He called. She answered. I thought for a moment it involved me but scolded myself, assuming the serenity and acceptance of the empty church had flawed my judgment. At least until they were both looking in my direction. I buried my focus in my Trig again.

The click of heels against the glossy chestnut-colored floor became louder, and I startled when the chair next to me was forced from its position, the moan echoing throughout the foyer. She was wearing a sweet and spicy fragrance with a sensual undertone. Though I didn't know her name and she had yet to speak to me, I trusted this woman immediately. The soothing air she brought over with her confidence was suddenly my dearest companion. She sat and spoke.

"Hi, Paige. I'm Maureen Little. I'm in charge of the counseling ministry here at Grace Community. I am thrilled to meet you."

"Hey." I averted my eyes, assuming they were trying to get me out of their hair.

"That probably sounds scary. But Pastor Robert asked if I could come sit with you for a while. He says he's sorry he didn't ask first. But he didn't want you to be alone. I hear you've been through an awful lot today." Her voice was medicinal. She was probably very good at this counseling thing. But so was the doctor that told me to kill my baby. No one could genuinely care about my well-being or even how my day was.

"Today was nothing." I sounded needy. But I was desperate to fill the void this peace had finally gained access to. I desperately wanted her to ask me to stay.

"I see. I hear you're waiting on your dad? Call and let him know you have a ride. I want you to stay for the Wednesday night service in a couple hours. We can go get some food before that, maybe?"

Powerful relief. This was far beyond asking me to stay. Oh, for a God that answered more than a prayer. For a compass that promised more than northeast. But denial came quickly, as usual.

"Are you sure you don't have somewhere better to be? I mean, that's really nice of you." I hated even the timbre of my voice as it pleaded.

"Paige, I am right where I want to be." Maureen made me believe her. Not out of manipulation or obligation, as I was used to. Out of love and genuine concern. That was brand-new to me.

Chapter 10

Trauma

Maureen took me out of the peace and across the street to a quiet diner, where she did nothing but listen to me as we enjoyed some of the best sandwiches and fries ever in the world. She didn't take notes. She just listened to my ramblings of school and homework, knowing I really wanted to say much more. It was as though I'd been spinning in circles in my own tortured head for years. I didn't realize how much I *had* to say until Maureen stepped into my life. I tried to hide the things I knew would make her run. When I thought I'd said enough, I allowed silence. And into the silence came Maureen's sweet but wise voice.

"Pastor Robert tells me that you feel like you don't deserve to be at church. He tells me there was some situation with a young man. Is that correct?"

"Yeah. Jake." I had been found out. I avoided Maureen's eyes.

"And who is Jake to you?"

"My boyfriend," I said before my mind caught up with my mouth. "Sorry. *Ex*-boyfriend. We were together for a year. He didn't take it well when I broke up with him." Why did I feel so compelled to speak to her?

"Is 'Jake' what happened to your wrist?"

"Yeah. . ." I stretched my lacy sleeve over the cast, embarrassed.

"Does he hurt you a lot?" Maureen gently encouraged me. I felt safe with her. When ordinarily I would have defended Jake's actions and told her it was an accident, I no longer felt compelled. Something told me this woman wouldn't have believed it even if I did.

I nodded and touched the hair that I'd cut above my shoulders the week before because so much of it was damaged. A change I wasn't used to. I had been accustomed to it flowing over my shoulders and tickling my inner elbows. I looked across the restaurant, then at my acquaintance's clasped hands. And then I looked into the compassionate amber eyes that begged me to bare my soul without the aid of her speech. Because I'd never said it, and because I needed to, I opened up with bitterness.

"You wanna know why I don't deserve to be in that church? I'm seventeen as of last month. And I was *pregnant.* But because of the way Jake reacted when I decided to dump him, I'm not pregnant anymore. They said the baby wouldn't have survived. But I made sure of that when I got rid of him." I was quiet, but the tears came without warning.

"That's terrible, sweetie. I'm so sorry." Maureen was visibly moved, shocked. But she believed something precious in the tears that no one else had even noticed.

"You and Pastor Robert are wasting your time on me." I moved a tear across a carpet burn on my cheek, and it stung.

"So, because you had an abortion, you think God won't forgive you?" Her tone was sympathetic, not condescending.

"Well, why should He? That's not half of what I've done. God has every reason to *hate* me."

"Probably." The word of a counselor? And said with such conviction.

"Yeah. . ." I trailed off, welcoming another hopeless tear.

"And yet, He loves you enough to sacrifice his son so that you don't have to worry about *any* of the things you've done. Good thing, huh?"

"He *loves* me? Why do people keep telling me that? Really, you have no idea. . ."

At this, Maureen smiled. Maureen's smile was mesmerizing. One corner of her mouth rose higher than the other, and there was a fiery warmth in her caramel eyes. The smile held compassion and strength and self-control. One could be sure that whatever secret she bore would not be released without purpose and calculation. The only truths revealed in Maureen's smile were truths about her. Her intelligence and confidence. Her wisdom. Her youth. All the sincerity within her. Yet all the sarcasm and mischief. Her smile contradicted itself in a manner that made Mona Lisa seem childlike.

In an instant, I knew that she was much deeper than the gentle one-dimensional counselor. A depth I could drown in. I loved the smile and how it made me feel like I was a friend, and we were laughing about an inside joke. And I hated the smile because I knew I could never earn a friend so superb.

With this first appearance of her smile, Maureen sat back against the yellow cushioned booth bench.

"Oh, I gotta hear *this*. Something so *awful* that God is too small to forgive it." And the dimension of sarcasm suddenly emerged. She fell just short of belittling me so that I would defend my stance. A conniving yet successful tactic to get me to share my heart.

"I will taint you just by saying it out loud."

Maureen's smile begged me to bring into the light all the things I'd never said aloud. "Try me."

"Okay. . .Jake? He's my longest boyfriend, but he's not my first. I've had a *lot* of boyfriends." I paused to read Maureen.

"Still not beyond forgiveness." The smile renewed.

"Even if I crossed certain unforgivable boundaries with *all* of them?"

"Oh, dear. You mean. . .?" She bobbled her head from side to side with a goofier smile.

I winced. "Yeah."

"And you said you're barely seventeen?"

I was offended, having shared my heart only to be ridiculed. "I'm a slut. I know that. Everyone at my school knows that. I'm probably traumatizing you."

Maureen laughed the laugh that gave her smile the most fitting of melodies, emitting from an upturned chin and eyes shut tight and a crinkled nose to ease me. "Traumatizing me? Sweetie, I've given birth twice and everything that involves— including little *boys* who truly are made of frogs, snails, and puppy dog tails. It would take a lot to traumatize me."

I released a single laugh, wondering how someone with her youth and poise could have given birth twice already. Maureen took a sip of her iced tea with natural lipstick around a straw. I tucked stray hairs behind my ears and looked to the table. She continued, immediately sensing my discomfort. She reached for an anecdote.

"I found out I was pregnant two weeks after my high school graduation. My boyfriend was in Florida, helping to move his parents there. David always knows the right thing to say. So I'll never forget how scared I was when I told him over the phone, and there was just. . .silence. Our parents taught us all the right things. We were smart. We knew better. But in all my wedding photos, I am six months pregnant. I was so scared I'd never be able to teach my sons the right thing after that stupid mistake. So I handed it over to God and begged for forgiveness. It's all I could do. Hope for God's grace. I'm the director of counseling over at the church. So, I've met a lot of girls in situations like mine and helped them conquer things they didn't think possible. If God, in His abundant grace, helped me do so much good after one mistake with one good man, imagine how much more He could do if you laid all of *your* sin at His feet." And Maureen's dimension of sarcasm sheered to let a passion come through that was undisputable in sincerity or truth. From where did she receive this power?

I nodded, feeling in my diaphragm a tingle and in my ears a twinge as she spoke those potent words. I couldn't begin to understand how to comply. How to lay down every shred of what I've ever done. But she made me want to try.

"Do you want to be *forgiven*, Paige?" Maureen smiled again that knowing smile. She leaned on her left hand, balanced by an elbow on the table. She wore a wedding set. A beautiful setting in white gold of emeralds and diamonds. She had a glimmer of a clue what I was going through, but she'd still married the guy. She was loved like I would never be.

"I've done drugs. I used to drink before I was pregnant. I poured vodka on a Christian girl at a bonfire. I lied about my age to get a tattoo. I'm telling you. I've done way more than just sleep around, as if that wasn't bad enough. I would understand if forgiveness wasn't, you know, possible."

"Emma McHardy. That was hard for her. The vodka thing." She noted dryly the obvious "aha," sipping her iced tea.

"Serves me right that you'd know her." I entered my own bitter sarcasm. "I forgot she goes to your church."

Maureen nodded with her smile. "Since she was a kid. Good family. The vodka wasn't hard for her, though. It was the money for a new shirt she found in her locker the following

Monday. She could see you were surrounded by darkness and pain, but she felt powerless to help you. You have people praying for you, Miss Ellis. Anyway, it seems like you've got the works when it comes to the rebellious teen thing. It boggles my mind that teenagers, or adults for that matter, think what they are *all* doing is any kind of rebellion at all. Either way, what the world says is just stretching our wings and finding our independence often ends up being what destroys us. If it were up to me, the teen years would be spent inside a cocoon until they could prove they had useful wings." Maureen was amused in her hindsight, but my age left me little to look back on with a smile.

My tears began again, but Maureen took my hand and continued, "Luckily, it's not up to me. It's up to Jesus. Without Him, we wander through life in agony. And then we cause ourselves more pain to try to fix the agony. But Jesus can fix *any* pain. And any side effects of your own remedies. My question is, will you let Him? Do you believe that He can redeem you? That He died so that you could be free of all this?"

Before I answered Maureen, I had to work to fight off tears. "There's no way God just, like, *forgives* me."

"Forgives. Forgets. In Christ, our sins are as far from His memory as the east is from the west. He *loves* you unconditionally. He wants to walk with you through this and everything else. Otherwise, He wouldn't have found you. And you wouldn't have found *me*." I had never seen such passion from such poise. She wanted me to hear those words more than she cared to finish the sandwich in front of her.

"I want to believe that. I've heard that. Just never like that, you know?"

"Well, listen, let's go to the church service—"

I protested immediately. "I can't go to church."

"It sounds scary, but you'll see very quickly that it isn't. You'll be a sinner in a room of sinners who are coming just as they are, just like you. The only reason we get to be there is because God, in His ridiculously infinite grace, forgave us. But you ran to our church when you were scared. So, if anyone deserves to be there? It's you." And she renewed me with the beauty of a crooked smile.

I find warmth in the sweetly familiar singing voice of my preteen companion. I am serenaded and calmed into staying awake through the searing cold throughout my body and chilling pain in my leg.

The songs are innocent. Something I lost just an hour ago. I never could comprehend how the loss of innocence can change a young girl. But now, I hate every girl who retains hers to give freely as she chooses. I hate every boy who seeks to take it.

I hate everyone and everything and the God that made me. But I find redemption and beauty and true love in the voice that sings to me and the arms she uses to save my life. I wonder how I would have done this without her.

She sings in time with the beep I once saw as an annoyance. She sings me out of pain and into deeper understanding. I shudder at the thought of making it through the woods alone.

Chapter 11

Communion

What can wash away my sin?
Nothing but the blood of Jesus
What can make me whole again?
Nothing but the blood of Jesus
Oh! Precious is the flow
That makes me white as snow!
No other fount I know
Nothing but the blood of Jesus

I'd heard the melody in various places. Mocked the words with atheist boyfriends. But that night, I finally understood that any song about a fountain of Jesus's blood was my own anthem forever. I was reduced to tears in the back row of a sanctuary with hundreds of other sinners. I wanted to live for Him because He died for me. Even if all I ever came to learn in life was that He saved me, I could finally be whole.

The pastor that had invited me to the church spoke to the room. Or, just to me, I couldn't be sure. He spoke about a woman who washed Jesus's feet, even though she had been just my brand of sinner. She had used her tears and her hair. My hair had been sacrificed because of my own brokenness. But I longed to dedicate the rest of my tears to my Savior. I fell in love that night with a Man powerful enough to send me away saved.

There was nothing more precious than what had become painfully apparent to me. That long before I knew His name, He had been calling mine. I had been compelled by the Holy Spirit to break up with Jake. To take a seat in a tiny hospital chapel. To purge my provocative wardrobe. And finally, to run with all my feeble strength through the doors of a church and into His arms. I was free in His arms—no longer bound by the sins of my past.

After the last song in the service, I wept uncontrollably in the company of the woman God sent to grab hold of me. I repeated a prayer after Maureen that changed the path before me and erased the one I'd already trampled. She handed me a Bible and took communion with me, which I didn't quite understand until that moment. I accepted His blood and His battered body as a stand-in for what *I* deserved. I thought I'd gotten what I deserved when I fell down those stairs. But my sacrifice was worthless and of my own earning. His sacrifice is worthy of the whole earth's praise.

I couldn't forgive myself for the things I'd done. I would always go to bed with the face of a little boy I'd never meet carved into my mind. But knowing that the Creator of Heaven and Earth forgave me for even that brought a peace that surpassed my understanding. In that peace, He'd beckoned me with a still, small Voice.

Before I thought of my never-to-be-born son that night of redemption, I held my compass in my hand in the constant dim of my bedside lamp. I considered the arrow pointing to the "E" and the one pointing to the "W." I marveled at how no matter what I tried, the two directions could never meet. Absolute truths, as I already knew them to be. As Maureen said, my sins were that far from my Savior's awareness. Forgiveness. And thus, my void was filled.

Part II

Symptom Relief

"Hatred stirs up strife, But love covers all sins."

Proverbs 10:12

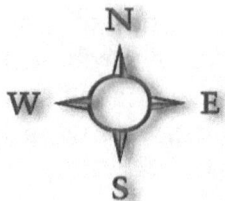

Chapter 12

Shrink

Jake was in jail, being held without bond until his trial since he swore even to a judge that he wasn't guilty. But I was still terrified to be at my house alone or to walk alone further than the church after school. So, Dad started picking me up there on his way home from work. I didn't want to be accused of loitering, so I often tried to help if I saw a need. Helping the worship band move sound equipment. Keeping the coffee cart stocked. I noticed the church staff was relatively small, so they all worked to meet needs, regardless of expertise. I jumped in wherever I could. But usually, my still-casted wrist would earn me a warm smile and a, "We got this! You go take a load off."

Logically, the three quiet hours I spent in the foyer each day would have been best used for homework. But even fundamental logic was different through the eyes of the redeemed. Therefore, most often, I spent the entire time reading the Bible Maureen gave me. I soaked in God's promises to the gentle click of a compass lid with a still-casted hand.

Maureen and I spoke a couple of times a week when she called me into her office or took a walk with me through the church. I was smart enough to know she was only a church counselor doing her job, but I was connected to her as if she was my friend.

One such day, Maureen recruited me to help her set up for a service with a single flick of her head and a smile. This meant she wanted to check up on me and knew she could use my desire to serve as an excuse. Maureen often multitasked by counseling me while I helped her with other jobs.

I followed her, and she knocked on a door to an office that intimidated me. The plaque on the door was a declaration of power, yet Maureen spoke to the man that opened it as an equal.

"Approval, please." Maureen handed Pastor Robert an insert for the program for that day's Wednesday night service. He took the insert and invited us both to enter the office.

I stayed close to the door and quietly looked around the office while Pastor Robert read the program insert aloud to himself. There were pictures on his desk turned so that he would see them while sitting there, and there was nothing on the walls. I knew he had at least one grandson and wondered why family pictures didn't overtake the room. A private man, I assumed. Part of me wanted to lean in and look at the pictures. But something told me it wouldn't be a good idea.

"How have you been faring, Miss Ellis?" He remembered my name, and I was startled.

I cleared my throat. "Um. I've been okay, sir. You have a beautiful church."

He smiled. "As do you, Miss Ellis."

Maureen found the comment amusing but rolled her eyes with some benevolent sort of disrespect in Pastor Robert's insistence on humility.

On the way back to our task, I saw a door hiding in a corner of the foyer opposite the information desk and a direct diagonal from my little table. The maintenance closet. There was a sign below the one that labeled the room. It was the kind of engraved metal plaque I assumed would contain some sort of profound scripture or commemoration. I'd never been close enough to read it, so Maureen waited as my eyes apprehended it.

Thou shalt maintain God's house—
But only if thou art capable of returning borrowed items
to this "office."
—Blessings, Mark

I chuckled, and Maureen smiled.

"That's awesome. Who is 'Mark'?"

"Mark is a lot of things. I guess his job title is 'Facilities Manager.' He gets a little help, but he pretty much single-handedly cleans and fixes everything in the church. He's here seven days a week. I'm amazed you haven't seen him." Maureen continued through the foyer as I allowed my mind to scan through the faces I usually saw in the church and the names that had connected with the handshakes.

"It's possible. I see a lot of people."

"You haven't seen him. You would know if you had met Mark. And *I'd* know. Trust me."

"Okay. . .?"

"Don't worry, it's probably a good thing." She snickered to herself.

"Oh, is he like a grumpy old man?"

Maureen turned from me to hide her smile. "We'll go with that one."

I was intrigued by the type of old man bold enough to engrave the saying on a plaque for all to see. I refocused my thoughts when we stopped at the information desk, where the woman there was standing with a stack of inserts and programs, joining the two into a third stack. Maureen took the stacks from the stout little woman and smiled at her. We sat at my favorite table and worked to finish the task. After a moment, Maureen started in.

"Have you considered making a commitment to abstinence?"

"Considered? I think that's a given after everything that's happened."

"I wouldn't be so sure. I'm living proof that a lot can happen between a 'given' and a 'commitment.' Maybe you should wear a purity ring to remind yourself."

I smiled slightly. "I'll skip the purity ring. I realize I'm forgiven and stuff, but that's taking it a little far, don't you think?"

"Is that what *you* think?" She paused a moment between stacks to stare intently into me.

"Spoken like a true shrink."

"Hey, the official title is 'biblical counselor.' I tell you what God thinks, and you make decisions based on that and the way you are moved by the Holy Spirit." Maureen smiled when I called her a shrink. It seemed she took some pride in that. "But seriously. You should make a *commitment* to abstinence, not just assume. If that's something you want to strive for, of course."

"Well, isn't abstinence what *God* wants? Does anything I want matter after that?"

Maureen took different pride with the next smile.

"Wow. I like you." It sounded fresh in her voice. Not something she said often. "I mean, yes. God tends to honor *any* choice we make to flee from sin."

I sighed in relief. "So, where do I sign up? I'm *so* ready to do things His way."

Maureen was astounded at my willingness to live for God. I was disgusted at my previous *un*willingness.

"If you want to honor God with purity, that's great. But this isn't a decision you should take lightly. It might be easy now, after your particularly horrible relationship. But it won't stay that way long. Eventually, you *will* be tempted. From my experience, faith is not faith if it hasn't passed the test."

"Are you doubting me?" I said it lightheartedly but with a tone of pure defensiveness. Many things were with Maureen. She was brilliant and understood, with precision, all tones of voice, and any kind of sarcasm like a science. Therefore, I was comfortable as myself with Maureen. But just then, she was trying to make me understand something and responded with sincerity.

"I'm not doubting you, Paige. I just—"

"No, I totally understand. I would doubt me too. But you're forgetting one tiny detail."

"And what's that?"

"'I can do *all* things through Christ, who strengthens me.' Jesus changes everything." I smiled. "Go on and doubt me. But don't doubt Him."

She paused in a silent revelation before she looked at me, nodding. The notorious smile returned. "A bit out of context with that verse, but you're a good kid, you know? Not a kid at all, as far as I'm concerned. Were you young when your mom left?"

"How did you know my mom left?"

"If I divulged my methods, you'd end up a better counselor than me, Miss Ellis." She smiled, and we collated papers in silence for a time. Again, this was a science to her. And as if I was some reacting substance in a lab, I suddenly gave her the exact results she was expecting.

"I was twelve when the divorce was final. She actually came home for my twelfth birthday, which she thought was my thirteenth, and told us she wasn't coming back. She's a travel photographer, which means she never 'left' because she was never home. Dad raised me. He says she'd come 'home' for short visits when I was little, and I wouldn't even recognize her. I never even knew her well enough to miss her. But Dad loved her enough to be okay as her last priority if it meant she'd keep coming home. So, the divorce was hard on him." I didn't remove my eyes from the task at hand and spoke only the truth.

"So 'Dad' is a bit of a workaholic, and you don't really see much of him. Loves you like crazy, but the only way he knows to show you is to provide for you, and he likely copes with pain by working, so it's sort of a vicious cycle. Strict and a *great* dad when you were a child, but at some point, he became pretty hands-off with the parenting thing. I bet you guys get along pretty well when he is home from work. And you cook and clean for him even though he never asks you to. You have some resentment for him, but otherwise, you want to please him. Am I right?" Maureen smiled, knowing she'd hit the nail on the head.

"There's no way you guessed all that!" I smiled a little, having a transient memory of ice cream with my dad as a child.

"It's pretty obvious if you think about it." Maureen painted a morbidly pleased smile on her face. Then she unexpectedly took what should be secret and made it known as if the whole world already knew. She took what should be painful and made it seem ordinary. "So, how old were you when you were raped?"

An intangible sheet of ice swept down my back, straightening each tiny orange hair in its descent. And despite the satisfied smile on my counselor's face, I tried to pretend I didn't understand. "I. . .what do you mean?"

"You're a terrible liar. Some of my favorite people have that same quality, so don't take that as an insult." She smiled, then concentrated her attention on the collating in front of her, though its mindlessness was even less so to the brilliant woman.

"Um, thanks?" I attempted to forget what she was talking about, but I knew she wouldn't let me. Her persistence was something worthy of a medal.

"Eleven? Twelve? That's certainly something we should talk about."

I sighed. Mumbled. "Twelve. I've never even put it into words like that. Nobody knows about it." I responded awkwardly to the adrenaline pumping throughout my body like a sudden molten betrayal.

Maureen winced. "Your dad knows."

I panicked. "I. . .Maureen, I hope you don't think he. . . because I'm sort of into psychology, and I've read that it's common, but my dad would never—"

"I know," Maureen assured me. "I emailed him. And technically, I'm allowed to counsel minors over fifteen without parental consent, but I always reach out to parents if it's safe to be sure they are aware. 'Dad' emailed and said, 'I think she could benefit from that, thank you'. An abuser usually tries to buffer or protest in some way. So, I know he's probably never abused you in *any* way. But I also think he knows someone did." She smiled compassionately but nonchalantly as if entering my head and searching out my darkest secret was to her like a trip to the mall.

"I didn't know you'd gotten in touch with him. But I didn't tell him about what happened. I don't know how *you* knew."

"I get that a lot." She laughed a little. It was suddenly clear why a twenty-eight-year-old was the head of the counseling ministry when there were several other counselors twice her age. Her insight into the human soul seemed to have no limit. I no longer felt safe around her, yet I wished to always be surrounded by her knowing comfort.

"Promise me you won't ask about that again. Like, ever. I *don't* want to talk about it. I'm serious." I was serious. And she sensed it but only accepted the terms with a bit of spirit.

"I'll wait until you're ready. Could be never. But honestly, it could be next week with *you*. God just grabbed hold of you quick, didn't He?"

I was speechless, not understanding what my desperate clutch on Christ had to do with talking about the more painful regions of my past. She rerouted the covert session to something slightly less uncomfortable.

"So just pray about the abstinence commitment, okay? I do have faith you can do it, but—"

"But what, Maureen? God's got this."

"*But* sexual abuse tends to cause a young woman to go one of two ways. Sometimes, she can't stand the *thought* of a man touching her. But sometimes, she subconsciously tries to take back the power he took from her, which results in a lot of choices that wouldn't normally exist within her personality. Usually promiscuity."

I took the conviction with a quick sigh and then defended myself. "But I'm done with that, Maureen. Christ conquered the *world*. I don't have anything to prove anymore."

"Amen. But old habits die hard. In the future, I bet you'll question a guy's *interest* in you if you aren't sleeping with him. That being said, do not *ever* hesitate to come to me if you have trouble with anything or want to talk. You have my number. Call me or text me *anytime*. Please. I won't have you going back to old habits just because you didn't want to wake me up. Doctor-patient confidentiality applies."

"So, you're *Doctor* Little? An actual psychologist?" I faked a dramatic gasp at the revelation, flattered by her heartfelt offer.

Maureen corrected me. "I suppose. But I prefer *Mrs.* Little. I don't think you'd confide in me if you had to put 'doctor' in my name. My *husband* is Dr. Little. He's about to become a board-certified neurologist, we hope. That would get confusing."

"Okay, Mrs. Shrink." I smiled at the irony.

"Maureen works fine." She smiled too.

"Thanks for sticking with me. I'm really cold." I speak only to keep my lungs from freezing. My hair is beginning to ice.

"You hear the water? Do you hear it? I knew you would make it." Maureen is more excited than ever. I notice her voice has aged a bit. She sounds more like a girl her age— well, the age we both are today —than a younger child like before.

She allows me to lean against a tree as the stream comes closer into sight. The moonlight takes over for the flashlight now. I look up and see about a billion more stars than I've ever seen at home. I hear a strange echo. A howling animal. No. A voice. A word. The same word over and over and over.

"Why are you young? Where am I really?"

"I love you. And you will see me again." I hear two loud beeps and then look back at the stars as a single word echoes through the trees.

Chapter 13

Test

Just like every day after school, I found myself making the trek across the parking lot. I always thought it was too big for the church until every inch of it was filled on a Sunday morning. Normally only a dozen or so cars were in the parking lot, with little variation except bookstore goers or midday prayer roomers. Maureen drove a pearl white Cadillac because the mother of two would never be the minivan type. For Pastor Robert, only an old pickup truck would do.

I smiled on those vehicles daily, loving the people that drove them. And daily, I stopped and admired one that had gone unclaimed to my eyes. Obviously, it was the vehicle of a church employee because of its constant presence in the row just in front of the main doors. It was a car born of patience, love, and dedication. A fully restored classic Mustang in emerald green with a white convertible top. Gorgeous. But a respectable kind of gorgeous. It was exactly what Jake Stone wished his Camaro—only recently towed from the back of the parking lot—could be, but he had not the patience or heart to bring the vision to life.

My father was beginning to wonder if I'd gone insane because I was at church so often. But I figured that if insanity is that peaceful, I was content with crazy. I knew that God could best teach me there in His peaceful presence. But where I supplied God with an invitation to teach me, under the confines of my Bible, of course, He decided instead to test me.

I was reading in Proverbs, rolling my eyes at how accurately my former self was portrayed as an immoral woman. It was almost funny to me and disgusting all at once. But I know I never, ever wanted to go back there. I secretly dreamed of becoming the woman in Proverbs 31. The virtuous woman. Though I doubted a husband or children would ever rise up and call me "blessed." And while I was lapping up each word, I seemed to hear a faint whistle from all around me. I first assumed it was Pastor Robert, who whistled beautifully with a wink whenever he passed. But this whistling was faster, breathier. Younger.

It was distracting, but not enough to keep me from the Word. Then it was, for some reason, accompanied by jingling keys and the occasional squeak of a sneaker against what I knew was the floor of the foyer. I looked up to see the reason for the interruption of my peace but didn't see it, probably obstructed by a staircase or two.

Finally, I sighed and took a break from reading because I could smell that the bookstore had a fresh brew of coffee. I set my Bible down and unfolded my legs, rejoining them with my flip-flops on the floor, and began the fated walk across the foyer.

Halfway to the fulfillment of my caffeine urge, I realized that the whistling was getting louder. And then I realized it was attached to my destination. What I saw was the back of a six-foot-tall male at the coffee station, whistling unabashedly. From behind, there were tell-tale earpieces and cords flowing from his ears to a device in his pocket. He was dancing to music no one else could hear.

I grabbed a cup from next to him, filled it with coffee, and replaced the pot. Then I looked around for packets of the natural cane sugar I liked, but it was missing from the usual stack. I sighed, trying to decide what substitute to settle on. And when I sighed, the whistling stopped, the jingling ceased, and the body beside me turned, to my absolute horror.

He was slender but not scrawny. His jeans sat firmly at his hips. Not sagging or skintight like many styles. His shirt was contrarily just tight enough to hint at comfortably chiseled muscles. And as my new purity demanded, I prayed before I looked up, hoping he was a brown bag special—great body to make up for a face in need of a paper sack. His hand reached up and removed his earpieces in one movement, distracting my eyes to his face more quickly than I'd hoped.

With all righteousness, I panicked, forgetting all about the body that rivaled the David. I made every God-fearing attempt to imagine the young man as a toad that didn't have toffee skin, and wavy hair combed back like a raven at rest. I tried to see his eyes as cold and harsh, instead of green framed with long dark eyelashes. My own eyes were green, but against his obviously exotic heritage, his were much more alluring. His features were strong and sinfully masculine but with the softness of youth, even with a shadow of a beard that only came with a neglected shave. *Breathe, Paige. Breathe.*

It could have been the abstinence talking, but I assumed that wherever he went, he strained necks and tested car brakes. Therefore, I prayed that he completed his coffee mission so that I could sugar mine in un-tempted peace.

But he lingered a moment. Why did he linger? First, I decided that he lacked intelligence because of the blank stare he was giving me. Then when he blinked a few times to return him to the earth, it was as though two flaming stars had extinguished for a moment but returned with radiant fire. Wisdom. Poise. I fought a smile when I looked away from the fires to see a thin layer of dark hair covered his arm until it met the snug Christian t-shirt:

Your friends hang out with you. Your best friend hung out FOR you on a cross.

I was irritated with God for the eyes He gave me to see. But thankful for the escape He provided.

"I like your shirt," I said in complete truth. And for the first time in my life, I decided that I should probably remedy the thoughts I was trying not to think with black coffee and a mad dash to Maureen's office.

She could see I was distressed when I entered her office within a panic and without a knock.

"You alright, Paige?" She was concerned for me and probably thought I'd gotten myself into serious trouble. As far as I was concerned, I had.

"You jinxed me! I am *so* never succeeding with the abstinence thing! You were right."

She cleared her throat. "Um. . . did you. . .?" She seemed hurt. Gravely disappointed.

"No!" I was offended she would even ask. "You said God would test me. And you know what happened? There's a guy out in the foyer that is out of the park, *insanely* gorgeous. I've seriously *never* seen a guy that hot. I *failed* the test! You jinxed me!"

"Oh, my! And when did this happen?"

"Two seconds ago, while I was getting coffee. I ran off before I could get sugar. He probably thinks I'm an idiot, but that's just as well."

"Good girl. You passed."

"What?! Did you hire a model to test me? And how did I *pass?*"

She chuckled. "Sorry, I'm not acquainted with too many models. So, this guy. Did you get his number?"

"Seriously?!" *Was she kidding?*

"Okay. . .his *name?*"

"No. I just told him I liked his shirt. Which I did. I've never been that *awkward* around a guy. Jesus is making me lose my touch. I suppose that's more of a blessing than a curse." I was distracted and tried to sip my coffee. I hated black coffee, and the attempt didn't go well.

Maureen was amused at the face I made. "God tells us to *flee* sexual immorality. That can be metaphoric. But in most cases, it should be taken quite literally. Joseph in the Bible actually ran off and left his clothes behind with a woman that was after him. Much like you and your unsugared coffee. So you passed."

I nodded, trying to catch my racing mind. Remembering Joseph and Potiphar's wife and suddenly feeling like I'd made a good choice for once in my life.

"What did he look like?" I was sure Maureen knew the deepest thoughts of every soul that entered the church. So, since she had to ask, she probably thought I was either hypersensitive to the physical beauty of men or that I was insane.

"Um, six feet tall or so. And he looked Hispanic, but maybe just half. *Beautiful* eyes. Green, I think. I'm pretty sure his shoes were green, too. But if anyone could pull them off, it'd be him." I tried to remove my pounding heart from the description.

Maureen snorted a laugh then giggled into her hand before faking a straight face. Then she blatantly lied. "That guy is *definitely* a figment of your imagination."

"Maureen! He was there! Otherwise, I looked pretty dumb fleeing from the scary coffee." I was irritated with the cruel counselor and her teasing.

Maureen smiled her usual smile in response to mine, but this time through lips that were pressed with an extra degree of secrecy. She thought a moment while she pretended to look at something on her computer.

"I knew you'd run to me the minute you met Mark." She smiled her smile but didn't look at me. "You are pleasantly predictable."

"Mark? From the sign? But you said he was old and grumpy."

"Did I?" Maureen winced but didn't seem to mind that she misled me. She simply began to justify it. "Well, old is relative. He's a few years older than *you*."

"Grumpy?" I demanded. Trying to trap her.

"You should see him when he runs out of Skittles." She snorted.

"Skittles?" I blinked my eyes at her randomness.

"Never mind that. Because in general, Mark is, by far, the nicest person I know." And here, she winked at me. "So, don't run the next time. He stopped biting people years ago."

"You're encouraging me to step into temptation after telling me to flee?" I stood, readying myself to exit the office of confusing counsel.

"I told you to flee *temptation*." She giggled through the rest of her words. "Before I knew you were talking about *Mark*."

I was highly confused, wondering what could remove a man of his countenance from my vast pool of temptation.

"What, is he gay?" The only viable explanation, in my mind.

"Nope." Maureen enunciated, distracted by her computer. She then decided she was unwilling to elaborate further about the young man and cut off the conversation with a panicked hiccup. "End of session, goodbye."

What I perceived as rudeness was likely something entirely different when worn by Maureen. But I took comfort in her reassurance. Not enough, however, to keep me waiting around in the church that day for the next sighting of temptation.

Chapter 14

Serve

Softly and without warning, God changed the very bearing on my compass one day in mid-November. I was rotating my liberated wrist with glee and a bit of stiffness, having gotten my cast removed midday. Since my dad was at work, Maureen had taken me to the appointment and then to lunch and to get a manicure in celebration. I'd never been happier to see the freckles on my hand again.

We exited her Cadillac, and Maureen watched me slow my pace as I passed the green Mustang, as I always did. She smiled as she commented.

"I love that thing. Sometimes I give directions to the church that include, 'Look for the green Mustang.' It practically lives here." She was amused. And once again, had more information than I did.

"It's beautiful." I was in a good mood, which always included a little fire. And I gave Maureen a feeble reply, even though she wanted me to keep talking about the car I relied upon to greet me. Probably to prove some point or counsel me somehow. But I didn't budge, just for the sake of being obstinate.

She sensed the fire, the purpose and all, and gave me an eye roll. "Suit yourself."

Pastor Robert approached me as I entered the church that day. Immediately, he spoke.

"Good afternoon, Miss Ellis. Welcome, as always. I see you are rid of that cast finally." He spoke against the deliberate flight of Maureen to her office in the hallway. The click of heels was much faster than usual.

"Hey, Pastor Robert." I adjusted my purse on my shoulder, smiling at my deep pink nails.

"What a lovely smile. You really like it here, don't you? You feel safe here. And I hear you have more than accepted Christ." His voice sounded odd in person after ordinarily hearing it projected from the stage in the sanctuary.

"Yes, sir. Is it still okay that I'm here?"

"Of course, Miss Ellis. In fact, I *count* on seeing you each day. Do you have a job?"

"No, sir."

"Do you *want* one?"

"Really? Here at the church?" I was thrilled at the prospect of a real excuse to be there.

"It would only be minimum wage. Just the few hours a day you are usually here. Three to six in the afternoon?"

"What is the job?"

"Our Facilities Manager could really use some help keeping the place clean and functioning. He kind of works alone, as things are. Help is hit or miss. Just the occasional teen fulfilling volunteer or community service hours."

"Your Facilities Manager *Mark?*" The name was said with the indifferent tone I'd hoped, having kept the hiccup of terror to myself.

"Oh, so you've met? That's a rarity. He tends to make himself scarce."

"Just in passing, I guess. No formal introductions." I smiled. The pastor seemed to light up when I did and continued even more cheerily.

"Anyhow, I hope you don't mind cleaning. It's not the most glamorous way to serve, but—"

"I *love* cleaning! You'd pay me? Really? I feel like I should be paying *you!*" What serendipity that the task I'd often chosen as penance should become my first job after choosing to live for righteousness.

"Which is why you are the woman for the job. I'll draw up the paperwork, and you can start today! That's if I can find Mark. Let's hope he doesn't have those contraptions in his ears."

I wasn't sure, and nor did I care if I officially accepted the job. In fact, I was smiling until he called the terrifying name in a volume and tone like a father might. I marveled again at the power of the pastor within the church and awaited the arrival of the Facilities Manager. I was struck with panic because I knew that I'd soon be met in the foyer by my greatest adversary, save *myself.* I'm not sure which I feared more.

I was suddenly beyond ecstatic that God allowed me to be in the presence of my pastor when I heard the fated jingling of keys and squeak of sneakers again. Even with all the warnings God could provide, I gasped inaudibly when I saw him approaching with a yawn from a hallway in all his glorious beauty.

Why, I wondered, was Maureen so confident in Mark's incapability of supplying temptation? But then, all at once, I understood when he arrived. Because the thing about his green eyes that gave them such undeniable splendor was not in their color or the way they shimmered fearlessly against the caramel hue of his skin. It was in their innocence.

He seemed in some kind of amused annoyance and glanced at Pastor Robert, then right back at me. He didn't speak, but he snickered and crossed his arms. I was screaming in my soul that I hadn't just agreed to spend three hours a day with him. But then there was a sort of peace. I had a sense that I was in the exact place God wanted me.

Therefore, I prayed feverishly for courage in the situation. It sounded something like, *"You've got to be kidding me, God."* And in looking when I'd rather not, a period of awkward silence must have occurred. Because Pastor Robert nudged the young man's arm and then cleared his throat.

"Paige, this is Mark. Mark, this is the young lady I told you I'd like to hire to assist you."

I took the hand the young man offered. A firm but friendly handshake, followed by a diamond of a baritone voice. When he spoke, my every breath was manually claimed.

"Mark Henley."

"Paige Ellis. Wait, *Henley?*" I looked back and forth between the pastor and Mark, realizing the grave mistake I'd made at allowing my eyes to see. I saw no family resemblance, but an audible sigh of relief came with my pastor's next sentence.

"Mark is my only son." Instant temptation removal. I was able to relax a bit. Even in my most seductive days, a preacher's kid would never have fallen victim. In a way, I guess I always revered those with godly morals. Pastor Robert reached up the few inches that separated them to put his arm around his son.

"He's great at what he does, but I'm tired of watching him try to juggle this with school on his own. I've been waiting for that cast to come off so I could pair up the girl always begging to help out with the guy that sorely needs it. If you think it's clever, I'll take credit. If not, blame Maureen."

"Can we blame Maureen just for fun?" I could see in Mark's quip that he was certainly acquainted with the insufferably brilliant Maureen and seemed to feel about her the same way I did.

A hum of an appreciative laugh was my reply. I nodded with a smile at Pastor Robert's wink. He squeezed shoulders of different heights that needed reassurance, then walked away to leave us shaking hands.

"I like to clean." I allowed the awkward words to unravel into the silence and then remembered the power I used to have over boys. I allowed a portion to save me in that instant. "It's therapeutic. Weird, I know."

"Right, yeah. I mean, no. I'm the same way. I don't know about therapy, but this is my favorite way to serve God." A genuine smile, dimples and everything. A lock of hair strayed onto his face until he shook his head to tame it into place. Torture.

"Well, in that case, I look forward to serving God with you." Joy for those words bubbled over into the hand I was still awkwardly shaking. I laughed and crossed my arms. I averted my attention to the information desk, where the woman attending it was shaking her head with a smile she couldn't hide.

We spent an hour writing down a rotating schedule that would help us clean the whole church over five days, three hours a day. Then a quick cleanup on weekends after services. He tormented me with the left hand he used to write. A bright silver ring engraved with a cross on a significant finger glimmered in the light of the open foyer. Married? But so young! Was that allowed? It brought another level of relief but some silent embarrassment. For the sake of posterity, I only hoped that his wife was at least half as attractive as he. I had certainly detected innocence, but wondered if purity carried into marriage still looked like innocence. Regardless, I wanted to work at the opposite end of the church as him. I wanted to flee. But we agreed that focused teamwork would get the job done faster.

I filled out paperwork and got a thorough tour, learning the nooks and crannies of the church not known by most. I'd undertaken quite a large task. I was overwhelmed as I met much of the church staff in our journey. Pastor Robert had introduced me to some, and Maureen others. But Mark took the time to introduce me to everyone we passed because most of them spoke to him. I was most pleased to learn Ruth Silverman's name. The woman who had watched me read my Bible and fiddle with my compass from the information desk. She was kind and frail, about sixty years old at the time, with a face that almost seemed familiar, but I didn't know how.

"It is great to finally be introduced to you, Ms. Silverman," I said cheerily as I shook her hand over the high counter.

"Likewise. But please, call me Ruth." Ruth whispered. Deeply. Almost like she was choked up. Eyes almost glistening. And at her joy of meeting wretched me, I felt forever welcome in that foyer.

I officially met the worship team, which was a great honor to me, and various other assistant pastors, counselors, and administrators. But regardless of honor or renown in their positions at the church, Mark's presence seemed to demand the respect of all. Perhaps because he was the pastor's son. But I suspected that he had done well to earn the respect by his constant air of kind confidence. Yet, in our travels throughout the church, he refused to look me in the eyes.

We opened a familiar door without knocking before I was about to walk home—my father having told me he was working late. Maureen was inside on the phone. Her reaction to Mark seemed rude to me. She held up a finger, even though the call was obviously personal.

"Uh-huh. . .No, we ate that two days ago, you trying to get me fat?. . .Well, because then the heels would be harder to wear, and I heart them. . .Ooo, sounds good. I'll be home soon. . .I love you, baby." She finished her call and then finally turned her rushed attention to Mark as she put her current large designer handbag on her desk, tossing things inside.

"I'm on my way out. What do you need?"

"I'm just showing my new *assistant* around." Mark was unaffected by her rudeness, speaking in amused annoyance yet again. And creating some look of quiet animosity that brought some odd tension into the room.

Maureen moved her neck to look around Mark through the slightly cracked door.

Her demeanor rose to cheeriness. "Oh, hey, Paige! I didn't see you there! Your dad has a meeting and called and asked if I'd take you home. I'm glad I caught you before you started walking."

"Oh, thanks. Yeah, it's kind of cold tonight." Which my father didn't used to care about. But I was distracted from appreciating my father. I glanced between Mark and Maureen when she sent some kind of silent signal urging him not to speak of the tension. The moment was painfully awkward until Maureen spoke,

"Alright. Ready, Miss Ellis?"

The ride to my house was silent at first. Then I verbalized my most prominent accusation but allowed my brand of humor to aid me.

"I don't know how you convinced Pastor Robert, but I know this was all your idea. And I hate you. Why would you make me *work* with him?"

"Well, you don't have to. We just didn't want you to eventually think you'd outstayed your welcome and stop coming. We figured a job would make you continue to grace us with your presence. And the only opening was with him." She tried to evade the altercation.

"You could have warned me! How am I gonna keep it together? I'm an immoral woman working with the hottest guy on the planet!"

"Formerly immoral. Who now guards her thoughts and lives her life to follow Christ. Yeah, I've met you, Paige. And I trust you and the accessibility of your counselor. And the God that strengthens you, remember?"

I was flattered. But then I turned to worry. "But do you trust *him*? Mark?"

Maureen laughed once. "I trust that kid more than I trust *myself* most of the time. Especially with 'keeping it together.' He's not just a looker. He has a good head on his shoulders, too."

I recalled a glimmer of silver in the foyer. "So, is he married, then? I saw a ring."

Maureen was happy to reassure me, "A *purity* ring. But it's as solid as the other kind."

"Pure like... *virgin* pure?" I marveled. "He's over twenty. That's impossible."

"More like never-held-a-girl's-hand pure. Mark and Jesus use different definitions of 'impossible' than you or I." Maureen chuckled, somewhat with pride, somewhat with envy. I was intrigued by a mixture of both.

I didn't perceive Pastor Robert to be the kind of dad that would be overprotective enough to keep Mark from all female kind or pursuing dreams. Certainly strict and demanding of respect. But more of a support system than a dictator. Which led me to ask the question of Maureen.

"And this is all his choice? Even the janitor thing?" I was still in disbelief at the paradox of Mark.

"Drives you crazy, doesn't it? He's studying to do something else, and he's certainly smart enough to do *anything*. And handsome enough to be walking a runway somewhere. But between you and me, I think he'll spend most of his life mopping those floors. Few people can find their peace as a true servant of God like that. There's only one Mark. You'll learn that pretty quick."

I nodded, anxious to see what a true servant looked like in action. But I wondered how Maureen could come to have such respect and trust for someone so much younger than her. Because I needed to know, and because I felt at ease to ask, I wondered aloud the thought.

"So, how do *you* know him? He seemed a little upset with you a minute ago."

Maureen bites her lip. "Oh, don't worry about that. Mark and I go way, *way* back. Kind of a love-hate thing, you could say. But it takes a lot to earn Mark's hate." We arrived in front of my house, and I wondered how Maureen could have earned someone's hate, even halfway.

I spent an hour choosing clothes to wear to my new job the next day. Grungy enough to get dirty. Modest enough to not tempt a boy or myself, especially in a house of God. But pretty enough so that he remembered I was a girl. My wardrobe was somewhat limited after the recent purge of immodesty.

About the time I heard my dad come in the house from work, I reached onto the back of my closet and pulled out a box. That's where Dad had stashed my mother's things she left behind. Things she abandoned earlier in my childhood for more provocative clothing that eventually led her astray. I found some well-worn soft jeans and a sea-green button-up cotton blouse. I tried them on just before my father knocked at my bedroom door.

"I brought home dinner. Wanna come down?" He had been trying to communicate with me more since the incident with Jake. Care for me and look out for me more.

I'd opened the door in my mother's clothes, and my father's face turned a dreary gray as if he'd mistaken me for a ghost.

"They suit you." His voice was sad, but he was probably happy I'd stopped flaunting the body that blossomed far too early.

Over dinner, I told my dad about the job, taking Maureen's advice to include him in my decisions more often. He was pleased and said he liked the people at the church and what they'd done for me. My father knew the Lord. But he had deep roots in the ways of the world. I prayed that he would walk through the doors of that church and know the peace I had learned to live for.

I begin to recognize the voice, the word it calls into the darkness. That word is my name. That voice belongs to my father. I look, and Maureen is no longer at my side. She has left me again. But I don't care. I'm elated to hear clearly now what I answer with great desperation and joy.

"Daddy!" I try to run toward the canvassing flashlight, and only then do I remember my ankle and cry out in anguish. And then again, with more desperation than joy.

"Daddy! I'm here!"

Chapter 15

Brave

I walked into the church and placed my backpack on a shelf in the maintenance closet where Mark showed me. I pulled out my bright pink handkerchief and tied it onto the red hair that floated lifelessly above my shoulders. I glanced at the schedule on Mark's tiny desk that was shoved against the back wall of the tiny room. I speculated that he'd never actually sat at the desk, considering there wasn't a chair in the room. There also seemed to be a pile of blankets and pillows underneath. I started to work before Mark arrived from his college classes.

I called out to ensure the emptiness of the men's restroom farthest north in the church and then put up a sign that directed people to other restrooms. After snapping on a set of silicone gloves, I started in. My guess was that this restroom had not shined in years like I coaxed from it. I dipped a mop in the water I'd made and realized the mop itself had turned the clean water brown. I grabbed a clean rag and started on my hands and knees, washing the floor.

The process, which should have been disgusting, began to be therapeutic right away. Not in penance for years of crimson sins. Jesus died for those. I was simply washing the feet of my Savior the best way I knew how.

I heard a chuckle behind me that both startled me and sent an electric pulse to awaken my heart. What a *gorgeous*, genuine laugh. I instantly saw Maureen's assessment of "the nicest person she knows." But I also heard truth and finesse in the laugh. And a hint of sarcasm. A lot can be discovered from a laugh.

"We have mops, you know, Cinderella." The witty teasing surprised me.

"Yeah, they're kind of gross. No point in putting more dirt *on* the floor." I stood and smiled up the eight inches that were our height difference.

"I'll see if the powers-that-be will let me buy new ones." His focused, contemplative nature came to light in the eyes that stared silently into mine. He was reading me. I inquired.

"Cinderella, huh?"

His eyes answered with a glance at the handkerchief on my head.

"Have you ever had bleach in your hair? When that happens, you'll wear one of these too, Boss." I was astonished at how the awkwardness from yesterday melted into such an effortless conversation. I was put at ease in the laughter of my sole coworker.

Mark was amazed at how well and quickly I made things sparkle. He liked the way I pulled out floss from my pocket to get dirt from around a faucet. I liked the way his lime green converse style sneakers glided across the floor as he mopped. Light on his feet and in his entire demeanor. He opened doors for me as if to mock me with respect. But I knew he didn't mock. He was actually giving me that respect.

"Go, team!" He said, giving me a freshly degloved high five. A day's work completed right on schedule. "This should work swimmingly."

I sat in an upstairs area that overlooked the foyer and removed my handkerchief, making sure to have my brush at the ready for my pitiful hair. Mark didn't miss a second of those actions. He was thinking, I could tell. I waited for him to speak.

"So, I feel like I should explain what happened yesterday. I'm sorry if I was rude. See, Dad took applications for your position starting when I graduated from high school. That was over two years ago. He's gotten a thousand applications, I swear. The job is posted on the church website. But on our application, you have to give your testimony and a bunch of other stuff. Dad said there were some solid applicants but that they'd all annoy me. So, yesterday when he said, 'This is the young woman I told you I wanted to hire,' he 'told' me he wanted to hire someone two *years* ago. I didn't know he hired you until *you* did." He snickered, sitting in a chair across from me.

"Oh." I cleared my throat. "I. . .I didn't actually put in an application. I don't even think I *would* have if I'd known there was an opening. No offense."

"None taken." Mark laughs. "Cleaning toilets isn't all that glamorous."

I giggled. "I'm not into glamour. I just didn't exactly feel worthy?"

"Of cleaning toilets?" Mark snickered.

"Of setting *foot* in God's house. I always feel like someone is going to kick me out when I'm here. And I always try to help out if people let me. Pastor—your dad—asking me to *serve* with an actual job sort of blew me away."

"Oh, well, that makes sense then that he hired you. And I'm glad to have an extra set of hands. So please disregard my surprise yesterday."

I snickered a little. "My counselor, Maureen? She told me you were old and grumpy and then tried to tell me you didn't exist. And then told me you were the nicest person she knows. And something about Skittles. I think she's confused."

Mark chuckled. Then he began rifling through his pockets for something as he sighed. "Oh, Maureen."

"She mentioned you two have a love-hate relationship." I put my brush back in my bag and gave him time to respond.

But instead, he released that gorgeous laugh again. "Love-hate? People always think she's so normal at first, but I swear she's from another planet."

I smiled, realizing I must not know her that well. "But she's really smart. Amazing, actually."

"Yeah. Love or hate, she's one of my favorite people." Mark stopped a moment and read me again.

"Mine too, I think." I smiled, nodded, and signaled a much-needed subject change. I pulled out a bottle of water from my bag and took a drink.

Mark finally found what he'd been digging for in his pockets. Half a bag of Skittles. He began throwing them in the air and catching them in his mouth. He looked at my backpack, taking the cue to change the subject.

"What's your major?"

I snickered and then realized he was serious.

"I'm actually a junior in high school. I just turned seventeen. I don't even have a driver's license." I smiled to guard him from embarrassment.

"Really? Wow. Sorry. You just seem older." He winced, trying to unsay what he just said.

I offered a friendly smile, flattered. "I *feel* older." I was comforted by my own assessment.

"Uh, what school?" He corrected.

"River Valley." I nodded. His face lit up.

"Shut up! I went to River!" He exclaimed.

"Small world. If I missed you, you must be at least. . .twenty-one?" I took an educated stab.

"Dead on, Cinderella! I, too, am a junior. . .in *college*." He smiled as he exaggerated the emphasis. "I'm a psych major. Math minor. At Hill U, of course."

I nodded with satisfaction at guessing his exact age. I fondly, then shamefully, remembered a guy named Josh who was a junior in college. I never knew his major. I smirked a little, then looked at my feet, wet from mopping in the skimpy green foam flip-flops.

"Psychology, huh?" I inquired. "You like it?"

"Yeah, God calls us to love people and heal the hurting. Most pain happens in the mind. The soul, really. And only God understands that. But psychology gets close to making sense of it on this side of Heaven, I guess. My courses are really interesting, either way." Mark explained.

"Even the math ones? You said math minor, right?" I grimaced.

He chuckled. "Math is amazing. It's not a soft science like psychology. There's always a right or wrong. It's a welcome contrast to psychology."

I nodded, understanding the need for absolute truth. "I thought I might go to college for psychology. I just recently decided to graduate early, so I better get on that whole college planning thing." I thought of Jake. And winced that I'd shared more than I was willing to explain.

"You're graduating *early*? That's *brave*." He supplemented his cheer with the crunch of a Skittle that landed on his tongue.

"Well, it isn't easy, but I'd say I'm the opposite of brave. Trying to run for my life is more like it." *Why was I telling him this?*

"And God is involved in this decision?" The first part of a point he'd make.

"I'm pretty sure *He* made the decision and then told me about it." I smiled, nodding.

"Doing something that huge just because God says so is brave. Doesn't matter what you're running from." I smiled at the irony as the mature young man coughed after catching a Skittle too far into his throat. Then he squeaked, "I think I just inhaled a Skittle."

His laughter was enchanting. I blinked to return to pure thoughts. "You might be one of the first people not to call me crazy for it."

"You seem sane so far. Just don't spend too much time with Maureen." He held up a Skittle, offering it to me as I giggled. I shook my head in a smile. He again threw his head back, to the rustling of his hair, and tossed the Skittle in the air before catching it in his mouth. An image that helped to both send me and carry me home.

"Uh-oh. You're not talking. Not another boy, is it?" My father's intruding voice over dinner offered little reassurance.

"No, Dad. No more boys for a while. Unless you count my boss."

"*Should* I count your boss?" Why was my dad suddenly interested in my contact with males? He sensed the question in my eyes. "I'm just checking in, you know? I haven't done that enough."

I nodded. Then chuckled. "No, Dad. My boss happens to be the pastor's son. He's not the kind of guy a girl's dad should worry about. I was actually thinking about college."

"Ah, I see. So...what have you decided to do after you graduate in May? I'm still not too keen on the idea, but I do trust you." I needed my father to be 'keen' on the idea. I wanted his full support in everything I did. I'd lived too long with his quiet discontent.

"I'll just go to Hill U. I'll stay home until you're ready to let me go, I promise."

I was, of course, speaking of Hillsboro University. A prestigious University that helped our city thrive. A source of a lot of delinquency for me, but also an excellent school in a few different areas of study.

"Well, that's sweet of you, Paige. What do you want to study?"

"Psychology. Like Maureen." *And Mark.* I silenced the unwelcome addition to my thought.

"I had worried about whether you'd waste that brilliant mind of yours. How are your grades?"

"Good. Really good. Top 10 percent of the class good. If I'd waited a year, I might have still had a chance for number two or three in the class, but I messed up for a while, so I don't have time to—"

"Oh, Paige. My little perfectionist. Welcome home." My father smiled with pride.

"Daddy!" I'm sobbing with desperate relief that I might be safe. With this, I crumple to the ground by the stream where I should have stayed.

I hear footsteps with a frequency that suggests a full run. An out-of-breath man puts his arms around me. I sob inconsolably into his shoulder. Finally, my nose accepts a smell other than stale cigarettes of raw violation. I smell my father. My daddy. My hero. The relief is intoxicating, and I barely hear him speak.

"I'm so glad you're here." His voice is unfamiliar to his face but familiar to my soul. It seems younger, as if he's a teenager. "We can't lose you too."

The heap of flesh and fabric that was my bleak loneliness is now a heap of sobs and love and acceptance. I don't tell him about my visit to a stranger's cabin. I refuse to mount more irreparable pain on top of the departure of my mother. The pain and blame are mine to bear for straying off the path.

Chapter 16

Age

"It's *ten* degrees outside. Why are we standing here, Mrs. Shrink?" I remember wishing I'd been warned so I could have retrieved the gloves from my gigantic purse.

"Because I am the riskiest, most unorthodox counselor you will ever know." She was telling the truth through a devious smile.

"So I'm told. You seem pretty normal to me. Until today, at least."

"Which tells me that my methods are working." She smiled the next smile to herself.

"Speaking of working, I like to get a head start before Mark gets here. Pardon my deviance, but Black Friday is no excuse to stand out in the cold."

"Well, sure it is! Mark stood out in the cold for hours last night. He'll be here any second with his treasures." Maureen confirmed this fact to herself using her cell phone.

"Why would he—" My thoughts scattered as I saw that beautiful emerald green classic Mustang swing into the parking lot. The first time I'd seen it in motion. The car whipped into the drop-off area right in front of Maureen and me, purring like a lioness. Because my heart was suddenly plotting escape, I didn't believe that part of my teenage girlhood would or should ever fade.

Maureen noticed again my unquestionable admiration for the vehicle. But she only smiled that terrible smile when my jaw dropped. I wondered about her counseling methods when a very tired-looking Mark Henley dragged himself out of the driver's seat.

"Hey, Paige," Marks said through a yawn. He walked around the back of the then-tamed convertible and popped the trunk with his key. I fought a smile with all my might, appreciating the match. The Mustang I adored was so obviously his.

"Did you get it?!" Maureen was a giddy schoolgirl as she bounded to the trunk of the vehicle.

"Yes. You owe me five hours of sleep and a bag of Skittles." Mark fiddled a moment with his left middle finger as he yawned again. He took notice when I began to walk around his tantalizing vehicle.

"Mark. Your car is *hot*. Maureen, how come you didn't tell me this was Mark's car?" My tone revealed my dissatisfaction over the car's unrecognized exquisiteness. I bent down to look in the window at the immaculate ivory leather interior.

"You didn't ask." She smiled, loving that she was getting me back for my previous silence over the car.

"Well, she'll be a lot hotter once we unload all the *paper* from her." Mark was irritated with Maureen.

"She?" I finally claimed Mark's smile when I invited him to talk about his pride and joy.

"Paige, allow me to introduce you to my best girl, Velma. She was born in 1967 and reborn slowly over the past several years. A little love and elbow grease go a long way." Mark looked over his "girl" and rubbed a smudge from her hood with the sleeve of his hoodie.

"Velma's an interesting name," I noted.

"My mom's favorite cartoon character," Mark smirked.

I grinned, nodding. "Well, *Velma* is gorgeous."

"Thank you. But she is a bit perturbed at the lack of gratitude after sitting outside of an office supply store half the night for one Dr. Maureen Little."

"Oh, giving in to a little blackmail never hurt anyone, Mark." Maureen flashed Mark her smile.

"Um, that's quite a blanket statement." Mark chuckled. "Paige, can you help me unload some paper, please?"

I finally moved to the open trunk that Maureen had been admiring. It contained one large box labeled as an all-in-one printer. Next to it were about fifty individual reams of paper.

"The printer was 20 percent off *and* the paper was pretty much free with the printer. Ruth's printer at the information desk died last week. Can you believe our luck?!"

"Yay!" Mark mocked Maureen's girlish enthusiasm before she punched him in the arm. He rubbed it groggily.

I'd already stacked three reams of paper onto my arms, confused by the odd flirtatious relationship of Mark and

Maureen. I raised an eyebrow at them within a smile as I made my way inside for a cart. They shot each other a troubled look, then we unloaded the "treasures" in silence.

Maureen announced that she was going shopping and asked if my dad could come pick me up that day, though Maureen was normally my ride then. I called him to confirm before I was left virtually alone in the building with Mark.

"How was your Thanksgiving?" Mark was still yawning every few minutes. He led the way over to the maintenance closet.

"It was great. I mean, the food was terrible. But my dad made it. Usually, he ends up volunteering for work stuff and/or doesn't stay in town for holidays." I smiled at the memory of gag dry turkey and nearly raw potatoes lovingly prepared by a father who was finally trying.

"That's awesome." I loved the heartfelt truth that inhabited Mark's words.

"Yours?"

"It was fun. My family is pretty crazy, but they can cook, so that makes up for it." He smiled at his own joyful memory. "I think I gained about twenty pounds yesterday."

I giggled. "Too bad you didn't get to sleep, though. I'm really starting to see how insane Maureen is. It's really random that she asked you to do that." I love her insane but wanted to see if Mark did too.

"Eh, not as random as you think. I owed her one. Or a thousand. Or she really is blackmailing me. Hard to tell with her." He shrugged as he reached the maintenance closet.

Mark unlocked the closet and grabbed a spiral notebook from the top of his desk. He flipped to an empty page as he leaned on the edge of the desk, clicking a pen as he crossed his feet.

"So. . ." He wrote some illegible heading on the paper. "There's nothing to clean today since no one has been here since we cleaned it last. On days like this, I look around for stuff that's broken and fix it or make a note to call someone else to fix it. And then we have to set up Ruth's new printer before we go."

I nodded, worrying there was infinitely more responsibility involved in this job I'd been in love with for a week and a half. I hoped Mark was good at fixing things. I couldn't even fix myself, let alone broken pieces of a church. I wanted him to tell me to clean something instead.

"I know you're on school break. The church is technically closed. That just never really applies to a few of us. We can get a lot more done when no one is here. But I can take care of things today if you wanna go hang with your dad." Mark yawned and blinked slowly.

I took pity on him. "You look so tired. Let me at least walk around with you. You look for broken stuff. I'll look for dust bunnies."

Mark smiled a little. "Deal."

We walked through each classroom and hallway, checking lights and other mechanical elements. I realized that every door had scuff marks on it and scrubbed away at them as we went along. Mark smirked at my attention to detail.

"So, what's your favorite color, Paige? Middle name?" Mark was deliberate with his icebreakers and had been since we met. He seemed to like piecing together a person from tiny snippets of information.

"Hot pink. Catherine-with-a-C. You?" I smiled, imitating his monotone questions.

Mark first gestured to his lime green shoes to indicate his favorite color. "You either love it, or you hate it. I *love* it... and you can't laugh at my middle name."

"What, is it something completely ridiculous like Eugene?" I smiled to myself as I feverishly scrubbed at a stubborn scuff mark at the bottom of Maureen's office door.

Mark snickers. "Not quite that bad. It's Ernesto." Mark's suddenly exotic accent stopped my scrubbing momentarily. And when I glanced at my arm, I saw the goosebumps I thought were in my imagination.

"That is totally random." And *hot.* I laughed a bit, which helped send the evil thought away.

He forced a distracted laugh, obviously not willing to explain his middle name. "I would have thought you'd be a 'baby blue' or a 'lavender.' But hot pink is acceptable as well."

"Is that some psychological assessment you learned in a class?" With sarcasm, but also intrigued that he cared about my favorite color.

His eyes questioned me, and sarcastically, he said, "Absolutely."

Mark set up Ruth's printer behind the information desk, and I stacked twenty reams of paper into a spot beneath the desk not fit to house them. In my frustration, and amid the sound of paper connecting with hollow wood over and over, I didn't hear my phone ringing at first. By the time I did, I was too entangled under the cabinet to reach it in time.

Ruth rose from her chair and struggled to fit her stout body in the space between where I was working and where Mark lay underneath another cabinet. In a glance at Mark, while Ruth reached down to retrieve my phone, I saw that one of the legs that protruded from under the desk was bent. He lay on his back, and I was using every ounce of my will to ignore that his shirt had lifted enough to reveal a two-inch section of tanned, toned stomach. I bit my bottom lip hard enough to feel pain and allow peace.

"Your phone, Miss Ellis." Ruth's voice was gentle, hollow, and distinct. Almost familiar.

She was bent at my side now, having been given a clear view of my extended glance at Mark. Her smile confirmed this fear, and I put a finger to my lips as I sat up and took my phone from her. I didn't even check my phone as I answered in the near-silent giggle I shared with Ruth.

"Hello?"

"Hey, Paige. How are you?!" A teenage-like enthusiasm was in his voice. Something I'd lost. My ears remembered they had known the young man's voice in darkness—in secret—as well as in public. My mind went over far too many names and faces before I settled on one I decided was worth responding to.

"Aaron?" But why would Aaron be calling me?

"Yeah," He laughed, "I bet you're surprised to hear my voice."

After Aaron told me of his remorse over the rumors he'd heard about Jake, I walked out into the foyer to avoid the eyes and ears of Ruth and Mark. It was in my ear in the foyer that Aaron tried to charm me. The charm of a teenage boy looked much different through the eyes of a woman who had seen the worst of the world. And from the wisdom of deliverance, his invitation to the winter formal dance at our high school sounded a lot more like he was after dark and secrets.

My logical mind had an answer at the ready. He had a point. What was the harm in a school dance? Aaron was always so good to me. But inside, I suddenly heard a still small Voice that urged me to find my end call button and use it with haste. Since I first heard it, that Voice had proven Itself worthy. Yet the dilemma was suspended in the awkward silence a moment. I realized I was pacing the foyer. I calmed myself, found my head, and breathed.

I closed my eyes and imagined the dark eyes that once hid with me in the night. I took compassion on the soul that was so desperate to simply connect with mine again. But then I realized the difference that was Jesus Christ. Aaron had mocked Jesus's blood. The peace I had found in just this foyer meant nothing to him, but it sustained me. Instead of using the wit he didn't possess to make him hang up the phone, I used a tool that was new to me. Truth.

"Aaron. . .dating. . .the way we dated. I'm not into that anymore. I've chosen to be abstinent to honor God. If I ever date again, it will be because I'm married to the guy I'm dating."

Aaron laughed at this. I responded with solemn silence. "You're serious. Paige Ellis, abstinent? That's ridiculous. I mean, that summer we were together, you and me were the opposite of that." Aaron had lowered his voice to a whisper. I assumed his mother was nearby.

"That summer was a lifetime ago." I paced the foyer. "I hope you understand why I can't go to the dance with you or anyone else." Words that were barely scanned by my own thinking as they came from the Holy Spirit.

"I'm sorry you'll miss it. Good luck with all that God stuff." Silence. I looked at my phone, and the call had ended.

I stared at my phone, searching for the disappointment I expected after turning down such a seemingly worthy young man. But I was only met with a victory dance God injected into my heart. No memory of Aaron's loving ways could ever compete with the pleasant peace of God's approval. I smiled unabashedly and bounced back to the information desk. Mark was standing next to Ruth and probably had been for a few minutes. I had been far away from the desk, but Mark was smiling a bit deviously as if he could have heard my half of the conversation.

"What are *you* so happy about, Cinderella?" Mark introduced me to a new tone in his voice. A tone that sought gossip.

Ruth smiled at us both and took her seat again in her chair behind the desk with a book. I finished arranging the paper below and decided to answer Mark's question since he smiled at me so eagerly.

"I'm happy because I'm a teenage girl and just got asked to winter formal by the most popular guy in school."

"Ooo," Mark jeered, "So Cinderella's got a date?"

"Well, I'm not very *good* at being a teenage girl anymore," I said with a liberated smile. I stood and faced my nosey supervisor. "So, no, I do not have a date. Never again."

This deeply satisfied his curiosity, and we both turned to the front door when it opened. I smiled again when my dad walked to greet me.

"Paige, I am so sorry. I think that kid Aaron might be calling you. He came by. My phone was dead, so I came a little early to warn you."

"I handled it." I couldn't stop smiling.

Mark chuckled at my peace and addressed my father. "I'm Mark Henley." Mark stretched out his hand to my father, who gave me an accusing look.

"Sorry!" I realized I'd forgotten my manners. "Dad, this is Mark. Mark, this is my dad. Paul Ellis."

My father took the outstretched hand and spoke, "*This* is Mark? Certainly not what I'd pictured from the stories." Even a middle-aged man could recognize Mark's blatant breed of handsome. I recognized his sheer panic at seeing it.

"Dad!" My hand went to my forehead, and I squeezed my eyes closed to distance myself from the situation. Mark was not yet rid of his inner gossip.

"Stories? Oh, do tell!" He teased me.

My father saw my embarrassment and attempted a save. "What I mean is. . .I guess I thought you'd be. . .older?"

"Age is a number, Mr. Ellis." Mark made my father feel at ease as he waved his hand. "For instance, I bet you have the cleanest house in the country because of this 'teenager' here. I've been cleaning the church for years, and it has never looked like it does now."

"That, I do. How many daughters yell at their father for not hanging up his coat? It's unnatural. But I certainly can't complain. She tried it on, but Paige is not like most teenagers."

"I agree. She's been a blessing. Lifted a huge burden off me. Thanks for sharing her with us." Mark startled me when he quickly flickered one eye in my direction.

Comfort, sealed with a wink. That's what I told myself, at least.

"Daddy, I think I broke my ankle," I say this after several minutes where my voice is only devoted to childlike whimpers.

"I can fix it. I'll fix it. We are together. That's all that matters." I look up into my own eyes that were passed to me. They are saturated as they have been for weeks. But I know that this moment of triumph has provided him some means to a new foundation. A family reduced to two. Together. Pain that is only my own. But the road will be long. And I've only made it halfway to my father's cabin.

Chapter 17

Storge

Even outside, I could hear that Christmas music was blaring over the master sound system. It was a Christmas album of Mark's favorite Christian band. An energetic swing style with a hard edge.

My mood brightened from the oppression of high school as I entered the church and saw him dance–mop across the upper foyer. He had attached bells to his sneakers, which I couldn't detect with sound over the music. He saw me and waved, but was unaffected by my presence. Mark is true to himself, regardless of his surroundings or company. He even added a little "mop guitar" into the mix as I carefully climbed the stairs.

I hated stairs. And those were treacherous. I sometimes had moments of morbidly wondering what it would have been like to be pushed down them. Only sometimes. Many steps were required to reach the height where the upper foyer sat. Only a metal-framed half wall of glass served as a handrail for the stairs and a barrier between upper and lower. Though I loved the transparency implied by the glass walls, they only served one purpose physically—to collect fingerprints that yours truly volunteered to clean every other day. I grabbed window cleaner from the cart Mark had upstairs because Monday was one of those other days. We both bopped and cleaned and sang along merrily to earsplitting modern Christmas carols in a house of God. I imagined God smiling in approval.

I glanced up at Mark once to see a new t-shirt. *Jesus has my back.* He turned to begin another row. The back of the shirt bore a simple cross. Under the cross was written: *See?* I shook my head, chuckling.

Mark finished mopping and began unlocking a storage closet off the upstairs foyer. I tried not to enjoy watching the towel that was swinging from his back pocket. He opened one of the double doors to the room and disappeared inside.

Just as I was finishing the glass, Mark appeared with several oversized wreaths, which all adorned large red bows.

A lifelong love of Christmas returning, I clapped my hands and jumped up and down, letting myself react in a volume that competed with the blaring music. The only holiday my father never forsook. Mark was amused at my reaction. He leaned the wreaths against the glass rail as he saw his father appear at the front door downstairs. Pastor Robert crossed his arms and glared up at his son, who ran to a soundboard on the wall and turned down the music to a livable level.

"Sorry, Dad!" The first words I'd heard from Mark since I arrived a half hour before.

"No, you're not!" I heard this from the pastor, who exited the foyer into his office downstairs.

We chuckled to each other at our harmless rebellion. Why hadn't I stuck to loud music my entire youth?

"How was your day?" Mark gestured for me to follow him into the open storage closet. I began to hear the bells on his shoes jingle as he walked.

"Oh, you know. It's high school, so it was terrible."

He snorted. "High school's the easy part. But if not, it'll be over soon."

I noticed, only after a double-take, that the storage area had a plaque on the door that was still closed, much like Mark's on the maintenance closet. This one, however, contained an error that I pointed out with a giggle. It said, *"The Storge Room."*

"Was this you?"

"One of the assistant pastors had a laser engraver, and I asked if I could use it for something with Velma. He and I went a little crazy with it that afternoon." Mark smirked.

"Well, are spelling classes included in your harder-than-high-school degree program?"

Mark merely smiled, well satisfied at my perceptiveness.

He flicked the light on in the storage area. The "storge" room seemed to be reserved just for decorations for numerous holidays and celebrations. Tubs and shelves were expertly labeled and categorized. One-third of the room was conquered by Christmas decorations.

"This place used to be a huge mess," Mark started, "But I got grounded the summer between my junior and senior years of high school. Organizing this room was part of the sentence. And then I had to clean the church every day. Two hundred hours in all. My dad thought he was punishing me, but that summer is when I found my calling. Finished the two hundred hours and then got paid from two-oh-one on."

"Grounded? Two hundred hours? What did *you* do?" I stepped into the storage room and examined the Christmas decorations, pretending not to be delighted at Mark's rare personal anecdote.

Mark lifted a tub, checked its weight, and then handed it to me and picked a heavier one for himself. He led me back to the wreaths, and we set the tubs down.

"I *allegedly* took my dad's truck without asking and *allegedly* ran a stop sign and got a ticket that he had to pay for because I was broke. . .allegedly." He smiled an innocent toothy grin before leading me back to the storage closet.

"But you had to have a good reason for taking the truck, right? You seem the goody-two-shoes type." I smiled, shaking my head.

He laughed. "'Goody-two-shoes'? What makes you think *that*, Cinderella?"

I wondered what would make me *not* think that. "Oh, please."

He chuckled. "Fair enough, I'll give you the goody-two-shoes version. I needed my dad's truck because I was taking my nephew to get ice cream—"

"Nephew?" I interrupted to clarify a word he hadn't used before, then thought aloud. "Oh, that's right. Your dad's grandson would obviously be your nephew. I think I met him briefly when I met your dad at the hospital. But he didn't seem old enough to have needed ice cream when you were in high school."

"Perceptive." Mark winked. "I have *two* nephews. You probably met the younger one. I was taking the older one for ice cream because his little brother had just been born, and he was feeling neglected. Now it's kind of a tradition. He might outgrow it soon, but I take him most Saturdays now," He explained.

"And you got grounded for that?" I laughed. He didn't. "Seriously? There *has* to be more to that story."

"There's more to every story." A repeat of the same fake toothy grin.

"I bet that's the worst trouble you've ever been in."

"Well, I like to live on the straight and narrow so that no one will suspect me if I decide to go on a secret killing spree."

We both laughed. His humor was as dark and dry as mine. Finally, I was understood.

"That's what I thought. Goody-two-shoes. Typical preacher's kid. I mean, except the loud music and the crazy shoes, and you totally speed through the parking lot. That's all a little more normal." I stepped out on a limb since he was in an anecdotal mood and asked a plaguing question that seemed to be taboo around those parts. "So is it your mom, then. That's um. . .Hispanic?"

Mark laughed heartily and seemed to read aloud my exact thoughts as a jest. "So basically, 'Why are you half Cuban and where the heck is your mom?' People don't ask that anymore. I forgot you wouldn't know. I can imagine your confusion."

"Ah, Cuban. That makes sense. Sort of." I giggled, happy I was going to be allowed in the loop.

"Well, apparently, my birth mother was the daughter of some pretty wealthy, powerful individuals with a reputation to uphold. She was a teenager and managed to hide the entire pregnancy. She died in an ambulance after giving birth to me on the bathroom floor. 'Ernesto' was her last word." Mark winced. "'Ernesto' was the gardener they'd recently fired for spending too much time with their daughter. He was here illegally from Cuba, and they'd had him deported. He has no idea I exist. And even though I was all that was left of their daughter, I'd have been quite the blemish on their good name. So they put me up for adoption. But that's all irrelevant. I'm at peace with all that now. Robert and Amelia Henley are my *actual* parents. They named me Mark because my dad can't do the accent thing, so 'Ernesto' wasn't happening." He chuckled. Then sobered. Sighed. "Anyway, my mom isn't around because she died when I was nine. An aneurysm that not even she knew about burst when I was at school one day.

She was the kind of person that made enough of an impact in the time she was here that God took her home earlier than *we* expected. She was only 38."

"I'm *so* sorry, Boss. I had no idea." I hated myself for asking what I was unaware had such a horrible answer. But suddenly, to my surprise, I saw Mark's dimples appear.

"No worries, Cinderella." He chuckled then changed the subject for something less painful. "So, Christmas decorations."

"I love Christmas. It's the only time people treat each other the way they should *always* treat each other." I followed the bells once again.

He snapped and pointed, pivoting gracefully to turn to me and walking backward. I wondered still if there was an awkward bone in his body. "I always say that exact thing! I *love* Christmas. Mom started this tradition of letting the junior highers decorate the church. Maureen is currently briefing a group of about twenty insufferable middle school girls who will still ask us to help them every ten seconds. I always end up doing the majority. Climbing up ladders and showing them how to plug in lights and such. I think preteen girls have some temporary brain shrinking disorder."

I giggled at Mark's ignorance and at the way the word "insufferable" sounded a little like something Maureen would say. He gave me an inquiring look.

"Seriously? Brain shrinking? You don't think maybe they just want an excuse to get excessive attention from *you*? Please tell me you're aware of that."

"Why do you say that?" He laughed, scrunching his innocent eyebrows.

"Wow," I remembered the poise and fearlessness I used to live by and explained to him what he was oblivious to. "Here's some perspective from a girl. I know it may be hard for a goody-two-shoes preacher's kid to fathom, but they are only 'insufferable' because they are twelve, and you are widely known to be exceptionally handsome. It's probably like getting to hang out with a movie star for an afternoon. I've seen females of all ages whisper and giggle when you walk by.

Tell me you notice this." With my smile, Mark looked away to avoid the flattery I'd offered.

"Whatever you say, Cinderella. But I think *you're* more of a goody-two-shoes than you think." He smiled, knowing I'd find this amusing. But somehow, I think he actually believed it.

As expected, I laughed robustly and extensively as the promised group of girls came into the foyer from their downstairs den, already giggling and pointing out Mark against the railing. Maureen followed them in and seemed confused as she looked up at me. I continued laughing when Mark winked and headed down the stairs to meet the group of girls. Maureen and Mark intentionally bumped shoulders as they passed each other on the stairs. As if they were passing some unseen understanding between them in the process.

Maureen reached me as I watched the girls coo and awe over Mark. We leaned against the rail and watched him lead them up the stairs again.

"I bet you have no trouble getting these girls to volunteer for this." I shook my head, wiping a tear from the laughter.

"Nope. When I was in middle school, Amelia Henley had an interesting time getting us junior highers to do this. Mention Mark's name, and they are all over that sign-up sheet. I hope they remember what I just told them. Mark's music was so loud, I could hardly think." Maureen laughed, and I joined her in cheery chortle. She once again gave me a confused look.

"What?" I inquired through my amusement.

"I've just never heard you laugh. Not like that. It's nice. I'm glad someone else enjoys watching him get ogled over by little girls. I'm *definitely* here *just* for this." Maureen smiled at Mark as he passed.

"Well, that and him thinking I'm a goody-two-shoes. He said those actual words about me. He's totally clueless." At my unforced laughter, I saw Mona Lisa's greatest rival in my direction. My laughter seemed to free me, but Maureen's smiled response reeled me back in.

"What's funny is you thinking *he* is." Maureen raised her eyebrows at me.

"But you said he was all pure and stuff. How could a preacher's kid not be?"

"You're obviously not very 'churched.' Otherwise, you'd know preacher's kids are quite often the worst rebels around. Mark is no exception. Pure, he is. He didn't cross *that* line, thank God. And he's got his head on straight *now*. But a few years ago? Goody-two-shoes would have been a *hilarious* label for him."

"It was probably still accurate, though. Even if he temporarily got into some trouble, I bet he only lashed out because of his mom. Amelia, was it? When you're a kid, losing your mom all of a sudden like that has to be rough." I assumed she remembered, even if she was just a teenager then. She confirmed this in the few more seconds of silence than she customarily allowed, coupled with a wince that started in some deep root of her soul.

"Rough?" She chuckled. "Understatement, sweetie. Now, if you'll excuse me from your amateur psychological analyses, I have a couple hours of entertainment to attend to." Maureen walked away as the secondary volunteer to help the girls with Christmas decorations. I tended to both Mark's and my duties for the afternoon.

As promised, Mark was asked for "help" often. While above doting preteens on a ladder for the fifth time, Mark shook his head at me as I passed by. He smiled at his unsolicited perspective. I was perplexed at mine.

Chapter 18

Family

"Mark, your nerdiness knows no bounds." The self-assured strut clicked to a halt in the upper foyer where my supervisor was helping me study for my Trigonometry final. "Seriously, who gets a math minor on purpose?"

Mark, who had no idea that he was saving me from losing all my scholarships by helping me pass this test, spoke through the Skittle in his mouth as he examined the next problem. "Says the girl that had a conniption when she *only* landed salutatorian."

"Valedictorian would have looked better on law school applications." Maureen sighed, plopping herself onto the opposite end of the loveseat Mark was sitting on, and turning her legs so that her red stilettos landed on my Trig book on Mark's lap. For this, he was forced with a grumble to sit back from my notebook, which was on the table between us.

I giggled at the two-sided teasing, still not understanding the history of my companions. So, I ignored their physical comfort with one another and requested to be let in a little. "Law school? Aren't you a psychologist?"

They both chuckled. Maureen spoke. "God had other plans."

"Valedictorian is more important for *med* school apps and scholarships, anyway." Mark provided additional cryptic information.

"We were totally tied for number one. That guy still owes me *exorbitantly* for consenting to that." Maureen yawned. And I tried to construct in my mind a scenario in which the competitive and overachieving Maureen would give up such a title for someone else's dream.

"What? Valedictorian or the thing that knocked you up?" Mark laughed gloriously, deeming my scandalous gasp well worth the punch in the arm from a classy counselor.

Yet, the truth of it didn't surprise me. Maureen was a powerful woman. But when it came right down to it, she drew her pride from her children and her husband. I'd been told of the medical resident who was soon-to-be a neurologist. The nine-year-old with a MENSA level IQ. The five-year-old with perfect pitch. These far more than the fact that she herself was a psychologist. Therefore, the damsel inside her would have only wanted the man that would both best her for an overachiever's highest honor *and* win her heart.

I delved into the scandal since Mark opened the door.

"Wait. . .so your husband. . .is he a Christian?"

Maureen giggled as she nodded and removed her shoes from Mark's lap. Mark was dramatically happy she did, stretching out and leaning over again with a groan and a sigh. I again let the wheels turn, trying to sort out a world in which a deliberately pure young man allowed a tall blonde to place red heels on his lap in a church and was unfazed by them. Either he was a celibate for life or found Maureen unattractive. Neither seemed likely. Maureen distracted those turning gears with a history that intrigued me more.

"My David is in *love* with the Lord. He leads both doctors and patients in prayer daily because he knows God has power over medicine. He even used to steal my volunteer hours from here at church before we were willing to do them together." She got distracted a moment in competition as we both chuckled. "But you want to know how two Christian overachievers ended up a teen pregnancy statistic, don't you?"

I tucked my lips and felt my face turn red. They were amused. I defended myself.

"That is a valid question!" I giggled. "I know we're all sinners, but you seem to really care what God thinks, Maureen."

"Of course, I do." She winced. Looking a little sheepish for the first time ever.

"Seriously, Maureen," Mark agreed, then spoke with a hint of sarcasm. "You'd think with all the support you had from the church to be abstinent, you'd have been successful. They even offered some accountability partners so you could make it through college still in love without crossing the line."

"Oh yeah," Maureen added, also hinting at sarcasm. "And all the 'support' we had from our high school and colleges to concentrate on our education and careers. Gosh, we even had full-ride scholarships on opposite coasts to make sure we were too busy for some silly long-distance relationship."

"Come on Maureen," Mark added, still with a wink in his voice, "You were set to get married, what… eight years after high school? That's not so bad. I mean, assuming Dave didn't fall for some California girl in the meantime."

Maureen rolled her eyes, then looked me in mine with sincerity. "There was *so* much pressure on us. They expected us to accomplish some crazy combination of time and ambition and abstinence. But no one wanted to consider that *God's* will was something different. So just once, on graduation night, we caved under all that pressure. And did what *we* wanted."

"Sinned. You sinned." Mark clarified, then clicked his pure tongue in disapproval with a head shake. Probably having no clue what sin was at all.

"You'd have made a great lawyer, Maureen. Are you saying it's okay to give up your dreams for sin?" I argued God's side.

"They all expected me to be a lawyer. But *David* was my dream and God's will for me. They cared about what I *did*. David is a part of who I *am*. God would have preferred we not sin, but. . ." She trailed off. Mark picked up the thought. A oneness of mind that made something click in mine before I knew what it was.

"God can even use sin as a course correction. They messed up, so God gave them Dillon, and Maureen eventually figured out she was supposed to be a counselor. Which she would have known from the start if she'd been listening to the proper advice." Mark was both covering for and scolding Maureen as if he'd been witness to said advice giver. But the math of time didn't make sense the way I added it up. Then I saw it clearly in the way Maureen rolled her eyes at Mark and pushed his shoulder aside as he laughed. A kind of love I hadn't experienced myself, but one that suddenly made me see how thick I'd been.

I closed my eyes in a chuckle. "Two sons. Two nephews. And Mark, you'd have been pretty young when Maureen had the first baby."

"Hey!" She took the math as a witty insult.

Mark then looked directly into my eyes with some kind of remorse for Maureen. "You're right. I was young when Dillon was born. I was only eleven, but you don't forget something like that. I was right outside the room with Dad and heard Dillon's first cry. I was this tough little kid, you know. But I cried. It's when I knew that if I do nothing else in life, I *have* to be a father." And he disclosed this time not only his lack of desire for celibacy but also the nature of his relationship with the woman in red stilettos. But if he hadn't, she did so with her furious huff.

"Mark Ernesto Henley, I am telling Dad! You promised!" She stood, about to storm off. But I spoke.

"Don't blame *him*, Maureen-Formerly-Henley. I'm the one that figured it out. Took me long enough, right?" I laughed a little. So many interactions that suddenly made sense. Perhaps it wouldn't have taken me so long if I'd been directly informed. But neither sibling was defined by the other, and thus knowing their relationship would not have changed anything. Would it?

"That's not the point, Paige. He made me a promise." Maureen, sheepish again.

"Oh my gosh!" I gasped at what hit me next. "Maureen, you lost your mom when you were…"

"Sixteen," she finished the sentence.

"I am so sorry if I've ever said anything that seemed insensitive." My heart dropped. "How are you okay?"

Maureen laughed once. "You hear this girl, Mark? I'm fine, Paige. We miss her, but it has been quite a few years. I definitely did end up pregnant, but other than that, I made it through."

I gasped again. "You're the pastor's daughter! I bet that was quite a scandal. What did people do when they found out the preacher's daughter was knocked up?"

But after the gossip queen emerged, the betrayal sank in with a sting. Why had they deliberately kept a member of the staff in the dark about an important family relationship? Perhaps I'd been mistaken about the way they cared for me.

"You made a promise too, Reen." Mark rose and walked off in one direction. Maureen stormed off in another. What I first assumed was abandonment was actually a direct order, though silent, from the man that came into my view from behind me.

"Quite a scandal indeed. A consequence Dave and Maureen hadn't considered in the moment, I'm afraid," said the pastor as he helped me to a stand. "If a pastor can't keep his own house in order, people question his teaching. Rightfully so. But people eventually understood how out of character and against my teaching this sin was. But more so that 'All have sinned and fall short of the glory of God.' Even my perfect little princess. But Christ died for her. And I eventually accepted that He died for Dave too." The rustic laugh of my pastor. Nostalgia, not regret. "Nevertheless, she hated that her sin could be so closely tied to my reputation. Won't you join me in my office, Miss Ellis?"

He led me to the place I revered most in the church. He was a father of two. A widower. But he was a shepherd above all other things. And he knew when there was distress, even deep within a heart. That always comforted me, especially on days I was the only one remembering things that ate away at my soul. On those days, he placed a hand on my shoulder and a word of encouragement in my ear. That day, he more than passed me by with the encouragement. He closed his office door behind us, pointing a stern finger through the window in his door as Maureen tried to approach. And every interaction they'd ever had suddenly made perfect sense.

"I just preach the Word around here. I have a stellar staff, including *both* of my children, that does most of the hard work. But because this office says 'Senior Pastor,' I also get to make decisions on a whim. Today, I'm stealing my son's assistant to help me hang my pictures." He chuckled. I complied without question, delighted at seeing a life in pictures.

First, he moved a large picture from behind a file cabinet and used the wire to hang it on a screw that had always been there. A portrait of a young woman, not much older than myself, with kind amber eyes. He took a moment to stare at the blonde woman who could pass for Maureen's sister. But no. In an instant, I realized who it was.

"Is that her? Your wife?" I asked with compassion.

"That's my bride. My Amelia." He confirmed with a sigh. "She had this picture taken for our first wedding anniversary since we didn't have any wedding photos to hang. She was just. . .perfect."

One by one, Pastor Robert turned the photos around on the desk. The ones that had intrigued me by being turned so only he could see them. A picture of a younger and very pregnant Maureen in a wedding gown. A photo of two young boys laughing and wrestling in the grass with Mark. Various graduation photos of both Mark and Maureen. Old family photos of Mark, Maureen, and Pastor Robert with Amelia. Pastor Robert took picture hanging Velcro from his desk, directing me where to put photos as he explained each of them.

I learned that the boy I'd met at the hospital the day I met Pastor Robert was Lane, Maureen's five-year-old. That Mark and Maureen had helped raise each other and heal their father after the death of Mrs. Amelia Henley. That Velma wasn't always so gorgeous. Dillon looked just like his mother, and Dave had a crooked nose. As I'd always thought would better suit the proud grandpa, the pictures were not all hung until all four walls were filled from nearly floor to ceiling with photographs he produced from seemingly magical places in the room.

In the two hours I should have been mopping after the brief study session, I learned that Maureen had thought she'd be a better counselor and the scandal of the pastor's daughter could be removed from his own witness if she kept their kinship a secret from the congregation, though the whole staff was aware. She had also grown weary of young girls using her counsel to try to convince Mark they were "God's will" to be his wife. She knew the secret would be unorthodox, but as I was learning, she did not operate under convention. The greatest shock, perhaps of my life, came when my pastor sighed and told me how he and Mark had convinced Maureen to tell me the secret. Not only that, he told me, but Maureen had planned to eradicate the secret completely, regardless of the consequences. All, he claimed, because of me. Because I was 'special.'

"Why am *I* special?" I nearly whispered. They didn't even know me a few months before.

The molten smile. "A timeless question, Miss Ellis. I'm half a century old and still include it in my prayers from time to time."

I smiled, appreciating the shepherd's form of whimsical wisdom.

"That's good to know. But this secret seems like a valuable method for her. Why would one wreck of a teenager cause her to change it? She's probably counseled a thousand girls like me."

He chuckled and moved to his desk drawer and pulled out a final picture, smiling as he looked at it, though I couldn't yet see it. "I assure you, Miss Ellis, Maureen has never counseled *anyone* like you."

Pastor Robert found a spot at about his eye level between the lone photo of Ruth and one of Maureen laughing. He placed the photo there. Maybe to remind me why I should forgive any perceived trespasses from the family. Or maybe just because of the way he smiled when he saw it. My memory was a day my coworker had decided to test out my floor cleaning method, and Maureen had caught us with a camera while Mark was complaining about his knees hurting. The result was a candid photo. Mark sitting beside me, watching me scrub floors. Me scrubbing floors in a Cinderella bandanna, giggling at Mark for sitting there. The picture described the joy we took in our day-to-day service, together in God's house.

I thanked the pastor for his love and insight, reluctant to step out of his office into a place of tension that was currently lacking its normal peace and solace. Mark gave a little wave before we both walked toward the maintenance closet from opposite directions.

"I bet he heard the whole conversation. This foyer speaks. When it's empty like this, you can pretty much hear anything anyone says." Mark's smile and random information melted away. "I'm sorry."

"Your dad is amazing. I'm not mad. At any of you guys. I get it." I nodded, and he sighed in relief. I took the opportunity to inquire of a long-wondered truth. "I always thought that preacher's kids were like your *sister*. Overachievers, you know? But she told me that isn't true. She also told me you were not a goody-two-shoes. So who *were* you in high school?"

"I guess we're even on the secret thing!" Mark shook his head, raising his voice after a victorious female laugh came from near the info desk, confirming the speaking foyer theory. What had I told that foyer? He sighed, then answered my inquiry in a mumble. "I was a jock."

I gasp. "Maureen just said you were a nerd!"

"I was a smart jock." He chuckled. "Sort of." He winced.

"What sport?"

"I was actually the 'star' pitcher in baseball until I quit playing." He gave a half smile for some embarrassment I didn't quite understand.

I snickered at the irony. "That's funny! I was a 'sort of smart' typical cheerleader until I had to quit." I winced, remembering that Jake forced me to quit. "Anyway, in the off-season, us cheerleaders would spend a lot of time watching baseball. So I actually dated the star pitcher once."

"Really? What was his name?" He counted years on his fingers. "I wonder if I know him."

"Um, Jason Fisher? The guy was a loser. He was *so* vulgar and talked all the time. The only time he ever shut up was to drink like a fish, so they called him—"

"J. Fish?!" Mark gasped. "*You* dated J. Fish? And you were a cheerleader? I—" Mark looked to the skylight and nervously cracked the fingers on his left hand with a wince. He was overwhelmed with disbelief for some reason.

"You didn't like hang out with him, did you? Because he partied *constantly*." I was in disbelief of my own and couldn't reconcile this portion of the awkward connection.

"Thus the 'not-a-goody-two-shoes' assessment." He chuckled in shame. I chuckled in wonder. "And the reason I quit being a jock altogether once God reminded me who I am in Him."

"Wow. Small world." I tried to end the conversation with a walk toward the stairs.

He growled as he followed me, reluctant to mention it. "I can't *believe* you dated him. I knew the locker room J. Fish, and maybe he was lying half the time, but—"

"My stuff." I blurted, not willing to mix my past with his purity. "It's upstairs, and I have to get home and study."

He cleared his throat and walked the few steps to the maintenance closet. He produced my backpack and purse and handed them to me with a smile.

"There was a creepy blonde walking around, so I packed up your stuff for you," He whispered. I giggled when Maureen scolded him from the info desk. Suddenly I loved them even more as a family.

Chapter 19

Gift

On Christmas Eve, we were scraping wax from the floor with razor blades, just outside the sanctuary doors where the ushers had stood collecting candles. Christmas was just hours away, and the entire church staff was gathering with their families in the senior high room, which was equipped with games and stocked with snacks. I planned to gather a moment with them but wanted to get home to the father, who refused to come. I was alone that night with my church family, knowing that they had helped heal me, even in this short time. God's many hands. Like Mark's hands. Strong and confidently precise in collecting wax from the floor.

I was in a simple red cotton dress, a red plaid scarf, and black leggings, abandoning my usual Cinderella garb for the Christmas Eve candlelight service and party. I'd even curled the hair that was starting to grow back healthier and traded my signature flip-flops for a pair of boots. Mark wore his usual jeans and a black sweater, fitted against his well-deserving chest. After Mark scraped, I used my usual rag and water to remove residue. He chuckled at this.

"I have something for you. You just reminded me."

"Oh, me too!" I remembered the item I'd seen in the church bookstore that reminded me of Mark. A wooden box with a hinged top, about the size and shape of a box of cigarettes. I'd painted "Mark's Addiction" on the side in lime green and included ten bags of his fruity obsession as refills.

I rose and headed to Mark's "office" to retrieve the carefully wrapped gift after we corrected the wax mess.

He followed close behind me and turned on the light when I could have emerged in the dark with his gift. I nearly stumbled over a second mop bucket where there was normally only one. It had a big red bow on it and was labeled on cardstock in bold marker "For Cinderella." The mop handle and bucket were both a brilliantly saturated shade of hot pink. My initials were professionally etched in the plastic with frilly black letters. *P.C.E.*

"Where did you find this? My present is so lame now!" I admired a simple bucket. The greatest present ever from someone I thought barely knew my name.

"You like it? I found it in a catalog after my phone died while I was in line for that printer on Black Friday. I hate that you clean floors on your hands and knees. That's why I asked your favorite color that day. Maureen said it would be tacky to buy you a mop, but you've been asking for a new one, so I hope it's alright." He spoke quickly and then waited for my reply.

"This isn't tacky at all! I *love* it. There can never be too much pink in the world. Thank you. I can't wait to use it." I handed him his gift bag as I admired my present.

He opened it and gently pawed the wooden box with some look of amusement but a little confusion. "How did you know?"

"Know what?" I joined him in confusion.

"This looks like a cigarette box," He noted.

"You're addicted to Skittles like a smoker. Thought you should look the part."

"Skittles helped me quit smoking." Mark smiled. "I used to hate fruity candy and anything that was mildly sour. So I let Maureen hypnotize me, and suddenly when I smoked, it tasted like Skittles. It didn't help with smoking. But Skittles did."

I gasped. "I had no idea you were a smoker. There I go being insensitive again."

"No, it's *perfect*, Paige. I needed something like this." Then he squealed in delight when he saw the ten bags of Skittles at the bottom of the bag. "And this is enough Skittles for at *least* a day."

We laughed at the justified exaggeration of his Skittle problem.

Maureen walked up to the door, and I admired her emerald knee-length dress silently. Classy to her core, I decided. Then she looked right at me.

"Wow, I *love* you in red! I bet this bonehead didn't say a word. Do you realize how gorgeous you are?"

"Thanks." I looked to the floor, never readily accepting a compliment. Even as fulfilling as they were coming from

Maureen. I pulled my hair to one side and stroked it a couple times.

"I didn't say anything because she always acts like that when people compliment her. So, Paige, you *don't*. . .look *great*." I looked up at Mark, who smirked a little before looking at the ground. I was again amazed at how perceptive he was. And flattered that he'd just complimented me. I didn't think he'd taken any notice of me beyond my mopping abilities.

"No thank you." We snickered at the interesting compliment.

"Party. Stop working. Let's go." Maureen was painfully anxious for us to come into the party. Her husband and sons had probably just arrived, and she had been dying for me to meet them ever since the family secrets came to light. Mark and Maureen looked behind me and took off together to the party at a comical pace, leaving me looking back to see the purpose for their sudden flight. A good purpose, I decided when I turned around to see 'Pastor Dad,' as they affectionately called him as of late. Looking kind, as always, in the suit and tie he saved for special occasions. He offered his arm, and I gladly took the most honorable escort into the party.

"Merry Christmas, Miss Ellis. What did you think of the candlelight service?"

"It was beautiful, sir. I felt like one of those candles." I laughed, not having shared these words with another soul yet. I remembered singing Silent Night as the candles lit throughout the sanctuary. A symbol of God's light spreading throughout the world.

"That is wonderful to hear! I should warn you about our 'wild' parties. First of all, Maureen's little one, 'Mini Romeo,' has no verbal filters. Nor is he very good at lying, so you are in no way safe as a lovely young woman. And, let me see, the praise band likes to play pranks, so just stick close to us." We both chuckled, though I was suddenly stricken with fear as I entered the party.

To my relief, no multitude of eyes found me at the door to accuse me. I was only met by Mark and Maureen. Maureen took my arm and led me to the back corner of the room, Mark and Pastor Robert behind us.

"Paige, I want you to meet my family." We stopped in front of a little couch. A man and a blond preteen were sitting there. I recognized both of them from my recent picture education. The tall, wide, and handsome mixed-race man stood and held out his hand. He towered over Maureen, even though she was a tall woman in the daily member of her beloved heel collection. The black in his mixture was most prominent, in all but the light brown hair. He looked down with a smile at me, and I noticed again his slightly crooked nose. Such a charming, kind face.

"This is my David." I shook the strong but soft hand of the doctor.

"Pleasure. But call me Dave. Only my wife calls me David." The voice carried into even in the crowded room. Its depth and character were stunning.

Next stood the young man from the couch. I smiled, seeing immediately that even far removed from one another, this young boy could be tied to Maureen without question, just as in the pictures. He bore her stark blond hair and caramel eyes, in which I perceived wisdom that did not match his stature. He only resembled his father in his slightly darker skin and wider nose, though his was not crooked.

"This is Dillon." I shook the young boy's hand. He smiled.

"He looks just like you, Maureen." The rest of the company laughed at the probably often-stated fact.

Mark looked nervous, which looked a lot like calm and collected, with only a slight tightness to his smile. And because he didn't have Skittles in his hands, he was playing with his left middle finger like he sometimes did. I envied his brand of mellow.

"Where's Lane? He was—?" Maureen began but stopped her sentence at the arrival of pounding feet and a full head of dark curly hair. The boy of about five rushed to the legs of his mother, nearly knocking her down. I crouched to his level, so the boy might remember my face. He turned to me and spoke.

"See, Mommy? I told you. Her *dress* is red. Her hair is *orange*. I remember from the hos-i-pal. Orange hair, Momma.

Not red. But I like orange better. You're beautiful, Miss Paige. And your face is all healed. God healed you! Mommy told me your hair is orange because God made you special. But she says I'm special, too." I was moved nearly to tears at the precious ramblings of the five-year-old. But he didn't stop there.

"Santa doesn't come to my house, Miss Paige. He goes to kids' houses that believe stupid things. But I still get presents, though from Grandpa and Uncle Mark and Mommy and Daddy. And my Daddy's mommy and daddy. But they live in Florida now. It's hot there at summer. Mommy has a mommy too, but she lives in Heaven with Jesus." The whole family was chuckling. Mark's laugh when he was amused by a child was nearly as handsome as the current child that elicited the laugh. I ignored the fact of nature and spoke to the child.

"I see God healed your arm, too," I recalled the sling that had been on his shoulder at the hospital. I was suddenly aware of my own lack of cast and rotated my wrist to a pop.

"Yeah, I broked-ed it, and Mommy drew dinosaurs on my cast. And then Daddy kissed it, and it got better. He's a doctor. Awww, you're so pretty, Miss Paige. Uncle Mark says that a lot. 'Cept he says 'dorgeous' or some word like that. Mommy says it means really, *really* pretty. So, I think you're dorgeous, too." I gathered from Mark's direction the sound a gasp makes when it avoids the vocal cords, and an attempt is made to muffle the rush of air with a fist. The sound, combined with the cruel but concealed chuckles of the family and the way the child stroked my 'orange' hair, should have scared me off forever. But I experienced a shockwave of comfort and peace in two little arms that gathered around my neck. "I love you."

Lane then ran to the opposite corner of the room to charm Ruth into submission. I reluctantly stood to the snorted laughter of the family, and Mark, who was making sure not to meet my eyes by putting his head down and using a hand as a visor. But beneath it, he was breathless with laughter.

"Okay, so *Lane* is adorable," I started, looking to Maureen.

Maureen giggled. "He is *that*, for sure. And honest." She winked.

"So, I'm told." Then I looked to Mark. "I'm trying to decide whether to let him live it down or not."

Mark finally looked up, face reddened, and met my eyes with rock-solid confidence.

"You should *definitely* let him live it down," he said of himself.

"But I heard from a verifiable source that you think I'm *pretty*. I can't just forget that." The laughter mounted around us as I barely got through the sentence for nervous laughter's sake.

"Actually, he thinks you're 'dorgeous.'" I was right about Dillon's old soul.

"Come on, at least let me clarify. Or install my nephew with duct tape at parties, I haven't decided." Mark shook his head with a growled sigh.

"I gotta hear how he gets out of this one," Maureen said in the direction of her jeering husband. Then she looked at me with a smile that forced me to remember my own first impression of Mark's physique. And a wink to suggest she knew it didn't stay at my first impression.

"So, you don't think I'm 'dorgeous'?" I asked sweetly in sarcasm, still against gut testing laughter.

"'Think'?" He bravely replied with a pretentious smile. "You need to clean more mirrors, Cinderella. It's not something you can speculate. Like, that compass you carry around. You don't 'think' north is north. It's absolute truth. North is north. And you. . .are gorgeous. It's not an opinion. It's *math*."

In an instant, after Mark spoke, the group was silenced until Maureen commented with wonder. "Wow. *That* was good."

I giggled. "And, by far, the strangest compliment I've ever gotten."

"You don't take normal compliments well, remember? But really, it's all God's. So, there's no harm in knowing it when you are gifted as 'out of the park, *insanely* gorgeous.' Love the baseball reference in that one. Or maybe it's a curse, I haven't decided. Since you sort of ran off the first time we met."

I gasped. He smiled at my warming face as I shot Maureen an accusing look. I was regretting the words I'd used to describe the coffee cart temptation months before. But finding it funny, knowing it was just Mark all along.

"I was hoping you didn't remember that!" I turned to Maureen accusingly but kept my tone light enough for present company. "There are serious holes in your concept of doctor-patient confidentiality."

"See?" She bent a hand at my face while looking at Mark. "She looks fabulous in red."

The others roared again in laughter, then a new voice joined the corner.

"Hi, Maureen." I didn't even need to turn. The conniving arrogance made the introduction.

"Well, hey, Dee!" Maureen answered brightly. More enthusiastic than her usual demeanor. I remember wishing I could hold the same enthusiasm for being in the presence of Dee Martin.

"Merry Christmas." Another voice—Emma's. She was sure to catch my eyes with a warm smile and a wave, which I returned.

"Merry Christmas, Emma," Maureen stated warmly.

"Hey, Mark," Dee greeted Mark as I might. As someone she'd known for years. For some reason, my heart lurched, but I didn't let on.

"Merry Christmas, ladies." Charming, cordial Mark. "Enjoying the party?"

"Yeah, it's great." Dee batted her eyes a little. "How have you been, Mark? Any plans for after college?"

"Well, I still have a year and a half for God to give me His direction, so I haven't given it much thought. How about you? Any college plans?" While Mark continued the conversation with Dee and her talk of Christian college and the like, I tried to plot my escape, feeling like more of a stranger to the Faith than when they'd approached my drunken former self at a bonfire. My ears reawakened when Maureen said my name during a lull in their small talk.

"You ladies have met Paige, right?"

"Yeah." Dee pretended to have to think about the answer as she gestured to me. "I think Paige is in the class below us in school." And in life. The Kingdom of Heaven. I could read between the lines. "It's really weird. . .I've never seen you at church."

"I just started coming in October." I reluctantly joined the completely fake small talk. Dee and I hated each other. Everyone at school knew that.

"Oh, okay. This is a *staff* party. I work in the nursery." She bragged.

"Yeah, I'm staff." I didn't elaborate. It was also well known that Dee had a crush on Mark. She talked about him constantly. I didn't want to appear to be competition.

"Oh! I didn't realize." I should have known she couldn't handle it for too long. "Odd seeing you without a. . .you know, a 'plus one.'"

"Well, I was planning to bring my dad, but he's kind of a recluse, so I—"

"Oh, I would have thought you'd bring Aaron." She interrupted. "Didn't you go to winter formal with him? I wasn't there, but in English, he was talking about how he was going to ask you."

Maureen, Mark, and their family were quiet, seeming to let things play out. But thankfully not abandoning me to go mingle.

"Yeah, no. He asked me. But I didn't go." I shrugged. I found a reasonable excuse because she'd never have believed the truth. "I'm actually *here* on Saturday nights. I'm saving for books for college, so I don't like to—"

"Oh. So, you just work here. I get it. But you have a while before college, though, right? I know you missed a bit of school with. . .well, we all heard about what happened with Jake. So, it's understandable that you'd slip out of range for scholarships. You have time, though."

I was embarrassed. Speechless and deflated, and nearing tears. My salvation came from an unlikely place.

"Actually," Mark's charm leaked even into what I could hear was going in a strange direction. "Paige is graduating in May. Top 10 percent of your class, so I think she and the college fund her dad set up managed to cover everything *but* books, right?" He looked to me.

"Yeah," I managed through a whisper, not quite making it past the fog of emotion.

"Thought so," Mark smirked a little before he continued. Emma was hiding a smile. "Sorry, we just talk about weird stuff while scrubbing toilets or whatever. Not that talking about Jesus ever gets old, especially if you're a new believer. I swear this girl devours a Testament a day. She makes me feel like the worst preacher's kid ever." He winked at Dee. Seeming to know exactly how to simultaneously get her goat and soothe her embarrassment.

Dee was suddenly the speechless one. Emma bit her lip, not knowing what to say or do.

Pastor Robert spoke up. "Miss Martin, that reminds me. I had an idea for the nursery I wanted to run by you."

He swept Emma and Dee off to a corner of the room before I understood what was happening.

"She seems nice." Dillon rolled his eyes in sarcasm.

"She means well, Dillon. We all have our own journey with God," Mark defended, then captured my eyes with an apologetic smile. He released the gaze with a beckoning head flick I was quite used to by then, having worked with him for six weeks. "You have to come try some of Maureen's truffles she always makes. This is the only time I can legally eat them. Usually, she yells at me when I steal them."

I followed Mark away from the crowd to a table against a wall, where he handed me a little round ball of chocolate. We sat in chairs that oversaw the entire room. We were silent for a minute, as I was still recovering. Then I turned to him.

"Mark, that was really sweet. Thank you. I don't have the best history with Dee—or at all, really." I sighed.

"Yeah, she's a little rough around the edges. But I really do think she loves the Lord," Mark defended.

"And she's pretty. That helps, right?" I teased. "I mean, from a mathematical standpoint."

Mark chuckled. "You and Emma get along?"

"Why?" I bit into the chocolate and attempted to get a rise out of Mark. "Do you like her?"

Mark laughed. "Emma has been dating Mike Overton for a year. From the worship band? He graduated from River last year." He lowered his voice to gossip level. "And he's proposing at your prom, so I hear."

I gasped. "Wow. I guess I didn't know that. Emma's really nice to me. Always has been. Dee, on the other hand. . .I hated Christians for a long time, Mark. If we're being honest."

"Except Josh Gerrick, right?" Mark winked.

My eyes widened. "Please tell me you don't know Josh."

"I totally know Josh." Mark snorted. "He saw you the other day at service and hinted to me that he um. . .knew you."

"Mark, it was completely illegal, please can we not?" I begged, the weight of yesterday overcoming me.

"Sorry." He saw the panic in my eyes.

"So, does everyone confide in you?" I wondered.

"Sometimes." Mark shrugged. "But the rest of the time, I have a secret weapon. Want to hear the song I like to listen to at these parties?" He finally procured a headset from his pocket and handed me one of the lime green earpieces. I put it in the ear closest to him, though I preferred to people-watch at parties, not seclude myself in a world of Mark's favorite music, which I'd heard all of in the past few weeks over the sound system. He put the other earpiece in the ear closest to me. And then I waited for him to start the music. He instead crossed his arms and leaned back in the chair, looking out at the room. And in case I should start to feel lost, he winked at me and smiled deviously.

He pulled the end of the earpieces from his pocket, which was not plugged into anything at all. I gasped.

"Are these *ever* plugged in?" I whispered, seeing he loved to people-watch as much as me. He smiled and shook his head, acting as if he wouldn't be able to hear himself speak.

"People like to talk to me. Which is great unless I'm working. One time I was vacuuming and put these in my phone because I was expecting an important call. I left them in, able to hear almost everything around me, and no one bugged me. So, I kept it up. I guess it makes me invisible."

"Plus, you get to spy on people." I snickered. So did he.

"Shhh. . .no one ever needs to know." He whispered dramatically with a wink and a smile.

Forgetting about my prior wish to leave the party early, I sat with Mark, and we were watched by Mark's family from afar. We watched and nitpicked and gossiped about every member of the staff, like two middle school girls. My jaw hurt from laughing. My gut ached from a unique joy. Far more meaningful than any returned flirtation or even the satiation of lust, I was suddenly connected. Wholly satisfied. Because staged in two chairs over two hours of my life, I met my best friend. But darkness entered as Dee Martin waved to Mark upon her exit, reminding me I wasn't worthy of such a pure friendship.

That's when Maureen approached with a yawn. "It's almost Christmas, and I still have presents to wrap. Lemme give you a ride, Paige."

Mark took my punch cup, and I stood, walking away with Maureen. "So, who gets to clean this up?" I asked, realizing that we were the maintenance staff.

"I'll take care of it. I've been doing it alone for years, don't worry." Mark replied.

"Are you sure? I can stay. Really." I wanted to stay. In fact, I would rather have welcomed the coming of Christmas and every single year and millennia with Mark than with anyone else.

"You could, but your ride home is leaving. I. . ." Mark was searching for the least offensive way to speak his mind. Kindness was always top priority to him. Maureen's, however, was to convey needed information, regardless of emotional risk.

"Velma, the emerald Mustang, doesn't like girls. Unless you're Mark's sister—or wife. It's one of his million rules that will keep him from ever *meeting* his wife." At Maureen's opinionated conveyance of information, I gave a shocked sort of smile. Not because I was offended that Mark wouldn't drive me home. But because I admired his dedication to purity.

Mark looked to his sister with offense and began to defend his rule. I spoke instead, quoting the counselor to her demise.

"'God tends to honor any choice we make to honor Him. Purity is one of those choices.'" I batted my eyes in teasing innocence at Maureen. Mark gave a half smile, basking in the rarity of seeing his sister bested. And as Maureen rolled her eyes and took me away, Mark winked a goodbye.

Maureen linked arms with me to lead me away. "Well played, Miss Ellis. But I bet you don't know *half* of his rules." She nearly whispered this.

"Merry Christmas, Cinderella." Mark managed just before I was out of earshot.

"Merry Christmas, Boss. Thanks for the mop." I turned a moment, long enough to catch him glancing at my orange hair.

My counselor usually disguised counseling sessions as rides home, even though I lived a four-minute drive from the church. That Christmas Eve, as she rambled, I pretended I was not actively fighting my tummy against the butterflies.

"It's weird, isn't it? I could tell you you're gorgeous all day, but the second a guy says it, you believe it. I bet in the past, you did *anything* for that kind of affirmation. Usually happens with a dad that doesn't always think to say it." I was pretty sure my counselor had secret footage of my past.

"Yeah. . ." was all I managed as my head dropped.

"My brother is something else, isn't he? I wonder if he has any idea what it meant for *him* to say that to you when he wasn't asking for. . .you know, *anything.*" She smiled.

I fought the smile as the car stopped, waiting for her to mention something about the encounter with Dee. For some reason, she never did. After the welcome omission, I reached into my coat pocket to retrieve a small wrapped box. I handed it to Maureen, and she asked me to stay while she opened it. Before she did, though, she surprised me. She handed me a box of about the same size.

Maureen opened her necklace bearing the label she preferred. "*Mrs.*" She laughed and thanked me. I unwrapped the box in my hands and opened a little velvet case. It, of course, contained a silver purity ring that bore a tiny symbol—a glass slipper.

"To remind you to wait for your prince."

"Maureen, I can't wear a purity ring." I mellowed my tone to a whisper, even in the secluded car.

"Someday, when you're ready, I want you to wear this." Maureen put her hand over both of mine and the ring. Then she lightened her tone and shrugged, not alluding to the splendor of her next words. "You've been washed in Jesus's blood. Tell me something purer than that."

"Thanks, Maureen. Merry Christmas." I exited the car and placed the ring in my bottomless pit of a purse, where it stayed next to my compass as long as God would allow.

Chapter 20

Pure

For months, I washed the feet of Jesus at church with a bright pink mop. To the church fellowship, I was invisible. A freckled, flip-flopped backdrop that was only there to make the church immaculate. A blissful Cinderella. I liked to be invisible because I could serve them and love them in secret. Maureen, the sister my childhood never allowed me, was my polar opposite. She was powerful. Important. In and through and of everything in the church. More so after she revealed her secret identity as the pastor's daughter. I was amused at the way it happened. Everyone in the large church assumed that they alone were kept out of the loop and that everyone else had always known. She let it birth and age like a rumor that no one would admit they didn't already know.

Everyone knew Maureen. No one really knew me. And Mark rode somewhere in the center with great effort. He tried to remain as hidden as possible and falsely plugged his ears to achieve my level of invisibility. But alas, as the Senior Pastor's only son, his cordial ways and stunning looks were impossible to miss.

Maureen was a loving friend. At least, through her loving counseling and warm acceptance, it would appear that way. Whether she brought me to laughter or tears with whatever type of conversation she orchestrated, I was accustomed to her. She brought life to all in the church, and I dared not claim her as a companion all my own. But Mark? Mark was different. The breaths I took in his presence were deeper. My laughter easier. My mind at ease, and my comfort complete. We worked hard and only spent three hours a day together. A little more on weekends. And only ever at church. But I'd never been closer to anyone else.

Yet somehow, Mark had built for himself an odd one-dimensional front without ever talking about it. On many occasions, a longtime churchgoer in search of putting a name with a new face for gossip's sake would introduce themselves to me.

I'd say, "I'm Paige. I work with Mark Henley."

And they'd inevitably say something like, "Oh, Mark! Pastor Robert's boy. So handsome and kind, isn't he? He's 'saving himself' for marriage. Admirable in a young man his age."

Handsome. Kind. Pastor's son. Pure. That is all they ever said about him behind his back. They never mentioned the lime green shoes or the work-ethic-earned callouses on his hands. His intellect, the fact that he was adopted, or even the death of his mom. No. Just the purity thing. What's worse is it was true. Maureen, I feared, was right. Mark's purity was deliberate. Calculated. The 'rules' were probably written down somewhere. And if they were, I knew that they would tell me I had certain stringent boundaries, simply because of being female. Because they made perfect sense and he believed in them with his whole heart, I respected the rules. But because he was my dearest friend, and I knew that he was a far more complex person than mere purity, I made fun of his rules mercilessly.

"Let me get this straight. You think there is actually a girl on this planet that won't want to go on dates alone with you until your honeymoon, won't let you hold her hand unless it has an engagement ring on it, won't kiss you until the preacher at your wedding says so, and you won't—"

"Whoa now!" He used humor to distance me from what he rightly assumed I was about to say. But with quick wit and an innocent smile, I redirected.

". . .let her ride in Velma until the wedding night? You're dreaming, Boss."

Mark laughed, coolly turning his attention to the water spigot handle in the maintenance closet. Not a question he preferred to answer, I supposed. "I thought you believed in abstinence too, Cinderella."

"Of course, I do. But the kissing? Hugging? Hand holding? What if you have zero chemistry with your 'dream' girl and don't realize it until you're joined to her for life? That would suck. I thought you said you wanted to be a father. You know how that happens, right?"

"Heh." He nasaled sarcastic amusement. He was often annoyed (therefore, I often teased) at the common misconception that purity was equal to ignorance. "First of all, I don't have a hugging rule. Hugs happen. Second, *chemistry*? Would you like a chemistry lesson?"

Mark moved to a shelf and searched for something. He found two bottles and then closed the door, shutting us both in the little room. This gave me time to read the bottles he'd set on the ground. One was concentrated bleach, the other pure ammonia. He crouched, opening the bottles next to the mop bucket. I was confused, knowing he preferred to use pine cleaner on the floors. Then I gasped when he made a theatric movement to pour them together into the mop water.

"Stop, Mark! Are you crazy?! That would kill us both in here if you did that!"

"Are you sure?" He faked a revelation of a gasp and put his hands on his hips. "How can you know that if you've never done it? And why don't I just try a *little* to see if the *chemistry* works?" I suddenly became calm at realizing his purpose. He replaced the caps for safety's sake, knowing I'd caught the analogy.

"Okay, Boss, I get it. Don't mess with chemistry...it's dangerous. But your analogy only makes sense if you know the chemicals and the reaction they'll have. How are you gonna *know* if she's bleach and you're ammonia?"

"If I'm trusting God to point out the mother of my future kids, why would He give me someone I had 'zero chemistry' with?" He smiled, putting back the dangerous bottles and pouring some pine cleaner in the mop water.

"Makes sense. Actually, you're smart. Looking for chemistry never leads righteous places." I winced, hoping I hadn't said too much.

"And we know this, how?" Mark smiled cunningly.

Until that moment, we had kept our conversations light and cheerful, often indulging in the guilty pleasure of gossip, made possible by the foyer that spoke. We delved into others' lives but never far into our own since I'd shied away at the mention of Josh. But he was intentionally playing with fire with his question. I'd gossiped enough with him to know how well he could read a person or a situation. He was kind, saw the best in people. So why, I wondered, was he toying with the worst in me?

"How else would I know?" I opened the maintenance closet door to allow some pine scent to escape. I saw in his body language that he was indeed joking but that he was eager to tell me something. My words had invited him to release it. Before he spoke, Mark glanced at my feet.

"Your shoes took forever to find that day. You'd think since I saw where you lost them that I would know where to look, right? Especially from up on the balcony where I was sweeping leaves. But it started dusting snow. Just enough to cover your flip-flops." Mark gave me a half smile.

"Pardon?" But I needed no clarification. I painfully recalled running across the parking lot from Jake. How silly of me to have not realized that the "maintenance man" who'd found my shoes had to be Mark.

"I called the police. Told my dad to meet you outside. I'm glad I was up there."

"I would have been fine." I almost whined the defense.

Mark chuckled. "Stone, right? Jake Stone?"

I startled. "Yeah, you knew him?"

He nodded, then smiled compassionately. "You wouldn't have been fine."

Mark knew Jake in high school, he told me. Not from a class. Jake was never fond of class. Not because Mark was a saint and witnessed to him. But because Mark smoked alongside him in high school, at the fence where the smokers all did. Mark had quit smoking for Skittles and Jesus. But he'd been left with chilling memories of Jake Stone.

So, when I asked if he knew *everything* that happened with *me* and Jake, Mark reminded me about Maureen's secret keeping abilities and the ears of the foyer. Maureen had told him about all Jake had done to me before we'd ever been introduced. The stairs, the baby, everything. Because the church janitor had watched me run and was concerned for the shaken-up stranger. I was floored. Because before I'd had the courage to let my best friend in on my darkest times, he had long since absolved me.

We worked as best friends those following months, which made us an even better team. And just as I'd still admire the chain smoker version of him, he was unmoved by anything he learned of my past.

Early February, he began to display severe trust in me. "I'll be gone the weekend following Valentine's Day. Psychology conference through school. Friday through Sunday. Think you can handle things alone if I don't find you help?"

"Yeah, I can do that." I was flattered at his faith in someone so broken.

"Earlier in that week, I could also use your help with something. You have no obligation at all. If you say no, I understand a hundred percent, okay?" He was asking with compassion.

"Okay?" I wondered at the need for compassion.

"There's a wedding on Valentine's Day. Normally they are only on Fridays and Saturday mornings, so I just do it myself since I'm here anyway. But this one is on a really crazy week for me, and it's a weekday. I could use help cleaning up."

"I can do that, Mark. Why have you never asked me to help you before?"

"Because you work seven days a week as it is!" Mark laughed. "And since we're part-time, there's no overtime. I get paid in food from the reception. I'm here until at least midnight after Friday weddings. This one will be the same. On a weekday."

"I'll do it, Mark. I'll help with weddings from now on. I can't believe you hadn't been asking me."

"This one is different, Paige. And I'll come up with some kind of an 'overtime premium' as a thank you. Or. . .maybe to apologize."

"Why?"

"Because it's *Josh's* wedding."

Of course, Josh would get married on Valentine's Day. The corniest day of the year. Josh Gerrick. A college guy I dated when I was fifteen. He was marrying a sweet Christian girl named Karris. Mark realized the dilemma before he asked.

Mark told me he'd known about Josh's tryst with an underage girl who could have easily pressed charges when Josh broke it off to honor God. And while shocked it really was me, Mark, again, forgave me freely. He told me it took integrity not to turn him in. And then Josh found Karris—the love of his life. Mark sifted through my darkest sins and found *integrity*. So, I told him the overtime premium better be good.

There were two things I admired in Mark above all other attributes. The first, his purity. It was the chief part of who he was in every corner of his life. But at an increasingly close second was his fire. On the surface, some might believe that purity and fire cannot coexist. Or that God prefers purity over fire. But I was starting to believe that Mark's purity was the direct result of the way the Holy Spirit collided with his fire. Maybe he'd once used the fire for rebellion, but he had since used it for righteousness and service to God.

One was drawn to Mark. And when one drew near, they realized that what looked like the boring facade of mindless obedience and self-righteousness was actually the subdued glow of a slow-burning fire of truth and humility. His tamed embers reminded me that God is not out to quench us. He loves the fire. He created it. And in Mark, I saw clearly that the only real purity is refined by fire.

Chapter 21

Overtime

"What took you so long?" I responded with a smile to Mark's approaching key jingle. I teased him because he'd been spacey and snail-like all evening in the midst of a long week. I was glad I'd chosen to help him with the wedding.

I'd been alone in the recreation room after we'd cleaned up the wedding ceremony. On my own, I'd already cleaned up a mountain of trash from the reception. I continued cleaning without even looking up since the confetti in the room would no doubt add time to the cleanup process. Mark spoke.

"I had to talk to the wedding coordinator about all the decorations and what belongs to the church and what doesn't. I made one rookie mistake one time with some decorations *years* ago, but now she makes me run everything by her anyway. And then I had to chew her out because she broke the news to me that she allowed them to use confetti. She knows I hate confetti. Sorry you had to realize that on your own." I smiled at the rant of a typical guy as I shook my head at confetti. And then I laughed at the overbearing woman he described.

"So Maureen's the wedding coordinator?" I chuckled, grabbing another trash bag.

He snickered. "Well, it was our mom's job. We haven't had one on staff since, but Reen does most weddings, and the other counselors help out too."

When I finally looked up at him to convey my understanding and remorse, I saw that he was holding a pink vase filled with a gorgeous array of pink flowers. He smirked and outstretched his arms to present them to me. Normally when a male person made this gesture, especially on Valentine's Day, he expected something from me. And normally, I gave it. Extremely uncomfortable that Mark bought me flowers, I couldn't respond but with a few blinks in the pauses of his explanation.

"Your overtime premium. Girls like flowers, right? And you like pink. Happy Valentine's Day?" Mark easily downplayed the sentiment, soothing my worries that the flowers beheld their traditional meaning for the day. Mark was more of an altar boy than a romantic as far as I knew, so I took him at his word and gave him a smile of a nod when he chuckled at my shock. Very much a girl, I thanked him giddily, loving the pink he'd added to my world.

After stashing the flowers safely in the corner, we got to work. The ceremony cleanup had been difficult. The multitude of fresh rose petals had to be individually picked up from the center aisle so they did not get crushed into the carpet. The carpet had to be cleaned because some of them got crushed anyway. Pew decorations were removed from the ends of chairs that also had to be moved back to their original position from some ill-conceived ceremony set up. When we had restored the sanctuary to normal, Mark told me the reception would be worse.

In an exhausted silence, we finished cleaning up the trash. After this, we moved to our least favorite task after special events. I gathered a handful of confetti off a chair in disgust.

"Promise me that when you get married, you won't include confetti in the celebration for my sake, Boss."

"Agreed." Mark grabbed another handful, also in disgust. "This is a really cold day for a wedding, too. We do a *lot* more weddings between March and October."

"I *love* winter weddings! Valentine's Day is a bit corny, but the weather is perfect," I spoke of my own childhood wedding plans.

"Yikes. See, at *my* wedding, I'll have to ride off into the sunset with Velma's top down since it'll be my bride's first ride in her. In general, a girl wouldn't be too happy with snot-cicles in her nose on her wedding day. So, I'm thinking it's a summer wedding for me." Mark seemed to have his own big day thought up as well.

"So boring!" I proclaimed to my companion after giggling about snot-cicles. "Summer is happy *without* weddings. More people should add something happy like a wedding to winter. To brighten it up a little, you know? That's why Christmas lights are so pretty. Because in December, the world is really dark. But obviously, I wouldn't want a Christmas wedding, because there are already Christmas lights.

"Psh," He agreed as a teenage girl. "*Obviously.*"

I thought a moment, looking between Mark and my handful of confetti. Finally, I smiled and then hurled the handful of confetti at my unsuspecting companion. He laughed and did the same to me with his handful. It was quite amusing to us both that while we threw several handfuls of confetti straight at one another, most of it floated stubbornly to the floor. Finally, Mark grabbed a handful and placed his hand over my head, watching the bits of silver confetti float slowly onto my handkerchief and hair.

Then his eyes met mine. I didn't understand what I saw. They were just Mark's eyes. But it felt like the gentle unswirling of a rose combined with the rite of the clash of antlers. Like refinement. Like fear. I feared the probable three and a half seconds of my life more than I feared death. Therefore, I took to removing my handkerchief and shaking confetti out of my hair with a playful smile, and he took to satisfied laughter.

Maureen saw the silliness as she passed the glass wall. She smirked and shook her head. Satisfied with herself, it would seem. She and I were both surprised when Dave came out of nowhere and lifted her off the ground into a hug, whispering something into her ear as he set her down again. She pushed him away with the most enthusiastic look of joy I'd seen from the woman.

"SHUT UP!" She screamed, obviously having received very good news.

Dave reached into his jacket pocket, handing her some type of official letter. She read it, then jumped up and down, heedless of the four-inch heels that should have prevented such behavior. I continued to watch the exchange. Dave held up a finger and reached into his inside pocket again, and pulled out a single rose, offering it to his wife and Valentine. Maureen responded with a version of her smile with intent like I hadn't seen in a church. Dave responded with a kiss that matched. Mark saw my interest in the sappy Valentine moment outside the transparent wall.

"Passed his board, I bet. That's a *huge* deal. Right now, he's a resident at a neurological group in the hospital. They love him and said as soon as he got his board certification, they'd take him on as a provider. At twenty-eight with a wife and kids, that's pretty much unheard of."

We looked out again at the couple, Dave holding Maureen close and telling her something in her ear that interested her. She giggled flirtatiously. A vulnerability I wouldn't expect from knowing the powerful spitfire of a blonde.

"*Mrs.*" I considered with a thaw of my heart. A position I'd also treasure if given the chance.

"Get a room!" Mark finally yelled through the door. He shook his head and walked over to the wall to retrieve the push broom. Maureen responded by giving her husband one last kiss and leading him by the hand into the room Mark and I had speckled with confetti. "So, did you pass or what? That would be worth hanging out with your kids tonight."

"Oh, and it's *so* painful for you to sugar up my kids, keep them up all night, and then send them back to me. But yes. WE PASSED!" The three hugged like a team of champions. Oh, to be part of a family like that.

I laughed to hide my envy of the group hug. "So prove it. Say something 'doctory.'"

They laughed at my intentionally juvenile tone. Dave thought a moment, then released his booming voice directly to my feet.

"Flip-flops are the worst shoes you can possibly wear. In time, they can wreak havoc on your feet and legs and spine. Mess up your feet, and you can mess up everything. How often you wear 'em?"

"Every day," Mark said just over his breath and barely outside a mumble.

Maureen hid her smile, confirming the truth of my footwear obsession to Dave. "Come on, baby. When you have pretty freckly feet like that, you gotta show 'em off!"

"'Pretty freckly feet' aside, if you keep wearing those things all the time, you will start to see side effects, not just in your feet. You have ankle problems?"

"I used to. I actually broke my ankle when I was twelve. It was a bad one, and I didn't get medical care right away. It just recently stopped giving me fits." I silently begged them not to ask further questions.

"It wouldn't have taken years to heal if you hadn't worn flip-flops the whole time." Dave's serious air was almost funny, and I responded accordingly.

First, I turned to the siblings. "You two are traitors!" Then I turned back to Dave. "What about your wife? She wears at least three-inch heels every day. Is that any better?" Maureen's beloved heel collection didn't faze her, but made my feet ache at the mere sight.

Maureen responded to my tattling by handing her husband the rose and then using the rec room as a runway for a moment, exhibiting her clicking black stilettos with a perfect model's saunter. Her ruffled deep purple satiny dress flowed gracefully at her knees, and when she removed her blazer at the end of the "runway" and swung it over her shoulder, I was giggling. Mark was rolling his eyes. Dave was enjoying every second.

"Now that I think of it, Paige, heels might be the death of *me*." Dave then kissed the blonde beauty's hand as he gave her the rose back. Mark was anxious at the silky tone Dave used next. "You're coming home with me, right?"

Dave winked at me before putting his arm around Maureen and pulling her away. The two lovers walked into the cold night, and Mark had begun sweeping up confetti.

"I bet that freaks you out." I challenged the limits of my pure companion.

"Those two had a rough marriage from the get-go. So, to see them still in love and fighting the fight after *ten years*. . . well, I really can't complain about however that works. Except that. . .ew, that's my sister." He crinkled his nose with a chuckle to escape the sappiness and winked at the laugh he coaxed.

He leaned the broom against the outside of the glass wall and came back in to collapse tables before he could sweep the rest of the room. I watched as he turned a table on its side and collapsed each leg, then rolled the table with ease across the lacquered cement floor, resting it against the wall. I attempted to do the same to the table next to it, with significantly less ease than Mark. He caught the table from crushing me with one outstretched hand.

"Stack chairs, Cinderella. I got this." I followed his request with an eye roll.

Mark shook his head and smiled. He started to break down another table but winced in pain and stopped. He fiddled with his left middle finger like he always did, balling up and stretching his hand a moment.

"Why do you do that?" I asked after months of wondering.

He gave the probably slightly modified generic reply. "You mentioned your ankle. Same here. I broke my finger pretty bad about a decade ago. It still bothers me when it's cold, and I've been picking up confetti and rose petals." He smiled, trying to falsely convince me of his mental presence.

I winced. "How'd that happen?"

He looked up at me and smiled. "Dillon turned ten a few days ago. So, I guess I broke it about ten years and seven months ago when we found out Maureen was pregnant."

"Oh, did you punch something?" I imagined a disheartened preteen version of Mark punching a wall.

"Yeah, something that's still crooked."

I gasped. "You socked Dave in the nose?!"

"Yeah. Wasn't a wise decision, but it felt right at the time. And now my finger is killing me. One of God's genius consequences, I guess. To remind me of His grace." He often put insight like that into a joke, but that one didn't move me to laughter.

"Like me cleaning up after Josh's wedding?" I offered a serious gaze, to which Mark apologized abundantly. I then smiled to put him at ease. "Speaking of Josh and Karris. Can you imagine the pressure on them tonight? Everyone knows *exactly* what they are doing right now. How does someone cope with that?"

"Good question. Not sure how I'd know the answer." He laughed, well obliged that I was tapping into his area of expertise, but at the same moment trying to escape *that* specific region of it. Still seeming like his mind was far away.

"Because you are Mr. Abstinence, remember? According to everyone but me." I rolled my eyes.

"Who am I to you?" He tilted his head, intrigued.

"Uh, Mark." I laughed once. "Who happens to have a better perspective than I do about purity."

"And how is my perspective 'better'?" He asked gently.

"I'm supposed to be seven months pregnant right now, so. . ." I crossed my arms, cleared my throat, and averted my eyes.

"That's an important perspective too. More than you know." The virgin part of my companion was uncomfortable, but he met me at the point of the theology. Something he had spent his life studying with all his heart. So, he sighed, giving in. "I see what you're saying, Paige. People sometimes argue that waiting until your wedding night causes more nerves and pressure than just letting it happen 'naturally.' I disagree. Compared to the fear and uncertainty associated with premarital sex, the fact that everyone knows you're handing over your purity is easy. Because it's all sanctified, and no one can really say anything to you. Something tells me that one day your perspective will validate that more than mine could."

I nodded. Smiled. Then I asked what he saw coming and dreaded with a laugh. "I'm gonna totally push the limits with this one. But you're the pastor's son. When you have your confetti-free, boring summer wedding, the pressure is gonna be ten times worse for you and your wife. Do you realize that?"

Mark said with confidence his explanation. Something he'd thought up but never had a chance to say, I could tell. "In baseball, I pitched most of every game. I *loved* baseball. What I loved most was the way the crowd just held their breath before every pitch. Half of them wanted me to mess up. Half of them were counting on me not to. But I could always count on them holding their breath and Maureen closing her eyes. *That* was pressure."

"So, how did you handle it so well?"

He shrugged. "I never get nervous. I just don't see the point. It never really mattered to me who was watching me do what I'd do anyway. So, in baseball, I waited to make *sure* they were holding their breath. And then I threw the ball at the greatest moment of pressure. I do the same thing in the rest of life. Some people want you to fail. Some have their hope riding on you to succeed. But all that pressure doesn't matter when you know you're doing God's will. That plays really well into abstinence too." He winked at me and the way I was nodding in a smile.

"It takes a real man. . ." I started solemnly, because my admiration demanded it. But then I smiled. "To use a *sports* analogy."

He laughed appreciatively and broke down another table. I thought a moment. And asked a far more innocent question.

"So did the broken finger help or hinder the pitching?"

Mark chuckled as he rolled the table to the wall. Then he squinted, seemingly considering the analysis for the first time. "I guess that depended on the weather."

Exhausted and close to midnight as I'd been promised, Mark and I stood just inside the main entrance of the church, awaiting my father's arrival, my flowers in arms. I was glad tonight that he was a die-hard night owl. The lone Velma awaited her companion in the dusting snow. The stargazer lily's fragrance was a welcome contrast to the moon-forsaken parking lot and the cold that beckoned me.

"Thanks for your help tonight." I was getting used to the sound of his voice through teeth that clenched a Skittle.

"No problem. Like I said, if weddings are normally on weekends, I don't mind helping. I don't have a life other than this church," I promised.

"I'll think about it. Flowers could get expensive after a while." He was distracted. Staring off into the distance. And instead of using sports analogies, I brought him around manually.

"You alright, Mark? You seem off. I was trying not to say anything, but—"

He blinked a couple times and returned. "Yeah." He looked down with a laugh. "I'm just tired. School's been crazy. I still have to go home and pack for my conference, and I missed getting to spoil my nephews tonight. I have a lot on my mind, you know?"

"You *always* have a lot on your mind. So, which one of those excuses was actually true?" I called the bluff with a straight face, to his amusement.

"Probably none of them," He admitted.

"Mark, come on! Don't you trust me? Are we friends or what?" I was begging him not to let go of how we'd always connected.

"*Best* friends, I'm pretty sure. I don't trust anyone like I trust you." He smiled with a wink. I could almost hear my heart singing. "I'm just walking through something, Paige. Could use your prayers, but it wouldn't be appropriate for me to tell you what's happening."

"Of course. I'll be in prayer." I replied with warmth. "You're *okay*, right?"

"I'm fine, Cinderella. Don't worry about me. Just pray for my safe return from this stupid conference, so you aren't stuck cleaning up after Maureen's confetti weddings on your own forever." He winked.

I rolled my eyes at the obvious evasion as I saw the lights of my father's SUV. I walked away as slowly as possible, watching Mark wave as he locked up the church. My father didn't inquire of the massive flower arrangement, except with his eyes.

"I've been eating purple monkeys recently. The red ones are a little tough." My dad's words were likely at the tail end of a nonsense rant, probably following something more important.

"What? I was ignoring you, wasn't I?" I buried my head in my hands. "It's been a long day, sorry. It was Josh's wedding, you know. He looks really happy."

"You told me that last night. I'm not worried about Josh."

"Please don't ask if I'm dating Mark again. The flowers are for helping him tonight. I'm telling you. He is not an issue. Velma is not accepting new passengers."

"What? Who is Velma? I was just trying to ask if you got that project done for science." My father gave me a knowing look. "But since you mentioned it. . ."

"Mentioned what?" I smiled in shame and slouched in my seat until the car was safely home.

Chapter 22

Eros

"Paige,
I didn't ask because I knew you'd say no. But I found you
some help while I'm gone. I apologize in advance. It was the
best I could do.
Blessings, Mark"

I didn't hear Maureen approach and lean in the doorway
of the maintenance closet as I read the note on the desk.
Where was the click of her heels? I startled visibly.

"What are you *wearing?*" I questioned Maureen's unusual
attire. She was in a worn-out plaid shirt, probably one of
Dave's, because she had it tied up in back to make it smaller.
She also wore jeans with a hole forming at the knee and cute
brown sneakers. I was unaware that Maureen even owned
sensible shoes. Minus my now reluctant flip-flops, she was
dressed just how I might.

"You like it?"

"No. Explain."

"Ouch. I'm not as 'gorgeous' as your boss, but I can push a
mean broom. Pastor Dad is making me help you for three days
while my little bro gets to spend a long weekend in business
casual learning about shrinking people. I require one of those
awesome Cinderella scarves if you have one on you. The outfit
really doesn't work without it."

"Weekends are intense. Especially Sunday. You ready for
this?" I tried to intimidate her and grabbed a scarf from the
stack I kept on the desk.

"I'm ready for anything. The question is, are *you* ready?"

Maureen tied her hair behind the handkerchief I handed
her. I was happy to work with her, but I knew that those three
days would become a marathon counseling session. She
started right in as we moved up the stairs in seated unison,
cleaning either side of the glass railing.

"Mark is probably so antsy at this conference. He's not
exactly an academic. The guy barely even studies." Maureen
rolled her eyes dramatically with the random information.

"I bet he'll get something out of it. He always tells me he learns more in short bursts than in a semester of a class." I said with confidence, trying not to worsen the dirty glass with streaks. "Speaking of Mark, he seemed off last night. When I asked him about it, he admitted something was going on but wouldn't tell me what. I assume you know, and I don't want to go behind his back and ask what's wrong. But is he okay, Maureen? I'm worried."

"Interesting." She said cryptically, then retreated to an unsettling, unprecedented silence for about an hour, completely ignoring my questions about Mark.

My heart nearly escaped into the toilet I was cleaning as Maureen suddenly broke the deafening quiet.

"I guess I understand why you didn't want to tell me." These were the words she chose after two shiny bathrooms of only scrubbing and running water to fill the silence.

"Tell you what?" I caught my breath and emerged from the stall to meet her.

"I just want you to know that whatever you tell me is safe with me. Meaning, I won't tell Mark your secrets. . .well not this one. . .not exactly." Maureen was attempting to use her fingernails through a rag to clean around the faucets. Because I knew she was onto me, I let her struggle with the task.

"You want me to talk about the thing I said you could never ask about?" A diversion. A fated night at a cabin she still hadn't asked about. I was unaware until that moment that something so sensitive and painful could be counted as a diversion for a greater secret.

"We're taking a break from cleaning to talk about this." I couldn't decide if she was talking about pain or my current panic.

I sobbed a laugh, my face warm with anger. "No, we're not. You're a lot slower than Mark. We have a lot to do today. I knew you'd do this to me. Mark was smart not to tell me you'd be helping me. I really can't stand you sometimes." I moved her aside and pulled out my floss, showing her the best way to remove the grime around the faucet.

"I bet Mark *loves* that." She was fascinated with the trick, ignoring the insults as always.

"Yeah." I smiled, even laughed a little at the thought of Mark. "Except I'm in charge of *all* the faucets now."

"Busted," Maureen declared in a sing-song voice.

"What now?" I was annoyed with her and the fact that she didn't quite understand the point of work.

"Well, I've thought you had a crush on him for a couple months—"

"I do not!" I interrupted her ridiculous prospect. Then I moved to excuses. "He's my best friend. That's probably what you're thinking. A *crush*? I'm not a third grader, Mrs. Shrink."

"No, you're right. I misinterpreted the signals." Maureen moved to the voice she usually used just before she blew me away with her wisdom.

I sighed in recognition of the tone and leaned against a sink for her revelation. She wasn't interested in either of us getting work done.

"Make it quick," I insisted.

For her, the feat was easy. She rattled off a thousand different ideas in a session, but it usually only took her a few minutes because of how quickly her mind worked and how well her mind connected with her mouth. I had to listen intently to catch it all, however, because everything she said was of the utmost importance. Quite often, she told me, *"I said that the other day, remember?"* In such cases, I thanked God for the memory He gave me for details.

"See, a crush is all giggles and butterflies and thinking he's cute. But if you ask me—" Maureen paused for my interruption.

"Which I didn't—"

She then continued, ignoring insults once again. "Tummy butterflies are no more than a predecessor to lust, further condemning the world's idea that true love is based on butterflies and good feelings. God didn't send His Son to die for *butterflies*. They are often the downfall of relationships and marriages when they find that the butterflies have flown off. I have a strong and unique approach to the way I teach couples about love in marriage. Would you like to hear it?" I allowed her smile to fill the silence before my reply.

"Right, so can we clean now?" I was slightly annoyed. Slightly terrified. I tried to stop the rant in its track. Not a chance.

"*Philia. Phileo. Philos,* whatever you prefer. Friendship love. It's that deep respect for who a person is. *Philos* is the way I love *you*." Maureen spoke with the determination of a swinging rag.

"Aw, how sweet." I snorted a laugh.

She smiled and continued the lesson. I wondered if I should take notes. "*Stergo*s, or *storge,* is affectionate love the way we see it in family. It is sometimes associated with obligation. But if you consider that it comes from parents and siblings that share roots with you, I think it runs too deep for obligation. I think it's pretty irreversible."

I shook my head at how eloquent her wisdom came through lightheartedness. Because my own could never rival hers, I allowed her to continue uninterrupted.

"And then there's *eros. Romantic* love." She let fly a dramatic emphasis and a sensual eye roll. "The long walks on the beach, butterflies, lovemaking, intoxicating, euphoric, marriage, babies kind of love. If you misdirect this kind of love, it'll burn you. But if you do it right, there's nothing like it."

My heart panicked, and I looked to the floor as she continued.

"Most premarital counselors will counsel based on *eros*, often involving *philos*, since the best marriages come from great friendships and certainly end up there if they didn't start that way. But I add in the *storge* love as well as the other two, because a marriage is a *family*. Affection, even out of obligation, can be the glue that keeps you together, knowing you are *family*. But even with friendship, romance and affection, love is not love until you have loved like *God* loves. *Agape*. Unconditional, sacrificial love. The kind that made God send his son to die. I define it between humans as our willingness to seek what is best for the other person, regardless of the sacrifice it involves for us. Even unto *death*. It is my experienced, professional opinion that a full understanding of all four types of love would *shatter* the divorce rate."

I looked around, confused, and whispered for effect. "I'm single and seventeen. Why are you telling *me* this?"

That knowing smile of hers appeared and simmered in the silence a moment. But even in its completeness, it didn't prepare me for the words that escaped it.

"Because you're in love with my brother," Maureen said nonchalantly and took the opportunity of my shocked open mouth to elaborate. "Regardless of the fact that many seventeen-year-olds stick with 'crushes' and a bit of *eros*, you love Mark with a powerful combination of *eros, philos, and Agape*." She suddenly changed from her serious countenance and backed down, crinkling her nose playfully. "And tummy butterflies."

My eyes widened, and I stopped everything I was doing and thinking. I hadn't even said it that way to myself. How could she be so bold to say it aloud? I peeked out the door to make sure the wind to the nearby foyer had not caught her nonchalant words.

"Don't worry, Ruth's alone out there, and she probably knew before you did. Can you imagine how much that woman hears in a day?"

I panicked. I was trapped, with no excuses. Not willing to lie and scared to admit the truth, I grabbed hold of my mop and mopped the floors of the current bathroom. I scolded my tummy for jumping when I remembered why my mop was pink.

"What, you aren't even gonna deny it?"

"Is there a point in that?" I said this with a laugh that also emitted some tears. "Just try to leave out the '*eros*' if you have verbal diarrhea. It would ruin the '*philos*.' He's my best friend, and this would pass easier if he didn't know."

"I'm bad with secrets, Paige. But I would never do something you think would put your friendship in jeopardy. Though, I do have some terrible news."

"Oh, there's something *worse* than being in love with someone I can never have?" I released an unexpected tear of relief. Not that he wouldn't find out, but that Maureen *did* and forced me to say it out loud.

She leaned against a sink with a gentle version of her smile. "Yeah, once you add '*Agape*' to any kind of love. . .well, they call it unconditional for a reason. You're stuck. It would be a painful lifelong journey to let it 'pass.'"

With a sigh, I found myself further proving for Maureen the truth when I tried to course-correct the subject.

"Mark said he's 'walking through something.' I'm really worried about him. I *care* about him. Doesn't matter in what capacity. Can you tell me what's wrong?" I denied further tears from falling.

And she laughed again, allowing with loving respect her proof.

"Mark is a great man. So young and so much figured out already. I envy his faith. He's willing to lay down his life for God's plan. Mark would have been the guy building the giant boat for an impossible flood. But until he gets the exact measurements and instructions, he tends to act funny. Don't worry. He'll likely be back to normal soon." Maureen's words were clear and true, but I felt as though I was missing something.

"So, what is God's plan for Mark in this case?"

Maureen smiled. Then nodded to herself. Then tilted her head, considering her words carefully. But that was not apparent once she snapped them out into the air like she was reading a grocery list. "Mark thinks he's found the woman God wants him to marry. And between you and me, I think he's scared to death."

First, I laughed. "Doesn't want to give up the purity, huh?"

"No, he *absolutely* does. You kidding? Mark has always been in love with the idea of being a husband and father. And he's a *guy*, Paige. Abstinence isn't something a guy *enjoys*." Maureen smiled. "That's not why he's scared. I don't think he quite anticipated loving a woman even more than his own life. It's terrifying."

"So, he's in love." I clarified, then removed my handkerchief. "Like, with a *girl*? Intoxicating, long walks on the beach, marriage, babies, etcetera, 'in love'?"

"Oh, yeah. Scatterbrained, excessively happy, stumbling, stuttering, beaming *idiot* 'in love.' He's been in this state *almost* the entire time you've known him, so you likely wouldn't have noticed the change in him. Until recently when God started telling him to *do* something about it." She nodded, finally coming to a recognition of the sensitive issue. Perhaps the way my heart was shattering was suddenly visibly apparent. "But the *eros* is just a fraction of it."

"We're really close. It's weird he hasn't told me. Do you guys approve of her? Is she. . .do I know her? Is he worried *I* wouldn't approve? Does he care what I think at *all*?" I cleared my throat of tears and turned away from her remorseful smile.

"Mark has made a handful of bad choices in his life. This is *not* one of them. Might very well be the best." And I hated her suddenly because I heard the betrayal of a smile in her voice. "But actually, Mark *knows* you won't approve. He thinks you'll feel betrayed that he's never said anything. I told him I'm 99 percent sure you'll try to talk him out of it and then try to quit your job. The other percent is the slight chance that you'll just *slap* him." Maureen giggled. "I do hope I get to be there when you find out."

"I don't *think* I'd hit him. But I also can't imagine Mark breaking your boyfriend's nose, so anything is possible." I defended my heart, hoping whatever nonsense she was speaking was some fleeting joke.

Maureen laughed in hindsight. "Those two were shaking hands before David's nose was done bleeding. It was more of a rite of passage than an attack. Guys are weird. Sometimes it takes blood and broken bones for them to realize they're brothers, not enemies. He'd never admit it, because his method was not very well thought out, but I swear he knew exactly what he was doing, even then."

My smile for the story was short-lived. Because I was suddenly in a worse place than stuck. I sighed. Shed a tear. I decided that perhaps it wouldn't be too painful to get over Mark, knowing he'd found someone who would follow his rules. Be pure for him and smile at his shoe bells and disconnected earpieces. But in that moment, my heart was in distress, disarray, though I should have known the day would eventually come.

"Can you just tell me who it is? Dee Martin? Please tell me it isn't Dee Martin. Oh God, it *is*, isn't it?"

Maureen laughed once. "I promised him I wouldn't tell you."

"Since when do you keep secrets and promises?" I guffawed.

"Since you," she complimented. Humbling me completely.

"What do I do, Maureen? I want him to be happy and do God's will. I just don't know if I can bear to *watch* it." Gently I asked, and gently she replied.

"This is a tough one, Paige. So God's answer will be better than mine. Take a cue from my brother. Hit your *knees*. And know that God is in control." Maureen flashed me a wince of a crooked smile and remained silent for the remainder of the evening.

In place of sleep that night, I prayed. I skimmed nearly half the Bible and waited impatiently for God to tell me what to do. But my answer didn't come in a verse or a passage. It came when I'd pondered them all in my heart, and my soul unified them as I fell asleep with a wee-hours headache, Bible in hands.

I dreamed a fitful, disjointed nightmare. Dee Martin taunting me. My old boyfriends chaining me to a cement block the size of the church. The entire congregation screaming at me as I tried to pull it wherever it was it needed to be. Maureen standing by helplessly. Pastor Robert reading to me from a Bible. Then I heard Mark's keys approaching, and the crowd hushed. I looked up, and Mark was crouching, searching for a key. He found it, then found where all the chains were locked together.

First, he unlocked the chains, then he took some and locked them again—to himself. He tested them for strength before smiling at the burden we were both chained to. Then he looked my way.

"Ready, Cinderella?"

His voice echoed like peace amid the impossible burden we shared. And even if nothing else was ever granted, including life-sustaining nourishment and youthful liberty, I could have lived in that dream, shared that moment for a lifetime.

So, it wasn't fair to me when I awakened alone and cold in the night. Back where my breaths were shallower, my laughter nonexistent. Back to tears I cried for Darian.

Chapter 23

Relief

"Tell me your deepest, darkest secret." An inappropriate greeting for most. But not coming from Maureen. She'd nearly flown into the classroom I was sanitizing after the Saturday night service. She was late and had barely changed into her cleaning getup. Just the sight of her reminded me of the way my heart was cracking under the weight of my love for Mark.

"I'm confused, Mrs. Shrink. Is this the secret you told the whole foyer yesterday, or the one I told you I didn't ever want to talk about? Let's save ourselves the trouble and talk about the weather tonight." I smiled, retaining my secrets.

"Oh, not the Mark thing. That's old news. Today, I want to be more like a doctor than a confidant." Maureen announced.

"A doctor? The last doctor I dealt with talked me into an abortion, remember?"

"Well, technically, the *last* doctor told you to stop wearing flip-flops." She smiled her smile at my feet. Then began her rambling. "And if you want to get technical, I *am* a doctor of psychology. It was a reasonably challenging program that took a few years of my life *after* my master's in counseling. I'm actually one of the younger individuals to have completed it, and I even took a gap year to give birth to Lane. I know you think I've no earthly clue what I'm saying half the time, but if you *do* want to get technical. . ."

"I don't actually want to get technical."

Unfazed, of course. "Well, anyway, when you get a cold, there's not much you can do about it, right? Except treat the symptoms and let it run its course. But when we get *really* sick, like with appendicitis, a doctor would be an idiot just to treat the symptoms. The pain. They want to treat the source of the pain and try to save your life. Sometimes a psychological issue, no matter how difficult, just needs some herbal tea. Take grief. There's nothing worse. There's also no cure. Sure, there's plenty of symptom relief. It really helps me to fill my mom's roles in the church. And Christ is our Comforter. But even He doesn't stop me from missing her because He knows there's something in it that drives me. But sometimes, an emotional issue needs emergency surgery, or it'll never *start* to heal. You follow?"

"Is this as difficult as the four loves thing? If so, I better take notes." I sighed, shaking my head at the way she explained things to my far inferior mind.

"In your opinion, what is your greatest *source* of emotional pain, Miss Ellis?" She moved right to my heart without warning.

I dropped a baby toy I was wiping off, and it made some obnoxious sound with lights as it rolled across the nursery floor. I was annoyed at first that the song it played was so cheery when I'd been asked about pain. And then I was reminded of that pain and how I should have been smiling fondly at the sound of a baby toy as a child grew and danced within me. So, when I bent to pick it up, my legs became boneless beneath me, and I was forced to sit on the classroom floor.

I removed the scarf from my head, feeling a sudden anxious urge to scratch my scalp. Maureen responded by sitting directly in front of me, crossing her legs like a young girl. She tilted her head slightly and let the long blonde ponytail fall in front of her shoulder. I swore she had powers over physics to make me feel certain things. Either that or God was with her in her endeavors and supplied the power for His own purposes.

"I think you know my 'opinion' of that." I lashed out, hating her for making me think of Darian then, amid so much other pain. And because I hated her, or maybe because I loved her, I allowed my sudden tears to speak for me.

"Mark says you mentioned you'd be seven months along." She nodded remorse.

"I didn't think he was listening," I recalled Mark being distracted at the time. Apparently by lovesickness. I cleared my throat. "I try not to keep track. But I probably always will."

"Did your baby have a name?" She was asking so that I would talk about him, which was odd. She knew everything about Darian *except* his name.

"Yes. But unless there's a reason, don't make me say it, okay?" I feared that Darian's name was a dam, holding in far more than an uttered label of personhood.

"That's fine. My mom's maiden name was Amelia Lane. My mini Romeo is named after her. Some people don't think much of names. A rose by any other name, right? Well, when I was pregnant with Lane, we almost lost him at around five months. That would have been terrible in itself. But Dave and I were high school sweethearts, and Lane had a name way back before we even got married or had Dillon. He was going to be named after my mom because I missed her so much. So, when they told us we might lose him. . ." Maureen's countenance faltered at a memory, a glisten in her eye. "It wasn't just that I'd be losing *him*. It was that I'd be losing my mom all over again. Like God was telling me not to even miss her. Even the thought of that was heartbreaking. So, my mom was the source of that fear, you follow?"

I nodded, being fully experienced with heartbreak.

"Paige, when you lost your baby, that was—I can't even *imagine* the pain you deal with, probably every day. Like I said, grief does need symptom relief. So, I've—we've *all* been trying to help you through it. We care about you. But what if I told you that the pain you had when you lost that baby was more than grief? I think it may be a symptom itself. Of even deeper pain."

I was offended that she would suggest something so absurd. That losing a child was a *symptom*. How dare she? No, I decided. She couldn't know what it was like. I retained my silence and added bitterness, beginning to build a wall. Her bizarre counseling techniques had finally crossed the line for me. But she continued as if that line—that wall—didn't exist.

"I want you to tell me the primary reason your baby was such a loss to you."

"Are you kidding me?" I said through tears with a twinge of anger. I began trying to untie the knot in my handkerchief.

"Please. It's important." Maureen allowed compassion. The gentle version of who she was.

Because I knew Maureen would get the answer she wanted, without me having to really try, I just opened up and showed her my heart.

"I would have been a teenage mother and scared. The whole nine yards. But he would have been the only thing I ever did *right*. I was so bad. So sinful. I didn't know Jesus, so I thought there was no turning back from that. But my baby was new. He'd have been a fresh start. He was *innocent*. I wanted him *so* bad. Stupid, I know." I finally untied the knot, just in time to release the tears for my son into my handkerchief.

"Beautifully said, actually. Let me clarify. You were devastated to lose him. But more devastated to lose your chance at *innocence?*"

"Yeah." I nodded, never having seen it quite so clearly.

Maureen tried to dumb down, unsuccessfully, the pure triumph in her brilliant smile. She leaned forward and hugged me with fervor.

"I found the source. And I know the cure. Would you like to know?" She said with far too much excitement. Even enough to make me cast away some of the pain for a moment.

"Please, oh evil Mrs. Shrink." I jested with a sniffle.

"Easy. When did you lose *your* innocence?" She smiled, bringing up what I told her I wouldn't discuss.

"Why do you ask questions you know the answers to?"

"I never ask a question I *don't* know the answer to. Or one I don't *want* to know the answer to." She smiled again. Then cleared her throat. "But to spare you the game. . .*this* time. . .tell me about your rape, Paige. Because if you're ready to let me, I want to meet you wherever you were that day."

I sighed and shook my head in a pained smile. I breathed once. And then twice. And then I said what I'd never said to anyone.

"I was taking a walk in the woods near my dad's cabin. He was concerned I'd get lost, so he told me to stay by the stream right outside his cabin because it could lead me home. If I had just. . .*listened*."

The dark classroom muffled the pain in my words. The silence of the church understood my tears. I knew I could trust Maureen to bring me meaningful comfort. So, I let her into a place I'd always traveled alone—a dark evening in the woods where I lost my innocence against my will. She cried. I don't think I'd seen Maureen cry like that. I explained to her the compass she'd seen me stare at on numerous occasions. I had started that day with so much innocence, I'd had to research exactly what had happened. I'd ended it filled with pain I still couldn't shake. There were a few moments of quiet filled with sniffles from us both.

Then I re-sobered. "So, you're telling me that all my pain is because of that?"

"Well, I think you caused yourself a lot of *additional* pain because of that. People tend to *say* that abuse like that is damaging. But unless you've lived it, you don't truly understand how difficult it can be to make that memory fade. I bet it lives inside your *bones*, Paige. All that stuff you did to try to forget was wrong. Made things far worse. You know that. But it wasn't completely unwarranted." To be finally understood was liberating.

"You said there was a cure?"

She chuckled. "You won't like it."

"It can't be that bad."

"It isn't. But you'll tell me in a minute that it's impossible. This cure is an interesting one. If you don't do it, your life will still be beautiful. After all, you do know the joy of the Lord. I foresee you being well-loved and appreciated your entire life, Paige. But it will just be symptom relief. There will always be a burden you'll carry, and the people who love you most might even feel that weight and have to help you carry it. You'll live in a fog and *miss* things. You already do. It's *already* hurting you. Eventually, this sickness could be your demise, Paige. But if you submit to the cure, you'll feel light enough to fly. And most importantly, God will be *immensely* glorified." Maureen was adamant, somehow knowing I wouldn't be happy.

"So, what's the cure?" I asked again, hoping it was not some other evil scheme.

A labored breath. A piercing stare of amber eyes. A squeezing of my hands around my crumpled handkerchief. And one passionate whisper of a word.

"Forgiveness."

I arrived home after a heated refute to a sobering truth. She told me that perhaps I should start the forgiveness with Jake, the reason for my greatest symptom. And that the effect of the forgiveness would be so liberating, I'd want to forgive my unknown attacker to his face. She told me if I forgave Jake, she'd find the man that hurt me. I told her not to bother. Forgiveness was not in the cards. She said that while everyone is accountable for their actions, the only way to truly understand *Agape* was to forgive. Unforgiveness adds conditions. *Agape* is unconditional. She said I should forgive because I am forgiven.

"Well, I know I'm forgiven, but—" I whined.

"*Do* you?" She challenged.

"Yes!" I had raised my voice.

"Then why do you refuse to wear your purity ring?"

After that, I had been silent.

And when I walked in the door, my father called me into the kitchen. He had made me a bowl of ice cream to my horror, relief, and tears.

When I was a child, ice cream fixed everything. My father was not an emotional man, but he tried. If I cried over something enough, he'd give me ice cream. When my mom left for good, ice cream wasn't good enough. He had told me that "only a cabin" would fix it. But since the fishing and hunting cabin he still frequented alone had only ruined me, there had been no ice cream until that night.

"It was the cabin, wasn't it? That's when it happened. Your, uh, therapist called me. Said you could use some symptom relief, whatever that means." My father stepped out in love as never before. And I stepped out in honesty, discovering from the hours-long conversation that he'd always known what happened at the source.

"Do you think I should forgive him?" I asked my father late in the conversation. Not because I needed a second opinion. But because I wanted to validate my stubbornness, and I knew Dad would enable it the way he enabled everything. I clarified when he didn't answer. "Maureen says I should forgive him. Jake too."

"I don't see what that would solve," Dad replied just how I'd hoped. "Sympathizing with a child molester? And what Jake did. . . *I* certainly don't have the capacity to forgive either of them. Maybe you shouldn't, either."

"Exactly." I concurred under my breath. Then my heart stirred me to seek honesty in my father. "Did you forgive Mom?"

He laughed once. Smirked. "Not until recently." He sighed. "I had every right to be angry with her. Just like you have that right in your case. But it had a side effect I couldn't see until recently."

"A side effect?" I wondered.

"You look just like her. The older you get, the more you look like her. Except she has brown eyes. Spitting image, Paige." Dad prefaced. Then sighed again. "It was hard to look at you. To trust you or ask you to trust me. I'd convinced myself you'd run away if I gave any opinion of how you should live your life. Just like she did. I'm sorry, Paige. The worst thing I've ever done is *nothing*."

"I forgive you, Dad. So does Jesus." My heart collapsed. Of course, I could forgive him. My father, who gave me a good life when my mother hadn't even wanted me. Human forgiveness can certainly extend that far.

He vowed from that moment to protect me enough to make up for all the things he allowed. I feared the new resolve, but welcomed it, knowing I'd probably never afford him the chance to protect me from another man. The only one I could ever see myself loving wasn't available.

I drenched my Bible that night with worry over the unknown. Would God ask me to just forgive the admitted greatest source of my pain? Or would He rather I keep my eyes on the future, forsaking the past that shaped me? I prayed, I cried. I hoped. That God would accept the easy path. I fell asleep in tears, as always. But I was distracted by the taunting fragrance of hot pink flowers at my bedside. And more pain from all around than I could ever conquer alone.

I try to rise, but every ounce of determination and strength has left me in one day.

"I don't think I can walk, Daddy. I'm so cold." This is said weakly. The world around me is fading into a beautiful fog of stars and tears. I worry that I may have to succumb to the sound of the trickling stream and fall asleep.

"It's alright baby, I'll carry you if that's what I need to do." My father's voice has changed. It is deeper. Smooth, pure, and genuine. It is more comforting than the sound of a cello in candlelight. But it still does not seem to match his face.

"Okay. . ." I feel myself fading away.

"No. No! You stay with me." My father lifts me, and seconds later, I am asleep to the sound of a deafening beep that I suppose is my pounding head. My failing heart.

Chapter 24

Capacity

I worshipped alongside Maureen and her family Sunday morning, and neither of us spoke of our conversations from the previous two nights. Dillon was in a classroom, but Lane was a bit under the weather and clung to me the entire service in the sanctuary. Between services, I sat coloring with the little one at my beloved table. He was impossibly precious and my only source of peace when Dee Martin and her minions passed me, leering and jeering. Except Emma, who bit her lip with a sorrowful sort of smile as she passed. It was excruciating, knowing that Dee Martin was an awfully good choice for Mark, and Maureen was right. I certainly didn't approve.

I shook off the all-too-familiar encounter just in time. Dave and Maureen approached with Dillon as Lane and I were laughing about the purple elephant boarding the Ark in his picture. Dave was about to take the children home so Maureen and I could clean together for one more day.

"I hate it. I'm not going anymore. These kids are still learning about Noah's Ark and the animals. They don't even touch on how the story relates to Noah's obedience or God's faithfulness. It's disgusting." I looked up, astonished to realize that these words were flowing from the mouth of a ten-year-old boy.

"Well, Dillon. When you are a pastor, you can change the entire Sunday school curriculum so that all the kids learn the same story at different levels. So that the fifth graders aren't learning about animals. Good idea, right?" Maureen smiled at how impressed I was with the young man.

"Actually, yeah. That's a good suggestion. I'll make a note of it." I was trying to recall if I ever "made a note of" anything at age ten.

"Mommy says not to tell my brother he talks funny." Lane echoed my sentiments exactly, to the amusement of us all.

"Pastor, huh? I think that's an excellent career choice, Dillon." I spoke to the young man nearly as an equal.

"Yeah. Dad wants me to be a doctor." Dillon rolled his eyes.

"You're ten, Dillon. With that mind, the world is yours. Don't rule it out yet," Dave's voice boomed.

"I don't want the world, Dad. I wanna serve God." Dillon's prepubescent voice was an almost humorous irony to his wisdom.

"Not the time or place, bugaboo. Take your brother to the car and start it, please." Maureen handed Dillon her keys, and we all watched the two boys walk out into the cold. A mother of trustworthy children.

Dave and Maureen shook their heads in laughter. Dave spoke to me directly, with a question that was far too simple. For someone of lesser intelligence, I would perceive it as small talk. But from Dave, I realized quickly it probably had some deeper meaning I didn't understand.

"You like kids, huh?"

"I *love* kids," I answered, but Maureen kicked Dave and then glared at him regardless.

"I apologize for my husband. He asks random questions sometimes." The word "random" was said between gritted teeth.

"It's fine. I'm used to random questions, Mrs. Shrink." Dave enjoyed this but received another kick and glare for laughing at the counselor slight.

Dave finally said goodbye and kissed Maureen before leaving the church with the boys.

They would be sorely and bitterly missed.

Maureen and I sat at "my" table and watched Maureen's family drive off. We had an entire service to wait out before we could fully clean the church. Maureen sighed, deciding how she would use her latest opportunity to prod, counsel, or otherwise "cure" me. She was silent a moment to allow the clicking of her brilliant mind. She never, ever quit.

Someday I'd see the beauty of it. Even if from a distance.

My heart was crumbling. With each crumb that flaked off and died, I made more connections that I assumed were God speaking. Without a word to my counselor, I rose to set in motion a decision that might kill me. But my expense, I decided, was nothing when considering the reward for Mark.

I made my way to the place of retreat for a pastor between services. Even knowing I'd be invading a probably precious few moments of prayer before delivering his final weekend message, I still couldn't convince my heart to send me elsewhere. That heart nearly erupted as I passed the maintenance closet in my journey. But I arrived at the office of pictures and power. It was unlocked. It was always unlocked. And I curled into a chair across from his desk, awaiting his arrival.

As expected, after only seconds, Pastor Robert entered his own office with a sigh before startling slightly at my presence. I immediately apologized.

"I know I shouldn't be here. I just needed to talk to you for a minute. I don't know what else to do, and I'm really sorry. Please forgive me." I didn't expect all the words or tears.

"Your being in my office unannounced only signals an emergency in my eyes. Don't apologize. What's the matter, Miss Ellis?"

"I'm a mess." My explanation for the obvious.

The pastor spoke, concerned. "You know our policy. I don't counsel young women, Paige. So, I assume this isn't a personal matter?"

"Well, it is. But I've already talked to Maureen. Probably too much. I'm here because I think I need to quit working here, Pastor Robert. Maybe even quit *coming* here." I surmised that vomit was more pleasant and savory in expulsion from the body than those words.

"I believe that neither you nor this fellowship would benefit from that choice, Miss Ellis. But it is indeed your choice. May I ask the reason?"

I sniffled once. Then twice. Shook my head, determined not to say it. Then all at once, it escaped into the picture-filled room against all barriers of my soul. "Pastor Robert, Maureen helped me to realize that I'm in love with your son. I'm sure you know the issues with that, so if I leave quietly, I think it'd be for the best. God's house is not a place for a scandal."

"Issues? Scandal? Care to specify?" Pastor Robert finally sat, taking a deep breath and collecting his thoughts for the shock I likely just delivered. But he had some odd smile on his face as well.

"Maureen told me that Mark found his soul mate. And I have so much respect for the perfect love story he's been planning all his life. He doesn't need a teenager around to throw a rock in things. I honestly prefer to leave before he gets back so that I don't even have to see him with her... but I know that isn't the right thing to do. So, I'm giving you two weeks' notice. Do I need to write it down?" I tried to steady my voice for the explanation.

He cleared his throat and narrowed his eyes with compassion as he leaned back in his chair. "Have you discussed this solution with Maureen? Worked through some alternatives?"

"No. Maureen's advice was for me to pray about it. Wonderful advice, but I think my feelings are getting in the way of me getting a clear answer from God. So, I'm being logical according to His word and fleeing the situation." I took a deep breath and a tissue from the pastor's desk.

"Paige, when you came to Christ, how did He speak to you?"

"He'd been calling me like a tug at my heart. Then when I came here and heard about forgiveness, I felt peace. Loving Christ and obeying God felt more right than even breathing." I described, smiling at the memory.

He smiled, nodding. "Interesting. It *felt* right. And before you were saved, when you were making a myriad of misguided choices, as we all do, how did that feel?"

"Terrible. I hated myself. I always knew it was wrong. I just didn't think I had a choice until I kept hearing that God loves me." I smiled again at the ease of wisdom in the man.

"Now, tell me how you feel right now."

"I told you I can't trust my feelings on this one. They are a bit clouded—"

"I understand. But humor me."

I sighed, dabbing my tears. "It doesn't make any sense. I mean, Mark is a little old for me. He's so pure and good, and I'm. . .not. But loving him feels *comfortable*. Like I could do it forever. Which scares me. And I'm sick just thinking about leaving him and all of you. I've never felt more peaceful than here at this church. But I don't have a choice. I have to go. So that—" I faltered a moment and sniffled. "So that Mark can have that same peace with the woman God made for him without ever feeling guilt about how *I* feel about him, because I know he'll find out. He's like that. It would ruin things for him. But he deserves perfect."

"*Remarkable*." Pastor Robert said with passion, at a near whisper.

"What's 'remarkable'?"

"'Therefore, I tell you, her sins, which are many, are forgiven—for she loved much. But he who is forgiven little, loves little.'" Random to my ears. But I somehow knew it to be a direct response to what I just said.

"Luke 7:47. You taught on that passage the night I accepted Christ." I smiled.

"I remember. A few months ago, my son presented that verse to me as if he was trying to talk himself out of something. When he asked, I agreed with him that in my own experience, it is the bonafide, bottom-of-the-barrel sinners that fall the absolute hardest for Christ. He asked if it was safe then, to assume that those heavily redeemed who understand the true sacrifice of the cross, also have a greater capacity for love. I knew from the look of him what he was asking me. So, I told him yes. Despite some challenges that may arise within the relationship, a formerly immoral person likely makes a magnificent spouse. Such a person is likely eager to repay to others the grace and unconditional love they were given through salvation.

"My son is wise. He'd been trying not to fall in love with this girl while waiting for God's best. But then he realized that if he chose a redeemed wretch over a garden variety godly virgin, he would be loved with a greater capacity. He wasn't quite sure if he *deserved* that kind of love. But he finally learned that it was exactly what he'd been looking for. Paige, there are dozens of young ladies in this fellowship who think that mere purity has earned them a claim on Mark Henley's left ring finger. But Mark fell for the one girl that felt she could never live up to his standards of purity, even though she, not purity, sets a standard none of the others can hope to aspire to. You see, in youth, Christ is best glorified when His children act with purity, innocence, self-control, and patience. But in marriage, which is what Mark is after, Christ is best served through love."

"So. . ." I sought clarity, admiring Mark even more. "He chose someone who could love him more than anyone else would."

"I believe she already does. And I assure you, Mark is in tune with God on this one. Because the young woman he's chosen is fully and unpretentiously willing to endure a lifetime of sorrow, loneliness, and misery—a veritable death of self—just so that Mark might experience momentary peace. I've seen her physically step aside when someone she deemed a better prospect approached my son. She wants what is best for *him* and respects him deeply for exactly who God made him to be. In my book—and my Book is God's Word—that is *love.* Because 'Greater love has no one than this, than to lay down one's life for his friends.' I can't think of one of the young virgins in this church willing to die like that for my son. There's nothing wrong with them. They just aren't for him. You see, then, why he thinks *himself* undeserving." The pastor's words disallowed my breath in place of a few tears, though my mind was lagging behind. Then as he stood and made his way into the bustling foyer to mingle, he placed that warm hand on my shoulder and proclaimed something just above a whisper. "Resignation not accepted. My son would be devastated."

The door shut me out of the roar of the foyer, and I sat a moment in the quiet office to collect my thoughts. In the quiet, encased in just a moment, I declared war within myself. I suddenly felt my limbs start to shake from a powerful source of anguish in my soul. And yet, every bit of my pain was eased. I experienced sheer terror. Unveiled delight. Because I loved Mark. With the fullness of a greater capacity than he could ever imagine. But I hated him because the wisest man I knew all but condemned him to a life with someone a lot like me.

I made my way slowly to the lively foyer through the dim hallway that housed the pastor's office. I listened to the flopping of my shoes, wondering what in the world just happened. Mindlessly, even through the crowd of people, I tended the well-loved coffee cart, directing my perfectionism at corners of sugar packets. Then I headed back over to my table as though I hadn't just silently said goodbye to it forever.

Mid-foyer, my heart left my throat when a thunderous thump occurred that silenced the overcrowded foyer. I turned to see that a few reams of paper had been dropped by a rather handsome young man standing atop the information desk. To intentionally get my attention. When all the breaths gathered before they realized the reason for the silence, Mark spoke into it in a voice all could hear.

"Hey! Paige Catherine-with-a-C Ellis! I choose *you*." When the awkward laughter and the coos came, Mark realized what he had just done and sought to correct it with church-worthy words that only added to the laughter. "Praise the Lord, Amen."

I was somewhere between hysterical laughter and a multitude of tears and not sure how to respond to the lock Mark had on my eyes from halfway across the room. I stood frozen under the eyes of the biggest crowd of churchgoers, including a wide-mouthed Deidre Martin and smiling Emma. But when he hopped down and made his way over to me, the foyer began to hum and then roar again, pretending not to watch. Mark arrived in front of me and didn't speak.

"I thought you were taking today off. Conference?"

"After two days of missing everything the speakers were saying because my mind was elsewhere, I called it quits." He joked, unclipping his own mass of keys from my side belt loop and returning it to his own. Easing my burdens. Sharing my chains. "God wanted me to tell you something."

"Well, you got that out of the way." I laughed, never understanding how Mark managed to float between wildly at ease and perfectly wild at all times.

"How was your weekend?" He asked. "I assume Maureen was absolutely no help."

"She was." I smiled. "Just not with the cleaning the church thing."

If the foyer wasn't at its fullest, between Sunday services, we'd have experienced an awkward silence as we walked up the steps to overlook the foyer. But, unable to handle the stares of those that heard, I made a beeline for some corner to die in somewhere, and wound up pretending to read the plaque outside the upstairs storage room like I hadn't read it a thousand times.

In nervous trembles, I stared at the "Storge Room," hating Mark for choosing to waste his love on someone so vile and unworthy. Maureen had predicted my exact reaction. At least I didn't slap him.

If love was this painful, I hated it even more. Now Mark probably thought I was insane when I looked at the plaque on the door, allowing the words to sink in again. And I smiled slowly, finding a glorious revelation of an occasion to change the subject.

"It's not misspelled, is it? It says '*Storge* Room.' Like *love*. The family kind. Maureen explained the four loves to me the other day." I chuckled. "That's cute, but how does your family feel about having their love relegated to a storage closet?"

He snickered at my realization, but even at my blatant denial of the new circumstances, he indulged my distraction. "Well, this room is a *reminder* of the love, not where it lives. Maureen has always ranted about 'storge.' But until that summer, I really didn't *get* it."

"Oh. The summer your dad overreacted and made you clean that room out for taking your nephew out for ice cream? Doesn't sound too loving." I snickered. Mark didn't. He shifted his feet around and re-crossed his arms. Offended that I'd joked about his overzealous father.

"As per the goody-two-shoes version, I suppose."

"Well, what's the full, un-cut version?"

Mark sighed and nodded, leading us to our usual lean at the railing above the foyer, where he began the heartbreaking full story.

"In case you've made the mistake of thinking I've never screwed up, you should know I was *drunk* that day Dad 'overreacted.' If you knew 'J Fish,' you knew about his crazy Saturday basement parties. I was at one of those, and I *forgot*

I was supposed to take Dillon to get ice cream until Reen called and reminded me. So, of *course,* I didn't tell Dad I was taking the truck because he would have seen how drunk I was. God got me to get Dill. To ice cream. And almost all the way home. Then I decided to smoke a cigarette, which Maureen hated me to do in front of Dillon. But hey, I was driving drunk with a five-year-old in the backseat. How much worse could it get? But it got worse. A stupid ash burned my shoulder, which made me run the stop sign because it hurt so bad. And somehow, the cop that ticketed me believed it was rum ice cream on my breath. God changed me that day. Started to bring me home. But the reality is. . ." Mark sniffled,

"I could have *killed* my nephew. God sometimes has to bring you all the way to your knees and make you crawl home before you see how sweet home really is. That happened when my sister cried her eyes out and held onto Dillon, knowing she could have lost him. And Dave ran baby Lane out of the room like I was some monster they couldn't trust. I *was*, Paige. For the first time, I was glad my mom wasn't alive to see me."

I stood, unable to look him in the eyes, even if he was lying. Terrified that he could have done something so heartless and idiotic. But before I allowed the hate, we accidentally met eyes with a stray movement of our heads. And instantly, because of their intensity, I forgave him. I decided that love was either blind or incredibly wise and gracious. He spoke again.

"They should have thrown me to the streets. Or turned me in. I wouldn't have blamed them. But instead, my dad got me up at 4:00 a.m. the next morning to start organizing that disaster of a storage room. I spent half the morning vomiting from the worst hangover in history. And when I was finally done hurling, Maureen decided to use a bit of positive reinforcement on me. A bribe. As if I deserved that. Dave had Velma towed to the front of the church as I was smoking a cigarette. I took one look at her, and they knew they had me. She wasn't too much to look at then, but I saw her how she is now. I knew she wasn't beyond hope. They let me see that before they threw the curve."

"Sports analogy." I smiled, sniffled.

"Of course, Cinderella. They told me if I wanted her, I was smoking my last cigarette—ever—and that if I was gonna turn my back on rebellion, I was doing it *all* that day."

"I'd say requiring you to quit cold turkey after three years with a hangover wouldn't be fair, but I suppose fair is relative, considering what could have happened with Dillon." I shook my head, not understanding fully that the same Mark standing at my side was the one that committed such a horrible travesty. "Like, why didn't Maureen *kill* you? She's quite a mama bear. Seriously, even if she was going for *mercy*, buying you a car is a little excessive." My own inner mama bear awakened.

"She wasn't going for mercy. She was going for *grace*. Mercy is what Dad did with the 200 hours of community service. Sin has consequences, and those were lenient. Maureen wanted me to understand something else. Because Christ, when He died, that wasn't just mercy. It was like giving a classic project car to a teenager after he drives drunk with your son in the car. Not just unearned. But *wildly* undeserved. She said grace is the best teacher. Because in response to the *grace* of that outlandish gift, I gave up a lot more than just smoking. I gave up baseball, and while all those guys were partying and dating, I was serving God. And restoring Velma, saving her for my future wife. Even though she was already exceedingly beautiful when I got her. My family helped remind me who I really am, you know? I'd almost forgotten." Mark's eyes glistened. My eyes glistened. And I loved the room, the plaque, and every person or circumstance that created them. But instead of giving him more than a smile for it, I turned in my soul to a place of defensiveness, not of God or love.

I sniffled. "I'm not your project car like Velma. You can't fix me just by—"

Mark chuckled. "Who said I wanted to fix you? I don't love you for what you *could* be, Paige. I love you for who you are *today*. Sure, you're a work in progress, just like the rest of us. But even so, I'm certainly not skilled enough to 'fix' you or anybody else. That's God's job. And if He thinks He has work to do in your life, I'm just hoping to be. . ." Mark shrugged. "A *wrench*."

We took a moment to lean next to one another in silence at the rail, just as if it was the previous Sunday and we were blissfully ignorant. And then I couldn't stand the lie anymore. I opened up to my friend.

"I almost quit my job just now because I didn't think I could handle watching you be in love." I sobbed, then laughed. "Your dad wouldn't let me quit."

He chuckled. "I heard."

"How did you talk to your dad in that amount of time? And why would he tell you?"

Mark guffawed. "Dad isn't the one with verbal diarrhea. I talked to *Maureen*."

"I didn't say anything to Maureen."

"Since when do you need to *say* something to Maureen?" He smiled.

"Yeah, I guess you're right." I sighed.

"It's really weird that you didn't know. I felt like I was constantly screaming it." Mark unleashed his dimples in a way that was more brilliant than all other illuminating entities in this human realm. "Maureen says she all but told you."

"All but," I said with sarcasm, then tried to stifle my sudden tears and remove my handkerchief.

"I could have killed her when she bought you a purity ring with a glass slipper. I thought for *sure* you'd figure it out." Mark chuckled.

"Cinderella," I murmured to myself, then faced him, biting my lip, humming a laugh. "Wait, didn't she bought that on Black Friday?"

"Um, yeah. She found out how I felt on Thanksgiving." He turned and leaned his back against the rail, laughing.

"Thanksgiving? Mark, we'd been working together like two weeks at that point." I laughed at his mistake.

He snickered. "Paige, as soon as you said the words, 'I like to clean,' I knew I was in trouble. Two weeks later, I was done. My family has been begging me to tell you since Christmas after Dave and the boys met you. But Song of Solomon says,

'*Do not stir up nor awaken love until it pleases.*' So, I held out until God insisted that I tell you. I got a little worried when I bought you flowers, and you looked at me like I had two heads. That was the test."

I giggled and explained. "Guys used to buy me flowers when they wanted. . .something I didn't think you'd ask for."

"Oh! I am so sorry." Mark winced. "If I ask you for *that,* there will be like rings and vows and stuff first."

"Good to know." I giggled. Then Mark watched as I tried to untie the bandanna for the tears. But only a moment before taking it from me, untying it, refolding it, and allowing me to give it another purpose. Tenderness I would never deserve.

"Mark. . ." Was all I could manage. Because his name alone set me to a tearfully trembling voice.

"Paige?" He replied gently, remedying my hair from the quick removal of my scarf. My name on his tongue was lovely, like a cello humming richly in the dimness of candlelight. Confirming for me his full affections and intentions, even in the one word. But I, of course, protested. As was so wisely predicted.

"You could have *anyone.*" I tried to open the world to him.

"I want *you* or no one." He determined.

I moved on to negotiations with a heavy sigh because I was still convinced the conversation was part of a dream.

"I'm seventeen!"

"No, you're not." He gave a half smile. "Time should fix the number, though. And love is patient."

"I've been with a *lot* of other guys." I winced. "I was pregnant. I had an *abortion.*"

"I'm aware." He tilted his head to soothe me.

"But you're a virgin!"

"Oddly, I'm aware of that too." He laughed with sarcasm.

I laughed along. "People are gonna freak. There is so much about this that is not what they expect from you."

"Don't care. I love you. And I *know* this is right. If God is for us, who can be against us?" He was passionate. More so than I'd ever seen. Enough to scare him into a calculated sigh and recover from the tension with a joke. "I prayed for courage today. Never do that."

A silence occurred, but only a few seconds before its greatest cure. The cure at which we excelled, though I'd been long deficient before I knew Mark. After we laughed the tension away, he inquired of his best friend, leaning against my shoulder.

"You okay? And. . .I mean, are *we* okay? I don't want this to ruin what we have. For all I know, you're still plotting your escape."

"I'm pretty sure you *know* that's not the case, Boss. I'm just trying to figure out how this is all gonna work." I leaned back against him with a coy smile as I took in his scent.

"Easy. We'll get married, have eighty babies, and live happily ever after. Let's not complicate this, Cinderella." He chuckled with a sarcastic matter-of-fact Skittle chomping air.

"That easy, huh?" I giggled, chomping on the Skittle he poured into my hand from a wooden box.

We were startled when a presence divided us. The incessant eavesdropper forced us apart and mimicked my lean against the rail. In heels again, leaving me with a far better coworker.

"Always leave space for good counsel, love birds." She reprimanded even the innocence of the closeness. We snickered at her ridiculous implication.

"This is a mess," I said with a smile, shaking my head, still in shock at all the uncertainty now taking up residence in my life.

"No," Maureen said with that smile and the exact counsel we needed. "That *foyer* is a mess. Don't people know how to wipe their feet? At any rate, someone should take care of that mud."

"Come on, Cinderella. There isn't a mess God and our mops can't handle." Mark winked cheerily before he led me down a staircase to remedy muddy footprints.

Chapter 25

Courage

There was a day when the turmoil was not overcome by peace as I entered the church. A day my table wouldn't do, and I ventured past the outer courts. I sat in the sanctuary after a midday flight from school, a notice in my hands, served to me in person in the lunchroom amid all my peers.

A hearing date for the trial of Jake Stone. A trial I thought I'd have much more time for which to prepare my spirit. But instead of time, there had been a timely investigation. And since he still claimed to be innocent, they were counting on my testimony to bury him at trial.

I was in agony. Just seventeen. And instead of my time being filled with prom dress shopping and other teenage frivolities, my life was overcome with a cleaning schedule to keep. A courtroom I had to enter. A love I'd never deserve. Overwhelmed? I thought for a moment I should check my forehead for sweating blood. As Jesus in Gethsemane. Yet how dare I compare myself to my Lord?

I sat where God's presence resonated best in the church. I knew He was there with me. But I longed for the calming smile of my friend Mark. For the cello. Instead, I heard different strings resonating beside me. And nearly as lovely.

"Miss Ellis." Two warm and rustic words. A wink. A box of tissues surrendered to me. Exactly what I needed. I thanked my pastor before he whistled back out of the sanctuary. I was alone only a moment before a voice of sugar and spice flowed from the row behind me.

"Oh dear." Maureen saw my obvious distress. "This has to be serious. You're playing hooky to sit in the *sanctuary*. Either you did something *awful* or you're one of the wisest women I know. So, what'd you do?" A motherly sigh.

"I know Jesus is in my heart, but sometimes I just want to be surrounded by Him too." I sniffled, partaking of a tissue from the box atop my crossed legs.

"Mmmm," hummed Maureen proudly. "That's what I figured. Wise."

I took a deep breath before revealing my distress. The verbal allowance liberated me, and I thanked God for sending Maureen. "They want me to testify against Jake. They're talking attempted murder, among other things." I handed Maureen the notice over my shoulder.

"You're seventeen. I have a pre-law bachelor's. I also have that 'Dr.' prefix they like in a child advocate. Not that you need one. But you're not doing this alone, sweetie."

I smiled as Maureen squeezed my shoulder.

"That would be *so* great, Maureen. My dad wants to support me, but he has trouble even *mentioning* Jake." I shuddered at the unwelcome memory of Jake's cold and hateful eyes and the thought of a courtroom of people to whom I'd have to tell my worst of sins. But found comfort knowing Maureen would be with me.

I thought back to a knock-down-drag-out in a classroom over baby toys and cures.

"Maureen, I don't know how I could ever forgive him. Maybe at the trial, you'll see why." I said with honesty.

"Well, I don't doubt this guy is a waste of the earth's oxygen, but nothing is impossible with Jesus. Start with Jesus, add time and prayer, and see where you end up." She concluded the subject matter by squeezing my shoulder. "Ooo, Paige. Got any gum?" Maureen asked as if she'd been searching all day for a piece. Odd, since I'd never actually seen her chew gum. Still, I nodded, which in her mind gave her permission to grab my purse into her row and rifle through it.

The sanctuary door squeaked, and Maureen's sighed eye roll included a tinge of peppermint. "Well, my presence just became obsolete. I'll talk to you later, Paige."

I understood what Maureen was saying when I turned to see she was rising and passing a handsome silhouette in the dim aisle. With some short exchange of a silly handshake and a moment of whispered information, they parted ways, and Mark headed toward me, carrying something the size of a shoebox.

When he came into view, I reprimanded him. "You have a class! Calculus at this time, right?"

A single giddy chuckle. "Aw, you have my schedule memorized. How sweet. But Reen told me someone important needed some cheering up, and suddenly math wasn't appealing to me." Mark sat next to me, setting his box on the floor. He left a chair between us and patted that chair with a demand. "Feet."

I, of course, complied, rotating in my chair and placing my feet on the chair between us. My flip-flops were bright blue that day, and they are included in the smile he claimed for my freckles. He removed the lid of the box on the floor, then put his middle finger and thumb on the sides of my left flip-flop. "May I?"

I nodded. He removed my shoe and tossed it behind him with all his strength. It landed somewhere mid-sanctuary, to my amusement. The second one was thrown within laughter and misdirected itself way up and toward the stage. I lost sight of it somewhere above the front row. I was amazed he'd thrown it so high but remembered all his sports analogies.

He startled, eyes wide, then placed warm hands on cold feet. "Holy wow, Cinderella. You have, like, feet-cicles."

"Well, I hardly ever wear socks, so they are just sort of perpetually cold. I'm really in need of a pedicure, so don't look too close. Your hands are warm. It feels nice." I giggled. He seemed to have some dilemma saunter past his eyes before he withdrew his hands. "What's wrong?" I asked. "Why are my feet naked?"

He guffawed once to the ceiling, then reached down again and brought into view a pair of shoes I could smell for their freshness and quality. They were closed-toed sandals—rough leather with laces and accents in hot pink. Slowly, Mark slid them onto my feet. They were the perfect size, and I fell in love with the shoes immediately. But more so with the way Mark's warm hands grazed my feet during the operation.

"When Dave said how dangerous flip-flops are, I had to find you something else to work in." He smiled, then dropped to a whisper and a wink. "I really care about your feet and the person they are attached to. You know, as your boss."

I smiled. Completely smitten and in far too deep to flee. I pawed the new shoes, and Mark waited for me to speak. But his loving perfection stirred my heart nearly to tears. And it is only with a squeak that I thanked him.

"I just heard you have to testify against Jake," He brought up. Not helping my effort to withhold tears.

"Yeah. I mean, I don't *have* to, but I don't want him to hurt anyone again, so prison would be a good place for him." I sniffled.

"Um. . ." He cleared his throat. "I just talked to Maureen, and she doesn't actually know what happened with Jake. I mean, I know you two were. . .whatever you were. And I know about the baby, and I saw him chase you across the parking lot. But what about that would mean prison? Maureen said you've been pretty vague about it."

I hummed a laugh through tears. Claiming another tissue from Mark's hand as I nodded. I'd told the story to the police and doctors. I'd forgotten by then that I'd never actually told anyone in my 'new' life. No one at all since my body had healed. Before I could speak, the tears came again.

"It's okay, Paige," Mark whispered. "The only reason I'm asking is because you have to testify in court. Maureen just suggested that I ask you to tell *me* what happened."

"I was. . ." I drew in a stuttered breath. "A different person, Mark. So much could come out at the trial. I don't want you to know that person."

"I'm in love with her." Mark smirked. "You can tell me anything, and it'll never change that. Why is Jake on trial for attempted murder?"

I laughed once in irony. "For trying to kill me."

"Did he really?"

"He would get really angry and do horrible things, Mark. Jake and I were together for a year. Maureen thinks I might have PTSD that'll come back to haunt me one day." I sighed. Calming the tears. I told him the story of the incident, sobbing through most of it while he encouraged me to continue. When I was finished, he spoke.

"You are far braver than I, Cinderella." His opinion of my bravery helped call me up from darkness not long before. It meant the world to me. He showed one of his dimples. "I don't have any doubt you'll be amazing on that stand."

I avoided his eyes, unable to accept his version of facts.

"In reality, I'm scared to death," I confessed.

"Of course, you are. Courage is a *reaction* to fear, not the opposite of it."

He captivated me in a loving stare. I didn't know how his eyes saw a light in my darkness. But I was prepared to spend my life being grateful if he'd only ask.

"Will you do something for me?" He asked within a struggle against his front jean pocket, and I assumed he was going to ask me to buy him some Skittles from the bookstore to refill his box.

"Sure, Boss. Anything." I laughed at the determined way he searched in his pockets. But I stopped when his hand emerged with something much smaller than a Skittle box.

Mark held between his thumb and forefinger my purity ring. And I knew that it was with Maureen's sleight of hand and "gum" craving that he acquired it from its case in my purse.

I sighed, more amazed by Maureen and enthralled by Mark.

"This ring is engraved with '*Forgiven.*' Maureen said you probably didn't even know that. Mine says '*Grow.*' Same person had them engraved. Which is completely irrelevant to my point." Mark sighed nervously. "The past is all forgiven. Washed through and through with Christ's blood. So, starting today, I'm asking you to take that grace and run with it. It might be uncharted territory for you, but you are *so* brave. So, I want you to wear this purity ring, and I'll wear mine. Until God tells me I can replace it with a different ring and marry you."

I smiled at my lovesick self. Because Maureen had begged me for months to proudly adorn the purity ring. Yet before Mark was done with his first asking, it was on my finger. He thanked me with a sigh of deep gratitude. But he should have known I'd do anything to retain his honor.

"Marriage, huh?" I flirted. "That's pretty serious."

"I didn't mean to scare you." He worried. "It's an eventual *hope*, Paige. I wasn't saying—"

"Paige Catherine Henley." I smirked, looking up, considering it. "My only objection—and this is pretty huge—would be that we'd have to be careful when we change the 'E' on my mop to an 'H' because if we mess it up, it'll look wrong forever."

Mark smiled sarcastically. "Yeah, we can't have you using a mop with an imperfect H. So, that *is* something to consider."

I took a deep breath and closed my eyes, realizing that when I released the next words into the vacant sanctuary, I was allowing an insatiable fire to ignite. Not a dangerous one. The kind that warms a house in winter or illuminates the buoyant smile of a birthday wisher. I nodded once.

"I love you, Mark." Words, I realized that offered but a sip of what might take a lifetime to pour out to him.

"I love you too," He proclaimed, and placed a hand on my shoe, still atop the chair. His line and limit. "I can't wait to see God's next move."

I allowed the new shoes to lead me home after work, using the chill and time alone to help me think. The breach of my front door greeted a sizzle of something my father was probably burning for dinner. I stepped onto the kitchen tile I'd cleaned in penance for years and washed my hands as I greeted my dad.

But my greeting was abnormal. A little insane, and completely unexpected. No hello was uttered. No jest about the state of the burning meal. It was something that flowed from my spirit in response to his recent promise to protect me. Because neither of us had really changed if I refused to be honest with us both.

"Dad, remember when I said you didn't have to worry about Mark?" I sobbed. Or laughed. It wasn't clear to me. "I didn't lie, I just didn't expect. . ." I sighed.

But my dad's response was far more relaxed. A sigh, then a chuckle. Then words were even more unexpected than my own.

"You really think I don't know how you feel about him?" Not with anger. But with a nod in his voice like I'd reminded him of my favorite color.

I met his eyes in a blank stare. Unable to respond for a moment. "But Dad, you're supposed to freak out or something, right?" I was trying to teach him how to be a protective father. I dried my hands on the towel hanging from the oven handle, then began stirring the burning meat.

"Well, I hate to ask. But do I have a reason to 'freak out'? Are you in a predicament again?" My father nodded at my stomach during the invasive question.

"God, no!" I hoped God didn't mind the vain of His name in that case. "Mark's never even kissed a girl. Look, we're wearing purity rings. It's not like that."

"But you're dating him?" My dad tried to clarify as he grasped my left hand gently to examine it.

"Okay, even if he or I had time for that with school and work and church," I cleared my throat. "Mark doesn't date. It invites undue temptation. I've told you that."

"Hmmm." My father allowed. "About identical to what he said on the phone. Except he mentioned that his eventual hope is to marry you."

"He *called* you?" I gasped and became the dinner-burning culprit.

"Yeah, over the weekend. You're seventeen, Sweet Pea. What is he, twenty?" The logical devil's advocate surfaced unexpectedly.

"He'll be twenty-two in July." I gave hopeless honesty. "I'm sorry. I don't know how I let this happen."

"I told him I'd like for you to concentrate on school for now. But if things pan out, we can talk marriage once you have a bachelor's degree out of the way."

"Dad, that's like four and a half years from now." At my gasp of a response, my dad took over the dinner-burning effort again.

"Yeah. But don't worry. When he asked, I told him he could 'court' you. Whatever 'court' means. I think he wanted to wait until you're eighteen." My father sighed. "I don't mind you dating the guy. But are you sure you want a preacher's kid? Does he know anything about your history? He seems a little naive, Sweet Pea. Something to consider." My dad was smiling about this. Like a joke. Like Mark was a child that had never tasted sin or experienced pain.

I was confused when it was with tenderness and joking that the will of the world surrounded the unquenchable flame with doubt and years and mockery. I refused dinner and sleep with hopelessness, scared that God's will was just as cruel.

There is a steady darkness and a deafening beep. I hear my breath and feel only calm and the darkness, heavy upon my chest. I fear my own death. I feel the cold within my spirit. I am alone, trapped. But I'm starting to understand. Starting to remember the truth.

Chapter 26

Trial

"I'll be there," Mark had said.

"There are things I'd rather you not hear. Really *bad* things," I'd begged. "I'm not who I was. But I *was* bad."

"I'm not asking. I'll be there. End of discussion." Mark had won the argument. I had welcomed the ultimatum in the peace and warmth of the foyer.

Now the only sound in the hallway of the musty building was the tiny creaking of my heels against the wooden floors. I was pacing, warming my uneasy hands with my breath and against one another. My pastried, caffeinated stomach grumbled against itself, and I was regretting the breakfast. In fact, that day, I was regretting a great many things.

"Everything will be fine, Sweetie." Maureen's voice sought to soothe, though the eyes of all my other loved ones immediately forced the opposite.

"Assuming I don't pass out." I continued my pacing outside the courtroom door.

I was banishing tears, refusing the gag reflex that would prove to ruin the way the olive dress brought out my eyes and made me look "youthful but mature." Maureen thought the jury would be sympathetic. I wished she'd have let me wear red with a target, as I'd requested after our meeting with the Assistant Dirtrict Attorney. At least then, my fate and perceived character would have been more certain.

"If you listen, you'll hear them hold their breath between a question and an answer. You can't hear it if you insist on letting your nerves do the talking. You don't have anything to be scared of." Mark's tone was gentle but firm. I took it to heart. *Let them hold their breath. . .let them hold their breath. . .*I whispered within.

"Just the truth, Miss Ellis. The truth is easy." The pastoral comfort stopped my pacing.

"Easy to *remember*. But not so easy to hear. I wouldn't think any differently of any of you for going home right now." I stood under the arm of my father and in front of a bench that housed Pastor Robert and his two grown children. Dave had stayed home with the boys. At my suggestion, they all looked to Mark.

He smiled. "*Agape.* I won't think any differently of *you* if I stay."

The peace in his eyes caused my heart a ripple or two. Maureen and Pastor Robert shook their heads at their lovesick kin, and my father was in blissful confusion.

As I was finally calming myself, we all turned to footsteps in the hall. The youthful doctor who'd talked me into and then performed a "medically necessary" abortion on me. She was an expert witness who would describe and provide an analysis for all the injuries the emergency room had discovered, though she herself had become an obestetrician.

I tried not to let her presence affect me, but suddenly I saw that Maureen had risen from the bench and dusted off her pantsuit unnecessarily. She suddenly took to confidently and flawlessly flaunting every inch of her height, the full sway of her hips, and the radiant fluidity of her hair as she walked to the young doctor. But only after some sort of self-assuring breath I'd never seen her need.

"Eva?"

The doctor turned, startled by the blonde beauty. She was petite, I realized now that she was looking up to speak to Maureen. She reached out her hand to shake Maureen's, narrowing her eyes a moment before gasping and covering her mouth.

"Maureen. Oh, my goodness. Um. . .hi. Small world. . ."

"Extremely. The ADA kept saying, 'Dr. Moreno.' I'd wondered if it was you. I'm Paige's counselor."

"It's me. You look great! How is your family?"

"David and the boys are great. We recently celebrated our tenth wedding anniversary. Lane is almost six, and Dillon just turned ten."

"My goodness, how the time flies!"

"I hear you're working at Mercy Main now?"

"Yes, I work at a women's healthcare practice that is located in the hospital."

"Oh, David works at a neurological group there."

"Oh really? I didn't even know. Small world, big hospital." She laughed. "So, are you a psychologist?"

"Yes. Well, church counselor with a PhD"

Maureen tended to know more people than knew her. But once truly acquainted with Maureen, she was impossible to forget. She also never forgot someone. Therefore, this type of encounter was not abnormal anywhere, but this one was markedly awkward. Both women seemed relieved when the bailiff came to bring us into the courtroom.

Officially, it was the trial of Jacob Stone. But the courtroom, the lawyers, and consequently, my heart, seemed to convert it into a trial against my character. Many questions didn't involve the incident at all. The prosecutor used this to my advantage, helping me boast of my grades and college scholarships, and involvement in church. I agreed to take the stand. Therefore, my word had to be perfect. I tuned out the pressure and listened for the breaths, knowing my nerves might compromise it all.

I remembered deep and intense shame as Jake's eyes stared coldly through me in the courtroom. I hadn't seen him since he was free to chase me with his car on a whim. But more so, I remembered the words of my loved ones and the Holy Spirit, Who urged me to simply tell the truth. I told the truth to an earthly judge, twelve jurors, and a courtroom of people. The truth liberated me. But it also came reluctantly, knowing Mark and his family were a captive audience to hear of my past.

I had to speak to every injury, old and new, discovered the day I arrived at the hospital. My father and my pastor became privy to the way a tiny pill was forced into my mouth the night I could have died from side effects of Ecstasy. I divulged my year of prison, whom they called Jacob Stone.

I was in tears as I recounted the horror of being dragged by my hair and pushed coldly down the stairs. Glad Mark had helped me practice telling it. I was one of only a few witnesses, and testifying first allowed me to hear all of the other testimony. Thus, the trial began with emotions running high.

As expected, the cross-examination was grueling. Jake's defense attorney asked about my previous lifestyle, boyfriends, my current "romantic interest," which I was astonished she even knew about. She tried to trip me up in something. Anything. But truth after truth after truth made it impossible, and she began running out of options. So, she brought up a far too valid argument. If Jake "saved my life" the day we used drugs together, why would he then try to kill me? I told her I didn't know. Even Maureen was worried about that. An assault charge wouldn't buy him near as much time behind bars as attempted murder.

And then the lowest blow of all. My faith was questioned. I was asked why, if I was afraid for my life the day Jake followed me with his car, didn't I stop at the police station instead of running to the church. She tried to get Jake out of the felony menacing charge against him.

"I guess I cared more about being forgiven than about my safety. But I knew I'd be safe in the church. And they called the po—"

"Forgiven? What had you done that needed forgiving?" I almost smiled, seeing a little Maureen in the manipulative questioning. Still thinking she'd make a great lawyer.

"A lot. But I'd aborted my baby. I hated myself for that."

"I'm confused, Miss Ellis. So now you are saying the abortion *was* your choice?"

"I suppose. . ."

"Are you sure you weren't just using the alleged incident with the defendant as an excuse to free yourself of the burden of teen motherhood?"

Maureen scowled at the question, and Mark shook his head in anger. Though we hadn't considered this question when preparing for the cross-examination, I already had an answer. A great use for my weapon of truth, I decided once I had the words from the Holy Spirit. I listened for the room to hold their breath. And then I saw Maureen nod with pride at my genuinely tearful response.

"I will *never* be 'free' of my son."

The "kind" doctor who convinced me to have an abortion was called to the witness stand after me. Mark averted his eyes as she showed photos of the injuries to my abdomen after I was unconscious, and the doctor determined they were most likely caused by repeated blows from a combat boot. That showed Jake's intent to end at least one life that day. Not surprisingly, my testimony had matched perfectly with Dr. Moreno's evidence of my injuries. Truth upon truth. Even I'd been surprised to learn that my wrist had broken so easily against the stairs because it already had a hairline fracture in it from Jake. One of many injuries that stuck around for the hospital's x-rays.

Dr. Moreno concluded that my pregnancy would have likely ended whether or not I had aborted the baby due to the damage inflicted on my womb. That brought me no comfort. The jury sympathized when she also mentioned something I had all but forgotten about waking up after my abortion: it would be difficult for me to become pregnant or carry a pregnancy to term in the future. Up until this point in the doctor's testimony, Mark had been clenching and unclenching his fists. Fiddling with his finger. Nervously shaking his leg. But when that conjecture was mentioned, all nervous movements ceased. And just before I began to think Mark might give me up since I may not give him children, he turned to me and smiled with compassion.

The presentation of the case took only the one morning, to my surprise. During deliberations, I shared a solemn lunch with Mark, his family, and my dad at a dim restaurant where people might go to celebrate. But I had nothing to celebrate, even if Jake was found guilty. The others ordered lunch, and I sipped water, my stomach in knots. Mark didn't order, either. We all sat in silence. I found myself alone at a table of loved ones when not even they could assemble the valor to look at me. I sat nearest the window, staring in the direction of the building that would decide my character for me. Mark was across the table from me in deep thought, looking out the window as well.

I searched hopelessly through my purse for the tissues I'd need any second. My hand fell upon a compass. I ran my fingers along it for a moment until I was startled by two lime green sneakers that enclosed my pumps together beneath the table. He had all but sworn not to hug me, hold me, or touch me after finding out he couldn't even think about marrying me for four years. Choosing not to tamper with bleach and ammonia. But I had never felt safer than in the embrace of Mark's shoes. I looked up at him. Always aiding God in the fulfillment of my needs, he had a package of tissues at the ready and was finally meeting my eyes with his.

"I'm proud of you." The compassion in his eyes was genuine, as always. Suddenly, the others nodded and mumbled in agreement when they realized I probably needed to hear something similar. They all seemed distracted for various reasons.

I sobbed. "I'm sorry. The only time she ever mentioned that was right as I was waking up from anesthesia, and then I had to talk to a cop, and I honestly blocked it because I never thought it would matter. I wasn't keeping it from you. I just *forgot*, Mark." The rant escaped at random, taking more breath than I had.

"Forgot *what?*" Mark panicked at my tears.

"I can't have kids." I sobbed. "What kind of an idiot forgets she can't have children?"

Mark shushed me, squeezing my feet again.

"I am not even a *little* concerned about that, Cinderella." He whispered to soothe me. "You shouldn't be either."

"Maureen told me that in school when they would ask the kids what they wanted to be when they grow up, you would say 'A dad' every time," I whispered intensely, and Mark's family chuckled in nostalgia. So, I abandoned the whisper. "But if you choose *me*, you could be choosing not to have children."

"I *still* choose you. Every time. No matter what. *Agape*, Cinderella." Mark insisted. Maureen cooed. Mark seemed nervous with my arm-crossing father seated next to me, staring him down, waiting for the explanation. He appeased him. "Which, until you finish college, has nothing to do with marriage or attempting in any way to have kids."

"The statistics rule in favor of that." My dad knew he was practically being addressed directly.

Maureen rolled her eyes unabashedly and laughed in sarcasm. "David and I were 'statistically' eighteen at our wedding and married our entire college careers. We somehow have two kids, and people still call us 'Doctor.' *Weird.*"

"Enough." The father and pastor, taming the shrew.

"You're obviously an exception, Maureen." My dad sought approval. "Back me up, Robert."

"Wish I could, Paul. And I certainly understand your position." Pastor Robert fiddled with a dessert menu, not making eye contact. Trying to maintain humility amid the snickers of his children. "But my late wife and I got married at eighteen, around the middle of our senior year of high school. Didn't tell a soul. Our parents are all gone now, and I'm sure we aided that when they only found out what we'd done when Amelia was listed as 'Henley' on the graduation program. When they confronted us, we also let them know that we were expecting a child. Statistically, we shouldn't have lasted a year. And it was certainly difficult at times. But we were married *twenty* years when she went home to Jesus twelve years ago."

"My condolences." My dad tried to avoid the injury to his pride. "The math tells me you two had a child older than Maureen?"

Math not my strong point, I'd never even considered this.

"No, we lost that one shortly after graduation." Pastor Robert then leaned forward and met my eyes directly. "After that, they told Amelia she couldn't have children. That no pregnancy would make it to term. Maureen was the only one of seven total that did. We lost most pretty early on each time. But one, Angela, was a micro-preemie in a less medically advanced world. Amelia is buried next to her." We were all in sudden mourning, though Mark and Maureen's was less pronounced, having been acquainted with this news. The pastor continued, looking even more deeply into my eyes. "Mark was a compromise. Amelia wanted me to have a son. I wanted us to stop trying since Maureen was a miracle alone."

"I wanted a *sister* after losing Angela. Don't forget that part." Maureen said like a child, which proved to lighten the mood.

"God gave us Mark, who is as much our son as if Amelia had carried him herself. And I promised my little girl that if we all did well raising Mark, she'd eventually get a *wonderful* sister." Both Pastor Robert and Maureen smiled warmly at me. My father crossed his arms again. Mark cleared his throat.

"Everything works to His glory, Paige." No one else saw the wink Mark gave me. "He already has *this* worked out, too."

"But how?" I asked, not seeing a way through all the obstacles. All voices sought to soothe in their own opinions and ways, but quickly saw that I was only asking Mark.

"I don't know." He shrugged. "But God knows exactly what He's doing. His ways are above our ways, so they don't always make sense to us. But if He was small enough to understand, He wouldn't be big enough to worship."

I was enthralled, wanting to dance for hours and soothed like I could sleep for years. It must have shown on my face because Mark sat back in satisfaction. The pastor smiled in pride. My dad was confused at how words unrelated to romance pierced my heart so perceptibly. Then Maureen answered a startling ringtone right at the table. She spoke into a cupped hand for a moment, and then her eyes deepened when she hung up.

"Sweetie, they have a verdict. We can finish eating, though. Because we have an hour to get back."

My stomach twisted. Eating probably would have been the worst idea for me. I buried my head in my arms at the table. My dad's hand caressed my back, and Mark responded with another foot squeeze.

The jury deliberated for one hour before finding Jake guilty. However, they could only surpass reasonable doubt on one count of aggravated assault in the first degree, two counts in the second degree, and felony menacing. All reasonable and relieving. But he was found innocent of attempted murder because no one but me saw the hatred in his eyes that afternoon. Based on his age at the time of the assault, the convictions would only earn him a total of fifteen to twenty-five years in prison. Maureen assured me that he should receive the maximum sentence when it was decided in a week. That didn't prove to comfort me. But I was proud of myself for keeping it together, even as Jake's mother gave me a death stare after a tearful goodbye to her son.

But whenever pride entered, I was slowly learning, God would snuff it out. He didn't want me prideful. He wanted me on my knees, broken before Him. Therefore, when the court was adjourned, Jake looked back shamelessly just before he was led out in shackles and chains by a man in uniform. He scanned my loved ones as if to memorize them. His eyes first stopped on my father, then on Mark, recognizing his former smoking buddy. Then his eyes settled on me. Jake's hair had been shaven close and clean so that I received the full view of the eyes that had grown much colder in the past several months. Yet he smiled boldly, chilling every part of me his eyes chose to examine.

The others were conversing among themselves and didn't notice immediately that Jake had begun staring directly into my eyes and was thinking. Jake thinking, I remember, shamed the silence into submission like an untuned orchestra. The opposite of Mark's comforting cello. I was terrified. When he spoke, though he was a full twenty feet away, my loved ones all took full and fearful notice, but were unable to come to the rescue when the words shot quickly into the air.

"You remember what I told you, Paige. Don't ever consider you and your family to be safe." At this, Jake was dragged away quickly where he would await sentencing.

Pastor Robert responded with a hand that ushered me out of the courtroom. I lost all control of my emotion in the hallway of the courthouse. I sobbed, trembling violently, glad I'd decided against eating lunch. My father embraced me, and I felt many other hands touch me as Pastor Robert prayed and thanked God for the verdict we did receive. He also prayed for Jake's soul, though it was the least of my worries at the time. Mark's hands were not among those around me, as he was agitated enough to have announced that he was headed to break a finger and get some Skittles.

As I was sniffling away tears inside Maureen's warm embrace, someone approached with an apprehensive throat clearing. And then a lovely Latina accent:

"Excuse me, Miss Ellis?" Dr. Moreno nearly whispered.

Maureen sighed, slightly annoyed. "You should really work on your timing, Eva."

Though confused with Maureen's rudeness, I stepped away from the embrace and smiled. "It's fine, Maureen."

"I apologize, Mrs. Little. But I will be quick." At Dr. Moreno's seemingly deliberate use of the word "Mrs.," Maureen relaxed her countenance to a smile. Dr. Moreno continued. "Miss Ellis, I could not help but notice the way young Mr. Henley looks at you. Not to intrude, but he's a good boy, that Mark. A good man, from what I see."

My heart leaped. Then fell. I cleared my throat. "Way too good for me, I know. Which I've tried to tell him, but—"

"No, no!" She corrected. "On the contrary. From what I know of him, he feels strongly for marriage. For family. Is that right?"

I nodded, devastated. "That's sort of all he wants in the world."

Dr. Moreno smiled. "Miss Ellis, last October, I was merely covering a shift in the Emergency Department when I determined that other children might not be possible for you. Shortly after that, I began working for an award-winning obstetrics practice in the hospital. We have all of the latest testing and equipment and procedures. And there are procedures I am no longer asked to do, as well. Children are a great blessing. If you'll allow me, Miss Ellis, I would like to take another look. To give you another chance at that blessing."

My father spoke up. "That won't be necessary."

"It will cost you nothing. To help you have children. Or to deliver them. I will never charge you anything." Dr. Moreno ensured. Quickly handed me her card. Cleared her throat to hide the tears I already saw glistening in her eyes. "I owe this to you."

Dr. Moreno walked away with a nod, Maureen hotly crossing her arms and pursing her lips. Pastor Robert first oozed compassion from his eyes when Maureen's were in some distant place. And when she composed her brief anger and smiled at us, Pastor Robert averted his eyes. I knew it was all too mysterious to solve that day, and therefore stepped backward from them.

"Did anyone see which way he went?"

"*He?*" Dad asked. Wary, if not livid.

"Yeah, 'he.' Mark, Dad." I tried not to smile when I said his name.

"Paige, forgive me for being concerned that you're looking for your love interest after another young man was just convicted of *assaulting* you." Dad made a valid point. I crossed my arms and sighed.

Help me out, God. He did. "Dad, my best friend just skipped all his classes for a day to hear all about how the girl he loves was assaulted. He was *here* for me. I need to be there for him."

I found him outside when I'd gathered up my broken soul. He was leaning against the building, popping Skittles in threes. He looked away when he caught the evidence of my recent tears.

"You alright, Boss?"

He laughed. "Am *I* alright? What is it gonna take for you to worry about *yourself?*"

"Apparently, I don't need to. You do it for me. You're really mad, aren't you?"

"I've never hated someone so much. Or felt so powerless. I wanted to *kill* him, Paige. Had the shot all lined up. . .in my heart, of course." There were tears of anger shimmering in his eyes as he nodded at me. But he was too much in control to release them. He ground each Skittle deep into his teeth before he popped another as we stood at the brick corner of the courthouse next to an unused ashtray.

"I think I can relate to that." I released a laugh or a sigh. I'm not sure which. "I'm thankful for your patience with all this, Mark. I don't understand why you aren't giving up on me. But it's admirable, however misguided."

"Thanks?" He bit his lip and chuckled. Sniffled. About to say something he wasn't sure if he'd regret. "Paige, I know he's going to prison for fifteen to twenty-five years. After that, you'd be safe with me. I hope you know that I'll protect you and *treasure* you. Starting whenever you say the word." We smiled at each other, abandoning anger for something better. Or tucking away the cure for palliatives. The tension began to augment, and I broke it before it set me crying again.

"That's only happening if you have teeth, you addict." I smiled at the would-be smoker who was tossing an empty Skittles bag.

Chapter 27

Prospect

I tossed my hat in the air and recalled, for a moment, what it felt like to be a teenager. But only a moment. Like them, my family stood nearby, snapping pictures. Like them, I said goodbye forever to friends I once knew. Like them, I was wearing a sundress beneath a forest green robe. But really, I was nothing like them at all.

Emma, newly engaged as of prom, just as Mark foretold, greeted me in courage and warmth, building with me a friendship I'd done everything not to deserve. She had grown apart from Dee and Marley, Christians less Christlike. But unlike me, she was still welcomed into a mold of young Christians that my past kept me from. Yet, my redemption didn't even allow me close to the mold I'd fit not long ago. They were giddy, all of them. Enjoying youth and liberty.

But the only freedom I experienced that day was an entrance into womanhood that being in high school hadn't allowed, even if my experience had. I was free to love Mark, but not really. Most of me had to ignore what happened to his eyes when he set a pale green button-up shirt against skin darkened by nature and sun.

Most of my classmates gathered at parties. None of them suited me enough to be invited, but I had my dad, Mark, Maureen, and their family. That night we celebrated as a family, or friends, whatever suited the moment, at my home. Into the evening, we ate and chatted and played games. It seemed so natural, celebrating that way. Like it could continue for years.

The graduation gifts came as a pair of lovely and practical shoes or sandals from each person. It was a game they invented that involved scissors and trips I took up the stairs to my closet in pursuit of a pair of flip-flops each time. The giver of the new pair of shoes cut the old foam atrocities in pieces. Together, with jubilation, they beckoned me into healthy adulthood with footwear.

Mark, of course, found the best pair. A thong-style ergonomically correct version of flip-flops for me to work in all summer. They called it cheating, but I secretly called it romance. Because I knew he loved me even in flip-flops.

The hour neared when Mark yawned and checked his phone's clock.

"Yikes!" Maureen said, checking her own. "We have an early morning, everybody."

Everyone grumbled and began helping to clean up and get ready to leave. Mark had a better use for the next few moments.

"Paul, is it okay if I have a minute with Paige before I go?" Mark asked my father.

Maureen rolled her eyes. "Paige, I don't know how you stand how old-fashioned this guy is."

"A welcome relief, in some ways," Dad replied with a smirk. "That's fine, Mark."

We were on opposite ends of the living room. But even through the little crowd of loved ones, I understood the flick of his head toward the door. When we both stood, the family didn't hold back until the relief of the night, and the closed door silenced the whistling and kissy sounds.

We moved past the protective peers out the front window to the shield of the garage and my dad's SUV. We sat against Velma's trunk in the driveway, illuminated by a streetlight. I crossed my arms to combat the chill of the spring night that had yet to give way to summer. And we stared, relishing each other's presence.

Mark sighed after a time, "We'll be working together. Like, all day. All summer. And it's wedding season. So, we'll even be together some nights."

"Yeah, I can't wait," I smirked. "Hopefully, we don't get sick of each other."

He chuckled. "I don't think that's possible. But I wish. . .I don't know. We'll be together. But we won't actually. . .I mean, we'll be working, so. . .I wish we could actually spend time together."

Having been brought to that sinfully suburban house as a baby from the hospital, my ears were attuned to even the slight cracking of the front door. I rolled my eyes and spoke truth, raising my voice with a laugh. "I just wish we could have a private conversation without Maureen trying to listen."

When the door closed again with a frustrated grunt, Mark smiled, then said something far too deep for a smile, cradling his arms as he turned to stare at the streetlight. "I wish I could kiss you."

"Mark Ernesto Henley, kissing is for *marriage.*" I managed to quote his strict purity rules after the gasp and the warmth that surrounded me at the mere suggestion.

"I know," he whispered intensely with a bone-deep suggestion. "I wish that too."

I sighed. Heartbroken. "What are you trying to say to me, Boss?"

"That I love you. But that I'm *scared.* My whole life, I've been gung-ho about abstinence, even when I was in that stupid party phase. I've *always* wanted to get married and to give everything to my wife. No compromises. So, since God wants me with you, and I'm in full agreement, I'm *willing* to wait as long as you need me to wait."

"So why are you scared?" I sighed. Knowing his rock-solid rules and plans for his life.

He quoted scripture after a trembled sigh. "'The spirit indeed is willing, but the *flesh* is weak.'"

I sighed. "Please don't say that to me. You were supposed to like, *be* my hope for abstinence."

"Well, *that's* a bit of pressure." Mark laughed, mimicking me. "But don't forget, you were supposed to like, *be* my hope for getting married."

My heart first jumped when he made clear with his tone the meaning of his words. He was suggesting *now,* not dreaming of the distant future. He was speaking in rebellion to my father's wishes for us to wait four years. Enough, when he welcomed my contemplative silence, that I knew he was asking whether I shared the same wish.

Therefore, I took a precious few moments to consider the prospect. Affirm for myself that I would love him still in ten years when the novelty had worn off. Twenty years, when the jet-black hair started to gray. Thirty years, when the middle of our lives demanded an adventure. Sixty years, when the adventures were all but over. I knew that through novelty and normalcy, black, white, or gray, he would look to Jesus. And with Jesus, years were a feeble obstacle for the endurance of love.

And when I'd decided my heart would still bend as long as there was still a tinge of Cuban timbre in the way he says "Cinderella," I wondered how long I could continue to breathe before I heard him wake me with it in the morning. Whisper it into the night. Let it echo across a foyer as he beckoned me "home" or muffled against the passing cars while we rode inside of Velma. I was liberated in the mere thoughts until my father's voice entered them, sickening me deep within. Words of statistics and education. Wisdom and wait. A tear fell in the soul sickness, when I remembered there were years still until kissing and private conversations—or even a joining of our hands—could be added to our love.

He saw the tear and sighed deeply. "If that's four years, that's four years. But I guess what I'm asking is, if it didn't *have* to be—"

I nodded and interrupted, beginning an anecdote of a response. "So, my mom cut my hair when I was six or seven because she was home for two weeks in a row and decided she didn't want to deal with it. After that, because my mom was never around, I grew it all the way past my waist to spite her. My dad used to call it my 'warning label' because, well, I had a wild side. All the boys *loved* that long red hair. I was a walking temptation, and I *knew* it." I laughed bitterly, and Mark chuckled, worried. I continued. "But it wasn't meant to hold my weight up a flight of stairs, so I had to cut it again. And I miss it, you know? I do want to grow it out again. When I was a kid, I always wanted my 'warning label' at my wedding if I ever had one. But. . ." My tone was glum. "It just takes *forever* to grow it."

"I've got forever." He shrugged, beautifully heartbroken.

I laughed once. "So, that's one option. Because in four years, I'll have my warning label back. But Mark, the last time I grew out my hair, it was for all the wrong reasons. When I cut it off, it was around the same time I came to Christ. Like a fresh start. The next time I grow it out, I don't want it to be while I'm knowingly a temptation again. I want to be the thing that keeps you *from* temptation. So, the ideal would be to have Maureen figure out what to do with my short hair for our wedding, and *then* you can watch it grow out."

Mark sighed in relief. Smiling brightly. "That's all I needed to hear."

"But for now, let's call it a night. We have an early morning mopping floor together like it doesn't mean anything." I sniffled, and we parted in a touchless 'I love you' as I retraced the walk up my front steps.

I couldn't even laugh when Maureen pretended to *just* be opening the front door again to exit as I heard Velma start behind me. I waved to them all in silent gratitude as they exited, invoking my right as a teenage girl to escape tearfully up the stairs to my room. But the flip-flops were destroyed, the girlhood escaping. And they all recognized my tears as those of a woman who heard her heart driving away in a green Mustang.

Chapter 28

Portion

Summer had begun that week, and Maureen found us cleaning a men's restroom. She had been calling, "Cinderella!" in a sing-song voice down the hall. I could hear that she had some wild scheme in store.

"Uh-oh." Mark had said under his breath before she arrived, having the same understanding of the situation.

"Should I be worried?" I called from a stall as I heard her heels enter the bathroom.

"Of course!" She said, and then explained that her "future nieces and nephews" would need their mommy to have a driver's license. Since Mark had his 'no riding together' rule, and my father was too busy, Maureen insisted that she would be the woman to teach me to drive before I turned eighteen at the end of the summer.

When I reluctantly agreed, her heels clicked in unison as the twenty-nine-year-old forgot her age. Maureen had a way of going from calm to hyper excited in seconds. She also had a way of remaining far too calm when she should have been livid. That was the case as I had my hands over my mouth behind the wheel of a luxury sedan. I'd just run the entire side of the vehicle down the cement casing of a light pole in the parking lot. The sound was deafening and unsettling to the teeth and nerves.

"So, you've never driven? Almost eighteen. Literally, never been behind the wheel of a car?"

"I never needed to. I always had a boyfriend that could drive. I *swear* I was in reverse." I was examining the controls that Maureen had just spent a half hour explaining. But it was not as if I'd never *seen* someone drive. Just never such a fancy vehicle as Maureen's. I felt like a complete moron for having de-fanicified it a bit.

Maureen was nodding. Then she smiled a little. Then she shook her head and revealed her full gorgeous smile. I smiled slightly in response, waiting to be reamed by the spitfire blond. But instead, Maureen laughed. Then she stopped a moment. Then she opened her mouth again and begged me to snicker with her glorious laughter. We sat for a moment in the injured car laughing at my injured pride.

Maureen retrieved tissues from the glove box for her to remedy the tears of laughter. My throat was aching from the last few moments of my life. When I returned to reality, Maureen pretended to punch my arm.

"Are we nixing the 'get Paige a driver's license' idea?"

"Are you kidding? I want my nieces and nephews to *survive*! We have a lot of work to do! And this is just *my* car. Mark has a certain classic stick-shift that he'd like to teach you to drive someday."

"You don't mean Velma. His *baby?* He doesn't want me to ride in it, so I'm not driving it either. Especially with my current 'skills.'" I took a breath. Addressing for the well-meaning counselor, a much-needed correction to her prospects. "About those nieces and nephews, though. . .You remember how Dr. Moreno offered to re-evaluate the 'no kids' diagnosis? I know you have something against her. But I went and saw her."

"She's a good doctor, regardless of anything else. What did she say?"

"She said at this point there's nothing she can do." I shook my head and fought the tears. Maureen understood.

"Have you talked to Mark about it?"

"Yeah. Just like before, he says he isn't in love with me for my childbearing capabilities. But he also still tells me how much he wants children. He's like the world's best uncle. Can you imagine how great of a father he'd be?" I sighed. "I don't know if I could live with taking that from him." I fought against the bitter tears.

"Paige, love isn't about what you can get from someone or meeting certain conditions or expectations. It's about offering up everything you *do* have regardless of what they have to offer you. That can look like everything from giving away the only two mites you have to laying down your life for the sins of humanity. So regardless of your medical issues—or driving ability—" Here, she smiled, "Mark is offering up everything he has, even if you don't do the same. He doesn't want you to be anything but what you are. That's what love is, and he sees it as a privilege and a blessing that God allowed him to love *you*. So, stop worrying that *you* are not enough for him."

"I'm sorry, it's just. . .no one has ever loved me like that. Especially if I'm not even sleeping with him." I laughed once. remembering that Maureen told me that once.

Maureen reminded me with a sigh. "Jesus loves you like that."

Each day during a brutally hot summer, I spent seven hours working and one hour behind the wheel of Maureen's car. The last hour was a lunch break. I spent it midday with Jesus and a Bible since Pastor Robert and Maureen insisted we leave that space and time for good counsel in the form of the Holy Spirit speaking to us as individuals. I got better at driving each day. Better at cleaning. Closer to Christ. More in love with Mark. But each day, a constant and piercing ache penetrated my soul deeper.

I had all a person needs and more than I'd ever had. Time to think, loving friends, and the blessing of serving God in His house. Therefore, it was a mystery why I went home at the end of a day and missed Mark more than I cared about any of it.

I suppose that's why weddings became not only tolerable but anticipated and treasured. It was a game we played. I wasn't allowed to see the wedding schedule. Mark would tell me there was a wedding that day by bringing a single rose to work in the morning. On Saturdays, it was already obvious when I arrived, as the weddings happened in the morning on Saturdays because Mark had a standing date with his nephews for ice cream before service. Regardless, we kept a vase on the desk in the maintenance closet to house the two or three roses a week until we had to cycle them out for death's sake.

Weddings were as close to dating as we got that summer. We were even allowed to have meals together during weddings. When Mark was young, his only request for cleaning up a wedding was a portion of whatever was catered. Since me, the price for cleanup was two portions. We'd dine in our office to be sure to stay out of sight while the festivities transpired in various areas of the church. It was during that time that we whispered gossip about the bride and groom and choices for decorations and dresses and use of traditions and the like.

Mark's birthday was near the end of July. A Saturday, and as I walked to work in the 8:00 a.m., already soaring temperature, I was looking forward to spending the day with him. When I arrived, I became sweatily aware that there was an issue with the A/C. Probably someone from last night's cruel confetti wedding tampering with the thermostat, I assumed. Then my thought was disappointed, and my fear confirmed when I approached Mark inquisitively at the thermostat.

"Why is it so hot, birthday boy?" I asked cheerily.

"Air conditioning's acting up again." Mark seemed extremely anxious. "And. . ."

He handed me a rose.

"Oh, when does the wedding start?"

"In three hours. The bride will be here any minute to get ready." He chopped off my words. "My normal HVAC guy isn't answering."

"This is really bad." I winced. "Did you check the filters? Because last time—"

"Yeah, Paige. I checked the filters." He snapped. "And everything else. No luck."

"I'm sorry. Want me to try to find another person to—" I started timidly.

"No, it's. . .I'll go check again." He stormed off in the direction of the utility room.

I heard Maureen approach and glanced at her as he rounded the corner out of the foyer.

"He's in a *mood*." I noted.

"Yeah, he gets that way about once a year. Mark hates his birthday." Maureen explained.

"Who hates their birthday?"

"Mark. Weren't you listening? It took me years to convince him that he isn't cursed. He's lost two mothers. The first one was on the day he was born. The second one was a few weeks after his 'gotcha day,' which we always made a bigger deal about than his birthday because that's when *we* met him. He honestly doesn't see a reason to celebrate *either* day now that both of his mothers are gone. But we love him, so we always celebrate. Puts him in this mood. The A/C not working probably confirms his 'cursed' notion." Maureen sighed. Closed her eyes and looked heavenward. Whispered. "God, please give him this one. He's had such a trying summer. In Your Son Jesus's name. . ."

"Amen?" I concluded. "What do you mean by 'trying'?"

"I'll let *him* tell you that one. Be gentle with him?"

"That has to be the first time you've suggested *that*." My eyes widened. I was genuinely worried for Mark.

"Not *too* gentle. He's probably slightly, you know, off his guard today? You understand?" Maureen, losing faith in me, yet again.

"Maureen. . ." Before I could fully scold, we both sighed in relief, stretching out our arms as flowers in sunshine in response to the air kicking on.

Mark let out a triumphant holler, praising God as he returned to the foyer.

"Thank you." Maureen mouthed toward the high ceiling before walking away.

"Brunch! Look at this. It's genius." Mark handed me a plate of quiche and croissants and other goodness and hopped up on the desk beside me.

After we blessed the food, we ate in silence for a time. Then I watched my love's mood shift again to sadness as he finished his wedding portion. He set his empty plate aside and crossed his arms.

"I'm really glad you were born." I expressed with gentleness, as instructed.

"Thanks." He chuckled, taking my plate and tossing it in the trash, then leaning against the wall across from me.

"I'm serious, Boss. Maureen told me how you feel about today. But you should know that God has used your life in wonderful ways, and He isn't done. So, you can feel like you're cursed all you want. But I'll still be here loving you." I smirked.

"Well, I appreciate the effort. But this might be my worst birthday yet." He laughed a little. Retreating inward again.

"Ouch." I stepped down from the desk, offended. Gathering cleaning materials to start on the vacant sanctuary.

"Paige, wait." He realized the error.

"I haven't done anything, Mark." I sniffled at burning tears. "Stop treating me like *I'm* the one that killed your moms."

"Whoa! Can we cut the drama, please?" Mark laughed bitterly.

"Can you stop being such a downer? That's not even you. You're stealing my job." I laughed once at the truth in the irony.

He snickered as well. Whispered. "I love you." Then, convincing me that I was speaking to a complete stranger, he reached out and placed a hand on my upper arm, stroking it with his thumb. "Come here."

The awkwardness of the next moment dawned on me when I remembered Mark had never given me a hug. But I saw that he was laying aside all qualms about it as he bridged the short distance between us in a blur and pulled me in for some healing intensity of an embrace. His chin resting on my shoulder where I'm sure his face was heedlessly overtaken by my crimson locks I'd temporarily un-covered. My heart was pounding and giving in when his very essence was included in my next breath. Since I could have accomplished both fainting and flying at that moment, I determined my favorite place in the world, and it obviously wasn't the maintenance closet.

His next words were but a mumble of voice and hair and shoulder to the rest of the room. Perhaps a squeak from the tears and relief and joy from being so far into my presence. But to me, they were a clear and precious cello against my ear. They were determined, meaning something far deeper than the limits of the language.

"I am *never* letting you go."

I giggled. "No one's asking you to."

Mark gently and silently released us from the embrace, leaning against the brick wall with his arms crossed. I leaned against the desk, crossing my own arms.

"I need to ask you something." I began with confidence. "When I was at the mall with Maureen the other day buying your present, the guy at the counter could clearly see that the wallet I got to replace your falling-apart one was for a guy."

"I love the wallet, by the way." He smirked.

I sighed, frustrated. "The guy said, your *boyfriend* will love this. And I honestly didn't know whether to correct him."

Mark shrugged. "I've encountered the same thing. It's like we're not quite that and way more than that at the same time. I've determined that in the vernacular, that's really the only way to describe what we have. I've called you my girlfriend to describe you to people that don't understand. Like to my professors when I missed class for Jake's trial."

"Does it ever bother you that we've talked about getting married, and there's not an English term for what we are?"

"That's a problem with the culture, Paige. Not with our relationship." Mark shrugged.

"Okay, but pretend you're talking to someone *from* the culture right now." I insisted. "And then tell me what I *am* to you."

"Um. . ." Mark smirked. "You're the woman I love, Paige. But there's not a label that really works right now."

"So, I'm your purgatory?" I rolled my eyes.

"Yeah, pretty much." Mark laughed bitterly. "Whatever it is, it's the hardest relationship I've ever had. I've never had to take cold showers for anyone else."

"You're too pure to need cold showers." I teased with a giggle. "It's not like I walk around half-dressed trying to seduce you."

"Thank God for *that*. I'd be done for." Mark admitted with a laugh.

"I wouldn't do that. I have a pretty deep respect for your purity, and I know how guys think, so. . ." I smirked. Then realized what he said. "You were supposed to *deny* that would work."

"Deny that a beautiful woman whom I love has the ability to make me forget everything I stand for with very little effort? Guys who deny that meet their demise. David, Solomon, Samson, plenty of others. I'm not as naive as you think." He admitted. "I *know* I'm a neanderthal. My Savior knows what he's dealing with."

His admission met my hysterical laughter, though I was terrified knowing how easily I could destroy him. He smirked when I finish laughing.

"I wanted to talk to you about something too." He said after a silence.

"Okay?" I nodded.

But before he began, we were interrupted by Maureen entering the room without knocking. Swinging the door open as quickly as possible and then giving us a look that suggested pride, disappointment, and accusation all at once.

"You know *anything* could happen in this room, right? You should leave the door open and eradicate the temptation." She crossed her arms. Then didn't allow a response. "Someone is here to see you, Paige."

"We were just eating and talking." I passed Maureen on my way out the door. Shame setting in. Hating that she was right. We were just discussing how easily it could all go sideways. "I'm sorry."

I reached mid-foyer and found Emma greeting me with a smile.

"Hey!" She said.

"Hey?" I smiled a little.

"Sorry, I'm in a huge hurry. But I wanted to get your phone number. Maureen just told me you're not allowed to spend your lunch with Mark during the week, so I was hoping to steal you away for one sometime. I want to ask you something. You're impossible to find whenever I'm here for church, and whenever I do see you, Dee is around." She rolled her eyes.

"Sounds great!" In the two-minute exchange of phone numbers, Mark and Maureen had made their way into the sanctuary, where Mark had begun ceremony cleanup.

They were whisper-yelling, and I sat in the back row, just out of sight, but not out of earshot.

"I just don't see what would possess you to do that? We were in our office, just like we have done almost every day since last October. It was *completely* innocent, despite what you *think* you heard during a private conversation. Shame on you for making her feel like she did or that she *would* do anything wrong." Mark argued, angrily tossing pew decorations into a plastic tub.

"Mark, you *love* her, don't you? You want to marry her, right?" She whispered.

"Like you wouldn't *believe*, Reen." Which warmed me to my toes, even in the now excessive air conditioning.

Then I shivered as Maureen laid into Mark like I'd never heard her do.

"Well, a husband is supposed to love his wife like Christ loves the church. Meaning he's supposed to sanctify her and present her as *blameless* before the Father. With any girl, you'd need to do that. But with *this* one it is a thousand times more important. If you two were to let some magical moment take you away, this *incredible* girl would spend your entire marriage thinking she wasn't *worth* you keeping her pure beforehand. If you *wait* for her, your purity will cover her. It is of the utmost importance that you don't screw this up, Mark." Maureen tried to be discreet, which she never did extraordinarily well. So, I heard each word with perfection.

I assumed Mark would cast her worries aside again. But what I heard was something entirely different.

"I know everyone likes to think it, but I'm not *Jesus,* Maureen. I'm keeping it together the best I can, and by the grace of God, I haven't messed this up. But if I'm supposed to sanctify her, I've *already* failed." Mark's outpouring silenced Maureen a moment. When she spoke again, it was with much more compassion.

"All you have to do is marry her, Mark. Boom, sanctified. You're not meant to do this forever."

Mark interrupted her with bitter laughter. "Just four years. Actually, probably closer to five. I've tried every angle with Paul all summer when we have coffee together on Saturday mornings. He's not budging. He wants her to have a bachelor's degree before I even have his blessing to *propose.*"

My heart dropped. I was already tempted beyond any limit I set in my past. And knowing that Mark wouldn't touch me for four years might be long enough for Mark to stop wanting to.

"Are you *kidding*?" Maureen gasped. "I knew you'd been talking to him, but I didn't know it was that bad. Mark, can you handle four years?"

"Honestly? No." He laughed. "And he told me to stop asking. But the worst part is, when I explained the whole temptation thing to him, he told me that Paige is at the age of consent, and he can't legally keep us from giving in to temptation. So basically, he doesn't *care* if we're abstinent. Just that Paige doesn't get married yet because he thinks she'll lose focus. It doesn't make sense to me, but he's adamant. I have *no* clue what to do. Because I'd hate to put Paige in a position where she'd have to disobey her father. Having her choose between him and me? That's not the kind of person I am. I want Paul's blessing and support."

"Have you talked to Paige about all this?" Maureen asked, devastated.

"I was about to when you walked in. It was just this morning over coffee when he told me not to ask again, so I've been praying about what I should do. I was about to let her weigh in." Mark sighed.

"Well, I'll be praying God reveals the next step in His plan for you and Paige. You may have to think outside the box to determine what's best for her." Maureen encouraged. "But she definitely knows what's going on now."

"Yeah, I *thought* I heard her walk in." Mark realized, then used his hands as a visor as I walked up the aisle.

We sat on opposite sides of the smaller aisle the wedding had created. Rose petals at our feet. Wedding decor everywhere. All of it taunting us.

Maureen sat on the edge of the stage, ready to counsel us. In the silence before I spoke, I decided she looked a little angelic with the way the sun streamed all the way into the sanctuary from the foyer in the early afternoon sun. But only because she was blonde and had left her hair down in curls that day. She shaded the sun with her hands but could still barely look at us.

"So my dad said no?" I asked timidly.

Mark smiled. "No, he actually said yes. He's never said he didn't want me to marry you or that he doesn't want us to be together. I'm four years older than you. He doesn't have to be alright with that. So, I'm thankful that he allows me to be a part of your life. I don't want you to think I'm at odds with him."

"But he told you not to ask—" I crossed my arms, confused.

"Just if I could marry you. We talk about a lot of things other than that when we have coffee." Mark sighed. "I think he doesn't know how serious I am. So, I'll keep trying. You weren't supposed to hear all that yet. I'll get it sorted out, Cinderella."

"How can you keep trying? You aren't supposed to ask him." I explained. "If you want me to wait, I can. Nobody has any faith that I can be abstinent. I was just being silly before."

Mark laughed. "Cinderella, I have plenty of faith in *you*. We discussed how much faith I have in *me*."

I was startled. Chuckled in disbelief. "Half the time, I think you don't even *like* me because you refuse to touch me. Like I'm toxic or something. I can count the times you've touched me on one hand. Your *father* touches me more than you do, and he's my pastor." By the end of the explanation, I realized there was resentment in my tone that I didn't intend to put there. Maureen suddenly painted on her face a look between utter satisfaction and the awkwardness of the conversation she was witnessing. Mark was visibly crushed.

"You remember bleach and ammonia?" He asked timidly. Then cleared his throat.

Conviction gathered my breath into a sigh. I nodded. "I know. 'Not even a little.' I'm just confused how I'm supposed to understand the difference between avoiding a 'chemical reaction' and you being so disgusted with me that you don't want to touch me. Do you seriously plan to avoid hugging me and holding my hand during prayers and kissing me hello and goodbye for four *years*, Mark? Leave bleach and ammonia open for that long, and they don't react the same anymore. I seriously doubt we could take things to the next level after zero contact for that long. We'd be miserable, probably forever."

Mark crossed his arms, defeated. I continued, teary-eyed.

"In four years' time, you could look around this church and pick out another girl and marry her and have two or three beautiful babies with her. I love you too much to take that opportunity from you. Please tell me you understand that. I want to see you making people sick with how affectionate you are with your wife. I want to see your face in a little boy running around this church like a little terror. I may *never* give you that. So *please* don't wait for me, Mark. Go sanctify someone who isn't a seventeen-year-old harlot of a janitor."

"Stop talking, Paige." Mark sniffled. Then sighed as he rose, then pulled me from sitting into a hearty hug. "I'd rather be miserable with you than disgustingly affectionate with anyone else."

"That doesn't make any sense. But I agree." I sniffled, calming in his embrace.

Maureen giggled, approaching us again. "On the contrary, that is a fine definition of what love inside a great marriage looks like."

"Miserable?" I laughed, wiping tears as I reluctantly came out of the embrace.

Maureen laughed. "Goodness, no. Because if you're determined to be together, even if you're miserable, chances are you'll spend time and effort working on *not* being miserable instead of just dismissing each other as failures. Happily married couples aren't necessarily exceptional people. Just exceptional forgivers."

Chapter 29

Perspective

I turned eighteen on Labor Day and yawned my way down the stairs, headed to work. I startled when Dad was in the living room on the phone. That happened sometimes when he got summoned to work early to navigate an error in a client's books. And from the apprehensive way he was checking the clock with a sigh and making a promise to someone on the phone, I assumed from echoes of the past that he wouldn't be making our date for my birthday lunch. He hung up and called me to him just before I was about to head out the door.

"They really making you work today?" He asked.

"Well, there was a wedding last night, and we were exhausted from the other weddings over the weekend. So, since the church is closed today, we decided to go in today to take care of it and get a head start on tomorrow when our classes start." I sighed exhaustion.

"Let's hope you can get some rest in too. Happy Birthday." He produced a box with a pink bow. Normally my gifts from him were monetary and impersonal or even over-the-top expensive to compensate for his indifference. So, the box—in my favorite color—was a surprise. As was the revelation of a silver cross pendant with a diamond at its center.

"Dad. This is beautiful." I was immediately in love with the gift.

As he asked me to turn, and I moved my still-wet ginger locks aside so he could clasp the necklace around my neck, he spoke. "I wanted to get you a car since Maureen helped you pass your test last week. But something told me to let you save up for one like you wanted to. Felt like the dad thing to do, and I'm really trying to do that. And you're head over heels for Jesus. So, I thought this was fitting."

"Thank you, Daddy." I touched the necklace, looking at it in the mirror by the door where I'd always checked my hair and makeup before going out on sinful dates or to make sure my bruises were sufficiently hidden. I wasn't one for makeup anymore. Or bruises or dates. And I was astonished.

Enchanted. That my father chose the gift that defined me best.

"You need a ride? I'll need a minute to shower, but I'm headed your way, apparently," he offered.

"Thanks, but I'm okay. It's a pretty day, and I want to get going." I smiled. "Love you, Dad."

As I approached the church on foot, I saw Velma had beaten me. But upon a double-take, I saw Maureen's car, too. It was rare for her to work on holidays. Pastor Robert's truck, also present, was an even rarer holiday occurrence. I looked around. Dave's sports car. Ruth's car. Emma's. A few others. Early, I decided, for so many cars to be in the parking lot, even if it wasn't a holiday. But my heart discerned the clues before me. They *wouldn't.*

"Okay, Boss! Show yourself immediately." I called into the foyer I breached with haste, hoping to be wrong. I was startled at the state of the foyer. It was covered in computer paper as if someone stood at the edge of the balcony and tossed down a few reams, sheet by sheet. I didn't put this past my church family in all their oddness. But before I began cleanup, I headed toward the maintenance closet to seek Mark, and swore I heard a female giggle from the balcony. The paper's culprit, probably.

I opened the maintenance closet and saw an eerie light emitting from under Mark's little desk in the corner. There was a vase on the desk with a dozen *new* hot pink roses in it. The dead ones from weddings disposed of. Before I could lean in for a smell, I tripped over a set of green sneakers that were protruding from under the desk. I leaned down to see Mark himself propped up against the wall with a pillow.

"You're under your desk," I observed aloud.

"Hey, Happy Birthday, Cinderella! Come here for a minute." The voice that caused my spine and my knees to betray me. Fortunately, I was already crouching to join him under his desk.

And I was beyond confused at first by the out-of-place pillow and blanket as I ducked to find a spot to sit. It was cramped there, hip to hip with our shoes outstretched. But then I caught a whiff of pine cleaner and Skittles and the unique pheromonic musk of Mark Ernesto Henley.

"You must spend a lot of time here. It smells like you." I laughed, nearly through a tear. How I loved his presence.

"Maureen calls this my 'secret place.' I've done my quiet time here every day since I was a teenager, and God roped me back in. Better is one day under the desk of a broom closet in His house than anywhere else. . .or something."

I giggled. Mark pointed up to the underside of the little desk. Taped beneath were half a dozen pictures of Mark's mom. A few of myself. And more of the rest of the family. There were also some Bible verses I knew were dear to him written on sticky notes. Sticky notes on pictures of prayer requests and praises. One such sticky note attached to a picture of me read, *"Please Lord, let her be my wife."*

"Hmm." I smiled. Whispered. "Did you want to finish your quiet time? I can go start cleaning up the newest weirdness in the foyer." I rolled my eyes with a smile.

"No, I'm done. I was just asking God for courage over and over. Paper likes to static cling to the foyer, so I thought I'd get prayed up before we spent an hour unsticking it."

"Courage again? When are you gonna learn not to do that? It's just paper. A lot of paper, but we can handle it." We both laughed, happy to be in each other's presence.

But I was a bit uncomfortable when Mark's eyes wandered down my body. "Wow. Somebody loves you."

I touched my cross with relief. "Yeah. My. . ." I winced for the probable sore spot. "My dad."

He nodded. "It's pretty." And then, Mark did something out of character and against the rules. He procured my right hand with his left, then threaded his fingers in between mine with confidence, as if he'd done it a thousand times. Enough that I was in ecstasy. But I knew it to be a first I thought he was reserving for his distant engagement.

"Mark, why—?" I was puzzled, but he was elated.

"I'm just hoping some of this courage leaks out to you. I think I'm overdosing." He winked.

"Okay, um, there's a bunch of cars here. Please tell me there's not a surprise party or something?"

"It's nothing major. Maureen knew you'd attempt not to do anything today, so she got donuts and coffee and stuff. When I got here, they had already done the wedding cleanup, too. Maureen loves birthdays," Mark explained. "Just humor her?"

"Okay," I whispered.

"Paige, do you trust me?" He said, in a place far from laughter.

"With everything up to and including my life, Boss," I responded, confused.

"And you *love* me?" He sighed, squeezing my hand.

"You're scaring me." I stroked his hand with my thumb.

"Just—"

"I love you." I laughed. "I tell you that and show you that every day. That isn't changing in this lifetime, Mark."

"Good." He nodded. Sighing relief. "I love you too."

As we went back out into the foyer, Mark hopped over the paper as if he was concerned about disturbing it. I was laughing at him but followed his lead. He walked to the electric panel on the wall, using his key and free hand to flip on the lights in the upper foyer. I looked up at his purpose for it and was startled at the lineup of familiar faces. Emma, Maureen, and her family, Pastor Robert, Ruth, and other various staff members. More than I expected.

I laughed when they immediately engaged in a chorus of the Birthday Song.

But Mark was elsewhere as he led me to the unoccupied info desk. He crossed his arms and sighed deeply, checking the nearby clock for the time. I thanked everyone when they finished singing. Then they began to talk and laugh among themselves but remained at the railing. I looked to Mark to fill in the gap of information I obviously had. He merely winked.

"I wish I'd brought my dad if there's a birthday thing." And nearly cutting off my words, to the almost crippling fear of Mark, a door to the church opened. Mark closed his eyes and took a step back, then opened them with a smile, and took two steps forward with courage not his own.

Then I saw the reason for the fear. My own father was storming into the church and was within feet of Mark when he stopped. He said he was going my way. Someone must have invited him last minute. But something else I couldn't explain kept me quiet about it. My dad looked up at the crowded rail and then at me, and then looked up the few inches to Mark's poised green eyes.

"Good morning, Paul. Thanks for coming on such short notice."

I was too panicked to speak, but I looked up at Maureen who turned, leaning her back on the rail with purpose. She couldn't even look. What was going on?

"Mark, I told you Saturday. And every week all summer. I'm done discussing this. I've made my decision." My father was firm but gentle for the sake of the many ears in the foyer.

"I know." Mark exuded some sort of respectful enthusiasm. Was he giving up on me?

"So why am I here, Mark?" Dad sighed with fatigue.

"Because I want to marry your daughter." The same enthusiasm. Which caused all in the room to chuckle. Including my father, even though Mark was openly defying his decision.

"I would *love* for you to marry my daughter. When she's a bit older and done with school." My seemingly exasperated father gave his obviously familiar reply.

"Great. But you know I mean within a year. So before she turns nineteen." Mark bit his lip immediately after the response to the response.

"No. Do you realize how absurd that sounds? Nineteen?"

"So, six months is out of the question?" Mark delved further with valiant bravery. At the thought of being married to him in six months, my heart leaped, and I met his eyes, not realizing how urgent his timeline was. But not caring, except to trust, as requested.

"Completely out." My father was desperate for Mark to concede. He got a cruel, smug look on his face. "If you loved her, Mark. Really *loved* her. You wouldn't be asking her to choose you over college when she's barely hours into adulthood."

Then the standoff began. I tried to interject into the torture of a silence. "Mark, it's okay. . ." I trailed off when Mark turned his attention to smile at me. Silence me. Beg me to trust him with his eyes. Then he looked back at my father.

"Paul, I called you here to let you know that I love our Saturday coffee, and I hope to continue that. I wanted to thank you for some good conversations this summer. And I really wanted your support on this marriage thing. But you can rest assured, I will not be bugging you about it anymore." Mark was passionate, falling just short of rebellious in tone.

My dad sighed. Tried to be remorseful as he began his exit speech. "I like you, Mark. You're a good, respectful kid. Good family. I don't deny that. I do hope we talk about this again in the future when you're both a bit older. It might put some perspective on things. Catherine and I got married at twenty. If I knew then what I know now—"

"You wouldn't have Paige," Mark murmured.

"I was twenty-*three* when Paige was born. I'm glad we waited to have her because things were even more of a mess before she came along. But at least we could cope financially. You two are *kids*. Step back and think about this for a minute. Do you understand, Paige? I'm not the monster you think I am."

Both men looked to me for an answer that began as a river from my eyes. I submitted, knowing it was what Jesus would have me do. "I understand, Daddy."

"Thank you. I'll see you later, Sweet Pea. We still on for lunch?" Both my father and best friend were casting my heart aside. But I nodded, letting pain soak into pain. Trying not to allow the tears.

Just like that, Mark had given up on me. It was only a matter of time. And he did it with a cool humor of confidence like marrying me was never a priority to him.

Somewhat in disbelief at Mark's words, Dad took a few steps back to exit the church, first checking to make sure I was alright. I tried to stop the tears, as they had witnesses. Mark gently removed my handkerchief from my head. Untying the knot and refolding it to hand to me, as he'd done before in tenderness. He reached up to tuck the now stray hairs behind my ears lovingly, which was like a knife to my heart. He looked at my dad, who was watching broken but stern-heartedly the exchange. We all heard frustrated sighs from the foyer above. Mark's sigh contained much more resolve and fear than anything I'd ever seen in him. And I watched as he fully unbridled his inner rebel with a completely out-of-place smile.

"Paige, don't cry, okay? Your dad is right. We need some perspective." His face fully lit up into a smile. "And Paul. Please stay. We have donuts upstairs for Paige's birthday."

Dad and I didn't understand Mark's demeanor and how it contrasted with seemingly icy words. My father started to inquire but was stopped by something nearly equivalent to a full run and a brick wall, though it was only tangible to the two men closest to me in proximity. Currently, their antlers clashed with power and iron will. And I stood in confusion as my father took a step backward, more for leverage now than retreat. For some reason, he wasn't leaving the church yet.

Dad cleared his throat. "I suppose I can stay for a minute."

"Awesome. Follow me," Mark said, grabbing my hand and leading me up the staircase closest to us. My dad followed, noticing the paper in the foyer and looking confused.

Then it occurred to me all at once. Holding my hand. Tucking my hair. "Mark, why are you touching me?"

Mark smiled. "Because you need me to."

"But is that the best idea? I mean, should I really string you along if—"

Mark chuckled as we slowly ascended the stairs. "Let's not finish that sentence, okay?"

We reached the top of the stairs, and everyone was lined up at the back of the balcony along the wall near a table of coffee and donuts, looking like they were about to burst with excitement. I grew nervous at the tension, especially as my dad reached the top of the stairs and stood with Pastor Robert in confusion.

"I wanted to show you something." Mark bit his lip to hide an enormous smile.

I sniffled at the tears I was fighting. And I argued with him, "Mark, I clean this church. There is nothing you could possibly need to show me that I haven't already seen."

He rolled his eyes, smiling, as we stopped midway between the random people and the edge of the balcony. He faced me and took both my hands in his.

"There is *totally* new stuff in this church today, Paige." He snickered, smiling.

I rolled my eyes. "Yeah, for some reason, there is paper all over the foyer. Which we should go clean up because even though we may not have put it there, it's our job to clean it up. Paper is like gigantic confetti." I looked to my left, where I knew Maureen to be standing. "Was it *you*?"

They all snickered, except Dad. Maureen gave me her smile. "I may have helped."

"I am so confused. Someone explain to me what's happening right now." I sighed, frustrated that they were all so joyful when I was crushed.

"Your dad just said it!" Mark laughed. "We need perspective. Because if you look at it from a tiny, human standpoint, things can seem like a really big, confusing mess. You try to juggle everything in your life, and priorities just seem all muddled together. But if you think like God— eternally—that's when things become clear." He looked into my eyes and moved his hands to my shoulders. "Wow, you are *really* upset right now. *Please* don't be upset. Please look at the big picture. *God's* perspective."

"I tried." I sniffled. Both relieved and stricken with emotion that he understood why I was upset. I whispered. Though everyone was listening. "God has been telling me something different from what I'm supposed to be okay with right now. I thought we were on the same page. But, I mean, I understand you not wanting to be defiant."

"I do try to be respectful. But there's a point where if that causes me to stumble and disobey God, I have to, respectfully, agree to disagree with anyone I may have gone above and beyond to get to see things my way—which is God's way in this case." Mark cleared his throat. "Because whether or not someone just thinks they are looking at a gigantic mess, I have an obligation to righteousness. And I just happen to be seeing things from a. . .*higher*. . .vantage point. Big picture, you know?"

He was repeating and separating the words like he was speaking in a code that I should understand. I stared blankly at him until my dad quickly moved from the corner of my eye to the edge of the balcony. When he arrived there, his sigh set the rest of the room on edge. Dad turned around, and I looked on, confused, as he sighed again, nodding at Mark.

The rest of the room breathed relief. Mark bounced up and down in excitement.

"I am *so* confused." I hipped my hands.

"The *paper*, Paige." Mark animated drama with his hands. Then he tapped my nose once. "Not mess." He tapped it again. "Message."

A light bulb went on. No. There was no way. But before I realized my feet had moved, I was looking over the edge into the foyer. He was right. What I saw wasn't a mess at all. The paper was arranged into two enormous words that I couldn't see from below. Only from a higher vantage point. The way I'd been learning to look at my entire life.

"MARRY ME?"

After a gasp, I lingered a moment in disbelief as two caramel hands grasped the rail on either side of me, and Skittle warmed breath met my ear.

"Please?" He rumbled lovingly.

"Are you serious?" I whispered, still looking at the words.

"Depends on your answer."

I giggled. Spoke quietly. "Well, that'd be an enthusiastic 'Yes!' with a few questions."

"Questions or conditions?" He clarified.

"Unconditional 'Yes,'" I reassured him. "But I'll be upfront right now that I really don't think I can be engaged to you for four or five years, Mark. I want to do right by you, and I'm scared that even with the power of God flowing through me, I'd mess that up. I really hope that isn't what you're asking me to do."

"And I was really hoping you'd say that," Mark whispered as he released the rail and I turned to him. Lane's feet thundered a little pink box to the hands behind Mark's back, and then he ran back to his tear-faced mother. Mark took a deliberate and smiled step back as he brought the box forward, preparing to diminish in altitude.

I gasped. "Don't you dare! I already said yes! You're just trying to make me cry." Everyone laughed at this. But Mark the rebel disobeyed me as he explained.

"I don't want you to be able to tell our grandkids I didn't do this. And I *definitely* don't want to hear it from Maureen." Then Mark took one knee, brought the box into my view, and opened it, revealing a simple sapphire and diamond ring that I'd come across in a giggled phone search over lunch with Emma when she asked me to be her maid of honor. Mark flashed his eyes at me. The cool calm of the Caribbean. All the passion in the universe. And words I never thought he'd direct toward me. "Will you be my wife?"

I sobbed a laugh. Glanced around me at the withheld breaths. Glanced at my father's sternly crossed arms. Then back at Mark, who was staying true to his respect for tradition as he knelt. I utilized the mind God gave me. I thought of priorities. Purity. I knew that I'd break one heart and bring relief to another. But I knew it would all be alright, as long as I stayed true to the heart of God. I knew that the best way to honor my earthly father was to honor my Heavenly One with my only chance at purity and righteousness, even if he didn't see it at present.

"I love you." Mark tilted his head as I said it, not knowing where I was going. When I regained control of my mouth through the tears, I concluded my response. "And, again, yes."

I couldn't decide whether sighs or gasps followed from the rest of the balcony, but I knew that Mark was near tears with relief as he stood. He first embraced me tightly against him. Then we watched with mixed emotions as he removed my purity ring and replaced it with one I much preferred. As he did, I spoke frantically against his ear. The others were cooing among themselves and probably thinking I was delivering sweet nothings they weren't privy to.

"My dad." Which Mark understood completely, I saw in his nod and labored breath. He already had a plan.

During the quiet words, Pastor Robert had prepared for my approaching father by shooing all but the family to their posts or back home. The family had come near, and no one was sure what was about to happen. Mark grasped my hand, and we both turned and faced my dad. Mark cleared his throat.

"Paul, I need to do what God wants me to do. And when I'm Paige's husband, I'll need to make sure I don't do anything that will compromise God's plan for *her*, either."

"Mark, she's *always* felt led to go to college." My hurt father seemed to have calmed a bit from his pompous annoyance. "I know my opinion has little to no value in this equation, but I'm looking out for her best interests too."

"I know, Paul. I never disagreed with you. Classes start tomorrow. And I promise you Paige will attend them and do great in college and earn her degree as you requested. But I want to marry her. . ." Mark looked at me with more of a demand than a request and squeezed my hand with sincerity. ". . .Today."

Maureen laughed and then made some sort of squealing sound, because as wild as Mark's words are, we all knew he was completely serious. The others were feeling the tension. Even Lane was seeking protection from my father's scowl behind Dave.

My dad sighed. "Mark, you seem pretty determined, and my daughter, who is now a legal adult, has a ring. You have all the cards. All the power. But is this up for negotiation at all?"

"Absolutely." Mark allowed though he knew he'd already won. "I was always willing to come to a compromise, Paul. I'm just not willing to compromise *purity* to do it. So, four years is *way* off the table. Paige and I are agreed on that."

"Alright, let's meet halfway. A wedding in two years." He cut the time in half for Mark's bravery and my defiance. Quite a compromise, I decided.

Mark was not satisfied. He let go of my hand and placed his arm around my waist. His voice, firmly with his heart. "Today."

Maureen covered the low laugh at the ensuing scandal with a hand. We were all loving this side of Mark.

"It's Labor Day. The county clerk isn't open to get a license. You want it legal, right?" My dad said with a chuckle, not realizing that Mark hadn't the means to bluff.

"Yeah, you're right. God wants us to go through the proper legal channels." Mark gave a little for the law with a clearing of his throat. "After our classes tomorrow, then. I think we both have half days."

"Two years. You can handle it." My dad stood his ground.

"You *started* at two years. I thought we were *negotiating*." Mark looked at me, considering the deal. Then he crossed his arms after a quick glance at his own purity ring. "And let's not test ye olde' 'Mark can handle it' adage. Mark is a human that relies on God. So, you're testing *God* at that point."

Our quiet counsel laughed at Mark's tone and what it implied.

My father sighed. "Okay. . .a year and a half?"

Mark clicked this tongue. "How about I let her get through the first stressful week of college. And we get married this weekend."

I giddily wrapped my arms around Mark, loving that I was the prize being bargained for.

"Come on, Mark. A year. Like you said all summer."

"Ooo, now we're talking. But that was before I had 'today' on the brain. So, a month."

"The end of the school year. That way, you'll have graduated, and then she'll have all next summer to get refocused again for school." My father was finally bending. As the only child that always got her way, it was clear to me that Mark was home free for whatever he wanted. I thought for a moment Mark wouldn't try anymore. But he prayed for courage, and courage he received.

Mark cleared his throat. "Now *that* is an acceptable timeline. However, Paige wants a winter wedding. So, it'll have to be the end of *this* semester or no deal." This was his most serious of requests. At the ultimatum of a tone, Maureen was gasping in delight.

"And what does 'no deal' entail?" Dad wondered.

"We get the license tomorrow afternoon. And I know like twenty pastors who would marry us." Mark shrugged. Completely serious. Dave and Pastor Robert chuckled.

"And how do you know she'd even agree to *any* of these ludicrous timelines?"

Everyone looked at me. I looked up at Mark and said it matter-of-factly, "Boss, can I have the day off to go home and pack? I might be getting married tomorrow."

Mark first melted as the others laughed, then laughed when my father sighed.

"It's September, Mark. The end of the *semester*? How can you manage your school and work schedule and plan a wedding in that amount of time?"

"Ooo! Pick *me*! I'll do it!" Maureen was shushed by her family at the interjection.

"She will." We confirmed in unison, to our amusement.

My father sighed. Bent. Broke. Then gave his final compromise. "Give me one more Christmas with my little girl."

Mark was glowing with excitement. "I'll throw in New Year's because I'm a nice guy, and Paige does NOT want a Christmastime wedding, and I'll promise to have her back from our honeymoon and completely 'refocused' by the time spring semester starts."

"So we're talking early January? Four months from now?" My dad caught my eyes.

"If that's alright with you. . .sir." Mark couldn't mask his giddiness with the overzealous respect.

"Only if I get to help pick the dress and pay for a wedding and walk her down the aisle. Dads live for that stuff. No more talk of this eloping nonsense." My dad bent, even to a smile at his terms. And I smiled, knowing that terms precede agreements.

Mark lit up. Bubbled over. And outstretched his hand to my father.

"January." The two men shook hands, and then Mark's bubbling made him pull my father into a mighty embrace of gratitude. After the embrace, and one between my father and me, our families retreated from us, allowing us to finally respond to our engagement. But as was their way, they looked on from the back of the balcony.

I heard my father speak. "Once a rebel, always a rebel, I guess."

Mark's family agreed with laughter. Then I spoke to my rebel of a beau in a volume only we could hear.

"You scared me! I thought—" My thought was interrupted by his desperate sigh of relief.

"You think *you* were scared?! No comparison, Cinderella. I need Skittles *bad*."

I pushed his shoulder playfully with a giggle.

He grabbed my hand before I could retract it and used it to pull me into his arms where I belonged. We were laughing and then crying inside the hug with a relief rivaling the beauty of the sunrise concluding outside.

What can wash away my sin
Nothing But the blood of Jesus
What can make me whole again
Nothing but the blood of Jesus

I am in and out of consciousness as I listen to the chorus sing through the darkness. A delusion from hypothermia, I presume. A lamentation of sorts. But such a lovely song. My favorite.

Chapter 30

Tradition

"We could have it at my house," Maureen suggested. "My living room would be great for a bridal shower."

"Your house is gorgeous, Maureen, but is a bridal shower a hundred percent necessary? I don't exactly have a lot of women in my life. It would be practical strangers giving me kitchen stuff and lingerie," I pleaded. "Why didn't we just go to the courthouse?"

"Paige, you're the one who decided to marry the Senior Pastor's son. The women who would want to be at your shower were my mother's sisters in Christ. They were at Mark's dedication when he was a baby. The shower isn't about you. It's about being a blessing. Anytime you have a chance to be a blessing, do it. Don't even hesitate. Don't worry about whether it makes sense logically. Yes. The bridal shower is necessary. And you'll get some fun stuff out of the deal," Maureen lectured.

I rolled my eyes and conceded with one request. "Can we invite Ruth, at least? She's the only woman in the church who doesn't treat me like a *doll* or something."

Maureen snorted laughter. "Paige, don't be stupid. Ruth is the *first* person on my list after Emma." She advanced to the next item on her unwritten agenda, "Mark tell you he booked your honeymoon?"

"Yeah," I replied sheepishly. Maureen and I were stuffing wedding invitations at my table in the foyer before Mark arrived for the day. A year before, almost to the day, the two of us were in the same place. Our hands busy, and our souls connecting. We had just met then.

"*Yeah*? Paige, David took me to Hawaii a couple years ago, and it was *incredible*. I think it's perfect. There's plenty to do if you want an adventure. And if not, just vegging on a beach or in your room is great too. Aren't you *excited*?" Maureen schmoozed.

I nodded. "Of course, I'm excited. I'm going to paradise with my best friend." I sniffled what I didn't say. The part that wasn't exciting.

Maureen sighed and lowered her voice. "It won't be weird. I *promise* you." She was keenly aware of my fear. "Marriage is this unique relationship that allows you to be both best friends *and* lovers. In fact, you need to nurture both if you want a good marriage."

"I can't believe we're having this conversation." I laughed a little.

Maureen giggled. "Because he's my brother?"

"Because he's *Mark*. You once told me that I shouldn't worry about temptation with him because he's so adamant about purity. So as much as I'm looking forward to marrying him and having a deeper connection with him, I'm having a hard time fitting him into the same category as the guys I've crossed the line with."

"So, don't." Maureen snorted.

"Don't?" I tilted my head, confused. Did I misunderstand marriage already?

"No. *Do*. Yes. Do that. *Please*." Maureen clarified with wide eyes. "But don't lump him in with the other guys. You're not 'crossing the line' with him. The line is moving." She lowered her voice again. "Paige, sex in marriage is not even close to the same thing as what you've done before."

I laughed, mostly from the nerves at her candid words. "I know. Because sexual immorality is listed among the worst sins, but suddenly when someone gets married, it's completely acceptable. Like this normal, mundane thing like mopping floors and scrubbing toilets. Except, you know, in secret. Because it's still kind of a not okay thing to talk about it. It just seems strange."

Maureen cackled. "Now, is this the version of mopping floors and scrubbing toilets like I do at home, or how you and Mark do it, which is not quite as innocent?"

I rolled my eyes. "How is it not innocent?"

"You flirt the entire time. And Ruth says she caught you *dancing* together the other day."

I bit a lip. "We had a few minutes until senior high let out, so we were practicing for the wedding. And she didn't *catch* us. We weren't hiding anything."

"I know." Maureen nodded. "Have you and Mark, you know, talked about it?"

My eyes widened. "You want me to talk about sex with *Mark?*"

Maureen laughed aloud. "You just told me it's weird that no one talks about it!"

"We've had brief conversations about temptation and stuff. That's what gave him the go-ahead to propose. But like I said, we're best friends, and we have a really pure relationship. I don't know why or how to open *that* dialogue." I sigh. "Maybe as we get closer to the wedding. . ."

"Don't stress out about it, okay? If you think it would be a temptation to have a discussion beforehand, I respect that. Just make sure you come up with a good icebreaker for your wedding night. I've heard horror stories from couples who pretend sex doesn't exist until it is sanctified." Maureen winced. "Sex is meant to be an illustration of our oneness with God through Christ. Something that draws you closer as a couple and closer to God at the same time. It's not a *secret*, Paige. And it's not mundane or boring. It's just that describing the intricacies of married sex is a lot like trying to describe to someone what your heart is saying when you worship God. It's not *unmentionable*. Just indescribable."

The front door spread light across the foyer, and Mark entered, on the phone. He winked when he reached us.

"Dad, she's sitting in the foyer. Yeah, I'm looking at her right now. She's probably been here for hours; how did you not notice the most beautiful girl in the world sitting in the foyer? Her classes end at lunch on Thursdays. No, don't worry about it. I'm here now. I'll ask her." He moved the phone aside. Spoke quietly. "Paige, Dad wants to know if you and your dad want to come to dinner tonight."

"I'll ask him, but that'd probably be fine," I replied, texting my dad while Mark headed to the maintenance closet, finishing his conversation.

"Have you ever been to the house?" Maureen confirmed suspicions.

"Mark accidentally left his Calc book upstairs one time last semester, and Dad and I dropped it off," I confessed. "I've never been inside. I feel like it's hallowed ground or something."

"You work in a church. . ." Maureen reminded me. Elaborated. "You vacuum a *sanctuary,* set up communion tables, and dust a podium where the word of God is spoken, and my childhood home is hallowed ground to you?"

I shrugged. Smirked. "Mark restored Velma there. Your mom took her last breath there. Dave got his nose broken there. It's this entire history I was completely unaware of until about a year ago. I don't exactly feel worthy to just *go* there. Besides, I don't have a car, and Mark has his rules for Velma, so he usually just comes to my place and hangs out with Dad and me on Saturdays. Just since the engagement, of course."

"There's history at your place, too. Some of it pretty serious."

"I don't mind Mark knowing my history." I shrugged.

"Most of it, right?" Maureen challenged.

I sighed, shutting down if she was going to interrogate and accuse me.

"Nevermind." She sighed. "Just don't be scared if Mark wants to let you into his history too."

"I'm not scared, I just—"

"Oh, Paige. I bet Dad is cooking elk. He is *so* good with game. You're in for a treat," Maureen rambled.

I rose when Mark was returning to the table, accepting his deep, warm embrace and satisfied rumble against my ear. "Missed you today."

"Whoa? What about side hugs? What is this?" Maureen teased.

"I've never had a hugging rule." Mark reminded his sister when our embrace ended, and he joined us both at the table.

"So," Maureen said, like an entire sentence, or like the end of a rant. Which meant it was the beginning of one. "I heard you two got approval from Dad to do your premarital with me, so I have a session log already printed up for your appointment tomorrow. That's the form I have to sign before Dad will do the ceremony."

"Oh, good," I commented. There was no way she was done talking.

"I just wanted to warn you," she continued, still stuffing invitations as she spoke. "You'll be extremely angry with me tomorrow. But not as angry as you'll be with Dad this evening."

"Whatever, Maureen. I can't handle the games. I'm on the clock." Mark stood, stretching.

"Let me finish this stack, and I'll be ready to start work," I told him. "These invitations need to go out like tomorrow."

"No rush." He shrugged. "I'll just get started on the north hallway."

I nodded at his enchanted smile as he got ready to walk off again. He was energetic and enthusiastic in those days. Like when we first met. I got nervous when his stare continued. "What?" I giggled.

"What do you mean *what*? I get to marry you. Am I supposed to get over that sometime soon?" He snickered, then winked as he walked off.

"You two are adorable. Which means you'll probably fight like wolverines when you're married," Maureen commented nonchalantly.

"Excuse me?" I laughed.

"You'll see. Go work, Paige. I'll finish these. I have some lag time before my next appointment."

After a hearty stew and apple pie, I happily helped Mark with the dishes. The kitchen and dining room were combined, and our fathers were chit-chatting in the dining room portion. We returned to where our fathers were sitting after the meal was consumed and cleaned up.

"Any luck on the apartment front, Mark?" My dad asked Mark of his current mission after the honeymoon was booked.

"Well, the family housing at school didn't work out because I'm graduating this year. So since only one of us would be a student, we'd have to move in May. That didn't seem logical. We'd also prefer to stay around this area—close to the church. The area around the University is pretty pricey. So, I'm still on the hunt," Mark explained.

"He hasn't found anything good enough for his bride, he means." Pastor Robert chuckled.

Mark rolled his eyes. "It likely doesn't exist, but I'm trying."

"Doesn't have to be fancy, Mark. We're at school or the church most of the time. We just need a place to study and sleep. I told you it could even be a studio apartment at this point," I reminded him. "Our budget doesn't allow for much more than that anyway, unless we go on a strict Ramen diet."

"I'm trying to find a balance, Paige." Mark crossed his arms over his chest. Wanting to provide the best he could. "I also want us to possibly buy a house in a few years, so I want to save."

"There's always the alternative. Offer still stands, son. Don't make me beg," Pastor Robert said warmly.

"What's the 'alternative'?" My dad asked before I could.

"*No*, Dad." Mark smiled with respect but seemed to have protested this quite a bit.

But his father spoke anyway. "Paul, my daughter got pregnant when she was eighteen. Wasn't married at the time. In the time it took us to plan her wedding without her mom around to help, Mark and I were able to finish the basement. It's a one-bedroom apartment with a kitchen, living room, and bathroom. The entrance is right off the garage, so anyone who lives there doesn't even use the front door most of the time. It's come in handy the past decade. I've been able to house missionaries that had to come back stateside and other people in need. At the moment, it's a bit of a, what do you call it, a man cave? Mark has his exercise equipment down there in the bedroom. It's fully furnished besides that. I told him he could just switch the guest room furniture upstairs with the exercise equipment, and these kids would have a nice little apartment. It suited Maureen and Dave for years, even with little Dillon running around."

"A full apartment, huh?" My dad was impressed.

"Pots and pans and everything. At their age, I'd have jumped at the chance. My parents kicked me to the curb when they found out I was married. I'm hoping to give my own son a head start in life." My pastor said to my father, or all of us.

Mark interrupted with a sigh. "Dad, seriously. I'm not living in your house." He quoted Genesis, "'Therefore, a man shall LEAVE his father and mother'?"

"My house is paid off. You two could have a few rent-free years to save for a house of your own. I'd leave you two alone. You know that." Pastor Robert persuaded.

"That's not the issue, Dad." Mark laughed. "We built that apartment in an emergency because Maureen and Dave messed up. They didn't have a choice but to live here. Paige and I are doing things a little more traditionally. I didn't beg Paul to let me marry Paige and promise to take care of her only to turn around and live at my childhood home with her. I want to do things right."

"But it's like a separate apartment, right?" I asked to Mark's confusion.

"It's still IN the house," He asserted.

"Miss Ellis, it is absolutely separate and private. From down there, you can hear what's above you, just like with most apartments. But Dave and Maureen used to have some spirited arguments, and Mark and I would be sitting above them in the family room and hardly hear a peep." Pastor Robert reassured.

"You're not considering this, are you?" Mark accused, seemingly heartbroken.

"Boss, I told you it didn't have to be fancy. You don't have to prove anything to me. And it's not like we have to worry about having kids anytime soon. But when we do, we'll need to have saved money," I reasoned. Our fathers looked at one another, confused.

Mark explained, timidly. "Paige and I have talked about adopting. Because of what Dr. Moreno said. It's expensive, but we're a little young for most agencies, so we'll have time to save."

"One step at a time, guys." Dad chuckled. Uncomfortable every time possible future children were mentioned.

Having already felt a tug in my heart and made a decision, I bit my lip, standing. "Can I see it? The basement apartment?"

"Yeah," Mark stood. "I mean it's. . .Maureen said she'd help me get it up to snuff for you if we did decide to stay there. She already has a color scheme in mind. You know her. But right now, it's really not much."

The house was a tri-level, and Mark led the three of us down a few steps into the family room, then into a cove with three doors. Mark opened the one to the left, which revealed a full flight of stairs that led to a second door at the end of a generous landing. Mark smiled and opened the door for us.

The living room was immediately apparent. I saw that once upon a time, great care had been taken to prepare and decorate the space for a family. I looked to my right at a dining area containing a little round table and four chairs. Then I looked in the corner at the full, but petite, kitchen. When Mark closed the door, a cozy kind of tenderness immediately filled my soul in the silence. A tenderness like home.

Mark cleared his throat. "So, there's a bedroom over here in this hall, and a door that goes from the bedroom to the bathroom and another one from the bathroom to the hall. It even has a big bathtub because Maureen wanted one for Dillon. But that's really all there is to it. It's garden level, so you get some sunlight, but there's not a door that goes outside—"

I whispered, interrupting his rambling, and my words seemed to fade as I spoke them, the response caught in the cinnamon air like a secret. "It's perfect."

"Maureen says the water gets way too hot, the bedroom is *freezing,* and the refrigerator sounds like a rabid bear sometimes at night. But I doubt you'll notice any of that." Pastor Robert smiled satisfaction.

"You'd really let us live here, Pastor Robert?" I wondered into his kind eyes.

"I'd be honored if you did, Miss Ellis. But only if you start calling me 'Pastor Dad' in a couple of months. That's what my kids call me." He flattered.

"And I guess I won't be 'Miss Ellis' anymore either." I shrugged.

Mark snorted giddy laughter. I giggled at him. Then his expression changed to sincerity. "Is it okay if I talk to Paige for a minute alone? We'll leave the door open."

A common request. Mark's rules allowed only semi-private conversations that couldn't easily progress to anything else.

"Absolutely. Paul, I have been meaning to show you that muzzleloader I told you about."

Our two fathers ascended the stairs together, chatting about guns. Also a common topic between the two hunters. When they were out of earshot, I turned to Mark.

"Don't even ask if I'm sure about this, because I am, Mark. Feels right. This place is adorable," I revealed.

"Well if you think so, I don't really have any complaints. It was just a pride thing, I guess." He shrugged. "But now that we have the apartment situation figured out, I had something else to ask you."

"Okay?"

"Um. . .wedding night. I have the honeymoon booked, but we don't fly out until the day after the wedding. So, we need somewhere to stay the night of the wedding." Mark explained.

"So, what's the problem?" I giggled at his nerves over the subject.

"So. . ." He sighed. "I don't care about your past. You know that, Paige. But I also don't want to take you anywhere that would remind you of it when it's supposed to be *our* time together."

"I see," I whispered in shame.

"See, and I knew you'd react that way. It's not like that. I just want to do the best thing for your heart." He sighed. Trying to be sensitive.

"You can't tell me it doesn't bother you, Mark." I pried, shifting the subject. "That it takes work to figure out a place a guy hasn't taken me."

He laughed once, slapping on his charm as he grabbed my hand. "Cinderella, I'm taking you to the *altar.* And then we're gonna take a ride in Velma. All I need to know is *where* so I can make a reservation."

I giggled. "This one is easy, Mark." I smiled and shrugged. "Why can't we stay *here*? It's just the one night before the honeymoon. No reservation required."

Mark guffawed. "You want me to not only live at my dad's house but bring you here right after our wedding? Tell me how that's romantic in any way."

"You said Maureen was going to help decorate." I shrugged. "No one's ever decorated an entire apartment for me to help me feel comfortable. That's totally *you*. We found a place to live together. So just take me *home* after you marry me. Trust me, it's romantic."

We entered Maureen's office for our first premarital counseling session, and she signed a slip of paper, then handed it to us. "There you go. Bye."

I was confused. She just signed off on one of the requirements to be married at this church—a minimum of ten premarital counseling sessions. We planned to do two a week with our short timeframe which was already a bending of the normal rules. But Maureen had just signed off on all of them.

"You didn't counsel us." Mark blinked his eyes in confusion.

"Mark, don't insult me," Maureen said, typing something on her laptop, practically uninterested in our presence, as she often seemed. Her mind able to perform two or more full tasks at once.

I sighed, frustrated. "I'm eighteen. I could benefit from premarital counseling. Dad thought the ten sessions was a little slim to begin with, and—"

"Oh, I agree with you there, Paige. So many couples take the plunge completely clueless as to what they are getting themselves into." She continued to type at her computer.

"Yeah, so—" I began.

"So, Dad and I started your premarital counseling the day after Thanksgiving of last year. Pretty close to a year now. By the way, I am so excited to have you and your dad join us for Thanksgiving this year, Paige." She smiled.

"We barely knew each other." I laughed, ignoring her attempted tangent. "We were friends at best. You can't do premarital counseling on coworkers."

"Shut up, you loved each other then. Mark had even verbalized it. It was painfully obvious. We knew *you'd* realize how serious it was late in the game and sprint for the altar, so we took the liberty of working on the requirements so you could get married here in the church. It worked out quite well. Well enough that I'm actually stealing some ideas from you two for future couples." Maureen pointed at me. "Especially the thing you told me about. Cabinet above the kitchen sink of your apartment, by the way. In case I forget to tell you."

"Maureen, we've never been in this office together for a session." Mark seemed to have to remind his sister of this.

Maureen looked at her brother. Sighed. Shook her head, disappointed as if he was missing something. "The best counseling doesn't happen in an *office*."

I nodded, knowing she could counsel a rock and give it purpose. She was certainly capable of covert premarital counseling. She continued.

"I'm not saying you don't need a counselor. Just not yet." Maureen winked, then opened her desk and pulled out a stack of paint samples, and spread them before us. "Before you go, I decided to go with the white duvet and a nice light green on the bedroom walls. Come pick your favorite shade."

I awaken to quiet. A warm and musty silence. I open my eyes, and I'm surprised by my surroundings. I'm curled up in a wooded shadow, back against a tree. I have been crying in shame, as I often do. Dreaming, I suppose.

There is a stream to my right. I rise and walk to its edge. I place my bright pink toenails into the icy purity of the water. I see a figure across the stream. I strain my eyes against the sun to recognize the face. There is a calm. A peace within the light that I work to understand. But no matter where He moves, I am unable to train my eyes.

Chapter 31

Clean

I watched another puff of steam escape my mouth and mingle in the dark January air with his. I smiled at the four lime green shoes rested upon the frosty metal table. I took in a whiff of the rented jacket that surrounded me before I moved the plastic fork to my mouth again, allowing the tangy lemon filling to melt against my tongue with the sweet icing.

I was thinking of the foyer's staircase my father escorted me down just hours before. The way Mark had been moved to both tears and laughter when he saw me approaching in the white dress. The purity ring he wouldn't let me put on his other hand when I replaced it with his wedding band. He had instead taken it, turned from me unexpectedly, and handed the ring to Dillon, his only groomsman next to Dave, the best man:

"To grow into, grow fond of, and then grow out of."

Cryptic instructions they both seemed to understand. I recalled Maureen's tears, even as Lane had chosen the moment to wiggle wildly because of the "itchy" suit that matched his brother's.

I recalled Maureen and Emma, in emerald gowns of my sister's choosing. Dave and the boys showed only their rowdy sides at the reception, despite the lack of alcohol. There was the hot pink bouquet Emma caught. The garter that hadn't been included in the festivities for modesty's sake. The dance with my father. Mark's surprise dance with Maureen that they spent crying and missing their mother.

I was thinking of my dad, who had accepted Christ long ago but then walked with Him fervently. Since the engagement, we attended church together, though I suspected it was mainly to keep Mark from holding my hand during service. He was the protector I always longed for. A little late, but never unappreciated. He had even actively aided Maureen in finding a mandated white cascade of tulle and beads that complimented shoes in "feral limeade," as Maureen called Mark's favorite color.

I was thinking of Mark's loving father, who canceled a Saturday night service for the first time in a decade for the ensuing joyful celebration. The afternoon, evening, manifesting with eerie flawlessness. My mind skipped from bowls of lime green Skittles on tables in the foyer to one green boutonniere and the way it had complemented a gray suit and green sneakers. Mark's unwavering eyes.

His voice disbanded the memories in progress, even though his bite of our shared cake plate muffled it. "You have cake in your hair."

We giggled, and Mark set the cake and forks aside. I moved closer to him on the balcony's bench, leaning into the crisply ironed curve of arm. He leaned in for a single, soft, lemony kiss, then released his enchantment into the air as a sigh.

"I could kiss you for a *living,*" he confessed with his tantalizing voice. Cozied up against my soul like bleach against ammonia as he kissed me again.

"No complaints here. Not sure who'd clean the church, though." I revealed my predicament with a giggle, melting submissively into his embrace and daring his eyes.

"So, I take it you're not concerned about chemistry anymore?" He rumbled.

I rolled my eyes at his teasing. He laughed a little, somewhat distracted. He wanted to ask me something. We were hiding from our remaining guests on the frigid balcony. All that was left for us to do was leave. So valiantly, my new husband's fingers brought warmth to the chill of mine. He cleared his throat. Speaking of fairy tales, because the reality seemed impossible.

"Velma is ready and waiting to help me take my wife home. If we wait any longer, she will turn back into a zucchini, Cinderella."

I laughed robustly. "Don't you mean pumpkin?"

He made a guttural eye roll like a preteen girl. "Velma is green, duh."

I hummed a laugh and then forsook his silliness for far too much sincerity. "Are you sure? There are still some people here, and the confetti was pretty mean. Maybe we should help them clean it up—"

My plea and remorse over the confetti ploy were cut short. Because he knew my motive for remorse included something deeper than confetti. Something like guilt over taking for my sinful self the purest of men. But Mark was again disbanding thoughts with some purity-altering kisses that were only corrected after a few moments by the squeak of a balcony door, the click of heels, and the annoyed clearing of a throat.

"Give us a minute." My husband was reluctant to stop the kisses we were finally catching up on after a year of avoiding them, even if his sister was looking on.

"I'm not trying to kill the mood. I just need you to *relocate*. With you gone, we can get started cleaning up your evil confetti stunt." This was probably the last place the exhausted Maureen thought to look for us, as intended. We turned to her and responded to her curling fingers with eye rolls. We headed inside, mindful of my billowing dress as we moved past her into the comforting warmth of the upper foyer.

"There they are!" Pastor Dad growled benevolently, not at all annoyed we'd escaped the overwhelming attention of the wedding.

"Last people I ever thought I'd find *canoodling* on the balcony," Maureen announced, to Dave's booming laughter.

"Canoodling is perfectly acceptable today, Maureen." Pastor Dad said with a chuckle.

My dad was also there with Pastor Dad and Dave. The minuscule sendoff I'd requested, and right on time. I didn't want more than those closest to us watching me escape into the night with my love. Mark fiddled with the balcony door, which never liked to close when told. A product of numerous windstorms. I removed Mark's jacket from my shoulders as I approached the family with Maureen. To my distress, my dad passed me, mumbling something about wanting a word with my new husband before we left. I looked back, and Dad was speaking close to Mark's ear as he worked on the door.

I tried to ignore the mystery at the door behind me. Maureen sighed, shaking her head at me as a mother might.

"What?" I asked of the sigh. Winced. "I'm sorry about the confetti."

"Oh, Paige. I was just thinking how proud my mom would be right now. *Gosh*, she'd have loved you." Maureen received a quick hug from her father as she pulled a hanky from the front of her gown and put it to use. "You alright, Mrs. Henley?"

"Not remotely," I confessed, glancing at a conversation by a now-closed balcony door. "It isn't good when Dad wants 'a word' with Mark."

"Be careful not to judge all conversations by the tense ones, Paige. You should be relieved that your husband and father have a positive relationship. Amelia's father hated me." Pastor Dad smiled.

"You're a pastor." I smiled, wondering how such a wonderful man could have been hated.

"Not when I was your age," he encouraged with nostalgic laughter.

My father came into view next to Pastor Dad with my suede winter coat in his arms. Then before I could turn to seek him, I nearly jumped when Mark's arms found my waist from behind, and his lips, my bare shoulder.

I felt it, and the whole of the family saw clearly the implication of the kiss, which was far more than an appreciation of freckles. But I lost sight of them a moment when I closed my eyes at the way his nose took in like the beauty of rain the section of my hair behind my ear. Then to shatter any fear at my feet and slice the tension like a warrior, Mark spoke sensually loud enough for all to hear.

"Your hair smells like cake."

As we all laughed, I turned to Mark and handed him his suit jacket. He placed it around his own shoulders carefully. The others were laughing, but his eyes caught mine, embracing them like unswirling roses and clashing horns.

Then all at once, I realized that the others had stopped laughing and were laying hands on us. The four of them prayed in turn over our impending vacation and marriage. When they said the final Amen, Mark and I were wiping tears and laughing and thanking the family. Then Maureen cleared her throat and governed as always.

"All your stuff is inside Velma. She's parked right out front. If you take the elevator and the side door, no one will see you leave."

"Did you do what I asked?" Mark inquired of his family with some wild excitement in his smile.

"You are completely insane as it is four degrees outside. But yes. Paul actually took care of it." Maureen gave Mark a loving smile and then hugged him goodbye.

My dad handed me my coat. "You'll need this, Sweet Pea." I took the coat, slightly confused, and my dad hugged me with warmth and a few tears. "Don't want you to be cold."

I hugged everyone goodbye, and then Mark did the same as Maureen helped me zip my coat so as not to catch beads in the zipper.

"You should have worn it like that all day," Mark commented on the clash of comfort and formality with the familiar cross of his arms. A wedding gown sets even the classiest of wardrobe pieces to shame.

One of this family's favorite things to do was talk and laugh while standing around, heedless of the time or obligations. I usually shared in this hobby, never having a family before to share in it with. The current conversation started with Maureen scolding Mark over the cake in my two-hour labored hair and was then consumed by a silly argument about who won a bet or something of that nature. But at present, I enjoyed much more the way Mark's breath rumored a whisper into my ear.

"Can you run in those things?" He gestured to my shoes with a wild sort of half smile.

Just outside the church door, out of breath from running and giggling and an elevator ride of secret kisses, I saw something enchanting. Our emerald and ridiculously decorated chariot, puffing steam into the frigid January air. To my joy, Velma's convertible top was down, heedless of the night or the season. Mark's excitement over the decision was well satisfied in the smile and girlish laughter I dared not hide from him.

"See, you didn't even need a boring summer wedding to do this. I don't mind snot-cicles for Velma's sake."

"Which is why," Mark said as he opened my door, "Velma and I chose *you.*"

When he lowered me as royalty into the freezing vehicle, it was leather and Skittles, I decided, that intrigued my nostrils. He took his seat at the helm and turned to me, watching me laugh a cloud of breath into the air as he revved the engine. Mark was euphoric at the spirit of adventure I'd shown him very little of up to that point. He smiled and finally showed me his. I adored the way a seemingly cautious young man drove so assertively.

And after a usual three-minute drive turned thirty minutes, we thundered in giggles down the stairs of the apartment about the cop that barely missed the speeding Velma. After closing and locking the door, Mark leaned against it with a deliberate breath. I flashed him a quick smile at his cold reddened nose before turning over my coat to the hanger on the wall. Then I sat on a chair in the living room, pulling up the hem of the bulky dress to remove my green heels.

"Those shoes are awesome, by the way." He offered to ease his own nerves.

"Thanks. They are *almost* worth the pain." I giggled. "You should take yours off too."

"Why?" He said with obvious jumpiness. I smiled, and he breathed himself to a quiet calm. "Sorry. . ."

I snickered at his sudden nerves. Then I offered him gentleness. "Just your shoes, Boss."

I rose and took my shoes into the bedroom closet, making sure Mark knew I'd keep the place tidy *and* that I was there to stay. I assumed Mark would stay in the living room to remove his shoes and spoke in a volume he could hear across the distance.

"What did my dad have to say when we were leaving?"

But as I emerged from the closet, I heard the crunch of a Skittle and the clash of keys against a dresser before I looked up. I was startled to see he was setting his shoes by the dresser and then leaning in the doorway, blocking my path. I giggled at my previous volume.

"Nothing of consequence," Mark said, almost rebelliously.

But when I returned the friendly smile he gave me, I could see that his mood had shifted, even in the short amount of time. With a kind of panic, I noticed he had turned even to his box of Skittles, with hands that shook visibly. At first, I thought maybe I wouldn't laugh. But then I remembered I was looking at my best friend.

"I thought you *never* got nervous, star pitcher." I teased, removing the Skittles from his hands.

"This isn't exactly baseball." He smirked. Cleared his throat a little. "Dave told me the other day that in a few months, we'll laugh about how nervous we are right now. And that in a decade, we might even *forget*."

"Can we just fast-forward to that?" I giggled, and he hummed laughter. Both of us valued comfort over the new and exciting. "Mark, I have something I want to do for you. You might think it's completely bizarre, but it's important to me."

"Um. Yeah. Whatever you want." It seemed the pressure finally caught up with him, and he needed some courage. And though I lacked my own, I took his hand and guided him to sit on the bench at the foot of our bed.

"I'll be right back. Just stay there, okay?" I backed away toward the door from his grasp on my hands. "No Skittles," I commanded as he reached for the box I left on the end of the bed. He chuckled as I exited.

Most new wives might have retreated to the bathroom to heighten a new husband's tension with alluring lingerie. I'd granted others the same, but Mark was worth much more to me. I instead headed to the kitchen and opened the cabinet above the sink, where Maureen had placed a few items at my request.

I retrieved a set of soft green bath towels and a musky bar of soap from the cabinet as I ran the water to achieve the perfect temperature. I filled a large, rustic wooden bowl, and when I shut off the water, my heart seized with nerves. Nerves in this situation were something unique and terrifying to me. So, I was assured that I was making the right choice.

I entered our bedroom, holding a wooden bowl of water against my belly, towels over my arm. Bar of soap and washcloth in my hand. Mark sat anxiously on the bench where I left him. I lowered myself to my knees and placed the bowl of warm water at my new husband's feet. I used one towel to cover my wedding gown, so as not to get it wet. It was while still in my wedding gown and he in his suit that I bridged the chasm between *philos* and *eros*. Between sin and liberty. Purity and marriage. With bare feet and water.

"Oh, Paige," He uttered when he finally realized the purpose of my strange actions and was moved to tears almost immediately. We were both overcome, and I lost the fight against my own tears. Tears stirred in me from a much different place than his.

I shushed him and rolled up his pant legs. And against the backdrop of gently displacing water, I served him in a way I believe is an art form that never should have died.

The skin atop Mark's feet, unlike the hands of the maintenance man, was soft, new almost. His toenails were well-groomed. This was the part of him they all accepted as his whole. But his calloused heels, rough enough to set the soap to lather, dug in deeper and told a better story. The illustration of the part of him they didn't bother to see. The carefree part. The broken part. At first, I was astonished to know how easily they could have all been made aware of more than just his surface self. But then my heart leaped. Because starting that night, he was only mine to know so deeply.

He watched with silent adoration as I used fragrant soap and a few of my tears to wash my husband's feet. I didn't deserve any part of him. But because he was so much better than me yet *chose* me, I sat beneath him, providing him the first act in a lifetime of service to gain the right to be loved by him. I was a harlot. He was yet untouched. I only wore white that day to honor him, but I washed his feet in hopes that he would wash from his mind all of my crimson sins.

After I washed and dried his feet, I kissed them, confirming the gentlest part of him with the most sinful part of me. I then looked up into his eyes. Mark laughed a little to ease the vulnerability of his tears. Then he joined me, lowering to his knees on the floor of our bedroom as if he had me on the same level as him in some delirious intoxication of his heart. He was reading me. My remorse and guilt, and shame. My love and unconditional admiration for him. In response, he sniffled and whispered, though no one else was in the whole house to hear.

"Paige, you should know that I forgave you the day I found your shoes out in the snow. You're a new creation." He found both of my hands with his atop a towel that covered a white-as-snow gown while my gratitude manifested in a sob.

The silence became terrifyingly tender, and we were left with a clear path before us, paved with time, tradition, and love. The bridge built and the path atop it, Mark leaned in slowly for a soft kiss like the newness of clean feet. Like joy and tears. Like forgiveness.

Chapter 32

Coffee

He lay beside me and covered my shivering January shoulder with a white duvet and my heart with honor. I had expected shame. But I had found sanctification. I had been accustomed to a sickening numb but had received instead peace. Now I knew he was the strength on which I could relinquish my insecurity. Forever my best friend. But now, my husband.

His first instinct, and the truest, deepest part of him gave me great relief to see. Mind blown and life changed, he laughed abundantly. But after some new flood of relief overcame me, I took immediately to weeping through the next few moments. His smile faded, but he seemed to understand the tears too, and he shielded me with sincerity in his embrace.

After I sniffled my last, we experienced a stillness against sea-green sheets. A stillness as powerful as it was strange. But not an unsettling strange. Rather, the kind of strange a newborn baby experiences when his eyes are cold and raw, and he finally sees the face that gives radiance to his mother's voice. We had lost mothers to spare between us, so we were instead rediscovering each other's eyes, the way they shimmered peacefully against the night. But the strange, for me, became an apprehension. The apprehension, a panic, though Mark seemed sleepily at peace.

I panicked because I watched my husband transform before my eyes with a strange sorrow. A righteous sorrow, which can often prove to be the worst kind. Since the day they frightened me over unsugared coffee, his eyes had been a window to his innocence. I searched frantically for that same innocence but didn't find it. The innocence I unveiled was something that quieted my spirit beyond protestation. It was a *daring* innocence like lime green sneakers. That was the moment I realized I hadn't ruined my best friend. I'd finally set him free.

"Eventually, one of us is supposed to say something, right?" He mused of the stare we shared for a full ten minutes.

"You just did," I whispered. Not sure if I was being ironic or just abrupt. And then I winced and asked something in the freedom of hopeless awkwardness before I knew I was speaking. "I was so scared this would make things awkward and ruin our relationship. Did we just *ruin* everything?"

But Mark smiled and rested his nose beside mine. "Well, if we did, we should definitely try to 'ruin everything' as often as we can."

I gasped at his boldness. Suddenly all awkwardness cowered and tiptoed from the room when my friend. My Boss. My counselor's brother. My pastor's son. Kissed me with glowing embers against secret laughter like I was his lover.

The laughter soothed me enough to ask a burning question. I bit my lip and ran my hand along his back, where I knew a cross of nails was shamelessly inked between chiseled shoulder blades. We'd laughed until we cried not too long before, realizing we'd both chosen the same spot on our backs to 'defile' with ink. That laughter had been what we needed to break down any remaining walls and nerves.

"So, a tattoo. Gotta say, last thing I expected from you. Does your dad, the old school pastor, know about it?"

Mark laughed his laugh. "Yeah, apparently, I was a *heathen* for a full week after I turned eighteen and wanted a permanently inked image of my devotion to Christ." I giggled at his eye-roll of a memory. I found relief knowing we still had the ability to converse, despite the stark turn of events.

"He got mad about a *cross*? Don't tell him about *mine*!" I whispered to Mark's delight. His hand moved to my mid-back, where a three-leaf clover sat just out of sight of both a short or low-backed shirt. Just so that when I got it at age fifteen, my dad wouldn't find out.

"It's very fitting, my beautiful Irish Princess. But why not *four* leaves?"

"I never considered myself to be 'lucky,' however Irish I appear." I snickered.

"Well, that's a pretty interesting coincidence because I bet there's something you didn't know about a *three*-leaf clover."

"What?"

"They say Saint Patrick used the shamrock as an illustration for the Holy Trinity. The three leaves represented the Father, the Son, and the Holy Spirit. So, your shamrock is *just* as cool as my cross, Cinderella." He smiled lovingly.

"The trinity has been a tough one to understand since I've gotten saved," I admitted.

"Well, no one fully understands it. But it's like three People and one Person at the same time. Pretty simple."

I giggled. Rolled my eyes in sarcasm. "Yeah, *totally* simple."

He smiled. "I like to think of it as Him being one God. But He's so big and complicated that each individual Persona had to be an actual complete entity." He yawned, blinking wearily, then began again. "So, I think of God the Father as an actual father or pastor. In my case, that's the same thing."

I giggled, wrapping up my hands with his and moving closer as he continued. He was right. Pastor Dad served as some image of God the Father to me. My own father failed me there. Mark continued.

"So, that makes it easier to understand that Jesus is like a sibling. Someone that's always there right there with you when you're growing up. No one knows a person's *humanity* better than their siblings. And my sister has been my closest friend a few times throughout the years," Mark explained. I smiled, knowing how clearly God spoke through Maureen to draw me in like a sister. I never had a sister—or knew Jesus—until Maureen.

"What about the Holy Spirit?" I whispered.

He smiled dreamily. "That one was always tough for me. I just figured there was no earthly representation for Someone living so deep inside you that they moved you to transform and serve God in ways you never thought possible. Because like, as close as I am to my sister, it's not like we shared a room growing up. There was privacy. And Dad laid down the law and *so* much grace. But we weren't *buddies*. It was hard for me to imagine the closeness of God until pretty recently."

"How recently?" I accepted the explanation and then saw his expression change to a smile that asked me to think. Then he used his hand to spin my wedding set around my finger.

Our two hands nestled in the few inches between shamelessly bare chests, under the warmth of bedding, between brand-new sheets we tested first with *eros*. Then I giggled, understanding. "It's so *weird* to think of God this way."

"How so?" Mark smiled. "He's closer to you than I'll *ever* get to be."

"I know. But for a lot of years, I didn't know Jesus, and I thought Christians were literally insane when they would talk about the Holy Spirit. God was the wrathful, judgmental old Man in the sky that was eventually going to send me to hell. A skewed version of the Father, I suppose."

Right on cue, a terrible and thunderous creaking of a sound demanded a startle and a clamor against Mark for safety. He savored me as he saved me with squeezing arms and an enraptured sniff of my hair.

He explained the sound. "The garage door sounds like the apocalypse from down here, sorry. Pastor Dad must be home. Which means—"

"I'm shunned forever," I whined with hopelessness. Just when I thought I'd escaped shame, adding my pastor to the mix caused it to rush back in.

"I was gonna say they finally got the church clean, but eternal excommunication was definitely my next assumption." He nudged me with sweet concern. "Dad adores you. Why would he 'shun' you?"

I beseeched his eyes for understanding. "Mark, we—"

"Made love?" He whispered. It was the first time either of us had given it a label. We'd both been counseled separately on the subject. But between us before that night, there had merely been an assumption that it would occur and never really a conversation unless we were talking about purity or cold logistics like reservations. So naturally, after the act was called by a name, I stirred. Wanting to run out of the room. He searched my eyes, which made me want to stay.

"Yeah," I whispered back.

"You act like he'd be completely shocked by that information." Mark chuckled. "He's a smart guy, Paige. Not that you really have to be in this case. We got married today."

I sighed. "I *know* he knows. And that he expects it. And condones it, or whatever. But what I don't know is how I'm supposed to look him in the *eyes* now."

With a compassionate resolve in his eyes and an affectionate hand on my hair, Mark smiled the wisdom. "The same way you always have."

A final few soft kisses denoted the parting of our wakefulness, and I was delighted that I could watch him succumb to sleep in the next few moments. One unwelcome tear fell as I remembered my son. But I spared the pillow of my past, knowing I was secure in the arms of my future. Had I but chosen Mark first, Darian might have been safe somewhere outside my mere memory. A sin that no amount of honor could undo.

Before I remembered falling asleep, my internal, inaudible alarm corrected the condition.

"Boss?" I summoned above functionally deaf ears for ten minutes before receiving a response. But I was far from annoyed. I was enchanted by the contrast of disheveled black hair against a green pillowcase. The strong arms curled beneath his pillow.

Finally, he lit up the room with the first opening of his eyes and saw that I was fully dressed and alert, facing him cross-legged atop the half of the bed I'd made.

"Did I seriously marry a morning person?" The velvet baritone was much more of a gritty bass before dawn, especially when a million reasons were calling him back to his deep slumber.

I sighed and gave him a painful truth. "An insomniac." I took a breath and then continued. "I really think we should leave a more detailed schedule for Maureen. I'm terrified for her and some volunteers to do our job for a week."

"It's called email, Paige," He mumbled. "Just correct the document and—"

"I'd rather deliver it ourselves and do a walkthrough." I bit my lip, concerned how the dust bunnies would gather that week.

Mark flopped himself sleepily over, replacing the embrace of his pillow with the boney denim my lap provided. There, I admired his soft, dark waves with my fingertips.

"Coffee," he grumbled.

Our kitchen lacked the commodity, so Mark convinced me to climb stairs and breach boundaries to acquire it. Within a few minutes of my lean against the counter, the morning was filling with her finest aroma, and Mark was sugaring my coffee to perfection.

He handed me my mug, then landed next to me in a lean, placing one of his socked feet between mine. Then, as we were sipping in the near silence we'd shared, he began clinking his purity ring's replacement against his mug, and his lips morphed into an elated grin.

"What?" I asked, nudging him gently with a side lean.

"Sounds different," he said with a shrug, barely correcting the smile for a sip of coffee.

We lived in the cliché of wedded bliss until I was suddenly alarmed at the lovely whistling that came trotting down from the upper level. Mark smiled at the panic, knowing my only escape was the mug of coffee I hid behind. I moved a couple feet away from Mark and crossed my ankles together. My husband shook his head with a sigh, somewhat bothered I'd shied away from his affection for a pastor's sake.

"Ah, I *thought* I smelled coffee. Is there enough for Pastor Dad?" The warm voice that had spoken God's wisdom to me from a vast stage was attached to only the sound of a mug contacting the counter and being filled just feet from me. I refused to look up into his eyes with reverent love as I'd done for so long. My heart was aching from the panic. I was standing in my pastor's kitchen with his only son before 8:00 a.m., unable to deny even the most scandalous explanation for it. Sheer nudity could not have added to that shame. How dare he be so unconcerned with my presence?

"There isn't enough coffee in the *world* for you, Dad," Mark joked with the caffeine addict in his chuckling father. I was gazing down at the tan and pink shoes that were almost at the end of their life.

"What time do you have to be at the airport again?" The gaze at the floor granted me a cold reality that the cowboy boots were crossing after the pastor leaned against the counter just on the other side of the "L" from me.

"Not until this afternoon. Paige thought we should go leave a more detailed list for Maureen and do a walkthrough before we leave." Mark reiterated my plan to his father verbatim but with an air of sarcasm in his voice.

"If either of you set foot in that church without sand in your shoes, I'll fire you both." This was said with all the rustic kindness in the pastor I loved.

"Told you." Mark sing-songed quietly in my direction. Both men were benevolently amused, but I was focusing my gaze on the weathered grout of the shepherd's kitchen floor.

Next, even in the transparency I loved about this family, we sipped coffee in painful silence for a full two minutes. I knew I was the culprit of building a wall between the men. Because twelve hours before, things were different. I could smile at them both with independent versions of love, without a worry that my eyes were as windows to this family. Twelve hours before, Mark was just a young man. Someone's son. Brother. The church janitor with no secrets he couldn't tell. All things he came into through *storge*. Now he would most likely be identified first for the fullness of his *eros*. As someone's husband. *My* husband. I couldn't even bear to look at the gentlest spirit in the family I stole him from. How I ever thought I could face the church staff and congregation was a mystery to me. The pain of the new arrangement began to well in my eyes until my pastor thundered through what was so obviously awkward and engaged his son in casual conversation as if it were twelve hours before.

"You know, Maureen really should have heeded your warnings that you'd get her back one day for all those confetti weddings."

"It was genius," Mark growled.

Pastor Dad laughed aloud. "Vengeance is Mine, says the Lord. However brilliant."

Mark laughed. "Hey, we had both the ceremony and reception in the foyer. Only one room to clean."

"One *big* room, two levels. Lots of confetti. About fifty people stayed behind to help, though. It really wasn't an issue. I barely lifted a finger. People kept saying it wasn't my place. Paul and I sat back listening to Maureen curse about confetti while we worked on what was left of the cake." I heard a belly pat next to me and a warm laugh.

"Fifty people?! Wow." Mark laughed in disbelief. "That's great, Dad. I know Paige was worried about leaving that mess behind. That's the exact opposite of what we prefer to do. Didn't feel right."

"It would have been wrong for you to stay and help." With a refreshed sigh, the experienced coffee drinker set an empty cup on the counter as quickly as he'd filled it. Then he cut me to my very core right when I thought I was safe. "Paige?"

I knew that my father-in-law was demanding my eyes, based on his tone and the gentle hand that landed softly on my shoulder. My whole being was unwilling, but my reverence begrudgingly granted him the favor.

"Yes, sir?" The warm and gentle eyes didn't read me or judge me. They offered the same comfort as the day they captured me in the tiny chapel of a hospital. Only now, with a hint of the way my own father looked at me. An unrelenting pride and something new. *Storge.*

"You were a *beautiful* bride." His truth, yes. But that wasn't what he meant.

"I agree." Mark winked at me through a sip of coffee. An *I told you so* wink.

"I'd be a little worried if you didn't, son."

Suddenly, a gust of cold air moved across the house from the front door with Maureen's voice as it grew louder and clearer.

"Dad? You still here? I'm headed to the church, but I got a notification that there were changes to the cleaning schedule, and I can't for the life of me see the difference. And I didn't get an updated email. Did Mark happen to leave you something different for me?" By then, she'd arrived in the kitchen but was looking down at her phone. She looked up twice before realizing with a dropped jaw that we were standing there. The jaw morphed into a smile that built as she looked me over first and then started at lime green sneakers and worked her way up the always even-keeled Mark Henley, ending the examination at his eyes. That's when she released a proud cackle from a full smile. "Um, why is Paige standing here looking like she's just a handkerchief short of working today?"

I sighed, moving a few freshly printed, stapled sheets of computer paper across the kitchen island to her. "I added a few details to the schedule, and we wanted to—"

"Oh, sweet Paige. I love and adore you. But there is absolutely no way this was a 'we.'" She batted her eyes after glancing again at groggy Mark.

Pastor Dad had been refilling his own cup, then retrieving another cup from the cabinet and filling it, stirring some creamer into it from the fridge. He handed the cup to Maureen just then.

"Aw, thanks, Daddy." She took a sip. Smiled. "So, they were up *before* you? This is Mark coffee, for sure."

Mark and Pastor Dad chuckled. I squinted confusion. Mark interpreted, but I didn't look at him. "Dad makes cowboy coffee. You can practically chew it."

"Yeah. . ." Maureen smiled into my eyes, changing the subject. "So, were you planning to *deliver* this to me at church?"

"Um, yeah. I mean, not anymore. I just—"

"There's no way you'd have made it to the front door without having a panic attack." She grimaced. "What was *that* thought process?"

"An incomplete one," I answered with a little laugh, hiding behind my coffee again.

Maureen giggled. "I see you managed to fish all those bobby pins out of your hair."

"No, I'm pretty sure I'll still be finding them next week." I giggled. Feeling even more comfortable with Maureen there, though I had expected the opposite.

"Where's your family?" Mark asked, shifting the subject.

"Home. Dave decided they were playing hooky. Lane was crashed on a stair in the foyer last night before we left. Oh! I can take your suit back with Dave and the boys' if you have it together." She smiled, then looked in her peripheral vision at the garment bag on the dining room table. "And, of *course,* it's together. You married Paige, who wakes you up the morning after your wedding to perfect a cleaning schedule and hand-deliver it to church."

"She wanted to make sure everything would be okay," Mark advocated.

"I know," Maureen admitted with a hand up. "Paige does the 'extra mile' thing quite well. How are your feet, by the way?"

"I'm sorry, my—" Mark started with a smile, then I watched the memory flood his face. He cut off the words and crossed his arms. "Maureen, that's private."

"Sorry." Maureen winced, then looked at me, leaning against the counter. "I swear I will attempt to learn the boundaries and when to hold my tongue."

The rest of us chuckled. Pastor Dad said it. "You're not *capable* of that, Maureen."

She rolled her eyes. "You're probably right. I'm bad with boundaries. But I do love you. And I'd die for you. Even pick up confetti half the night for you."

The three of them continued their smiling conversation, but I saw something different. My pastor. My Sister. My Husband. None of them perfect. But all of them so godly and so close to me in so many ways. If they accepted me that morning, well enough to share coffee with me like family, after all that had changed overnight, perhaps I'd been mistaken. Perhaps forgiveness was on the horizon. Enough that all three all-powerful Beings in one perfect God might commune with me together. Or that they already had been.

I must have released a convicted sob of a laugh because they all stopped and looked at me. Then the tears came.

"Um. . .okay. . ." The brand-new husband began to panic.

"It's fine, Boss." I sniffled. "God's just big. And I'm exhausted."

"Well, I better let you two get back downstairs where you belong." Maureen giggled. Gulped the last of her coffee. "You two have an incredible week and tell me all about it when you get back." She hugged us, then grabbed the new schedule and

Mark's suit and made her exit. "We have things well in hand here. Be safe."

As the door closed, Pastor Dad put his and Maureen's mugs in the dishwasher, then smirked.

"I better get going as well. You two have a *transcendent* day, and do *not* tell me about it when I come back to take you to the airport later." The pastor went to his little entry table that housed his hat, keys, and coat on the hook next to it.

"Thanks, Dad," Mark said. Not cheerily, like would be expected in the gratitude of an airport ride, a cup of coffee, and an extra day off. Deeply. Like he was pouring into the words a lifetime of gratitude. In his family, the depth of love was as rampant as the sarcasm and teasing. Seeing that clearly for the first time, I was humbled to have been made a part of it.

With a tilt of his hat I finally understood, Pastor Dad whistled out the door. Mark took my hand and led me from the kitchen.

It was Sunday, and normally Mark and I would have been worshipping and cleaning the church, if there was a difference. But if there was ever an excuse to watch the clock turn from morning to afternoon in a too-cold bedroom, aiding insomnia with coffee and *eros*; We found that excuse that Sunday.

Chapter 33

Sand

A clean freak from fingertips to the heart, I despise sand's busybody nature. Yet I giggled as Mark buried me in the miscreation from collarbone to toes. Pure silliness, laughter, and random acts of adventure claimed our time on an island thousands of miles from home. If we were only best friends then, we had been strangers the week before. We walked barefoot at the end of the carefree day, hand in hand, back to the room we shared.

Just like every day that week, we were drained of energy and daylight, and hours. But I sighed as we re-entered our room, wishing that week was our way of life. Wishing the wicker chairs facing the glass wall were the place we could forever contemplate life, staring out at the great expanse of ocean. Wishing the door in that wall, to the resort's private beach, was the only door we need open to the world. The unnecessary vastness of the bed overwhelmed by pillows and fine linens, the only place we could lose one another. If only all of life was as simple as the meaning of a kiss to my shoulder. That kiss was the call. My hum, the answer. His strength, my weakness. My love, his sigh.

And yet, there was a chill in the night when he was lulled to sleep in peace I couldn't attain. It was then I felt the most unworthy of the pillows and the wicker chairs and the vastness of love. When Mark slept, I mourned. Alone in the night when all was still. That's when I cried for Darian. Because I was his mother as sure as Maureen was Dillon's. And I loved Darian the same as when Maureen lit up at the depth of Lane's embrace. But no one would ever know the way I loved him. So, when no one could perceive it, I mourned him. A few minutes. Every night without fail. Maureen assured me this was healthy. And I wished I was doing it for therapy and not out of the anguish of necessity.

That night, I cried against a duet between crashing waves and the click of a compass. It should have been beautiful. But I hated it all. Because I didn't deserve for even one grain of that wretched sand to cling to me.

I didn't hear Mark rise from bed. I only knew of his presence as he gently pulled me onto his lap in the chair beside mine.

"Hey," he greeted peacefully.

"Hey." I was trying to hide all my tears for the sake of what was supposed to be only bliss.

"I love you," he promised, as always. And from his squeeze, I knew he was fully aware of all the tears.

"Why?" I whispered rhetorically. I forced a tiny laugh and curled up in my own chair again. I opened and closed the compass as I looked out at the ocean in complete defiance of my husband's concerned presence. But with his own stubbornness, he reached out and enclosed my hands, compass and all, within his. He spoke gently above a whisper.

"My dad warned me that you might cry yourself to sleep at night." Mark shook his head in a laugh at the memory, "I was so sure that my love would somehow make you stop. But Dad told me you might *always* cry yourself to sleep. And that sometimes I'll take it personally and feel helpless. But that the greatest gift I could ever give you would be to let you do it. He says Mom stopped mourning the babies they lost the day she got to hold them again." Mark's eyes glistened.

"Angela," I whispered, remembering the story of God's will.

"I can't wait to meet my other sister in Heaven." He confessed as he leaned back in his chair, taking with him the compass we'd been sharing the responsibility of. Then he looked at me. *Into* me. Read me. Haunted me. Like Maureen would never be granted. And he was devastated to have set my heart to breaking with the invasive question I saw coming for many miles. "Your baby had a name, didn't he?"

I nodded. "Jake and I talked about keeping him, so I had a name in mind. It was stupid. Jake hated it. I only mentioned it once to him."

"Then mention it *once* to me, too. Maybe the kid's stepdad will approve of his name." He smirked. "Let me in, Paige."

I hesitated for far too long, releasing tears that had built up on the other side of his name. I imagined the face, the hair, the fingernails I'd never touch, just like every night. I'd rarely said it aloud, and I barely remembered what his name sounded like. Suddenly, I wanted to hear it. I wanted him to be real to someone else. So, I scraped together all the courage inside me to wipe my tears. I sniffled once and looked Mark in his anticipating eyes.

"Darian." I paused and then looked away, not wanting to receive criticism. It was beautiful still to me. Not a name. But someone I knew. Someone I loved. I was relieved to finally share it. "It means 'upholder of good.' Because before I knew Christ, Darian was the only good and purity I ever knew. I wish someone else could have met him and loved him, you know?"

"Well, Jesus is loving him right now." My heart faltered and tears fell with Mark's simple but profound resolve. "And that's *not* a stupid name. It's beautiful! I'll ask God to kiss your Darian for me every time I catch you crying at night." He smiled.

"Thanks, Boss." My husband. My soul sharer. Willing to help bear even my heaviest burdens.

A short allowance of the waves against the silence occurred before the bout of insomnia demanded one of those impromptu adventures. Mark turned and pulled me onto his back for a piggyback ride. He ran out the door and across the sand with me like we were not adults in bathrobes. He set me down where the tide kissed our toes, and we tried to catch our breath amid laughter.

My heart suddenly startled when I heard a chillingly familiar click at Mark's side. The action that took me two hands, he accomplished with one. He had apparently brought my compass to the earth's edge with us, not having set it down before our spirited run. But what would be mindless to me was deliberate to him. So, he held up the compass in the moonlight to openly confess its presence.

"'As far as the east is from the west. So far have You removed our transgressions from us.'" He chuckled with sincerity as he plopped down onto the sand. "That's pretty far."

"Psalm 103. Maureen told me that the day I got saved." I sat next to him with a wince at my hatred for sand. "I stared at this thing for hours that night. That blew me away."

He nodded in appreciation of the sentiment, but with some weight on him and made a slight subject shift, I knew he'd reconnect eventually. "Your dad and I used to have some good conversations over coffee. Hopefully, things calm down, and we can start doing that again. Anyway, he said you've always been a neat freak and worked hard. He thinks it's funny that you tried to hide your tattoo from him. At the time, I thought he didn't know what he was talking about. And he told me all about your warning label, just like you said."

I giggled in nostalgia until Mark sobered suddenly and continued, reading the inscription. "*'To My beloved Richie.'* I took the liberty of asking your dad who 'Richie' is, thinking he was likely some great-grandfather or something. See, I was wondering where you'd have gotten an antique compass like this. But he said you got this compass the night you got raped and that it helped you cope." I was stunned and silenced beyond words or even a gasp to accompany my open mouth. Luckily, Mark continued.

"Don't freak out or apologize for not telling me. I'm almost done with a psych degree. I actually took a seminar once about recognizing the signs. I've known since about the time we met, and the closer we get, the more obvious it is. I know you're not ready to talk about how you got it. But something about this compass has been weighing on me."

He reached around me and squeezed my shoulder when I sighed with nerves and shock. And though I was scared he'd require some craziness of me, he was the one person in the world whose crazy I trusted without question. So, I nodded for him to speak his mind.

"Your dad knew. He *knew*, Paige. But instead of risking whatever semblance of a normal relationship he had with you to help you heal. Get counseling. See a *doctor*, even, he kept quiet. He kept quiet when he knew you were trying to cope by being promiscuous. And then you finally ended up with Jake, who almost killed you. If you ever wonder what made me decide I was marrying you even if we had to run away, it was that I want to protect you by any means necessary because he didn't. The only reason I respect him at all is because he prayed over you when you slept. He said he used to sneak in your room early in the morning and pray for God to—"

"Bring me home." I finished the sentence and explained. "Sometimes I was only *half* asleep."

"He never even taught you about the refuge and strength of Christ. So, there you were, a *child* who had to grow up all at once, against your will. And all you had was this compass."

I silenced him by grabbing his hand and placing it on the cross that never left my neck. "He realized his error. I hated him for a long time, Boss. But I loved him enough to forgive him."

He nodded to assure me that he had forgiven my father's neglect in years before. Then he removed from his apparently endless robe pocket the case I gave him to hold his Skittles. He helped himself to one, savoring it immensely, and then closed up the box. Something fond and familiar to me by then.

"That secret drove you and your dad apart, Paige. I won't allow that to happen with us. I know you're still in pain. But you carry this thing around like you're telling it all your secrets." He sighed. Hurt? "Honestly, I'm jealous of this thing. I want to be the one that knows your secrets. In fact, I don't want us to have *any* secrets from each other." He was adamant. I knew when I agreed, I'd be signing in blood.

"No secrets. Agreed." I sighed. Relieved that my life was fully shared with him.

"Good." He said with satisfaction. Then he did something strange. He took the hair tie from the end of my French braid and ran his fingers through until my hair was blowing annoyance into my face with the ocean breeze and a smile onto his face. He used the hair tie to rope together securely my compass and his Skittle box. Our habits of anxiety and regret together as one.

"What are you doing?" I smiled in confusion as I tried to tame my hair to the side.

"These are crutches. I Skittle crunch. You stare at this thing. They are both things we do instead of handing it over to Jesus. And if you or I have an earthly crutch at all, it should be each other. You promised." Like I thought. Signing in blood.

After I nodded, he stationed himself on his knees and took my hands so I matched him. Our knees and the hems of our hotel robes are wet and frigid in the moonlight. Mark closed his eyes.

"Lord, be our only refuge. Bring us closer together and closer to You in the years to come." This prayer was said quickly and with purpose before the kiss and the spark in his eyes.

"Mark, you are so random." He helped me to my feet.

"Mrs. Henley, do you trust me?" Mark kissed my hand and then stepped closer to the earth's edge, taking the compass and Skittle box bundle with him.

"Mark, what are you doing?" I had a strong suspicion and pursued him quickly, fighting the freedom of my hair. He *wouldn't*. But with a flash of his wild eyes, I saw Mark's intentions are set. Oh yes, he would. I protested fervently but backed down when his eyes demanded my trust. He smiled and got into his left-handed pitcher's stance to coax a laugh from me. It worked. Because I'd always wanted to see it.

"Are you ready?" Before I got a chance to answer, Mark convinced me that he was indeed a star pitcher. I watched the moon reflect against my beloved compass and that old Skittle box as it spun out of control about one hundred yards into the Pacific Ocean. I didn't even hear the splash amid the roaring tide. Mark was as satisfied with his pitch as I was with the way he looked in the moonlight, seeking the other side of the ocean with his gaze.

I answered only with tears as I imagined the crutches and secrets sinking down, touching the mysterious ocean sand where no one would ever find them. *That* deep. *That* far. Is how God had removed my sins from me. Maybe with that compass gone, I could work on real healing. I breathed a sigh of relief, and Mark pulled me close against his chest. I thanked him in tears as we stood in dripping hotel robes, staring out together at a great vastness of God's glory.

Chapter 34

Home

Velma's faithful driver opened the door, exposing me to the chill of January and back to the "mundane" regions of life that were far from a burden to me. An island paradise with my love had been excellent in every way, but not even jet lag could stop our hearts from sighing as we ventured hand in hand across a quiet parking lot on Sunday morning.

Yet when we reached the front doors, my free hand reached for the handle first, and the tell-tale symbol of my monogamy pierced my heart. What a week away didn't suggest about us, the rings would declare to the world. The last time his feet touched the foyer, they were as pure as the floor we'd both washed countless times. What would happen now that they'd been washed by his wife?

"I don't think I can do this," I finally allowed, though I'd really no choice in the matter.

"Yeah, that door is a tricky one." Mark used the sarcasm to reassure me. Then he swiftly opened the door and leaned against it to let me walk through. But he stopped me when I started to pass him, lifted me off the ground, and carried me inside, in case the rings were not enough fuel. I was giggling when he set me down on the other side of the most appropriate threshold. Mark smoothed my hair and started in on our greatest purpose at home.

"We need to find Maureen for the keys."

Atop his words, a familiar sound entered the omniscient foyer. Speaking of the devil almost always preceded the click of heels in those days. But since the click of heels often preceded healing, our talk of evil sentiments almost never disappointed.

The heel click stopped in a feminine pose of her height and authority, a familiar mass of keys hanging from a recently manicured index finger. We'd missed her. She shamelessly nudged his shoulder as he took the keys and winked.

"Missing paradise yet?"

Mark smiled. "No. She came back with me."

"D'awww. Excuse me while I vomit." Maureen teased.

After they laughed together and Maureen failed an attempt at pushing Mark down, I shifted the subject matter with a smile.

"How were things here?" I wondered.

Maureen cleared her throat. "Well, the church is still standing."

"Barely." Grumbled Pastor Dad into our presence with a fresh mug of his caffeinated lifeblood. "The ten volunteers said the work you required of them in four hours each day was impossible and were amazed when I told them that's *your* schedule for *three* hours."

"We're a good team, Dad. We have our routine figured out." Mark shrugged.

"You guys are beasts, and you know it," Maureen commented. Finally wincing at the state of my skin. "You certainly got some sun."

"The curse of a ginger, I'm afraid. Mark comes back looking like exotic tanned man candy. I come back a lobster. He didn't even wear sunscreen. So typical." I sighed, rolling my eyes at Mark.

"But you're a *cute* lobster." Mark laughed appreciatively, touching a finger to my bright red nose.

"I'm sorry, '*man candy*?' Not familiar with that one." Pastor Dad asked his son.

Maureen snorted and giggled. "Highly technical term, Dad. Translated loosely for you, it means: 'grandkids.'"

I gasped, cheeks warming in the presence of my pastor. "Maureen!" Instead of standing in awkward silence with Mark and his family, I made an exit. "I'm gonna go work on some name change stuff before this place gets crazy." I smiled the excuse at Mark's loving wink before heading to the info desk. I arrived, and Ruth was simply beaming.

"Well, aren't you a sight for sore eyes!" She breached the desk, and I leaned down to hug the petite and plump joy of my heart. She walked back around, and I leaned at the desk.

"How was it here without us?" I inquired of Ruth at a whisper.

"Oh, an absolute nightmare. But from the sight of that awful sunburn in the middle of January, it seems your absence was worth it." Ruth said with benevolent honesty, and I giggled. She lowered her voice, whispering as she gave me an employee name change form to fill out. "Is Mark still good to you like he's always been?"

Finding the question odd, especially the way she asked in such sincere secrecy, I hesitated at first. Then I gave her truth. "Of course, Ruth. He's Mark. He's always good. All the time. To everybody."

"It's still a comfort to hear, sweetheart." Ruth nodded.

The two of us allowed the foyer to speak when we heard Maureen's voice addressing her little brother mid-foyer.

"You know I'd never upset her on purpose." Maureen was apologizing.

"I know. But she's just a little overwhelmed with everything right now. It's been a tough morning." Mark cautioned. "She's excited to be back. But she keeps saying everyone will stare and think differently of her."

"No one is going to think differently of her," Maureen said. Then sighed when Mark and Pastor Dad chuckled. "Okay, that's an overreach. But she doesn't need to worry. They'll eventually stop staring. *Or* she'll stop caring. Maybe both. It's something time fixes, Mark."

Pastor Dad hummed agreement at his daughter's prediction. "Most of us have just missed her, Mark. She makes an impact. Paul was saying just yesterday how quiet his house is."

"You saw Paul yesterday?" Mark asked, almost nervously.

"You were unavailable. Someone had to buy him coffee. And then I had to take Dillon to get ice cream. My waistline doesn't keep up with your schedule as well as yours, Mark. I'm glad you'll be getting back to it." I heard Pastor Dad chuckle, then walk off to tend to pre-service business. His children mumbled a goodbye to him, then Maureen began to whisper. I still heard.

"You're nervous about seeing Paul." Maureen snorted and burst into giggles.

Mark gave a high-pitched laugh. "Well, he and I haven't spoken since we were leaving the wedding. We had a slight— it wasn't a fight or even a disagreement. Just a thing. I don't know. I'm just not sure we left on the best terms. It's really hard to tell with him."

"Paul loves you. I wouldn't worry."

"But did he mention anything?" Mark worried. What had I missed?

"Maybe. He seemed pretty nervous about what'll happen if this Dr. Moreno diagnosis turns out to be not so accurate."

"Yeah. He won't ease up about it." Mark admitted. "He's pushing this 'family planning' thing like he's a politician."

"It wouldn't hurt, Mark. Stranger things have happened than a healthy eighteen-year-old and her love becoming parents." Maureen sighed, cautioning him.

"Stranger things and *worse* things," Mark said in a low voice. "God's been working on our hearts. We were thinking adoption, which would still be great if God had that for us. But I'm not sure."

"Mark, that girl would do *anything* for you. It'll destroy her if you ask her to do something she physically can't do."

Mark hesitated with an emotional sigh. Ruth pretended to have something to do and walked away, leaving me to listen alone. Mark explained. "Maureen, you have to know I'd never do that. We've even talked about how much we love your boys and how blessed we are that we have them to love on. But Paige's only experience with having her own child ended *really* badly. I pray every day that it won't be her only chance. But what kind of a prayer would that be if I also tried to prevent God from any chance we *do* have at a miracle?"

"Okay." Maureen backed down. "I support you; you know that. And Paul will too if that's God's will."

"I got quite the father-in-law, didn't I?" Mark chuckled.

Maureen sighed. Mark never having used the term to describe my father. "You have in-laws. You got *married*."

Mark chuckled at her wonderment. "Paige has some interesting in-laws too."

"I know. I was talking to both of you. You two take care of each other. I'll be around for *post*-marital counseling when it gets tough." Maureen's heels clicked away just as I handed Ruth a completed name change form with a smile over my husband and my counselor.

I met Mark mid-foyer with my opinion. "Let's just be sure to not *tell* Dad that we're hoping to have children? He'll blow a gasket."

"I think we're in agreement there." Mark smirked.

"But we have to do what God wants us to do. His perspective, remember?"

"And this is why I love you." He said, taking my hand.

After we walked hand in hand across the foyer, Mark inserted his key into the maintenance closet door and froze, wide-eyed with a gaze at his feet.

"Um, tricky door?" I joked.

He shook his head in some kind of shock as he pointed to the base of the door. I gasped when I saw what he saw. A few dozen familiar flakes of foil. Confetti from our wedding grew in intensity as it got closer to the door. Still in shock, Mark slowly opened the door to the maintenance closet. Everything was in perfect order and maintained. Except that there were five pounds of payback confetti littering shelves and desk and floor and mop buckets and sink. Apparently, our temporary replacements had not found the confetti stunt funny. Or they thought they'd found a funnier one. We quickly identified the mastermind.

After returning in a terrified run from dumping a bucket full of confetti onto the desk of the hopefully reformed confetti wedding planner, we chose to ignore the massive mess for something better. We decided to walk the church to see how loosely our schedule had been translated. Mark performed some calculated surgery on his desk drawer to grab his trusty notebook and a pen and smiled as we exited the sparkling maintenance closet.

"Broken stuff and dust bunnies?" He suggested our beloved tradition. Then clicked his pen with the hand bearing a black titanium ring that suited him.

"You got it, Boss." I grabbed a rag from a shelf just before I closed the door.

After trying to assess and complete our work despite confetti, lazied muscles, the busiest day of the week, and various staff members' versions of, "You left the wedding so fast, I didn't get to say. . ." we are looking at a much later clock than normal. Mark sighed with fatigue when he locked the maintenance closet for the day, as he'd done hundreds of times before. Then he turned to me with some internal conflict on his face.

Normally at that point, we parted ways for a painful twenty hours, only to rejoin again with boundaries and time and stress ahead of us. Normally the sound of Ruth's printer and murmurs of other staff echoed in the foyer as we found a table and waited for my father to arrive. It was no quiet ritual, as until then, we had no secrets from the foyer. But today was different. And they were all pretending not to watch. But they were testing us. They wanted to see the other side.

Instead of shuddering at the recent memory of our desperate desire to display purity, Mark rebelled against it. He pulled me into an embrace that included a soft kiss and a few tantalizing words beneath the foyer's ears.

"Let's go home, Cinderella." Then he turned and bent, pulling me with my hop and his strength into a carefree piggyback ride. The way he'd often carried me across sand too meddlesome and hot for freckles and my last pair of flip-flops.

Maureen told us that marriage would be hard. But even as the foyer's purist scoffers gasped at what they perceived to be a provocative display of affection, we were heedlessly in the grasp of sanctified love.

Part III

The Cure

"You will guide me with Your counsel,

And afterward receive me to glory."

Psalms 73:24

Chapter 35

Pain

I searched the event arena floor for the black cap and gown that I knew to frame my husband. We were above the sea of them against a rail that overlooked the floor, not wanting to get lost in the post-ceremony bustle below.

"See him yet?" Maureen asked, ducking her head in and out of different views of the room below.

"It doesn't help that they're all dressed alike." I joked dryly, though slightly distracted by a nervous ache in my belly. Probably should have skipped the second cup of coffee.

"Yeah, this process was a lot easier last year with you and your red-headedness." Maureen started. "But I'm not worried. I'm sure he'll find *us*."

My memory as I was searching for Mark moved to a year before when I wore the cap and gown, though it was supposed to happen the same year as Mark. I was in awe at what God accomplished in my life because I obeyed His call to graduate early. That day I was waiting for my husband of five months, still getting butterflies as I thought of him. I was in a form-hugging red dress and silver shoes that Maureen picked with the express purpose of being a human beacon for my lovesick husband to find us in a crowd.

Maureen was never gifted with a little sister or a daughter, and I hadn't a mother willing to treat me like a dress-up doll. So, every excuse she could find, Maureen handled my wardrobe choices. Rarely did I object, considering she did so with her own pocketbook.

Maureen looked at me again with a smile and a camera in front of her face. "You always look like you have a secret." I blinked to remove the flash burst from my vision.

I smiled, irritating Maureen the easiest way possible. I shrugged, with no other response. Then I walked down the rail to get a better view of the area just beneath us and to escape the attention of the dozen or so people from church that attended the graduation. After a moment of searching intently, I heard Maureen's giggle echo in my direction. But before I could turn to see the purpose, I felt a hand slide onto the section of red lace covering my abdomen and a warm whisper behind my ear.

"Who are you looking for, gorgeous?"

I smiled at the butterflies that took flight with his presence. "Some *summa cum laude* college graduate of whom I am excessively proud, even though he's as stubborn as he is handsome."

Mark first chuckled at my response. "Yikes, how handsome is he?"

"Extremely, I'm afraid." I turned to see him in the glory of the cap and gown. The black shirt and lime green tie peeking out of the top. A smiled a little at the sight. He made me so proud.

The whole gathering of family and friends awaited his greeting where I left them but watched us share a momentary heart to heart from a distance.

He sighed and responded to something deeper than a spat that morning, yet unresolved. Mark, knowing even Maureen's line of sight had ears, was wisely succinct with his words.

"You win. You're right. I'm wrong. I love you. You're beautiful. I'll do the dishes. Those are my good husband lines, right?" He joked, though he was conceding after some serious bull-headedness that morning. He was fiddling with my hair, buttering me up with a wince.

I grabbed hold of his other hand that was reaching out to touch that same spot of lace again. "You need to fire your writer if *those* are your lines."

He smiled. "Why, what are *your* lines?"

"I love you too. But half the church came to see you graduate. I feel like I'm married to a celebrity. Can we talk about this later?" I nodded my head at those talking among themselves, trying not to listen.

"Later it is." Mark sighed in disappointment but smiled in loving submission to my pleas. First, he kissed me softly, which earned him some coos, a whistle from Dave, and my father's stern throat clearing. Then we walked hand in hand back to the curious crowd that was waiting to congratulate the graduate.

He was bombarded by hugs and congrats and picture snaps. I was left only with his empty diploma cover and a loving wink as I became the last priority.

After a ride in Velma shared with rowdy nephews, we celebrated Mark's graduation with a cake in Pastor Dad's part of the house with church staff and friends that met there after the ceremony. I chatted with Emma and Mike about their upcoming wedding as Mark succumbed to fond stories of his childhood from the female church staff, as always.

After only family remained, Mark and I took to our robotic task of event cleanup, even though we were not at church. We had the help of my dad and Maureen, and Dave, so the cleanup happened quickly. Then, having realized it was dinnertime, Maureen ordered pizza. Still having a deep ache in my stomach, that did not sound appetizing. But I nibbled off Mark's plate after the pizza arrived. Then, though I was tired from weeks of studying and finals and working and party preparations, someone suggested a family poker night.

My only stipulation was being allowed to change into clothing more fit for *storge*. Mark followed me down to our apartment for the same purpose, or so he told them. When we arrived in our room, I plopped onto my back on the bed immediately, only slightly pretending to be giving up and falling asleep forever. Mark chuckled as he unbuttoned his shirt and disappeared into the closet for a more comfortable one. I sat up slowly, trying to banish the tired from my eyes and the ache from my belly. Mark, well attuned to me, saw my discomfort as he emerged from the closet. His shirt was the one I got him for Valentine's Day: *"I love my wife."* He was buttering me up again.

"Feeling okay, Cinderella?"

"I'm fine." To feed that lie, I rose from the bed and began to pick out clothes from my dresser. I reached back for my zipper and sighed, frustrated, having untrained myself by then to do it on my own. "Could you—?"

Mark was at the ready to carefully bring my zipper into my grasp as he often did. I remembered his nerves the first time I'd asked, and I'd been wearing a much different color. That day, though he still smiled, it was routine to him. "So, uh, this dress. Maureen? I know she loves to put you in red, and you only wear heels if she forces you to."

I rolled my eyes. "Yeah, we went out yesterday after my last final when you were at graduation practice. She thought it would help you find us. I told her I wanted something a little more modest, but—"

Mark chuckled. "It's not immodest, Cinderella. And you look *incredible*. It definitely didn't take me long to locate my smokin' hot better half."

"Thanks, Boss. It's weird to be home this late on a Saturday."

Mark rolled his eyes at my subject change and avoidance. "Yes. But we do have other part-time maintenance staff that we trained after the honeymoon volunteer fiasco if you recall. And Dad has assistant pastors that like some time in the pulpit every now and then."

"I wonder which one of them will take over if he ever retires." I forced the bland subject further.

"Dad has another solid decade on him, Paige. And I doubt he'd appoint another old geezer in his place." He bit a lip, frustrated with me.

"What did I say?" I asked.

"Nothing. But is it 'later'?" He asked with some timidity so as not to repeat the fight we had that morning. "We have a second alone, so I was hoping we could talk—not about work and stuff."

"Go ahead." I sighed, pulling on my favorite yoga pants. "Talk."

"Come on, Cinderella. Think about it. They're all together. In good moods. Proud of me. . .It's a perfect time to tell them. Your dad might even decide not to murder me." He was pleading with me, which was what sparked the spat that morning. Recognizing this, he added gently, "I don't see a reason not to. It's just them now. It wouldn't be the whole party like I wanted to do this morning. I want to *include* them in this."

"We don't even know for sure, Boss." I argued weakly.

He laughed and referenced an item Maureen bought an abundance of as a joke and put in our bathroom while decorating it. "How many of those tests have you taken since last night?"

"Two or three," I mumbled a lie as I pulled a shirt over my aching stomach. Then Mark tilted his head. "Three or four." I corrected. "Have you seen my brush?" Mark shook his head as I searched for my brush on my dresser. I sighed. "Five. Then I had to pee at four in the morning, and I didn't want to waste it, so Velma and I went out while you were sleeping and bought the most expensive, sophisticated one I could find. All of them were positive," I whispered the last words.

Mark was amused. "You know I've never actually *seen* you sleep? In five months of marriage. Are you secretly a vampire?"

"That depends. Can vampires get knocked up?" I said bitterly as I walked into our kitchen, seeking my brush. Mark followed.

"I'd give them the same odds Dr. Moreno gave *you*," Mark said with a wink, procuring a green apple from the fridge. He took a bite and spoke through it, almost incomprehensibly. "Your brush is in the bathroom. Why would it be in the kitchen? Got preggo brain already?"

I stormed to the bathroom. "I promise we will tell everybody once I go see Dr. Moreno. Okay? Please? Is that a compromise?" I was removing bobby pins and brushing out my crimson locks in front of the bathroom mirror under the peaceful watch of my green apple-eating husband.

"You're scared," he finally determined.

"Out of my mind." I nodded.

"Think about how *cool* it'll be. And then you won't be scared." He cooed, melting as he placed just four fingertips on a belly that had caused me nausea and cramping for the past twenty-four hours, which sparked the first test to be taken. It had been an "Aha" moment alone in the bathroom, staving off nausea. Mark had been concerned over my discomfort. So, I'd emerged and sat on the couch with him, plastic stick in hand to uncloud the mysterious symptoms for him.

"Well, I guess I'm pregnant," I'd said plainly.

"You're *what?*" He'd responded, caught off guard like a penguin awakening in the Sahara.

"I mean, probably not. I'm gonna take another test as soon as I can. Did you grab milk when we were at the store?" I'd continued onto my next mission.

"Yeah, it's up in Pastor Dad's fridge, though. I had cereal up there. You did say *pregnant*, right?" My detachment had confused him. But I'd risen from the couch and ventured up the stairs, not allowing him a chance to absorb or react.

What I still hadn't told him was that while the plastic sticks had been clear, I had a sickness in my spirit as if something was wrong. I was highly tolerant of pain, and even I was beginning to want to take something for the cramps. And *that* is what sparked the fear.

Maureen dealt us into the poker game at the dining room table with a head shake of a smile. Mark winked at me before tossing his apple core in his father's trash in the kitchen. Pastor Dad cleared his throat and snapped his fingers before Maureen filled his flatted hand with a ten-dollar bill and a frustrated grunt. Dave chuckled, and my dad pretended to be oblivious to it all. Dillon was counting poker chips out for each player, not really caring what was going on. Lane was in the other room, singing to himself amid the sound effects of superheroes in battle.

"What, the apple?" I tried to sort out the reason for the current ten-dollar bet as I sat in the empty seat between Maureen and Dillon. Mark took a seat between my dad and me after silently intimidating the eleven-year-old out of it by standing with a stare. I loved that he assumed he should always get to sit next to me. And that even in the worry of my father's ultimate disappointment, Mark still sat next to him with entitled confidence.

"Yeah. It means Mark is stressed out, as Dad predicted. A few years ago, it would have been a cigarette, and a few months ago, it would have been Skittles. I was getting a different vibe than 'stressed out' earlier when Mark found us at graduation. Probably letting my feelings get in the way. It happens. But since nothing stresses out Mark like being at odds with the woman he loves, the apple has provided a clearer vibe. You know, a little tiff can become a nasty fight if left unresolved." Maureen was bitter over losing the bet and taking it out on her closest counseling victims.

"Keep your vibes to yourself, Reen," Mark said with gentle scolding, as he always did when Maureen butted in.

"Oh, come on! You don't even want to know what *I* thought it was?" Maureen pleaded.

"Reen, please don't shrink me." Mark sighed.

"You of all people should understand the temptation to shrink, Mark. You are, indeed, a recipient of a Bachelor of Arts in Psychology. *Summa cum laude*, might I add." Pastor Dad added, winking in pride. Mark laughed a little.

"After the distraction that is *Paige* came on the scene, I was concerned you wouldn't quite make *summa*, Mark." Dave commented.

"I wouldn't exactly call her a 'distraction,' Dave." Mark laughed, looked at me. "Paige reminds me of *Mom* when it comes to studying. I got an 89 percent on a *quiz* a couple of months ago, and she saw it and *freaked*. She made me study that material all evening. Before the wedding, we spent breaks at work with Paige critiquing my papers and me tutoring her in math. Now we have a lot more time to do that because it happens at *home*."

Maureen giggled. Nodded. "Dave, I remember you and me taking turns working on papers while the other one walked around with colicky Dillon."

"Tough times." Dave sighed, shaking his head at the memory.

"But good times." The optimist winked at her husband, who took up her hand and kissed it tenderly. I loved watching their weathered old love story whenever it ignited for a moment. It made me wonder if "weathered" was only the age, not the state.

"Ew," Dillon forced a shudder at his parents' affection.

My dad looked at me as I giggled at Dillon. "Did you get all the results from the finals, Sweet Pea?"

"Yeah, I almost didn't make it with math, but everything else was fine," I confessed.

"By 'almost didn't make it,' she means it *almost* wasn't a solid A," Mark teased lovingly. "We should talk about your math tutor. I think he's more of a distraction than a help."

The room tittered with laughter, and I was glad for the momentary distraction from my own secret. But when I looked at my cards and Dillon handed me stacks of poker chips, I noticed the cramping again. Even stronger this time. Mark inquired silently to me, and I shook my head to remove him from worry. But he persisted in a whisper,

"Want some water or something?"

"I'll get it." He rolled his eyes at my hardheadedness, and I rose as an excuse to escape the suddenly awkward but loving tone of the room.

"Seriously, though. Is everything okay?" Maureen whispered to Mark.

"Maureen," Pastor Dad scolded, silencing the intrusion.

I walked into the kitchen, just over a few feet from the table that Mark and I used more than our own. Somehow a private basement apartment turned quickly into sharing equally a large house with a pastor. We shared most meals and conversations, as if I was adopted in, instead of added by marriage. I loved the arrangement—we all did. Even my father, who lived on his own, spent many evenings there. And I was hoping with all my might that the shock of the positive tests didn't coincide with the pain that worsened when I stood.

Mark was right. It was foolish to try to keep such a secret from such a tight-knit group. But I was determined. The next few moments of my life began as a nagging ache that came in waves, worsening as I got myself a glass of water. Mark glanced over at me several times as I leaned against the counter, wincing in pain, sipping water. But he heeded my "warning label," knowing it might be more trouble than it was worth to check my well-being in my current mood.

So, it wasn't until a moan-worthy pain came from nowhere, and my glass of water clattered to the floor from hands that were known to be steady, not clumsy, that my husband was at my side in an instant. In fact, they all sprang into action. A doctor palpated my belly, a father's hand tested my temperature. A pair of worried nephews were ushered out of the room by their mother. My forehead leaned against my husband's chest within his concerned embrace. I was in immense pain and fighting nausea when Dave stopped touching me and cleared his throat, annoyed.

"What? You know what's wrong with her?" Mark wondered how Dave could find annoyance in such a worrisome situation.

"Mark, you know nothing irritates me more than a patient that doesn't give me all the information before expecting a diagnosis. I talk about this all the time. There are a few possible diagnoses. All of them are concerning. I need more information, so I know which of my colleagues to call." I heard the big brother in Dave's rarity of a scolding. Obviously, he'd come to some conclusion.

I assume Mark felt some sense of shame, if he was able in his unruffled way, when our fathers awaited some resolve from him. For the shame and for the sake of a compromise, he didn't speak readily, which brought Maureen fully into the room again with fervent curiosity.

My eyes were watering, but I looked up and blinked away tears, met by the intense stare of Mark. He was begging me with his eyes. And then, me in pain and him in worry, our antlers clashed, and the battle we'd only postponed ensued in front of God and everyone. Maureen saw it coming and winced, then bit her lip in a quiet, high-pitched moan to warn everyone.

Mark was the first to lose his head.

"You're seriously *still* not going to tell them? What is the *point* of this, Paige?"

"We agreed! Why are you being so selfish?" I demanded. Mark was taken aback at the words and the tone.

"*I'm* being selfish? They are *worried* about you, and you don't seem to care. I think *that's* pretty selfish." He defended, trying to keep his cool.

"Why can't you just trust me, Mark? I'm not ready to tell the whole world. I shouldn't have even told *you*. I knew you'd do this." My voice raised through a wince of pain. Enough combined with my warning label that the family stepped back a few feet.

"No secrets, remember?" He was deeply hurt. Took to quiet passion. "What logical reason would there be for you to not tell your *husband* and the people who love you most about this?"

"Why is *my* body everyone's business?" I was in tears over the pain. Lashing out.

He gave a hurt laugh and acted in defense. "Alright, since we're politicians now instead of, you know, one flesh, I wouldn't dare make a decision that might impact 'your' body. But that *baby* is half mine." He crossed the line and completely defied my wishes. Releasing cats from bags and shaming me into silence. He had remorse and immediate regret in his eyes. But only until he saw the relief in mine.

Amid the dropped jaws of the room, Maureen's face lit up. She enunciated, "*Baby?*"

"Thank you. All I needed to know." Dave removed his work phone from his belt. The phone we hated the sound of when he was on call and had to rush to the hospital in the middle of a dinner or church service. He hit a few buttons and left us in awkward silence as he exited the kitchen. Maureen took the liberty of speech once again, even in the brutality of the silence.

"You're *pregnant?*" Maureen clarified gently. "Here I thought my vibe was completely insane."

"We just found out last night," Mark answered, deflated. "So, Paige wasn't ready to tell anyone. Including me, apparently."

"While I'm not ignoring *that* red flag," Maureen's eyes narrowed. "Paige, you told me a *year* ago that you went and saw Dr. Moreno, and—"

Mark turned to his sister with a smile. "She said this wasn't possible. We went *again* recently because Dr. Moreno wanted to see if anything had changed. She said it hadn't, and that it would be a miracle if we ever conceived. This came out of left field, Reen. But Paige just told me she took like six tests."

"Left field?" My father's expected reaction began. "Why didn't anyone listen to me about this?"

"Paul, can we not do this right now?" Mark begged.

"Mark, you knew this could happen. This 'unexpected,' unplanned pregnancy will throw a rock in her schooling. This is exactly why I wanted you to wait on this marriage nonsense."

"Yeah, but if I recall, you didn't really care whether we were abstinent. And people used to ask if *I* understood where babies come from," Mark reminded.

"It's not that I didn't care. It just wasn't my business, Mark. But in either case, I expected you to be more responsible," Dad argued.

Mark's tact and poise and all his filters shattered in the place where that glass of water didn't. The way it always did when he was defending me.

He turned from me to confront my father. "What is 'responsible,' Paul? Is that your way of saying 'prevents Paige from being blessed with a child'? Because in that case, you're right. I've never even *tried* to be responsible for that. The person 'responsible' for Paige having to give up her firstborn child and being told she'd never get another chance at motherhood is behind bars for how 'responsible' he was. Maybe think a little harder about your wording, Paul. Because I consider myself to be plenty responsible. As a husband, I feel like I'm responsible for Paige's *life* and well-being and even her grade in math. Also, for *loving* her just as Christ loves the church. That means I will literally let you *kill* me before I let you continue to make Paige feel like she should be ashamed of *anything*. At all. Ever. No *wonder* she was so terrified to tell you."

"Son. . ." Though impressed, Pastor Dad attempted to calm Mark, to no avail. Maureen attempted to hide her smile.

Mark continued, "And by the way, I've learned a lot more about God and the human psyche from five months of marriage than in any class of that stupid *summa cum laude* degree I got today. There are a lot more important things than *schooling*."

"Maybe so, but you two have *drive*, Mark. Dedication. Beautiful minds. I'd hate to see that wasted on a child you're not even close to prepared for." My father softened. Mark continued.

"You're right. The world needs a few more old, ignorant, careless parents to usher in the next generation." Mark's vicious sarcasm caused Maureen to cover laughing lips and my father to silence.

"Boss." I whimpered through a pain that nearly brought me to my knees. And then I unleashed a sobbed rant once Mark returned me to his arms. "I love you. I'm sorry I didn't want to tell anyone. I just know something is wrong with this pregnancy, and I didn't want everyone to get their hopes up." My voice became high and pained. "Please don't be disappointed in me if I fail at giving you this baby."

Mark took me into his arms, shushing me as I sobbed. He didn't know what to say or do.

Maureen came near, touching my hair. "David is on the phone figuring this out right now, sweetie. But Paige, the only opinion you need to worry about is God's, and He isn't disappointed. It's a miracle you're pregnant right now. Not a *mistake*. So even if this miracle is temporary, you should be thankful and trust in the Lord. Don't worry about a bunch of imperfect humans and our quirky reactions. We love you, okay? That's the foremost thing in our minds." Maureen used her gentle counselor voice. The one that beckoned me to Christ at my lowest point in life. But I didn't know back then the part of her that accepted her ten-dollar bill back from her father, even as she spoke of quirks.

"Thanks," I heard Mark whisper to his sister, knowing she calmed me down. Then he kissed my head and whispered exactly what I needed to hear. "I'm with you through anything and everything, Cinderella."

Dave re-entered the kitchen with quiet compassion in his eyes. Dave was the proof to my theory that those of us with a stern and strong shell often have the softest centers. I knew this from Maureen, though I was usually only witness to the serious, logical man. She told me that "David" had been commended time after time for the beauty of his bedside manner. He was the perfect doctor. Both a man of science and a man of God. He would use the science to help a patient heal physically. But it was the man of God I feared I was about to finally meet. With a sigh, I heard his first few words.

"I got in touch with Ev—Dr. Moreno. She agrees with my diagnosis, and let me know that it would probably be best if we headed in. She's on call in the ER, and they are expecting us." This drew from the whole kitchen an adrenaline-laden gasp. No mention of an emergency could be without one.

"The *emergency* room? Are you kidding? Why?" And then Mark pulled me tighter. In worry. And guilt. And fear that he couldn't protect me well enough. But his tone was still much calmer than mine.

"What? No! Just give me some Tylenol. I'll be fine." I protested with fervor, realizing I almost wanted to vomit after I finished speaking. I squinted, forcing the feeling away just as another wave of pain hit me with panic.

Dave ignored my opinion. Then he whispered something I didn't comprehend to Mark, who was rubbing my back to comfort me. I couldn't decide if he was speaking quietly or if it was muffled for the pain. Mark replied in a similar volume and tone, still incomprehensible. They went back and forth like that for a few moments as I moaned in pain. Our two fathers were in proximity to hear as well, and I heard them all whispering through my excruciating pain and moans. Then Mark's voice startled me as if he was waking me up.

"So, should we drive or call an ambulance?" What had made him concede so quickly? I suspected I may have lost time.

"We can drive. Dr. Moreno said this is not considered life-threatening for Paige unless she loses consciousness. Then we should worry about internal bleeding. Either way, you need to be strong for this one, Mark." Dave explained. Then he began asking my dad what my blood type was, but I was having trouble comprehending the answer.

Mark lifted my head to see into his eyes with a curled finger under my chin. Which coincided with my head swimming, my eyes drooping, and a peak in the intensity of my pain.

I heard Maureen gasp. "She's as white as a ghost."

Mark had some sorrow in his sternness as he addressed me. "Let's go get in Velma." Then I lost the ability to read his face and stumbled back against the counter as I tried with all my strength and focus to unblur the concerned image of my husband's face.

"Boss, what's wrong with me? I don't feel. . .Mark?. . . Daddy?" Everyone was talking. Panicked. All at once. But why were they not talking to me? Why was I struggling to stand and sort out words? Mark commanded something I finally heard but didn't quite understand.

"Paige. No-no-no. Don't you dare!"

But his words faded first, and then his beautiful countenance, and then the kitchen and people I loved quickly gave way to black.

Chapter 36

Hope

I awakened and panicked immediately. I was alone in a hospital room I'd been in before. I woke up in the same recovery room after my abortion. And with an attempt to sit up in the bed, I experienced a similar soreness. Not the pain from the kitchen. The kind that came after surgical instruments had invaded my body. I remained lying on my side.

What now, God? I pleaded inside, then felt my lower abdomen. Deeply sore, with a few strips of tape to cover tiny incisions. An IV had taken up residence in my left arm. And my only comfort is that my wedding set was still on my finger. At least the redemption and love had not been a dream.

I looked out of the glass wall, where a doctor I recognized was talking within a huddle of people. She was my kind and caring OBGYN, but my heart was somehow caught in darkness. I recognized the rest of them with much more comfort. Mark was standing in his position of emotional distress. Hands clasped atop his head. Maureen and my dad were listening to the doctor with intensity, nodding every few seconds. There were questions mouthed by Dave to his colleague, but the leftover anesthesia would not allow me to read the lips.

Then Dr. Moreno said something that caused a strange reaction. It caused both tears, sad ones, perhaps, and smiles that conquered other recent tears. Mark was the most affected, burying his head in his hands a moment, and then coming out of it by embracing the petite doctor to the amusement of the rest of our family. Not sadness, I decided. But that full depth of gratitude Mark was so good at expressing. In fact, they all looked to Mark, patted him on the back to encourage him. Maureen embraced him long and became the woman that raised him, whispering into his ear. Mark nodded and mouthed what I could finally see. *God is good.*

Either out of instinct or spiritual oneness, Mark suddenly looked into my room, which seemed to lift his mood even more.

The others didn't see the reason for his smile until he returned my feeble wave. The rest of the huddle turned in unison to see that I was awake. Dr. Moreno began to enter my room, but my father placed a hand on her shoulder to stop her. I assumed my daddy knew that I'd return to a darker time if subjected again to her bedside manner in this room. I assumed she was convinced when she nodded at whatever he was saying. Though probably unorthodox, she handed my chart to Dave. The two colleagues locked eyes and held the chart as one in what would have been an awkward exchange if it weren't but a nanosecond. They nodded solemnly before Dr. Moreno let go and walked away from the family.

My heart sank, even without knowledge of the situation when my family bowed their heads for a quick prayer. Then it would seem a compassionate sort of quarrel ensued. They had something to tell me and were deciding who would come into my room and do so. Knowing them, the father wanted to be fatherly, the pastor, pastoral, and the counselor wanted to counsel. The doctor had the facts and felt the most qualified. Mark rolled his eyes at the argument, coming my way with a half smile while they continued the quarrel.

He opened the door and took advantage of the husband size space I instinctively left on even the smallest bed.

"Hey," he said.

"Hey," I replied. "I don't like waking up in the hospital."

"But the good news is you're not a vampire. I finally saw you sleep." He took my hand with a sigh and then a sniffle. "I've probably never been more scared than when I couldn't wake you up. My mom collapsed in that same kitchen and never *did* wake up. I was preparing for the worst."

"I lost the baby, didn't I?" I whispered, realizing my throat was mysteriously sore.

Mark sighed. "It's not always good to start with the empty half of the glass, Cinderella. Because I also just found out something *really* cool." He nodded with a smile.

I sighed and squeezed his hand. With my other hand, I soothed the messenger by hooking my finger on his belt loop. However sick I was, I still had some power over him. He

296 | R e b e k a h   T y n e   M c K a m i e

responded with a hum of a laugh. I inquired. "No sugar coating, okay? Tell me what happened."

Mark nodded, and his eyes glistened a moment before he could muster the courage to say his first words.

"It really helped me to imagine that Jesus and my mom and Darian are showing our baby around Heaven right now," he said in tears, but somehow with a smile.

My heart lurched. "Oh. . .I'm. . .Did I. . .was this my fault? If we had come sooner. . ."

Mark shook his head with fervor, a hand on my face. "Never do that, okay? Because," Mark's voice turned to squeaks and tears. "You were bleeding inside, and we almost lost you too. So maybe it's selfish, but I'm counting this one a victory. I don't think I'd *survive* losing you."

"I honestly didn't know it was that bad. I thought miscarriage symptoms were different," I apologized yet again.

"Well, you didn't *exactly* miscarry."

And when my heart didn't know how to comprehend this, I waited for him to give me the rest of the story.

The story of how my scar tissue was so severe that the path to my womb was structurally deformed. And so that baby had attached inside my fallopian tube instead—an ectopic pregnancy. I heard of how Dave had diagnosed this in our father-in-law's kitchen before he ever called his colleague to confirm. A neurologist, yes. But a photographic memory for all things medical and a graduation at the top of every class he ever entered. Dr. Moreno, I learned, had also been in the top 10 percent in Dave's same medical school that year.

They had seen the baby in the ER. A five week "fetus" they weren't sure if it didn't have a heartbeat as of late, or just not yet. Either way, my beloved family had spent the time during my sedated ultrasound to coo over and love the then lifeless baby. The tech had thought them ignorant. Mark had named her "Hope." But then he had been forced to make the hardest choice of his life. I stopped him there.

"So they just automatically asked you? Or did my dad try to butt in?"

"In this state, if you haven't officially decided on one before you're incapacitated, an assembly of 'interested persons' gets together and chooses a proxy decision maker. We were all here and they all looked at *me*." Mark sighed. "Even your dad."

They all had input, he told me, but it was Mark that signed for them to remove my ruptured fallopian tube, including the baby that had been inside. It took him some time to be convinced that there was no way to save the baby. She was already gone. But his timely tear-filled signature saved my life.

Then Mark told me the remarkable half of the news. Dr. Moreno had caused my scar tissue during a procedure she performed on a battered womb. After seeing she couldn't save my tube, she was devastated. And instead of removing her scope, she went on and performed a surgery that all but eradicated the danger and infertility involved with my scar tissue. It was a newer procedure she could see clearly from inside would work in my situation.

"So, Dr. Moreno says you'll spend the next few weeks feeling like you got hit by a truck. And with one tube, the chances of pregnancy are cut in half, so it could take years before it happens again. *And* any pregnancy will automatically be high-risk." Then a smile overtook Mark's face. "But we can have *kids*, Paige."

I gasped. "No!"

He laughed through a sob. "Yes."

The procedure was a success, but the young doctor had not been given prior permission to do it, and when she performed it, she'd put her medical license on the line, hoping Mark wouldn't sue. Mark, as I saw, had hugged her instead. It was probably how Eva Moreno had felt when she'd been accepted to medical school. Or when Pastor Dad had been appointed Senior Pastor of Grace Community Church. Because all Mark had ever wanted was to be a father.

It was Sunday, midday I learned. But my family members had kept a constant vigil over me. The night had been full of uncertainty. I'd received blood from my own father, the prayers of the entire congregation at church, and a multitude of songs and kisses from my littlest nephew. But since I woke up so quickly after the ordeal, they had high hopes for my full and fertile recovery. Mark concluded his revelations with a sigh and some silence. I sniffled because I'd been crying for most of it. He waited, with extraordinary patience, for my response. I processed it all, the best I could while recovering from anesthesia.

"You named her Hope?" I asked.

"You cry at night for Darian because you say no one ever got to love him. We made sure to love Hope while she was here. And to cry for her when we knew she was gone. We all loved her. And we know that she wasn't here long, but God used her in an incredible way while she was. Because of her, we can have other babies. So don't cry for her except this once. Praise God for her. For Hope."

I nodded and sobbed within his embrace a few moments. And when I regained composure, I sought the best of Mark.

"So did you and my dad duke it out again? I was concerned he might end up with a crooked nose." I gained a smile from the broken spirit.

"Oh, he's busted! He was so adamant about you not getting pregnant, but you should have seen the way he ogled over that baby during the ultrasound. And just now when he found out we could have other babies, he said he wouldn't mind having one or two grandkids to spoil. No matter *when* they come." Mark smiled.

I sobbed at the relief, the new prospect. The joy. "Let's have at least *three*."

"You got it, Cinderella." He showed the kindness of his dimples, then kissed me with remorseful tenderness. The cue, apparently, for the entire family to enter. Mark helped me sit up. And I mentioned how terrible I probably looked and laughed with pain. Maureen tossed Mark a brush, which he snatched back when I reached for it.

Then he did something he'd never done. Something I'd never ask for, but almost brought me to tears. He served me by brushing my hair slowly and gently as the family laughed and conversed. Sometimes about the situation. Sometimes not. But always reminding me how much I loved and required the presence of each of them.

Chapter 37

Risk

I spent half the summer recovering from surgery. I had been worried I'd be isolated in the basement, watching YouTube videos while the rest of the world played out in the sunshine. I despised sitting still for more than an hour or so, regardless of the reasoning. But my husband knew that. Since he worked full-time at church as of graduation, he made sure to send a constant flow of visitors in his absence. So many people asked about me every day that it wasn't much of a task.

Emma came often, to my joy, and let me help her with her wedding plans as I could. I knew that when her August wedding arrived, I'd be plenty healed. As her matron of honor, I encouraged her lovingly as she prepared for marriage. But in reality, my own marriage was something new to me again.

Though ecstatic at the prospect of children, it also awakened a new fear in us. What-ifs that involved college and money and housing. Our only vehicle was not fit for children. Things we never considered when we'd set up our lives for two. We were promised that it would likely take us years to conceive. But rising above the fear and what if's was the joy that came with hope.

Maureen came to visit almost daily that summer and usually brought her boys, placing a deep longing in my soul. One day just before Mark was due home for the evening, while the boys were upstairs playing in the backyard, I told her about the longing.

"I hope you know how lucky you are to have two healthy, living children to love."

She of course, smiled her smile. And then dropped on me something fear did not quite cover.

"Do you know how my mom died?"

"An aneurysm, right? Mark doesn't really talk about it, but he told me a million years ago."

"She never even knew about it." Maureen sobbed a little within her smile.

"I'm really sorry." I had nothing else to offer.

"She was a sweet lady. Everyone loved her. But she was stern, you know? She and I fought like a couple cats. But she was always right. And Mark was her perfect little angel. *Such* a mama's boy. There's a reason that he doesn't like to talk about it." Maureen reminisced.

"Because they were so close?" I asked against the quick sigh.

"Brain aneurysms are inherited. I have one too. David forced me to get tested as soon as Dillon was born. He wanted to know, I guess. But mine isn't like Mom's. It's bigger and it's meaner. Doctors can't figure out how I even lived until they intervened. Through childbirth and everything. One time my blood pressure shot up when I was pregnant with Lane. That's when I almost lost him, because they almost put me into preterm labor with all the drugs they gave me to bring down my blood pressure. Mark doesn't like to talk about Mom's death, because he knows one day he'll probably re-live it. With me."

"But if you know about it, can't you fix it?"

"I had surgery and they put in a coil to cut off blood supply to it. So the risk of a rupture is pretty low most of the time. My blood pressure was pretty high that night." She laughed a little, distracted for a nanosecond, then returned. "David couldn't decide on an area of medicine to specialize in. After the Lane incident, that's when he decided to be a neurologist. He says if I try to leave him, he'll save me. It's kind of an understanding we have. I've known about this over a decade, so I hardly think about it anymore."

"But there's still as risk that—" I clarified, my heart pounding.

She interrupted first with a snicker. "That I could get hit by a bus? *Something* will eventually kill all of us. I just probably have the burden of knowing *what*. I don't want you to worry, Paige. I just want you to understand something."

"And what's that?"

"I was a different person before life hit me at about sixteen. When Mom died? I played by all the rules. I never stepped on toes and respected all boundaries. I was a perfect princess and did just as I was told at all times. Minded my own business, for the most part." She smiled her smile. I laughed, not being able to envision Maureen as anything but all sass and spunk and curiosity.

"You're kidding, right?"

"When life gets hard, you can let it cripple you. Or you can let it *improve* you. When Lane was born healthy, it was a miracle. My prodigal brother came home right after that. It was the beginning of a less intense life for all of us. When all that came together, I decided that I was going to use my life to help people get through theirs. Love people. Change people. And follow hard after Jesus. No matter what anyone thought or said. So, if you ever wonder why I'm so intense? It's because life is too short to be *polite* about saving souls. And if you wonder if I realize what a blessing those boys are? Well now you know that I realize it *every* day."

"Understood, Mrs. Shrink."

"However, after all you've been through, I think someday you'll be twice the counselor and mother I could *ever* be. Because somehow, you're so much more amazing than me even though you still play by the rules. Don't even waste your time disagreeing. Just wait and see."

In tears, I hugged my sister. My counselor. Because she had once again shown me the light. Then she jumped back.

"So, have you gotten any hospital bills yet?" She winced.

"Yeah, it isn't pretty. Fortunately, Dr. Moreno never charges us, like she promised, but the hospital still has to, and the insurance through the church is not that awesome. It's okay, we have the money. I'd been hoping to buy a car, but God obviously knew I'd need that savings for something else."

"Didn't Mark have a savings?" Maureen wondered, surprised.

I giggled. Wiggled my wedding rings at her, then rolled my eyes. "And Hawaii. Then he recently put some money into Velma since we've been sharing her, and it was starting to show. But it'll be easier now that we don't have to coordinate our school schedules anymore. I'll just drop him at the church and—"

"Okay, you can stop talking now." Then she pulled from her purse a key ring. A simple black band beheld two keys, two remotes for automatic locks and a strange keychain. It was a transparent plastic square with a handwritten description of a car. A brand-new car of some kind in white.

"Um...?" I was confused as I pawed the set of keys.

"Think you're well enough to climb the stairs?" She stood and slowly helped me to my feet, supporting me up a flight of stairs with an arm at my waist. Mark walked in the garage door just in time to scold this action.

"Reen, she's not allowed to—" He took over supporting me. My entire midsection was still sore, even sitting in a chair. But when Mark's wedding banded hand replaced Maureen's around my waist, the pain nearly ceased.

"Hush, she's fine." Maureen reached her hand into the closing garage door to reopen the automatic one I'd just heard Mark shut.

"How was your day, Boss?" I smiled into his eyes, still loving that his tired sigh was for the comfort of the home we shared.

"It was good," He answered, though he was distracted. "You get a new car, Reen?"

"Yeah," I answered, producing the keys she'd handed me.

"As you know, my Caddie was a few years old, and David got a new-car-sized bonus and wanted me to splurge because I'm *completely* spoiled. Come out and see it." She said with a bright twist of her smile before heading out into the sunshine.

I started to follow, but my hero of a husband instead lifted me gently and carried me past an emerald beauty and an old pickup truck in the garage. When Maureen stopped at the clean white crossover SUV in the driveway described on the key ring, she turned around and gagged playfully at Mark's loving gesture. He set me down and we both admired the new vehicle. A vehicle with plenty of room for her family of four. Something that caused Mark a twinge of worry just at the possible need of procuring something similar.

"It's nice, Reen. My wife is supposed to be in bed, can I take her back in now?"

Maureen ignored the request. "I think you should call him Vinnie. Mark, I gave you Velma so you'd grow up and stop smoking. It was only a matter of time before she fell in love and got married."

Mark and I gasped in unison. Mark protested, "Maureen. This is crazy. This thing is brand-new. We can't—"

"You can. And you will. David and I insist. It's yours." She shrugged. "I love my Caddie. This thing isn't exactly 'me.' Totally screams 'Paige,' though. Paul picked it out. We were all slightly disappointed they didn't have one in pink."

"This isn't fair," I whined. "How are we supposed to thank you?"

"Or *repay* you?" Mark fretted.

"It comes at a price, of course. Just like Velma did." Maureen giggled at our surprise.

"Mmmm." I winced in pain and leaned against the new vehicle, in a bit of shock, but rolling my eyes that everything was a game to her. "And what's that?"

"Fill it with babies." Maureen giggled and shoved her shocked and concerned brother's arm teasingly. "Oh, and I'll need a ride home."

For quite some time, I watched in faith. I prayed. My body healed. My spirit waited. My heart smiled as I placed flowers in the hair of Emma's much younger surprise of a sister at that August wedding. Heather was her name. She and Lane represented the innocence of children I borrowed then.

I congratulated Emma on the ultrasound picture she showed me just two months later. I watched her grow to ridiculous proportions. I cooed and cuddled outwardly as she eventually brought in a tiny, precious being. They apologized for Mikaela's spit-up and colic. I bowed my head when Pastor Dad prayed over them to raise the baby in Christ. My past haunted me in new ways as I missed the children no one could see. I longed for the spit-up, the colic, and the dedicated promise to give a child Christ's love above all other things. Obediently, I did not cry for Hope. But stubbornly, I still cried for Darian.

I granted myself the truth that I'd been given by the greatest husband on earth. "In God's time," he told me, as months, *years* passed. I diligently put my efforts into my schooling and worked part-time with Mark. We were a team, and happy serving together, even if always just the two of us. But my heart cried out each time a baby erupted in a church service. My soul ached every time I started up Vinnie and the rear-view mirror showed me an empty back seat. And with every month, every negative test, I traveled further and further into a darkness that started to become as constant and hopeless as comfort itself.

"I was there." The voice is not one I recognize, nor can I describe it. Except to say that it comes from all around me. It is warm and bright. Three words that evoke great peace. Greater understanding.

"I know." I say this and then feel as though I'm being pulled. My eyes pulse and my breath is taken as I am removed from my perfect tranquility. My feet are icy, and I am again in a darkness with beeps and lights my eyes will not open to see.

Chapter 38

Time

"Nothing." I ground into bitter teeth as I was taking out my frustrations on a minuscule scuffmark in the youth recreation room.

"That's a really mad 'nothing.'" Mark was backing away.

"I'm proud, Mark. I just hate that you didn't think you needed to *tell* me before you applied for a master's program or scholarships or anything. You know, your *wife*."

"I wanted to surprise you. I didn't think it'd be an issue for us to both be in school. We've done that before, remember? And it's a full ride. We don't even have to *pay* for it. You like our little apartment. I thought it was a no brainer."

"A no brainer? Mark, our little apartment was cute and romantic two years ago. Now it's starting to feel a lot like living in your dad's basement. You said you were taking that counselor job at Dillon's school. You interviewed and everything. You said maybe we could buy a house. How is that even close to the same thing as launching into a full-time degree again? Sorry for assuming you'd stick to your word."

"What is your deal today? This is like the fifth time I've gotten chewed out. It's not like you to be so irritable." At this, Mark opened and began to pour some pine cleaner into the mop water. The smell I usually welcomed made me extremely nauseous and I concealed it by storming into the next room to begin emptying trash. Mark was calling after me. He appeared at the doorway to face me. I accosted him first.

"Irritable? How about you don't even care what I think anymore?" I said, bitterly removing a bag from a trashcan and replacing it with a fresh one. To escape Mark who was not letting up, I headed toward Maureen's office in a huff. I decided to allow sister dearest the counseling opportunity she had no doubt heard. Mark followed me.

"Oh yeah, that's it. While we're at it, is there anything else you want to be mad at?" Mark was fuming.

"Ending your sentence in a preposition." I used the ridiculous words to make him storm back down the hall. Mark was livid as I slammed the door to Maureen's office behind me. She looked up a moment from her crossword puzzle of the day and was barely able to hide her smile.

"You are so juvenile sometimes!" I heard muffled from the hall.

"I'm twenty years old, what do you expect?" I cracked the door and yelled it into the hall again, hurt. After re-slamming the door, I collapsed into a chair on the other side of Maureen's desk. I buried my head in my arms on her desk to fight nausea and tears.

"Marriage is hard." I muffled into my arms.

I heard Maureen chuckle a little.

"How is this funny to you? Did you hear what he did?"

"He told me yesterday about his once-in-a-lifetime opportunity that he thought you'd be excited about. He's been spoiled because you're a preposterously supportive wife. A year ago, you'd have been excited about it. Heck, a *month* ago, you'd have been kissing and congratulating him."

I sat up completely in my chair and glared at Maureen a moment until she smiled fully and knowingly. She was still working on her crossword as she spoke.

"You have two options here. You could act like a complete you know what and let him believe he's made an unwise decision. Continue leaving him out of the loop so he thinks you're simply insulting the home he's provided, his career direction, his grammar, etcetera, etcetera. Which is all quite entertaining for *me*." She finally took a breath. And softened her tone to reveal the actual counsel. "Or you could do the loving and honest thing and just. . .tell him."

"Tell him *what?*" My tone was much more accusatory than seeking of clarification.

She smiled. "You're funny. And looking rather green at the moment."

I buried my face again, moaning. Happy to not have to put on a front anymore. "How did you know?"

"If I divulged my methods. . ." She began the familiar mantra. I finished it with the bitterness of a spinning head and churning belly.

"I'd end up a better counselor than you. Got it."

"Mark, on the other hand, is a guy and has no idea. So, you should go tell him. This little spat would be over in about ten seconds. Ah!" I looked up to see that Maureen's exclamation was over a crossword she'd figured out. "Arduous. Duh." She growled under her breath.

"You know he won't go back to school once he finds out. He'll want a steady job. It'll crush him."

Maureen laughed, chin up, eyes squinted. She imitated her version of me with flailing hands. "'Oh no, my doting, providing husband might make sure he continues doing so!' You hear yourself? I bet you ten bucks he screams loud enough for the whole church to hear. 'Crushed' is not what he will be. He wants this about four thousand times more than any master's degree."

"Probably not the *whole* church." I agreed weakly.

"It's alright if you don't have the cash on you. I'll take an IOU."

"What if something *bad* happens again?" I asked with sincerity.

"You'd want to go through that alone? If I were you, I'd want the support of the second best husband in the universe either way. And the rest of us, too." She smiled. "Go tell him. Now."

Maureen helped me calm down. When she opened the door and let me out, Mark was looking hurt and pacing a few feet away in the hall. Then I smelled that before he did this, he mopped the room down the hall with pine cleaner. Far too much pine cleaner, because he was stressed. Mark looked up and began to speak.

"Does your *husband* get to talk to you now?"

The pine scent was overwhelming me, and my eyes barely saw the women's restroom before my feet bolted past Mark to take me there. I heard over my vomiting the voices echo into the restroom from just outside. Mark's was in panic.

"You okay? Paige, I didn't know you were sick. We'll talk later, okay?"

"I'll go get her purse. I know she keeps a toothbrush in there." I heard the heels click away and flushed the toilet, feeling well enough to stand.

I exited the stall, hand on my belly, seeing that Mark was leaning against the doorway looking into the bathroom. I smiled at his grace as I washed my hands. He was looking concerned, watching me intently for a reply as I dried my hands. The heel click returned and Maureen handed Mark my purse, then punched her brother's shoulder and giggled before she returned to her office.

I turned, leaning against the sink, watching Mark. He reached into my purse and handed me my toothbrush. I took it, and brushed my teeth, still watching Mark in the mirror. I watched him realize he was being left out of some loop. He despised nothing else in life like secrets. He liked to be informed at all times, though he loved to surprise others with things like early flights and master's programs. Therefore, I was amused at his distress.

"Please tell me the narfing is not from us arguing? I would feel really bad if this was my fault. I didn't know you were so upset." He spoke with compassion, as he often did, of my common reaction to severe emotional distress.

I was glad the rinsing of my mouth concealed my smile. I finished drying my mouth with a paper towel before I answered. "I'm not upset with you, Boss. But the 'narfing' is *totally* your fault."

"I didn't use *that* much cleaner." Mark was joking as he examined a scuff mark on the ground, knowing every eye in the church was watering from lingering pine scent.

I giggled, putting my travel size neat freakness back in the purse he was holding. "It's not the pine cleaner."

He caused the silence to bend as he looked up, calculating. His forehead wrinkled and he looked me dead in my eyes. He smiled a little, then shook his head. I nodded. And he lost all composure, dropping my purse and lifting me from the ground into a hug.

"I am *so* sorry. When did—? Oh my gosh, you're *sure?*" He carried me to the bathroom counter, where he set me down and leaned his forehead against mine.

"I'm sure, Boss. But wait, you're not mad? Your scholarships and the program. You'll still do it, right?"

He laughed, tapping my thigh, humming giddily through a smile. "What program? I'm a high school counselor who is buying a house for his family. Why didn't you just tell me?"

"I had my reasons," I whined.

"Why do you *do* that, Paige? We're in this together." Mark ran a hand through his hair, then clasped his hands on his forehead, shaking his head at the ceiling, but smiling bright enough to shy away any bitterness from the fight. He embraced me. Kissed me with tenderness. Then led me by the hands to hop off the counter and touched his knuckles to my stomach timidly. "Do you have any pain? And have you seen Dr. Moreno?"

"I went yesterday. I'm sorry I didn't take you, but I wanted to be sure this time before I got your hopes up. Anyway, I'm seven weeks. Strong heartbeat. Everything looks healthy. No pain. I'm just *so* sick, which is a good sign. Dr. Moreno was as relieved as me, I think." As I was speaking, Mark's tears were welling. Overflowing.

"So this is really happening, isn't it?" He sniffled and hiccuped the words. His tears aided my hormones in the failure of my own floodgate.

"I think it is."

Suddenly, I had to cover my ears as Mark let out a war call of a woo-hoo that caused office doors to open all over the church. And the click of heels down the hall. Then he squeezed me again and pulled back suddenly, touching my stomach.

"Oh! I'm not hurting you, am I?"

The heels reached the doorway. "She's not made of glass, little bro."

Mark laughed at Maureen's smile and then dropped to his knees in front of me and kissed my belly once before he embraced it. During the embrace, Maureen mouthed *"Ten bucks"* to me and I rolled my eyes.

A familiar whistle came from the hall and we gave each other smiling winces as Pastor Dad arrived and began the silent reprimand. Mark stood from his knees and held me close enough so that my cheek was safe in his chest.

Pastor Dad saw our smiles and our embrace in the women's bathroom we'd already cleaned and rolled his eyes, reaching into his pocket with a smile. "It seems I'll need to make some space on my office walls."

The pastor handed his daughter a ten-dollar bill. Maureen took it and forced an evil laugh. Then she jumped up and down.

"I'm buying some itty bitty socks with this," She squeaked. "Oh, ye of little faith, Daddy. I *told* you!"

"Come on, Pastor Dad. You lost the same bet two years ago. When are you gonna stop betting against Maureen?" I received a kiss on my head as I spoke before Mark transferred his embrace to his dad.

"The day I die first and win *that* bet." Pastor Dad winked at me. "Call Paul before someone else does."

Maureen laughed fully as she walked back to her office. Pastor Robert journeyed back to his.

"This is a good thing!" Mark pulled my nails from my mouth but stayed his eyes on the television from the old leather couch.

"I was assuming this would never happen, so I didn't plan accordingly. I wanted to finish school. I'm due in January. I *knew* I should have taken more classes. I could have graduated by now."

Mark smiled within the dream world, ignoring the tone of my worried rant. "January. Our anniversary is in January."

"Mark! Aren't you worried about this at all?" At this, Mark paused the television and turned to me.

"Worry and fear are really just a call to trust. They are faithless emotions, Cinderella. *His* time, remember? Apparently, that's now."

"You were *totally* scared when we told my dad today."

He laughed. Pointed at me. "*Concerned.* For the life of my baby's father. But I survived to trust another day."

Mark nonchalantly un-paused the television as if he wasn't a gift from God. I curled up under his arm on the worn leather couch. I had a profound thought where regret had lived so long ago.

"I'm sure a lot of women say this to their husbands, but I actually *know* that this kid is really, really lucky. Really blessed. That *you* are her dad."

The television paused again as Mark felt the weight of the words. But he gave me a comical smile with a wink. "*His* dad. A boy." He corrected me with rootless confidence. "Robert Paul. For our dads. We can call him Robbie."

"Girl," I rebutted, with not even a gut feeling to back it up. And actually loving his name idea. "Amelia Grace. For your mom. And the church. But we could call her Mia."

"Ooo." He fell in love with it immediately but continued the banter. "We will have to consider that when we have a girl later."

I tapped his leg. "How many times do you expect me to do this?!"

"At least three, remember?"

I looked around dramatically and sighed. "So, about that house."

Chapter 39

Invitation

"Please, my sweet Cinderella honey bumpkins? *Please?*" Mark was on his knees on hardwood floors in a vacant house. We were accompanied by an amused churchgoer who was our realtor.

"Mark, I *despise* stairs. This house has stairs going right through the middle. Your sweet Cinderella honey bumpkins says, 'no way!.'"

"But what would be the fun of yelling 'Robert Paul Henley, get your butt down here!' without stairs? Come on. You know you've always wanted to do that."

"Boss. . ." I whined.

Mark rose and took my hands, swaying me side to side. He'd have been embracing me, but something more than a bump on my abdomen separated us, and hugs were awkward.

"Hardwood floors, fireplace, lots of bedrooms to fill. And it's a steal. We won't find anything else like this, Cinderella." Mark's voice was never far from convincing me, even to my own demise if he asked.

"Fine. *Amelia* and I will take another look around." The friendly battle continued.

Mark talked details with the realtor while I ascended the stairs again, entering each of the four bedrooms. Imagining toys and cribs and tiny angels to fill them. The previous owners had painted each room a different color. I entered a yellow room that brightened my mood at the top of the stairs. I walked across the hall to a light pink room with a large closet. Something I wouldn't change, as there was never enough pink in the world. I entered the master bedroom and smiled in warmth as I imagined a white duvet and rustic dresser to complete it. Then across the hall from the master bedroom I felt compelled to release a yelp when a butterfly flapped its wings inside my belly in the baby blue bedroom. Not the pre-lust kind. Something physically tangible.

I was scared. Worried, as I was with every sensation, symptom, or lack thereof in the pregnancy I never thought I'd get to experience. And nineteen weeks in, I just knew the baby was doomed, though everyone told me not to worry. We'd seen a heartbeat. Something I almost thought could cover my sin. But now I was scared to death, knowing the baby was lost because of the sensation. When it occurred again, I moved my hand to the spot, and felt the flutter against my fingers through my stretching skin. In an instant, I was on my knees in tearful worship.

Mark, who heard the yelp, ran immediately up the stairs, inquiring of my well-being in the panic of an overzealous father-to-be. He pulled me to my feet, and I explained.

"You *better* buy me this house, Boss. Robbie already picked his room."

"Huh?" Mark asked of my smile and concession. I moved his hands to the spot on my belly. Mark was suddenly filled with wonder when the baby proved his presence to his daddy as well.

Months later, when I realized the pain would lead to Robbie's birth, I was overjoyed. But the child had then come into the world with pain I couldn't have imagined. Dr. Moreno had cleared her schedule for the delivery, knowing something could still go wrong. She had been scared to administer an epidural to be sure my fragile womb would not rupture without me knowing. Mark had trusted her. But in the end, after two days of fruitless pain, Maureen had lost her cool with Dr. Moreno. And at that point, a scalpel was necessary to free my son from my womb.

I was witness as Mark changed before my eyes. He became a father at first grasp of his son. And when I thought I'd finally be content, something was triggered in my gut, and I didn't want to lose sight of my brand-new son. A mother is in love from the beginning. And childbirth is only the beginning of the pain. Because when the child must suddenly live outside her, she learns that love that deep is excruciating. Every threat was felt within me, and I wanted to change the world for him. For a year, I felt every vaccine needle, every bonked head and bruised shin as deeply as I experienced his enchanting laugh when Mark raspberried a belly or threw him far too high into the air. The black hair and dimples gave little clue that I was Robbie's mother. But the pain of my love for him left me no doubt.

My greatest fear was a promise once made by a broken young man named Jake. My son was over a year old, and as was ritual, I stood at the door of the room Robbie had chosen before birth. I watched his chest rise and fall with irrational anxiety that each breath could be his last.

I nearly jumped when arms wrapped around what newly made me insecure. Under my loose-fitting wardrobe were wrinkled and scarred freckles that had distanced me for good from any notion of a body that once adorned a lime green bikini Mark bought me on our honeymoon. I fretted constantly over a layer of fat my teenage years never saw. But Mark embraced them all warmly, seemingly unaware of my blatant flaws. He set his chin on my shoulder, watching the rising and falling chest with me in the dim nursery.

"Let's go try for the next one," he murmured, because he fell naturally into fatherhood, loving every moment of it. Hating even the eight hours a day when high school students called him "Mr. Henley" and he had to be away from his own son to counsel them. But I laughed nearly loud enough to wake the child when he suggested the further destruction of my body and pain in my soul. I had thought I'd start school again the next semester, should I find a trustworthy day care provider.

"One miracle is plenty, Boss." I smiled as Robbie made a little cooing sound in his sleep. But cringed in loving pain once again. Mark noticed.

"Jake is locked up for at least ten more years. If he's dumb enough to come find us then, I keep my nine loaded. Nothing is more important than you and Robbie. You know that. At the moment, I'm particularly focused on *you*, but—"

"I hate guns," I mumbled under my breath. We both knew full well my only firearm memory was of a shotgun in firelight.

"And stairs. And sand. And the cold. And me, apparently. Or you're completely oblivious—" He yawned through the rundown of my many earned fears.

To the counselor in him, my fears were warranted. But as he always told me: Sand borders the ocean. Stairs were the centerpiece of our church. It snows when it is cold. And Mark had extensive firearm training. Since Velma was now fully restored, he and the other men in the family made full use of Pastor Dad's treasured gun collection. I trusted Mark's levelheadedness more than most laws of physics. Therefore, my husband with a gun was more of a comfort than a fear. He knew this, and didn't entertain my fears with more words.

He instead sought to distract me. He inhaled deeply against my hair, squeezing me tighter as he kissed my shoulder. It was painful. Agonizing. The way his kisses moved from my neck to my heart like tiny electrical pulses. I smiled that once upon a time I'd worried whether the chemistry would follow easily after purity.

But I was stuck. He'd put purpose to his intentions. Purpose I may not be able to fulfill. He felt me tense up but knew I'd never do so without good reason.

"What's the matter?" With finesse he never lacked, he first closed Robbie's door with near silence, then turned me around, looking down into my eyes in the dim hallway. Following the "no secrets" mandate, I spilled.

"I don't mind just living our life and welcoming whatever work God wants to do. But it took so long to get Robbie. I don't know if my heart can handle actually 'trying' again. I don't want to feel like I've failed every month when we pick the right days and do the right things and still turn up not pregnant for years. It's already been a year since Robbie was born. I know it would be difficult again. If it meant not going through all that again or risking another *Hope* incident, I could be happy just having Robbie. He's perfect all by himself." I sighed, relieved to have released the burden.

Mark startled, scrambling in his heart for a way to un-mention having another child. Then when the words failed him, a smile spread across his face. Like the child wasn't his purpose at all. He backed up, trying to get me to follow him into our room.

Mark. So beautifully subtle and wildly clear all at once. There was a time when I had a powerful radar for such advances. A time before Mark. A time before Jesus.

"You're not actually asking me for another kid." I sighed the realization in a laugh, closing my eyes, embarrassed. "You just want—"

"Yeah, bad way to ask," He admitted with a smiled wince. Then snorted, stroking my hair. "Your warning label hasn't quite grown out, apparently."

I laughed, then sniffled. Took his hand. Whispered. "I love you."

"I love you too. If we'd never had Robbie, I'd love you. If we *only* have Robbie, I love you. Whatever work God does in you or me or in us both, I *love* you. You're still my bride, every day, no matter what. But. . ." Mark kissed my forehead tenderly. Kissed my hand before leading me into the room with the white duvet. "There is nothing wrong with giving God 'invitations' to work."

Chapter 40

Calling

I hobbled down the stairs onto the hardwood floors of what had become a disaster of a house. I was disgusted and tearful at the sight of the overflowing laundry and lack of counters due to dishes in the kitchen. I had always been considered the worst kind of clean freak. Yet today, I expended every ounce of energy descending the stairs against a doctor's orders. Dr. Moreno hadn't considered my responsibilities in the bedrest order.

I reached the bottom, only to be head-butted in the bladder by a little girl who I was sure would be a red head. I groaned as pain shot from my bladder in all directions, causing me to hunch over and seek the bottom post for support.

I looked up and a toddler was turning his back at the top of the stairs to slide down them on his stomach.

"Good job, Robbie!" Every perceived enthusiasm was only a result of the Holy Spirit preserving my soul in the hardest of times. When one awakens with zero energy to a demanding toddler and a baby that is not quite due to be removed from a broken womb, she has seen the hardest of times.

But God's glory is certainly shown when hard times begin to near the point of rock bottom. If we are delivered from there, we can be assured a powerful lesson in faith where God can speak. As Maureen said, our faith is not faith until it's passed the test.

After a day of chasing a frustratingly mischievous and energetic toddler, I put him down for his nap, then took to a slink on the couch that called my name several times that day. Not realizing I'd succumbed to sleep, I awakened when the front door opened to reveal an even more defeated and exhausted high school counselor. Today he looked more troubled than usual.

"Hey, Paige." His lackluster attitude recently made me believe that I truly did destroy him by marrying him and being perpetually pregnant.

"Hey, Boss." There was a question in my tone, knowing he was about to spill his guts, venting as usual.

He gave me a kiss hello, then sat on the couch next to me and looked around to make sure our son was still napping as he usually is upon Mark's arrival. He promptly unloaded.

"I'm helping people, right? Kids trust me to help them plan for life and college, and they come to me when their hearts are heavy. I point kids to Christ every day. I have a meaningful and fulfilling profession."

"Yeah. Am I supposed to disagree with that? It sounds like I am. What you do is important, Boss."

"Then why do I *hate* every minute of it?" Mark was near tears as he uttered it.

"Mark, you've wanted to be a counselor your whole life. Sometimes I think if you had gone back to school like you wanted—"

"No, Paige. My career and life choices revolve around my family, not the other way around. Obviously, God is in control of *all* of that, and I think maybe I wasn't listening to Him about this career. I just saw how happy Maureen was and wanted to be fulfilled like her. Paige. . .?"

"Yes?" A rare tear escaped his eye, and I used all my strength to sit up and take his hand.

"I had a student come on to me today. I should have seen it coming. I didn't see it. I mean, she's a good kid. At the top of her class. Strong Christian family. She's pretty spunky, but this was way out of character. And so, when I responded, or rather, didn't, she told me she was going to accuse me of being inappropriate with her."

"Mark! Boss, you would never do that. I know that, you know that. God knows that."

"And then she told me she figured out somehow that we've been married five years and you're still only twenty-three. She says no one will believe I don't have a thing for underage girls."

"Did she *seriously*?! We never had a *thing* when I was underage. Especially not an inappropriate *thing*. Even still, you're only four years older than me, and I was the age of consent. That would have been *legal*, even if we'd messed up the 'appropriate' part. *"*

Mark raised his hand to stifle my anger. "In short, I hate my job. But that's okay because I may not have it too much longer."

"Oh, my gosh. How old is this kid?"

"Fifteen. Just a hair younger than Dillon. She's a *baby*, Paige. I can tell there's some pain there, but it's like foggy. I don't understand these kids sometimes. I'm not like my sister. But I *can* see exactly why Dad doesn't allow people to be counseled by someone of the opposite gender at church. I don't know what to do. What proof do I have?"

I heard Robbie trying to escape from his room upstairs and started to stand up. Mark gestured for me to stay seated and got up to retrieve his son.

"I have to do *something* right today. And you are on bed rest!" He was also able to mask his pain and fear with enthusiasm at the top of the stairs when I heard him exclaim, "Hey, buddy!"

I stayed up an hour after Mark went to bed, praying over the situation and seeking God. Suddenly I received a clear message directly into my heart. It was slightly out of my own character, though well within the character of Christ. I was hesitant for a moment, wondering if I was mistaken. But when I felt more compelled to birth the instructions than the child inside me, I set my sights to obey.

The next morning, I dropped off Robbie at the church with Maureen, who prayed for me before I continued on my mission. I entered the office of a Christian high school and spoke to the young receptionist.

"My goodness, Mrs. Henley! You should be at home resting." She was not the only one who was shocked that I could even walk, whale-like as I was.

"I know, but I've been told I need to speak to a student. Angela Holley? Is she present today?" I heard the click of keyboard keys as I looked around the office to avoid my husband. "Is Mark in?" I added.

"No, he is over at the community college dropping off some paperwork. Angela. . .is in Chemistry right now. Want me to call her up?"

"Yes, please. Just send her into Mark's office, if you could."

I opened the door and sat behind Mark's desk, smiling as I saw the order and organization that defined my husband. Complete with dustlessness and nondescript stack of papers in a tray. I heard a knock at the windowed door and watched a beautiful young girl enter. Her skin was a gorgeous shade of deep brown. She completed her outer mask with extremely long false nails and purple contacts. I saw barely a shred of what she actually looked like under the makeup and the red wig she wore. I also knew she was barely within the code associated with her uniform. When baby Amelia began to dance within me, it was clear I'd been led to the proper decision.

I stood to greet her with much effort. "Hello, Angela. I'm Paige Henley. Mr. Henley's wife. It's wonderful to meet you." I shook her hand but looked into the shocked and shameful eyes. She refuted defensively.

"Wow, you *are* young. You know I could have you arrested for talking to me without a parent here?" Her voice had a deep, sultry timbre that her attitude did not do justice.

"I'm not actually sure about that. Regardless, I just wanted to *meet* you, okay?"

"You think your fat belly is going to stop me from reporting your nasty husband?"

"Angela, while I'm fully aware of what the truth is, considering my husband is the most decent person I know, I didn't come here to get you to pity me so you'd do the right thing. The truth will come out. I'm not as worried about it as he is." I smiled at her. "Can we just sit down for a minute? It's pretty painful for me to stand." I ignored any emotional response my hormones attempted to bring out.

She complied, searching the ground for more insults as I sat in Mark's chair again. "You only know what he *told* you is the truth."

"Actually, the truth I know came from the Holy Spirit. And from experience. Mark—Mr. Henley, bless his heart—is so *blameless* in this respect that it went right over his head." I saved the air from more bitterness and falsehood.

"*Blameless?*" Angela snapped spitefully. I was determined to reach past her cold outer shell. I did so with honesty. I waited for the breath of silence, then began with that I didn't know how, but I knew to be true.

"Angela, here's what I'm pretty sure is going on here." I sighed. "You're pregnant. It's early on in the pregnancy, but you've known for a couple of weeks. Your parents are strict and would likely not be very accepting of their fifteen-year-old being pregnant. Also, the father of the baby, who probably looks at least a little like Mr. Henley, is being a jerk and doesn't want to claim the baby as his. But your parents don't like him anyway. You're realizing why about now, so you were looking at your options."

"How—?" Her deer-in-the-headlights face barely asked it.

"At some point, or maybe over the course of your entire life, your parents must have made it abundantly clear that if you become pregnant out of wedlock, there would be severe consequences. Is that. . .?" I wondered.

"When my parents were growing up, people around them had babies out of wedlock all the time, and they made sure they did better for me. They've always told me if I made that mistake, I was no daughter of theirs. They'll kick me out when I tell them." Angela shared, showing some remorse.

"Unless, for some reason, it wasn't your *fault*." I nodded understanding. "For instance, if the baby's father was thought to be someone in a position of trust. But someone with enough integrity that if he'd been weak enough to give into the wiles of a teenage girl, would also claim the baby as his without a paternity test."

"It sounds really stupid when you say it like that." Angela rolled her eyes.

"'Stupid' isn't the word I'd use." I smirked. "From experience, I'd use the word 'desperate'. But stubborn, righteous Mr. Henley wouldn't sleep with you. Frustrating. Trust me, I know. The guy wouldn't even let me ride in his *car* before we were married because of the slight *chance* that someone might *think* he might be *tempted* to be inappropriate." I released in one comical breath. "Because even to be accused of something like that follows you your whole life. Even when you're a man like Mr. Henley, who has fought his whole life to not be that guy."

"I know. I *am* desperate, Mrs. Henley. My parents burned all their bridges when they got married and left home. I have no other family besides them. Nowhere to go. Gabe broke up with me when I told him. All my friends stopped talking to me when I started dating Gabe. I don't even have anyone to *tell*. I'm completely alone." Angela sniffled. "I didn't know what to do."

"I figured as much. Someone with someone to talk to wouldn't be near as desperate," I whispered. Sniffled. "I've been where you are. It broke my heart, Angela. I just wanted to come talk to you and let you know that you're *not* alone."

"But I *am*. You're so lucky. You have a good husband like Mr. Henley. I'll never have that. I made stupid choices, and I'm scared to even ask God for forgiveness because I never thought I'd stray so far." She sobbed. "I just have to have an abortion now. That's the only way to fix this."

At that point, every passion in my soul caused me to reach out and take hold of the young girl's hands, demanding the focus of her eyes. I barely took notice of the swollen freckled hands that wouldn't even house my wedding rings at that point. I was desperate to speak into this young woman's life.

"Angela, there is no 'just' about an abortion. Mark said you're an outstanding student. So, you might go to college, have a successful career. You might find yourself in a fairy tale romance one day. You might have more children someday whom you love deeply," I didn't control the change in my voice that came with the tears, "But you will miss that one baby every day for the rest of your life. You are not. *Ever*. Alone. This sucks *really* bad where you are right now. I won't sugarcoat that. But God has something better in mind for you. I *promise*. Please let me help you see that."

Angela believed me, and I wrote down Maureen's name and phone number to give to her. I consoled an inconsolable student and felt a flare explode in my spirit when she thanked me through tears. A few minutes later, she walked out of the room, running straight into Mark outside his office,

"Morning, Miss Holley."

She looked up at him. "I'm sorry, Mr. Henley. I wasn't *myself* yesterday."

Mark squinted into her eyes. "Forgiven. Is everything—?"

"Congratulations on your new baby." She walked quickly away as Mark looked at me, stunned.

"Did you threaten her? You gotta be careful with stuff like that. She's a minor, Paige," he whispered with intensity.

I laughed at my fearful husband. "No. It seems she has a strained relationship with her guidance counselor, so I pointed her in the direction of a more suitable one. She's a good kid, like you said."

He looked at me, blinking and squinting, unable to find words or understanding. I stood on my toes with much effort and kissed his cheek. "See you at home, Mr. Henley."

Just outside the office, I watched Angela walk right into a passing period between classes. I had to do a double-take when she accidentally bumped shoulders with the barely sixteen-year-old Dillon. Even with braces and buzzed hair, the boy eerily resembled his mother.

"Hey, Aunt Paige. Normally 'bed rest' means you use a *phone* to contact Uncle Mark." He teased. I gave him a sarcastic squint of a smile.

"Funny. You're getting better with the 'joke' thing." I teased right back at his rare deviance from stoicism. "Anyway, I had to sort something out. Talk to a student. How's school?"

"Well, I still don't believe that continuing at a Christian high school instead of accepting my already earned diploma is going to help me understand the true dynamics of teenage culture as my parents hope." He chuckled a little. "But these kids can still be pretty bad, so I'm learning a lot."

"You know, most people *hang out* with their peers, not observe and study them." I laughed at Dillon, who would always be a beautiful mixture of his parents' evils.

"I don't get along with most of my peers. Angela Holley? She came out of the office just before you did. Is that who you were talking to?"

"You know I shouldn't tell you that, Dill."

"Well, I get along with *her*. She's not like the rest of the girls. We used to be friends. I really wish she'd observe more and '*hang out*' less." At that, Dillon's warning bell rang for him to get to class.

I headed out the doors of the school, seeking the innocence of my two-year-old boy back at church. Dillon's innocence was only slightly less apparent than Robbie's. He happily adorned his uncle's old purity ring and had since our wedding. I decided it was my wish that all teenagers would share in Dillon's innocence. Often at night, that desperation sent a spear to my heart. But I knew I could never help them all. As an extremely pregnant stay-at-home mom, I couldn't help *any* of them.

I entered the church to find Robbie laughing wildly, being chased around the foyer by his Aunt, who had probably dosed him with the candy she kept on her desk for him. When I reached her in all my waddling, I told Maureen about the young woman I spoke with and that she should expect to hear from her. But knowing Maureen, she would find a way to approach the girl on her own. She confirmed it by asking her name, pen at the ready.

"Angela Holley? Angela. . ." She hummed a fond laugh. "That was. . ."

"Your little sister's name, I know."

"Well, yes. But Dill used to have a crush on Angela Holley until she started dating someone not-so-awesome and broke Dilly's heart."

"Oh. I bumped into him in the hall, and he mentioned something like that. . .in his own way. He was also complaining about you not letting him graduate early. Angela *is* a good kid, Maureen. Dillon is a good judge of character."

"And she's *gorgeous*, isn't she? He had her over to work on some project a while back. I do see the appeal. But now she's pregnant. Whew. Dodged *that* bullet. Exceptional work, Paige." Maureen always said things in just the right way for me to believe her. To feel whole and needed, even if for a moment.

"Let him graduate, Maureen. It's really the best thing for him." I slid in my thoughts on the family-wide debate. "He's not a kid. Like, was he *ever?*"

"They grow up so fast, Paige." Maureen tried to tell an eternally pregnant woman. "I'm still a scared unwed teen and feel Dillon moving inside me, so I don't know who that teenager is that keeps trying to become a young man. You spend so much time begging them to grow up and be independent, then by the time they do, all you want them to do is slow down and be your colicky baby again. Someday—and it'll feel like tomorrow—that'll make sense to you."

Mark arrived home an hour late but in the best mood I'd seen in years.

"You are so amazing. Ah! I'm so stoked to tell you everything that just happened." He leaned down and kissed me.

"I wish you'd called. I was worried." I whined.

"Paige, a woman almost got mugged in the parking lot before the women's study just now." Mark could not contain his out-of-place smile.

"And we are happy about this?"

"*Almost*, I said. I just felt like I needed to be standing outside for a minute after I talked to Dad about stuff. And all I did was walk over when I saw something was wrong. The guy ran off."

"Wait, you stopped a mugging? At church? And I didn't get a phone call?" I teased him in my pride.

"My dad gave me a job at the church. Full time. He says he'll pay me every penny the school has been giving me. I'm so excited! I get to clean toilets *and* carry a gun as a security officer since I have my permit. He'd been considering training a few of the ushers. The current security guards have missed some important stuff and don't actually *care* about the church."

I laughed approvingly, "That's great, Boss!" It's as if he was returning to his love.

"I love people. But I'm no counselor. I just want to serve God. To be something important without people knowing I know all their secrets. But you? What you did today is something my *sister* would do. What got into you?"

"I'm sorry. Are you mad? I really felt like it was what I needed to do."

"Mad?" He chuckled. "Dad wants to hire you immediately. But he prefers you finish your bachelor's first."

"I'm in no state to clean toilets again." I frowned at the swollen feet atop the coffee table.

Mark laughed a little, "He wants you to be a full-time counselor. Maureen says you did something today that none of her staff have ever done. She said it took you five minutes to earn a girl's respect, figure out she was pregnant, and talk her out of getting an abortion. If that's true of the pistol that is *Angela Holley*, you are extremely gifted. And we know Maureen's a Daddy's girl and gets whatever she wants. She wants you. ASAP."

"What if it was a fluke?"

"How did it feel? Doing all that for Angela?"

"That was all God, Boss. I still don't even know what I said. But it felt so good. It felt right. Like how it felt when I walked in the church the first time. Or when I met Maureen."

"Like when Robbie was born?"

"No," I laughed. "Not quite like that. But pretty amazing."

"So, it's a done deal, then? You get six weeks to recover after they cut this baby out. And then you go to school next semester, and I clean and protect the church. And we tag team with the kids from here on out."

"This is crazy! Are we really considering this?"

"Insane. But I've learned it's futile to argue with the Holy Spirit."

Her cry was robust and unrelenting. Her birth, right on schedule. Her hair was redder than mine. Her daddy, lovely in even a hospital blue hair cap, did not lose sight of her. I knew that in a couple weeks of sleepless nights, I'd be annoyed with that demanding cry. But as I watched Mark comfort brand-new little Amelia in an operating room, her cry covered a void. It was a love song. A hymn. A joy.

I laughed in joy, even amid drugs and discomfort as I was repaired upon a cold table, especially at the blonde woman who was standing just outside the operating room, peeking through the glass. Just like she was *not* supposed to do. And yet there she was, bawling her joyful eyes out, following her own perfect set of rules.

We arrived a few minutes late for my graduation rehearsal after a morning of rushed showers and wet hair, diapers and tantrums and stress. I ran inside while Mark took the children to save spots for the whole family for the graduation. During the ceremony, I glanced up at them with exasperation when I saw that Mark was struggling to keep control over the children. It was the children's cousins that saved him from insanity when Amelia, or "Mia" began screaming at the top of her lungs, becoming "that disruptive child" at the ceremony. Lane took Robbie, the wild taming the wild. And Dillon took Mia. One gentle spirit, reminding another of her place.

I met up with them all after the ceremony. They found me easily because of the crimson braid beneath my cap. I hugged them all with happiness.

"Well, it took me a little time, but I told you I could do it, Daddy." I addressed my father. Proud of not only finishing a psych degree, but adding a counselor certification program.

"I still can't decide if I'm more proud of the degree," He replied, "Or of the grandkids you gave me. Either way, I'm proud, Sweet Pea."

I kissed my proud husband and children and hugged my nephews, who had both surpassed my height at that point. Then I looked with dark circled eyes at the ones which had conquered all.

"How did you do this, Mrs. Shrink?" I inquired of the school and family combination. She, of course, was delighted to answer the question.

"Same way you did. I went almost completely insane, and every day I failed miserably at something. But we are both alive, right?" Mark and I both appreciated her raw truth with tired sobs of laughter.

"Alright kids, let's go celebrate the newest member of Maureen's counseling ministry. With food and stuff." Pastor Dad hugged me, and we walked together toward our vehicles.

Mark hipped a red-haired toddler. I took a rambunctious three-year-old's hand. And we both left room for our hands to join together, to fail a little less that day. But in Christ, it was all a success.

I open my eyes. By the power of Christ, I finally open my eyes. But all is bright around me. I cannot delineate walls from ceiling from floor. All is a white blur. Am I indoors or out? And is the difference significant when I'm uncertain of my whereabouts in either case?

When my eyes adjust, I see that a person in white is sitting in front of me. A woman that was difficult to see. She is blonde, wearing colorless clothing that causes my eyes pain in its splendor. Her hair hangs as golden strands on her shoulders and it takes me a moment to recognize her.

"Maureen?"

"Paige."

"I think I'm confused. I thought I woke up."

"You're not confused. You are where you are."

"That's confusing." I stand and look around. I am no longer a child in the woods. But still, I hear the stream in its tranquility. Outdoors. Near the stream, I decide. Yet as my gaze shifts in all directions, I see only white.

I feel Maureen touch my hand. "Walk with me." She says this and takes my hand as a mother to her child. As a sister to lead a sister.

Chapter 41

Blind

"You got a Valentine, mini Romeo?" The thirteen-year-old opened the door as I entered the church.

"No. I have a girl I like, but someone else sent her a rose at school today." Lane headed to a sanctuary and group of musicians that awaited him, bike helmet under an arm, guitar strapped to his back. His talent and work ethic had landed him on the worship team nearly full time.

"Bummer. What about that Heather McHardy? She's sweet, right?" I asked about Emma's not-so-little sister. Heather and Lane grew up together in the church and had always been buddies. The tomboy was taller than all the girls *and* boys in her grade with dark curls like Emma's, dark mysteries of eyes, and a heart of gold in both beauty and purity.

"Well, yeah. Feather's my best friend."

"Feather?"

"Yeah, it's just a nickname. . .thing." Lane laughed a little. "She likes feathers. Long story."

"Like how Uncle Mark calls me Cinderella?" I smirked.

"No. Because Feather is my friend. And *that's* some weird lovey-dovey pet name. Feather's not really my type." The handsome young man flipped a wild curl from his face with juvenile conviction. His voice was in a fragile state, but I suspected it would end up rivaling the depth of his father's in a few months. I giggled, because to me, he was the five-year-old who had stolen my heart and made me long for motherhood just moments before, it seemed.

"You're thirteen. How do you have a type?" I couldn't contain the laughter, never having given into the sensitivity society says is due a young man's heart.

"Aunt Paige, I have to find someone at *least* as pretty as you, or I'll be sad forever." Lane put his hand to his chest at the flattering joke and walked backward toward the sanctuary with a half smile. I snorted a laugh but worried that he bore far too much charm for his age, just as he always had. I considered telling Lane that Emma, of enviable height

and countenance, was awkward and plain at age 13. Just like
Heather. I also thought to tell him that Mark called me
Cinderella when he was only my friend. But I suspected that
in a few years, or maybe months, I wouldn't have to tell him
any of that.

Ever since I cleaned up after a wedding with my best
friend at age seventeen, Valentine's Day made a stark turn
from the shallow indiscretions of my youth. That day, I
expected my annual pink roses and a fancy dinner out with
my husband, sister, and brother-in-law without the kids. I
had returned to the church from dropping off my three- and
five-year-old children with my dad. I waited impatiently for
my companions for the evening to arrive or become available.
But God put in my path a task before I could enjoy my
evening. I obeyed.

Angela was becoming frustrated with the two-and-a-half-
year-old that was running about the foyer. She was working
alone at the information desk, as it was Ruth's afternoon off.
Though I was finally receiving a break from my own children,
I was reminded that the barely eighteen-year-old was a single
parent, and breaks were rare.

Angela was ten times more beautiful than she was the day
I met her in my husband's old office. She had given her life to
Christ. She had abandoned her purple contacts and wig, and
a Light shone through her. At the birth of her son, she began
a journey of tiny dreadlocks that now grazed her shoulders
gracefully.

"Hey, Tucker!" The beautiful little boy ran and embraced
me.

"Babe!" His precious version of my name.

"Let's go see if the band is playing!" Angela thanked me as
I walked away with her son in my arms.

Tucker belly laughed heartily as I bounced him up and
down in my arms. I'll never understand how his father made
a choice not to claim him as his own, leaving a scared teenager
to raise him. Or how Angela's parents threw her out as soon
as her belly's plot became obvious. But I thanked God for
bringing the little family through the doors of a church that

forgave her without question. She and Tucker quietly occupied a basement apartment of which we were all fond.

Maureen counseled her until about six months before that Valentine's Day, when she started coming to me. I suspect that had something to do with the way Dillon looked at her. While Angela was eight months pregnant with Tucker, I remember Dillon asking her about the baby's name in the foyer that spoke. She had decided on Tucker, her late grandfather's name.

The conversation, I remember, had brought a rare smile to the young woman's face. The then sixteen-year-old Dillon had thought the name was meaningful. And even though the pregnant teenager had been at her most shameful and awkward, Dillon had thought Angela was radiantly beautiful.

He'd been a friend to her when no one else was willing. He was there for her. Helped her move into his grandfather's basement. He'd been just outside the room when Tucker was born and driven them home from the hospital and gotten them settled. Dillon insisted that Angela be included in Christmases and family events. He usually refused to respond to questions about the relationship. But he was in love with her. That much was clear to me.

When I exited the sanctuary after dancing to worship music with the child, I saw a precious sight that Maureen would be frantic over. The barely nineteen-year-old Dillon leaned nervously at the information desk, gently waving a rose. The rose was intended for Angela. The two were alone in the foyer. My jaw dropped as I canvassed the area with my eyes for the gossip buddy with whom I shared my life.

I silently begged Tucker to remain quiet as I listened from behind a staircase. I could only make out a few words.

"I have a son, Dillon."

"Come on, Angela. You know how much I love Tuck."

"He's a handful."

"He could use a *Dad*. Jesus Christ Himself was raised by a stepfather."

"Stop, Dillon."

"You're going to start running out of excuses, Angela."

"Not until after you run out of patience, Dillon."

"Love is more patient and powerful than apprehension."

I could barely contain the gossipy bubbles inside me. Even at twenty-six, nearing a decade of marriage, I flipped for a good love story. But I was surprised at the irony. Dillon was finishing Bible College, having gotten bored of high school and accepting his diploma two years early. Angela was a struggling single mother who barely obtained her own high school equivalency, and only with Dillon's help. Of course.

A pair I couldn't have guessed would find one another, but one that worked quite well. Angela could be a spitfire at times. Stubborn and enigmatic. But Dillon was taught about leadership and respect from Dave, who certainly knew how to handle a spitfire of a wife.

At that moment, Dave was walking in the front doors of the church with his own set of roses to unload. I released Tucker, who bolted toward Dave, yelling some adorable version of his name. Dave, who would turn thirty-eight that year, picked up the boy with ease as I came from behind the pillar. Angela recognized that I had to have been there before.

As the bold counselor I'd become, I went straight to the place of greatest tension in the room. Angela scooted the rose she'd received under the overhang on her side of the information desk. She and Dillon smiled at me far too innocently. Dave walked over and placed Tucker in Dillon's arms before tiptoeing toward his waiting wife's office in the hall.

Tucker lay his head on Dillon's shoulder. He had danced and sang with me. He had run to Dave to be turned upside down playfully. But with the nineteen-year-old Dillon, he had found his safety. Dillon swayed slightly from side to side with the young boy in his arms.

I smiled among them and nodded approvingly before two strong caramel hands joined each other around my waist with hot pink roses tied with a ribbon. He was in something freshly pressed and collared. But before I responded with more than a smile, I met Angela's eyes. Something in my spirit beckoned and commanded me to speak into the mounting silence. I realized somehow that it was the right time, and that I was the only person who could speak the truth from within my husband's embrace to a young woman's heart.

"I suppose you are only as worthy as your Redeemer." Simple words for me to say. But Angela seemed to breathe them into her lungs like medicine. She nodded through a tear, and Mark pulled me away, one arm still securely around my waist. Maureen and Dave met us in the hall.

"Ready for our date, you two?" Maureen was all crooked smiles.

"Unbelievably." I expressed my need for a break and yawned in my nonchalant expression of gossip. "Did you know about your Dillon and Angela? I knew there were some pretty serious *feelings*, but I didn't know—"

Maureen and Dave glanced at one another before we were violently pulled to a corner that was out of view of the foyer. Maureen whispered. "Is he doing it again?"

"Doing what? What did I walk in on?" I was worried, especially when Mark seemed to understand.

"She's been torturing him for a week!" Mark whispered. Maureen shushed us to allow the foyer's ear canal a voice.

"Dillon, you can't keep asking me that. I don't need you to rescue me. God is taking care of me." Angela was speaking quietly, with intensity and determination.

Dillon matched her intensity. "Well, what if God *wants* me to rescue you and take care of you? It would be the highest honor to be used in that way, Angela. But that isn't even the primary reason I want to marry you."

I gasped, feeling a bit betrayed, but more in wonder. "You're kidding. Why didn't I know about this?"

"Maybe she's just really not interested," Dave whispered, disappointed for his firstborn and almost ignoring what I said.

"She is," I whispered with complete confidence. My three companions looked to me for an explanation.

"Did she tell you? In counseling?" Maureen's whisper was intense. A desperate plea to find the truth. She never "saw" a situation when her sons were involved. She had looked at individual photos of strangers and determined they were in love with each other. But she honestly had no idea how

Angela felt about her son. To irritate her fully, I addressed the rarity.

"She didn't have to." I smiled at the five-minute-old memory of the way Angela had smiled at Dillon cradling Tucker.

"Alright, Junior Shrink. My Dillon has *proposed* to this girl at least three times now. If she is *so* interested, why is she humiliating him and letting him believe she doesn't love him?" Maureen rebutted in quiet, hurting for her son.

"The only reason Dillon wasn't valedictorian is that he was halfway done with a bachelor's degree when their class graduated. He's well-liked in college. He's handsome. *Pure.* He'll probably be a Senior Pastor somewhere in a few years. He's bright and godly and accomplished. Angela dropped *out* of high school the same time as him, but because she was a teen mom. She was an outcast. By most people's standards, she's not worthy of being a pastor's wife. She is letting him believe she's not interested *because* she loves him. Wants the best for him. She doesn't believe that it's her." I exited my explanation and turned to them with a jest. "She is a firecracker! Can he handle her?"

Maureen and Dave chuckled. But Mark didn't just hear what I said. He saw the mirror to our past that we were hearing from the foyer. I knew this because he squeezed me from behind suddenly.

"He can handle her," Mark whispered to me, and the four of us were fondly reminded of a love story long ago.

Then we looked back at the foyer when it erupted with a rare, if not brand-new sound. Dillon, always prim and proper, laughed uncontrollably. At first, I assumed that Tucker was being Tucker and bringing Dillon to such joy with his actions.

"You better not be joking with me!" Dillon bellowed with jolly.

"Why would I joke about this?" Angela said with her usual hip sway of an attitude and then an unusual giggle.

"I don't want you to make a rash decision just because of my eavesdropping family." Dillon still had a smile in his voice, and we allowed the snorted laughter from our corner.

"Dillon. . ." Angela sighed, and then pulled him by the wrist into our vision. She took Tucker from Dillon's arms and let him run into the hall. Dave grabbed him up and held him when he arrived. Dillon was confused but stayed with Angela a moment in the foyer as we watched now with permission.

"I *love* you. You know that. Are you sure about this, though? Marriage is a huge thing. And Tucker is still my first responsibility." Angela glanced over at me a few times as she spoke to Dillon. I smiled warmly when she did.

"Oh! Here's your ring. And I have something else to ask you." Dillon said as he was taking a ring from his coat pocket and placing it on Angela's finger, to our absolute delight.

"Something else? This was hard enough, Dillon." Angela was concerned.

"Where is Gabriel these days?" Dillon winced a little. We were equally as taken aback as Angela.

"After he gave up all parental rights when he refused to pay child support, I haven't heard from that jerk. I don't have any ties to him. It's long over, you know that. Why would you even ask?" Angela was worried Dillon was accusing her of something. But I saw exactly what was going on. I turned and whispered to Maureen and Dave.

"You guys have an amazing son."

"Well, of course. But why do you say that?" Maureen's blind spot was ever so amusing. I simply smiled and nodded at the foyer. Dillon answered.

"Angela, you're stubborn enough that even after I marry you and we hopefully have other children, you'll still consider Tucker to be *your* responsibility. But I don't just want to marry you. I'd like to *adopt* him." At Dillon's words, Angela was overwhelmed. He stood with a smile, and she backed up, covering her mouth with a gasp as tears welled in her eyes.

She squeaked a whisper. "Why are you doing all this? It's completely 'illogical.' Most guys would have given up by now." Angela knew Dillon well.

"Well, love isn't always logical. And it certainly doesn't 'give up.'" Dillon chuckled his usual confident snigger as he pulled Angela against him into a loving embrace with the difficulty of awkwardness. Something I was willing to bet he'd never done. "Just stop breaking my heart, okay?" He cooed the resolve almost too close to her for it to echo our way.

"I'll do my best." Angela cooed right back. And I knew what was coming, though it wasn't the way I saw this day going.

The shock occurred with ease. The romantic in me smiled. Dave chuckled. Mark laughed and squeezed me. And Maureen let out the most horrified gasp I've heard from a human being. Because her prospective pastor of a son was setting aside all reason and logic and using the passion of his soul to let us witness his very first kiss.

At its conclusion, we stormed the foyer before the bewilderment left their eyes. Mark and Dave nearly tackled Dillon, who was looking more like a man these days. Angela threw her arms around me. She whispered a tear-filled "Thank You" in my ear.

Maureen questioned me with her eyes. I smiled and pointed up to the ceiling. Maureen rolled her eyes and shook her head, just like every time she begged me to take the glory for something that was all God's. Dave invited the third couple on our double date.

"But what about Tuck?" The young mother had her priorities in order. We then heard a whistling man and called his name in unison.

"Pastor Dad!"

My father-in-law came into view.

Dillon had collected the toddler into his arms. "Want to watch your soon-to-be great-grandson?"

The man laughed his rustic laugh and jostled the shoulder of the young man with a comforting hand. "Of course! But one of these generations has to let me retire sometime!"

We spent dinner laughing, wedding planning, and advice giving. The generations provided no gap at all for a memorable Valentine's Day. We looked forward to a wedding the following summer. I'd been given permission to conduct premarital counseling for the young couple, but as was routine, Maureen would coordinate the wedding.

Mark scooted me out the restaurant door before dessert, in enough time for a quick trip home before the promised pickup time for our children.

"Did I ever tell you about how my family found out I was in love with you?" He crooned, walking backward into our bedroom and unbuttoning his shirt.

"You've told me a lot over the years, Boss." I reminisced, following him willingly.

"It was over Thanksgiving dinner," he continued, looking me over. Deciding his next move. He pulled me close. "We'd been working together just a couple weeks, and Maureen asked me how we were getting along. I told her and the rest of the family I was *marrying* you whenever God said the word. They thought I was joking. Then they told me I was confused. Then crazy. Because it was just a couple weeks. But I honestly don't remember knowing you and not *loving* you." He spoke between kisses to my neck. A common occurrence. Wooing me with all his soul, as if I'd have made another choice than to welcome his love.

That time the words distracted me. He'd taken me back to a time when I wasn't aware that he and Maureen were siblings. And as we fell into our silent ritual of *eros*, my heart filled with betrayal because questions had plagued me all evening. Because of my distraction, I felt shameful when it was over. Something that hadn't occurred with Mark. Not ever. We weren't supposed to have secrets, and that made my blood boil.

After a time, I found myself brushing my hair, and Mark remade our bed before we headed out again. And the lament made its way to my lips.

"Why didn't I know about Dillon and Angela?" I finally asked. My voice trembling.

"Dillon isn't like me. He doesn't exactly announce things at family gatherings. But he and I are really close, and he told me in confidence. That's the only reason I knew. They've been discreet, and they're not like 'dating,' which is why the proposal caught her off guard, I think. He told me Angela didn't even want to tell you how they felt in sessions. So, don't feel bad for not picking up on it." Mark carelessly tossed the accent pillows onto our bed. I walked over and fixed them, irritated that he could never remember their arrangement.

"That's not what I meant. I mean why didn't *you* tell me? When did we stop talking about everything and everyone? Do you not trust me anymore?" He heard my tone change to fit the wound.

"Wait, are we *fighting?*" His eyes widened, and he first panicked, then got defensive and sarcastic. "Because yeah. We should definitely start a fight on *Valentine's Day*. This was supposed to be romantic." Mark was embittered as he tied his black converse sneakers against the bed.

"Oh, you mean the day I found out my husband keeps family secrets from me despite our clear 'no secrets' rule? *So* romantic." We both married rebels. Fighters. Masters of cruel quip. And amid the many benefits of that, it could turn nasty quickly. Fearlessly, I declared war.

But Mark began laughing. Some closed-mouthed, high-pitched, bitter mockery of a laugh. "Oh, *secrets*." He said with cruel sarcasm. "Wasn't gonna bring this up tonight because we were having a good time together, but now that we're accusing one another of *secrets. . .*"

My heart was pounding at his accusatory tone. Some dormant memory alighted, though it came in through my spirit, not my mind, so I couldn't explain my sudden fear. I swallowed hard and avoided his eyes for the rug below. "What, Mark?"

I heard him approaching me slowly as he spoke. "You were in the shower this morning, and I answered your phone when you got a call from the hospital. They were confirming your appointment. Your *hysterectomy*. I told them it was a mistake! My wife would surely not schedule such a drastic procedure without telling me. But they said the order came straight from Dr. Moreno's office. And they had all the consent forms signed and everything. How's *that* for a secret?"

I panicked. And sniffled at tears. "I was gonna tell you."

"When?" He snapped off the end of my sentence. A level of anger I'd never seen in him. Meekly, I responded.

"Doc. . .Doctor. . ." I started in a stutter, plagued by that unspoken memory. Then I spoke quickly, so I was heard before the tension snapped under the hostility. "Dr. Moreno said I was on borrowed time, and another pregnancy might be disastrous. She said I was already showing signs of some serious problems."

"Would've been good information to tell your *husband*. We could have planned this together. Instead of, 'Hey honey. How was your day?' 'Oh, it was great. I let someone cut out my womb. Meant to tell you.'" His anger was rising, and he was stepping toward me. I took some steps back, but I knew the dresser along the wall would soon block my escape. The memory was moving into my limbs as a reflex. I'd never been more scared of him.

"Mark, I'm sorry. She said she wanted to do the surgery herself, but her schedule was filling up fast. And that I needed to make an appointment or I could be waiting a *year*. I did, but it hadn't been confirmed. This was last week, and things have been so crazy. . .I was going to tell you. I promise. It's a major surgery. I know that."

"I thought we decided to let God work when it came to having kids. He's been so good to us. What happened to that, Paige?" Mark's anger was mixed with sadness. The combination moved that phantom memory to a chill down my spine.

"It would be extremely dangerous to have another one." I was trembling. Terrified. And backed, now, against the dresser. He was now inches from me, and lifted his hand quickly.

Before I realized I was the cause of the bloodcurdling scream, my ears and heart perceived the sound with sheer terror. I found myself in the fetal position on the floor in front of the dresser before I realized that Mark was merely reaching for his car keys—which at present, he dropped with a crash on the hardwood and used both his arms to embrace me.

He and I were both in tears. He was startled by the scream but realized its purpose immediately. He gritted his teeth and muffled into my shoulder.

"Paige, you *gotta* believe I'd never hit you. Why would you even think—"

"I know. I know. . ." I squeaked in a sob.

"You've never done that before." He was as shaken up as I, squeezing my trembling shoulders tighter.

"Neither have you. You were *so* mad at me." At this, my blurred vision met the glisten. And the intent of the stare was obvious to us.

"I'm not *him*. I don't care how mad I am."

"What is happening to me? It's like I was. . ." I trailed off, not knowing exactly where I'd been or what I'd been thinking.

"I'll make an appointment for us to see the shrink, alright? Nip this in the bud."

Both loving and hating Mark's solution, I agreed.

There is comfort in her hand. A whole and secure perfection that causes me great relief. A fulfillment of a nostalgia that haunts my every breath.

"Where did you say we were?"

"I didn't say," Maureen offers some purer version of the smile that knows all. "Walk with me."

I am weightless and have nothing solid on which to plant my own gravity. I walk for an eternity. I walk for a moment. I do not see it approach. But yet I am upon it—stream in the woods.

Chapter 42

Secret

"If you tell me what Angela left their premarital crying about, I will give you a raise." Even the worst of her manipulations was spoken as honey. Resistance was difficult at best.

"Not only would I do this job for *free*, but I'd be breaking *so* many rules if I told you that." I was masking emotional exhaustion with the laugh. I wasn't prepared for Maureen's intrusion into my office just moments after her son and his fiancée left a rough session.

"Gah!" Maureen plopped into the loveseat across from my desk. "You and your rules."

For some reason, against all anyone had ever told me, the mixture of work, church, family, and personal life had been nothing but a comfort to me. I always thought it refreshing to not have to tell the same story over and over because what happened at work followed us home and to social gatherings that usually only involved family. And yet, conversation was never dull. I never got bored with my family.

Our foundation and glue was the Lord. But often, we found our strength in Maureen. She was my best friend and sister. Still, after many years she served as my counselor in her covert ways, but was a mentor who believed I would surpass her abilities. I knew she was simply speaking honey when she said it. But I thrived on the honey. Such a strange convoluted, yet simple, compact life. I would not trade it, except at that moment I was feeling rather sick, physically and emotionally, after the session I just counseled. I faltered. And sighed. Her sons' secrets may have escaped her. But never a stray sigh.

"That sounds like shame, if I've ever heard it. I would *love* to help you clear that conscience." Maureen was shameless, and became more intrusively perceptive with age.

"Leave me alone, Maureen." I rolled my eyes and opened my laptop to take some notes about the recent session.

"Maybe someday." She softened as she leaned in. "You alright, Paige?"

I bit my lip as I typed, trying to decide whether to take the counsel. A similar, recent choice had caused the dilemma. I'd sought counsel and found a truth much harsher than honey.

"I'm great!" I lied. "I'm just trying to take some notes before I forget—"

"You're not getting any better at lying. Like when you tried to tell me last week you were actually considering forgiving Jake? *That* was especially terrible. I let it slide then because my brother was with you. . ." She trailed off. She was certainly in a cruel sort of mood.

"Maureen. I have to get this down so I can pray about what direction to take with your son's counseling. So, bye!" I tried. But she was unmoved.

"There's the sore spot," she growled out in satisfaction. "So, let me lay this out. Angela still hasn't forgiven Gabriel, has she? For abandoning her? And knowing my Dillon, he doesn't find that logical since he's been around since day one helping raise Tucker. Rough way to start a marriage. A lot of trust issues can come from unforgiveness. But I told you that when you thought my teddy bear of a brother was going to *hit* you." Maureen surmised or recited my exact memories and assessments. I wasn't sure which. "A good biblical counselor, which you are, would tell her that she can only truly move on and give all she has to her husband if she forgives her ex. And she *should* forgive because Christ first forgave us. Angela is close to understanding that, so she left here crying. Am I right? You're not even close to forgiving. So, you want to vomit right now after telling someone to do the very thing you won't. Thus, the shameful sigh."

Near tears, because we both knew how right she was, I was angered that she wouldn't let up. Seething. Fuming. And I launched a personal attack.

"What have *you* ever had to forgive? Did little brother cut your dolly's hair when you were little? You don't know a thing about forgiveness, Mrs. Shrink. If you did, you wouldn't ask me to do it like it's nothing. I can tell Angela how hard it is because I have *plenty* to forgive. You let me know when you can think of something harder to forgive than rape or attempted murder. Excuse me, 'aggravated assault in the

first degree.' *Then* we'll talk, oh great expert of forgiveness."
I attacked her with a fiery sort of bitter sarcasm before I
returned to my laptop, thinking I'd finally won. But just as
soon as I reset my hands at the keyboard, they were almost
crushed by the slamming screen. I looked up into a face filled
with the worst of a roaring fire. A head tilt that stopped my
heart. Then she simmered just as quickly, sitting back down
slowly from the stand required for the assault. Why did she
have to summon such self-control?

"How many times have I told you never to ask a question
you don't want to know the answer to?" She said as a mother.
"I don't say these things to waste my breath."

"Was that rhetorical?" I had not yet backed down. The
strength of my will was not yet broken.

"Unlike you, Junior Shrink, I would never ask someone to
do something I couldn't do myself. And you, regardless of your
talents, education, and life experience, do *not* know
everything." Maureen said this in the clenched teeth of anger,
which I couldn't say I'd ever seen her use in my presence.
Then she coughed once to cover the tears in her throat.

I was silenced into shame, regretting the mere thought of
picking a fight with Maureen. She inhaled. Looked around.
And for once, I felt I might finally become privy to her
methods. But she asked an odd question instead.

"How is Dr. Moreno these days? I haven't spoken to her
personally since Mia was born. I know you and Mark had your
pre-op consult. You did take him like I suggested, right?" Like
small talk. Like her hair wasn't just more aflame than my
own.

I flinched, searching for the best way to answer the
random questions. "Yes, we went together. And Dr. Moreno is
fine. Why do you ask?" I tucked a nervous hair.

"I'm sure glad she's taken such good care of you these past
several years. Angela, too. Can you imagine how much money
she's lost not taking a penny from either of you? Especially
with all *your* high-risk pregnancies and procedures. Tens of
thousands of dollars, I would imagine." She said with some
nasty form of sarcasm. "You've never wondered why?"

"Because she's nice? And feels bad about being instrumental in the loss of two of my babies?" I was trying to understand. Think on her level. But I took cues still from my hair, not relieving myself of fire.

A hum of a laugh preceded a conversation right-angle. "David and I were eighteen when Dillon was born. That was never the plan. We loved our life, but we had a rough start to our marriage. If you're not focused on God's strength, Satan likes to get into those rough areas and twist you in your weakest moments. For instance, the season Lane was in my belly and we knew about the aneurysm. I had to be on bed rest, so I took some time off school after my bachelor's degree. David was in med school, which requires a ludicrous amount of studying. Most years, we studied together, but since I was somehow running a household and taking care of our son while on bed rest, David found a brilliant fellow student as an alternative study partner. She was over pretty much every night for dinner. She and I got along like sisters, and Dill loved her. Sweet Christian girl with a pretty accent. And *so* intelligent. Her name was Eva. Eva Moreno."

"Yeah, I heard they went to med school together." Because of her demeanor, my anger changed to reluctant compassion, and I shut my mouth.

She leaned on my desk with an exasperated sigh. "One night, David and Eva relocated to the library like they sometimes did. He was usually gone for hours. So, I didn't wait up for him after putting Dillon to bed. That was all pretty routine then."

"Okay. . ." I questioned her detail-oriented self. She continued with the sniffle of a fight against tears she eventually lost.

"I have an impeccable memory, Paige. And my David doesn't cry. Drives me insane how even-keeled he is. He didn't even cry at our wedding. He shed a few tears when the boys were born, but other than that, he doesn't cry. With the exception of that night. When I woke up to him on his knees at the edge of our bed. Praying. And bawling his eyes out. I asked him what was wrong. I was really worried. He cried harder. I asked if everyone was okay. I thought maybe we'd lost someone. He looked me dead in the eyes. And told me the worst news I'd ever heard. I'd lost my mom. But that wasn't her choice, you see? Betrayal is something *so* much harder." Instead of waiting for my reaction with pleasure, Maureen looked to the ground, taking a tissue from my box. And she need not even say it before I sank into my chair with a burden of a sigh.

"You are—" I hiccuped for air. "*Not* about to tell me that Dave had an affair with her."

"I guess I don't have to." She smiled a little. "It lasted a month was all. David broke it off when she started to ask him to leave me. I'm grateful for the choice he made."

"And they—?" I was a counselor and knew that they varied. So, I asked her definition of an affair.

"My parents always taught me that a man who will sleep with a woman before he marries her has only proven he is capable of sleeping with someone who isn't his wife. He'd given into temptation with me, so. . ." She nodded. Tried to smile. And failed. "The *library*. How did I fall for that?"

"Bu-wha-how?. . .He did. . .and. . ." Some conglomeration of all the questions came forth before I chose to process in silence. I wanted to deny it. But I instead internally analyzed before I reacted, as Maureen had taught me. And every interaction she and Eva Moreno had ever had pointed to something deeper. Some glance I once perceived between Eva and Dave was explained. Eva's free and supreme care for me stemmed from something deeper. She had made sure I was healthy and could have children. Cared for *me*. But done it all for Dave. But even penance didn't run that deep. She still *loved* him. I waited for Maureen to look up at me again, so she could see I was done fighting and that I believed her. And when she saw, she spoke.

"I have never told another soul. So, everyone thinks my blood pressure shooting up so high that we almost lost Lane was a *freak* thing. I wasn't sure what direction I'd take in a career at that point. Until I decided not to see a counselor about this. I was so scared someone would tell me *not* to forgive them or to even suggest I *leave* David. And it was already hard enough to forgive him and stay *without* the opposition."

"Maureen. . ." I squeaked out in comfort, trying to summon my own inner counselor.

"I wouldn't want to be in your shoes, sweetie. But what happened to you when you were twelve happened once. And Jake is in prison. It's all in the past. Which can be hard to forgive. And that affair is in the past. So, I thought if I just forgave them once, I'd be free. But I realized I was wrong. Because *every day* when my husband heads off to work, I have to forgive him again. Otherwise, I can't trust him to work in the same hospital as her. Every time he reaches for me, I have to forgive him *again*. Otherwise, I'm convinced he really wants *her*." She swallowed hard. "And I do it all without anyone ever knowing except the Lord who forgave *me* first. You're so much better than me, little sis. If I can do it every day, you can do it *once*."

"Why didn't you tell Pastor Dad or Mark?" That's what I asked. But I was thinking of the depth of Maureen and Dave's love. Something I admired about them and had never questioned. I'd never think the seamless teamwork and constant sensual glances were born of something as simple as forgiveness. She always said that grace is a good teacher. And in going over the years of *philos, eros, Agape* and *storge* and abundant grace they shared, I barely remembered my question by the time Maureen answered.

"Mark was still a kid and had his own problems and Dad was dealing with that. This was mine to bear. And Mark doesn't do the secret thing." Maureen sighed, returning to herself.

"Me neither! How am I going to keep this to myself?"

"I didn't ask you to." And her smile came on like she hadn't experienced the worst parts of life. "I do, however, have a price for you knowing."

"I should have known." I rolled my eyes.

"A Paige secret."

"Yes," I chuckled in both sarcasm and awe at her perceptiveness, "Because I have one you don't know..."

She didn't skip a beat. "When I mentioned Eva, you flinched. You didn't do that the other day. What happened at your pre-op consult?"

"I don't know how I'm going to look her in the eyes again, but the other day she just wanted to postpone my surgery a bit. Til the end of the year or maybe the beginning of next year." I tried the half-truth with half open eyes.

And Maureen's happiness bubbled through moments after her worst confession. She smiled, counting aloud and on her fingers from a few weeks ago to the "end of the year." She of course came up with some convoluted way to land at forty weeks—gestation.

"You're pregnant again." She squealed when I rolled my eyes in agreement.

"Yeah, still in shock. We didn't even know until Dr. Moreno did a routine check at the appointment. She was pretty worried because it's extremely risky to carry another baby in this womb. That's why we were doing the surgery in the first place. How do you *know* this stuff?" I tried to say over her childlike clapping.

"I'm a super genius. *Or* my brother is worse with secret keeping than you are with lies. I'm just good at releasing them from others." Maureen nodded. Inhaled. Exhaled. "So are you. You're better than me, Paige. In so many ways. You don't even need me. You just need to deal with the source. Or it'll *destroy* you."

I rolled my eyes. "Can we not with that? Not today. I'm feeling awful, okay?"

She nodded, seemingly having to give in to devastation. Then brightened up just as quickly. "Oh! I can't wait to hold the new baby! It's been way too long since we had some symptom relief around."

I was feeling the onset of sleep as my hand was losing feeling from the grasp within my husband's. But in a habit we had never overcome, we were whispering into the night, far beyond what our children assumed was our bedtime.

"And she let you tell me that?" He asked, eyes drooping.

"Well, in her own way, yeah. Hard to believe, huh?"

"Yeah," he seemed in awe. "I figured with her Jedi powers, she'd have picked up on it by now."

"Huh? Dave told her when it happened. What was there to pick up on?"

"I'm sworn to secrecy." Mark showed his sleepy dimples.

"When has that ever stopped you?" I giggled, readjusting my aching hand.

"I actually hate secrets because of *this* secret." He didn't share in my jolly.

"Oh?" I didn't quite understand his meaning.

He took a moment to release his hand, running tender knuckles along the outer protection of his newest child.

"'The things you think you least deserve should be the things you treasure the most.' It's what Dad told Dave that night. Dave told us *never* to tell Maureen. But Dave came to us *first* after breaking it off with Eva. He thought Reen would leave him and wanted to make sure she'd be welcome back home with us if she wanted to. We weren't surprised when she ended up in the hospital that night. Anyway, since she didn't leave, he hasn't stopped making sure she never has a reason. Same reason you're so scared of something happening to the kids, even before they're born. You treasure them, because you think you don't deserve them." Mark met my eyes in the near darkness.

"Of course I treasure them. They're my babies! They are everything I'll never be. But I'm not protective because I don't deserve them. I protect them because you *do* deserve them." I paused for his kiss of gratitude. "I'm glad God is allowing us to do this one more time."

"Can it be a surprise? The gender?" Mark requested as a child. "And can I name this one and not tell you until the baby is born?"

"Putting aside the fact that, no, you probably can't keep that secret. That is a lot to ask of someone who likes to plan everything." I said through a laugh.

"We get to schedule a cesarean again and we have baby clothes from both Robbie and Mia. The bedroom is yellow. How much more birth planning do you need?" He laughed, then kissed me. "Please?"

Chapter 43

Breathe

I remember sitting at my desk, head against a photo-printed desk calendar of my children. I awakened to an alarm on a phone from Maureen's office. I looked at the clock and it was about a minute past what I remembered. Which meant I could finally leave for the day. I forced myself to get up out of my chair amid a backache to make the journey home. I was listening to Maureen moan and groan through the wall between our offices. I had just turned twenty-seven. She was just thirty-eight. Why did we sound and feel like a pair of elders?

Maureen eventually knocked on my office door, as she did when it was time to lock up, and I realized Mark was probably going crazy with the kids trying to finish cleaning. I wondered how much longer I could carry on with this pregnancy fatigue as I opened my office door.

"Hey." I blinked a sigh. Then squinted at Maureen's rub of her forehead. "You okay?"

"Am *I* okay?" Maureen giggled. "I left my migraine meds at home today, and I'm feeling it after having to tell a couple they should never get married. How are *you* feeling?"

"Awful. I think the baby is mining for gold in my spine today."

"Lower back?" Maureen wondered.

I nodded.

"Keep an eye on that. With Lane, I never really had a proper contraction. Just back labor until he turned at the very end."

"We have a while to go, Maureen. But thanks for your concern. I think we both just need to go home and get some rest." I surmised.

She agreed with a tired nod. Maureen and I walked into the foyer where I took a welcome lean against the information desk to combat the back pain. I remembered, only when Lane approached, that youth group was that night. He was with a familiar companion who was eager to come see me.

Heather retained all her sweetness, often displaying it in her angelic singing voice at the high school she and Lane attended. This would be their first youth group meeting, just barely Freshmen that September. Both of them split the weeks between youth and worship team.

Something often happens in the warmth of the summer between middle and high school. Lane had spent it at a church camp, playing in their worship band for younger campers. Heather had spent the summer in Pennsylvania, where Emma and Mike lived with their four stair-step children. All gorgeous curly-haired little girls.

Both fourteen-year-olds had succumbed to traditions of their formative years over the summer, just as I'd predicted. Lane left a tenor and returned a baritone, six full inches taller. Heather had left a scrawny little tomboy. She returned in a fashion that made mini Romeo's jaw drop upon their reunion. Today she was approaching in athletic pants hugging her hips and a plain gray t-shirt overtaken by free-flowing hair. But with beauty like hers, a paper sack would do her justice.

The two teens arrived at the counter. Heather was bursting with some manner of excitement but refused to tell me why. Lane translated in his monotone humor. "Feather wants to touch your belly, Aunt Paige."

I giggled. "Of course, Heather! Maybe you can wake the baby up!"

Giddily, she put her hands on my extra-large belly.

"Is it a boy or a girl?" She asked in her gentle, sweet tone.

"Mark won't let us find out. And I've yet to beat his name choices out of him."

Heather cooed, and Lane rolled his eyes, pretending to be too tough for the sweetness. The exchange was one I saw in any loving marriage, and I decided to give the two "friends" five years before they took the plunge. A bet with Maureen I decided to make later.

"I guess the baby doesn't wanna move for me." Heather took her hands away, disappointed. But Mark ran across the foyer, placing his hands on my stomach.

He felt around for a minute and then grabbed Heather's wrist and placed her hand on my upper right stomach.

"This one likes to hang out right here. Baby. . .wake up, little one." He said to my belly. Still no response. Until my children ran after their Daddy and stopped at my belly, talking incessantly. The baby, boy or girl, loved the company of an energetic brother and sister. This was to Heather's gasping delight, when she received a hard kick directly to the palm of her hand.

Heather thanked me and then ogled at what she probably perceived as her own little dream of a family and the way Mark looked at me.

"Hey Feather, we better. . ." Lane called her away as he backed up toward the senior high room.

"Yeah, I'm coming." She smirked.

"Hey, Lane. Do me a favor, and help Pastor Owen reset the room after? It really helps me out." Mark requested of his nephew.

"Sure!" Lane smiled, and the two friends were off.

Maureen peeked from behind the staircase and pretended not to see what was blatantly obvious. I said it aloud when the couple was out of the foyer's earshot.

"Five years. Ten bucks." I sing-songed into the nearly empty foyer.

"Hush. My baby Lane is never growing up or getting married. And by never, I mean *seven* years. He'll likely try to tough it out and finish college. . .and almost make it." Maureen said, creeping out from behind the place where she'd been spying on her smitten son.

"She's sweet, though," I told Maureen when she arrived.

"Precious." She put her hands over her heart. "I *love* that girl. But I have to pretend not to. It's my job as a mom."

"I'm pretty sure *Angela's* onto you."

"Shhh. . ." This received a roar of laughter from several people, because Angela was standing three feet from us with Ruth at the info desk, listening to the whole conversation.

But within the roar, I suddenly felt compelled to bury my head in my arms against the information desk. A sharp pain had afflicted my back, just like all day. Ruth, the first to notice, inquired about my health.

"Oh, I think the baby wants to be involved," I said with a wince—glad this was my last pregnancy.

Mark, however, was not convinced. He rubbed my back as he laughed with the others. I listened as Maureen asked Angela the whereabouts of both of their sons, Dillon and Tucker. Together, we learned. Running errands like a father and son. And then another pain set me to a lean against the desk. But this one subsided slowly, moving toward my belly button, turning everything in its path to stone. A bona fide contraction, out of the blue. But of course, when asked, I lied.

"Braxton Hicks. The fake kind. No worries." I then set my eyes to the clock on the wall, so I could time the next contraction. In just eight more minutes of wedding talk and Mark heading to the maintenance closet for all of the children's things, the next one hit.

"Mommy, are you okay?" My Mia was smart. She earned the right of her "warning label" but softened it with her father's charm and keen perception, even at three.

"Yeah, I'm okay, baby," I said just before another sharp pain hit me. Enough pain for me to groan.

"How many weeks are you now, Junior Shrink?" Maureen inquired.

"Thirty-three and a half. We've got a couple *months* to go, almost." I wondered why Mark was taking so long in the closet with Robbie.

"Right, so why are you having contractions?" Angela said with attitude and from a mother's experience.

"I'm not." I lied with a laugh. "My back is just killing me."

"Mmmhmm." Angela and Maureen said in unison with a raised eyebrow each.

"Maybe you should sit down a minute, dear," offered Ruth, leading me by the arm behind the info desk.

"How bad is this? Do I call David for advice or an ambulance for an emergency?" Maureen asked, helping Angela lower my vast pregnantness into Ruth's beloved chair.

"Um. . ." I pretended my wits were about me as the raw ripping of an active labor contraction overtook me. Longer this time. The baby kicked my ribs, as this particular child preferred to do. Then, halfway through the contraction, it was cut off by an unsettling pop and a gush of warmth that soaked into Ruth's favorite chair. I answered Maureen's question. "The janitor—for a mess."

"Mommy," Mia whispered, the first to notice the predicament. "You're a‑pposed to pee in the potty."

The three women gasped, and Maureen set to delegation. Before I was aware, I was breathing through my disbelief of another contraction, and Mark was at my side in complete panic. So far beside himself that neither of us was thinking.

"No, no, no. It's too early. I haven't put the crib back together. And. . .you can't. . .you have to have a cesarean. Oh my God, we have to get you to the hospital."

"On it." Determined Maureen. "But for now, take this blanket" (Angela arrived at the desk with one). "And get her to my office. I'll call David and see if Eva is on call. Angela, can you keep an eye on the kids?"

Mark carried me with ease to Maureen's office, comforting me with the blanket and pillow from his secret place. This was a blessing, because as I'd never seen, he was unable to comfort me with anything else. All the beauty of his peace in our other birth experiences had left him for the blatant fear for his unborn child. Mark was simply pacing and sniffling while I squealed through three more astronomical contractions about a minute apart.

Then Maureen entered. Mark addressed her with panic.

"Did you call? Did you talk to Dave and Dr. Moreno? Is she gonna be ok?"

"Yes, Mark! What is with you?"

"Well, what did they tell you?" He was fiddling with his finger.

Maureen cleared her throat. "They told me to wash my hands. Which I did."

I was glad for her words as she dropped to her knees at my side. Because with the next contractions came an overwhelming urge only felt at one time of life—the urgency and loss of control far beyond the realm of words. And I breathed, so as not to push prematurely.

Mark, knowing the tell-tale fervor of breath, peaked within his panic. "Paige, do NOT push. You have to wait for the hospital. You've had two cesareans. And you tried for hours to push with Robbie. Dr. Moreno said your insides could rupture."

I was nodding, fighting with every ounce of will. Listening to the cello.

"Mark, shut up or get out." Maureen, in just a few words, brought us both to the place we needed to be. Mark came to the floor and his senses in time to hear Maureen's questions. "How far apart were the last few?"

"A minute, tops. She had three, maybe four, while you were gone." I took immediate ease knowing Mark's mind had always been somewhat in attendance.

Maureen nodded and moved in front of me, moving aside the soaked broom skirt. She placed her hands on my freckled knees. She was reluctant but sure all at once. And she closed her eyes a single moment, then opened them with her classic smile. Maureen told me in one deliberate word my next instruction with the cool of her amber eyes.

"Ready?"

My next contraction came, and with it, with one long push, I felt the relief from what I count as the greatest of sensations. When I thought I'd deliver Robbie this way, I'd done research. Some counted it nauseating. Agonizing, like a ring of fire. That day, I called it *storge*, at its very finest.

When I breathed again and lay back against the pillow and wall, Mark sighed through tears with one word. "Boy."

But something was missing, apparent in the fear on my sister's face and the stark silence of the room.

"S-see if Dad is out there, Mark." Maureen never stuttered. And Mark never obeyed her readily, but he opened the door as Maureen replaced my skirt feebly with her free hand.

Pastor Dad entered with an odd collection of items. Hand sanitizer, shoelaces, scissors, and Mark's old lime green hoodie. My wits finally about me, I could see what they were doing and what was missing. I sat up the best I could and peered over my legs. They were all in a quiet panic, suddenly with skill of hands like a team of experts. They cut a cord and then wrapped the minuscule, bluish child in a hoodie. Because he had yet to cry. They rubbed his lungs. Patted him, turned him, and whatever else they could think of in silence.

"Oh no. . ." I squeaked, and Mark came to my side, finally tending to me. I realized I was shaking violently.

Maureen finally did something odd, though I'm not sure any part of the last half hour of my life had been normal. She held the baby to her shoulder and turned her head to whisper in his ear. No one could hear what she said as she rocked the lifeless child. But she said whatever it was with purpose. Less like cooing a baby to sleep, much more like the way she whispered to me the night I got saved. Like it was the most important thing she'd ever said.

Pastor Dad prayed aloud for the child's life, though we were all in streaming tears, knowing his size, timing, and speed of entry could not be reversed for a better outcome. My worst of fears, and the very reason I had wanted to stick with two children. I finally heard the end of what was probably a well-thought-out rant to a child that could neither understand nor respond.

"So, you see, sweetheart, it's not so much to ask. All I'm asking is that you *breathe*." As if Maureen was talking to us, we all took in and held our breath. And just before we all gave into the cruelty of the world and exhaled, we heard a high-pitched squeal that didn't belong to any adult in the room or any child in the foyer. This was followed by a fervent and beautiful sound I knew better than any. Nothing mundane had been more welcome than the cries of my far-too-early baby boy. Or the sigh of relief from my husband. Or the way Maureen smiled knowingly into the baby's eyes. Or the rustic laughter of my pastor.

They were all interrupted by the storming of the office door. My own OBGYN quickly assessed the situation before Dave even reached the doorway, calmly spinning the key to his newest toy. Dr. Moreno was at my side in an instant, asking me a hundred questions. Some, I preferred not to answer in the presence of men who hadn't caused my predicament. So Maureen mouthed a "Thank You" to her husband as she rubbed the screaming baby, and he and Pastor Dad exited the makeshift maternity ward.

Dr. Moreno tilted her head sideways as she murderously massaged my belly. Her accent flowed forth, and Maureen was painfully quiet. "This does *not* look good, Paige. Let me have Dr. Little book us an OR for an emergency hysterectomy. Are you still alright with that? You may not have much of a choice, but I still need consent."

I looked to Mark, who nodded. My doctor asked for a verbal response. "Sounds good," I told her, still loving the baby's squeaky cries.

"Mark, could you go tell Dave affirmative, please? He already knows what to do," The doctor requested. I whined as Mark rose, but realized he was the only person with free hands at the time. And he exited, leaving me in an extremely awkward little space. My doctor spoke again to me.

"A boy? I peeked at your ultrasound results and didn't tell you." She tried to soothe me with her smile as I nodded with mine. Then she turned to Maureen and the two met eyes in what I feared would be a horn clashing of a fight-to-the-death battle. But there was instead a strange peace. "How is he?"

"Looks to be pretty alert. He's just really tiny. Have you alerted the NICU? He hadn't come yet when I talked to David last. We weren't sure he'd make it." Maureen staked gentle dominance immediately.

"The NICU is ready for him." Eva started to speak a few more times before her mind and heart put the words together properly. "I knew he'd be in good hands."

In the next moments where my consciousness started to fail me, I wondered if she was talking about the baby at all.

When I awakened after surgery, we visited the baby in the NICU. He weighed four pounds and was all alone in an incubator. Six weeks early. They told me I *may* be cleared to hold him soon. A darkness entered at the prospect. Because just that morning, I was finalizing nursery decor as he danced happily inside me. I missed him and needed him near me. I held back tears as I caressed the tiny child through gloves on the side of the incubator.

But God knows all. And before the darkness could take hold, Dr. Moreno entered with the Neonatal doctor. A favor, once again. The doctor almost demanded that I hold the baby, because the skin-to-skin contact would help him grow and heal. His lungs barely worked. His blood sugar was irregular. There seemed not to be an ounce of fat on him. I sat in a glider in the nursery and exposed my freckles to his scant blond hair beneath a blanket. Immediately tears came. Perhaps it was me that needed the contact for healing and growing.

That day in September, all generations were attracted to the arrival of new life, as it should be. I looked up at the NICU window to see my sister-in-law searching for a tissue in her purse. Dave was in his doctor's coat, as he had been at the church. I saw Mia, who understood completely that this was her little brother. I saw Robbie shoving his cousin to rile him up. But since Heather was standing there with Lane, he had to play it cool. I looked into the eyes of my beloved. They were as emeralds above the blue hospital mask that hid the rest of his face. But I could see he was smiling.

"D-A-R-I-A-N, right?" Mark asked suddenly.

"I guess. I never wrote it down," I answered casually.

"Well. . .I sort of. . .did. I filled out the info for this guy's birth certificate while you were asleep. His name is Darian." He knew I'd protest.

"Mark! You didn't! I can't just replace him like that. It doesn't work that way."

"Of course not. But it's a great name. I use it every night in my prayers when you cry. It grew on me. *He* grew on me. We both miss him. So why not name our son after him?"

"Dare I ask what his *middle* name is?" I sighed, scared I didn't have what it would take to properly love this baby.

"Um. . .Richard."

In response to my gasp of disbelief, Mark winked and exited the two doors securing the sterile room. I watched joy unfold, silently to me, in the hall. Dave wrapped his arms around Mark and lifted him off the ground for a moment. Mark was then tackled by our two other babies and received warm, gentle hugs from his father.

Maureen was communicating with me with humorous gestures during this time. She lifted up her arms at the elbows, fingers spread as she opened her mouth in a dramatic surprised face. I nodded at her, rolling my eyes. She was then hugged enthusiastically by my husband, who seemed relieved to see them all. I watched as my father arrived and stood next to Maureen. He was also victim to a violent hug from his son-in-law.

I couldn't comprehend the movement of the lips, but all eyes were on Mark, who moved his mask below his chin to reveal the remainder of his magnificent jawline. Once, he looked at me and winked while talking to our family. Suddenly, Maureen turned, excited by something Mark must have said, "Darian?" She mouthed, putting her hand up to her heart. She gave me thumbs up and searched for another tissue. This, before bolting down the hall after Robbie. My Mia caught my eye. She was waving and I saw her lips saying, "Hi, baby."

At that point, a nurse told me to go talk to my family, and took away my little angel. Mark came back in and retrieved me in my wheelchair.

We stopped at the window to admire the tiny miracle once more. Maureen's arm wrapped around my shoulder and she sighed. Words I hadn't the chance to say in the whirlwind suddenly surfaced.

"Thank you, Maureen. Mark was a mess. Without you. . ."

"I needed a victory like this. Don't thank me. When you get a chance, thank Darian for me." She squeezed me.

Mark got me settled in the room and ordered me dinner, then sat a moment before he joined the family in the cafeteria with our children. Maureen stayed behind with me, claiming to not be hungry. She sat in the corner looking exhausted.

"How are you so civil with Dr. Moreno?" I asked what had been plaguing me since before the hours started again.

"Civil?" Maureen laughed. "God used Eva's hands to save my little sister's life tonight. She's one of my favorite people right now." She lifted her head and became a bit more alert, knowing I needed my counselor. "That's what forgiveness is, Paige."

"So, does my new son's name have something to do with Mark wanting me to forgive?" I sighed. "I assume he told you since he hates secrets and couldn't tell *me*."

"He told me the same week you two found out. Verbal diarrhea, that one." Maureen giggled. "He thought it was a shame that your first baby didn't have any kind of commemoration or memorial. So, he gave him a namesake. I thought it was precious. I was secretly hoping for a girl because he was *still* going to call her Darian."

"Darian, I get. I approve. I've always loved that name. But Richard? From my old compass, Maureen. 'My beloved Richie'? I might actually have that changed. I know he meant well, but 'Richard' destroyed me. I literally *hate* him. Why would Mark do that? He's the one that threw the thing into the ocean."

"I thought Richard was audacious, to be honest. I suggested 'Jacob.' Mark wasn't as into that idea." Maureen laughed. "He needs to do some forgiving of his own. But Richard is a good strong middle name. And it will be impossible for you to hate this one."

"Well, I just won't use it," I mumbled. "What did you say to Darian when. . ." I sighed, remembering the fear. "Before he started crying?"

"I did the counselor thing. I think he felt guilty for being born so early and ruining Ruth's chair and my office carpet." We both snorted laughter. "But I told him you *needed* him, and that with you as a mom, he'd be treasured just exactly as he is. I also told him I keep candy on my desk for nieces and nephews."

After the painful giggle, I looked closely and saw that Maureen's eyelids were slowly rising and falling, and her head was in her hand.

"You okay, sis?"

"Says the woman who just accidentally gave birth and was relieved of her womb? I'd say I'm good. Just tired, you know? Little tension headache is all. I never did take my meds. Crazy Day. But I'm sure if you tell David, he'll stick me in an MRI anyway." She chuckled.

"Probably, Dr. Little." I made fun of her self-diagnosis, looking again at the picture of my new son on my cell phone. "That's Mrs. Shrink to you."

"Why am I here?"

"To see." The woman of many words has suddenly taken to saying so much with so little. "To remember."

"Darian. My Darian. Jake hurt him. He kept his promise. My Darian is gone, isn't he?" Words that would cause tears are simple to say in this warmth of life. No emotion is predominant because all are running wild at once.

"Who is gone when God holds us all?" With these words from my sister's sweet voice, I am soothed. I suddenly know that nothing is as it seems in life. Even life and death, seemingly the greatest of extremes, are trivial when it comes to the glory of God.

"When did you get so smart?" A friendly jest.

Maureen only smiles, reaching up to touch my hair. Looking deep within me, I finally see the truth. It comforts me. It frightens me.

Chapter 44

Trust

It was much too soon after childbirth and surgery, but I was feeling well enough to entertain. So, with a home-cooked meal, I rounded up a family that found every excuse to be together. That day's excuse was Sunday and wedding plans, though Dillon's wedding was still many months away.

Darian was still a beloved resident at the NICU. He rarely went a few hours without a visitor. I thanked those visitors that day with pot roast, even though the October weather was acting much more like July, and every man and child was playing in my backyard between dinner and dessert. Angela and Heather were among them, leaving Maureen and me to admire and laugh at the improvised baseball game through my sliding glass door.

Mark took the mound and held back one of his greatest strengths to underhand balls to Robbie, who was at bat. He did it for every batter, not counting strikes or fouls or anything at all—only pitching and letting them run the bases. But when Lane was at bat, Mark began to stretch dramatically, to Maureen and my amusement.

We perceived that the reason for the change was the way Lane was trash-talking Mark. Accusing him of mediocrity. And saying he'd go out for baseball that spring and make varsity immediately. Such was the way of Lane. He was joking and showing off for his ever-present companion, 'Feather' as he called her. Egging Mark on. Because he'd heard stories of Mark's glory days. Seen the holes in his grandfather's fence from years of Mark practicing. And probably witnessed a pitch or two. I was the concerned wife, however, of a thirty-one-year-old man who should have in no way been pitching a fastball. But regardless of my feelings, he was getting in position with that footprint still in his soul from many years before.

The adults held the children out of harm's way while Mark stared down his opponent, waiting for the hush of the crowd. And they hushed, because they'd all heard the same stories or seen the same focus in his eyes. Even Maureen and I watched, wanting badly to see if he still had it in him. Then Mark caught Lane nearly off guard with the finesse of a curveball, which thudded against the fence, swishing right past Lane. Immediately, Lane was ridiculed, and the little crowd went wild. Mark was rubbing a shoulder, laughing at his foolishness.

But the mood changed when a little voice spoke from excitement. From the purest opinion. Of a child.

"Whoa! Daddy, that was SO awesome!" Robbie determined at the top of his lungs. And then Mark ignored the shoulder injury and called his son to the mound for his first lesson.

Maureen and I cooed. And then she sighed. Every time I thought I knew Maureen, she revealed new caverns of her depth. Just then, something emerged from her that I didn't know was there to emerge. Some half-concealed state of panic like when a teenager confesses a menial crime. What she said seemed so innocent at first.

"Lane has always been too big for his britches. Always wants the next adventure before he's ready. I love that about him. I really think he'll be a good man someday, sooner than we think." She smiled. "Both of my boys will make wonderful husbands and fathers. I have no doubt about that."

I nodded. Somehow, I knew I didn't have permission yet to speak. She smiled and inhaled to share a story dear to her. I knew the look and drive.

"When Lane was five and still pretty shaky on a bike, he *insisted* I take off his training wheels. I didn't want to. But even at five—well, you remember how he was. Bull-headed but charming enough to get his way."

I laughed, remembering all too well the nature of the mini Romeo who had begun helping Tucker to hold a bat.

"That morning, Ruth had picked up a nail on the way to work and got a flat tire. Gosh, I think it was her first day working full-time, too. Poor woman. Of course, Dad ran home and grabbed all the tools he could possibly need for the job, and changed her tire in the parking lot. Shortly after he left, I got to his house. Because David owns about two tools to this day and didn't have what I needed to take off those training wheels. My brother, on the other hand. . ." She tilted her head, and I rolled my eyes at the only approved use of my garage—Velma and her tools. "I even loaded up the bikes because Pastor Dad's house is up on that hill, you know? And Dillon was dying to ride down it. Lane wanted to be just like his brother. So, I took off those training wheels and watched my baby start down that hill." She chuckled. "Lane fell *right* off and broke his wrist."

I gasped through a chuckle. "Oh no!"

"It was some teacher workday at their school, so I was home with them. David was assisting a surgery, getting ready for his board exam. Unreachable. Mark was in a seminar about victims of sexual abuse. It was worth three credits and offered that one day. I couldn't call him. So, I called Dad in a complete panic on my way to the hospital. And it was cold that day, so I asked Dad to go by his house because I'd left my boys' coats there in all the confusion. He was trying to get there so fast, he pulled his truck into his garage, where I'd left out all the tools and training wheels. And his front left tire was done for when he hit them. So here I am, in the ER, and they are telling me my baby needs pins put in his arm. Poor Dillon was trying to calm me down, but I was hysterical when Dad told me he'd be a few more minutes. Which turned out to be hours, because *all* the tools he could possibly need for putting on a spare were still at church. And still, no one was available to get him." She grunted in frustration after the quickly-spoken memory.

"Come on, Mrs. Shrink. You're superwoman. You can handle a little broken arm on your own." I encouraged her hindsight panic.

"Ha!" She guffawed. "Just you wait until one of *yours* gets hurt and you know it's your fault."

"I have a preemie! How is that different?" I argued.

"It just. . .hush, I'm not done with the story." She demanded.

"Hushing." I smiled, awaiting enlightenment.

"I was alone with my nine-year-old while they worked on Lane. I'd never been more scared. Not even the night I almost had a *preemie* or worse. Then, he was my baby. But at five, he was so full of life. One of my best friends. I was so in love with that boy, just like I still am, even though he doesn't hug my knees anymore. To lose him. . ." She sighed with more weight than expected. "Dave didn't get out of surgery until Lane got out of his. And by the time Dad got there, we were on our way out. So, we wheeled Lane out the side entrance, by the chapel? To meet up with Dad."

"That's an insane story-"

"Life is crazier than stories sometimes." She sighed before rerouting. "See, Dad wasn't waiting outside the chapel as discussed in text messages. He was *in* the chapel because he's a magnet for those things. Especially when he noticed the broken, beautiful redheaded teenager in the pew. He says he felt drawn in, like talking to her would be life-altering. I felt the same way when I saw him in there. And I thought that when Lane ran in all loopy on pain meds, that he had ruined the opportunity for Pastor Dad to minister to this girl. But I found out not long after that God hadn't missed a beat."

I sighed in a revelation that sent shockwaves up and down my spine. Set my ears to tingle and my mouth to drop open at Maureen's knowing smile. I remembered the day well. That day had been the beginning of my ascent out of the deepest parts of hopelessness. In disbelief, I tried to connect only one whispered word with my lips.

"Wow."

"God has a perfect plan. Sometimes something as little as a nail in the road or training wheels sets the whole thing into motion. He orchestrated the whole thing so I'd have to rely on Him, not other people. It was a hard day. Lane still doesn't have full range of motion in that wrist. He learned guitar to help it heal. And now music is his life. God *knows*, Paige. Even if it had been multiplied by ten, all that pain and stress was worth every agonizing minute. Because it led us to you. We need you. *They* will need you. Never question the means. In the end, it all works to God's glory." Her tears had been mounting. Ending with a cough of a sob that made her lean and grab a tissue from my kitchen counter. I panicked.

"Maureen?" My tone did not hide the fear. "What do you mean *they* need me?"

She sniffled and fussed with her tears a moment. And we watched Robbie throw quite a pitch for a little guy. They all cheered.

"I've been having headaches." Like a confession. Like the climax of the story. But an odd one.

"Yeah, you mentioned that."

She tucked her lips and looked away, which stopped my words immediately.

"I'm a psychologist. An honest to God doctor of the human psyche. I have a documented IQ of 153. I've counseled everyone from abused children to divorced couples for fifteen years. Since *I* was a kid. I have two beautiful boys who I think I raised quite well. I can talk anyone into or out of anything. I recently talked a preemie into *breathing*. I know people's hopes, fears. Their pain. Long before they ever speak. And sometimes. *More* than sometimes. I can help God *fix* it. He gave me a gift, and I used it for His glory." Maureen began to speak through passionate tears, which I'd never seen her do in all our years of acquaintance.

"That's all true, Maureen. But I've never known you to need validation. You and Dave are doing okay, right? Is this about Dillon? Their counseling is going great. We only have one more session." Maureen held up a hand to interrupt as if she had precious little time to speak her thoughts.

"I'm capable of *anything* with God. Why can't I fix this stupid little rogue blood vessel in my head? My coil isn't working anymore. And I need to have surgery to try to correct the damage. Turns out, they weren't tension headaches or migraines." She laughed in irony with a glistening tear.

My mind calculated. My hands began to shake at words my mind had not embraced yet. "Brain surgery? You've had it before. It'll be nothing. I just had surgery, and I'm already back at work."

"This is the kind of surgery they recommend you get your affairs in order prior to. Even if I don't suffer a massive hemorrhage and wake up in Heaven, I could be permanently mentally disabled."

I gasped. "Maureen, why would you even say that? And even if it is true, what kind of an idiot gets that surgery knowing that?"

"The kind of idiot whose aneurysm is bleeding, and she'll be dead in a month or so *without* the surgery. For the tiny chance the surgery might save me, I *have* to try." She started softly. Ended in a whisper. And then the silence of my home engulfed it entirely. It was she that broke the silence I'd not the presence of mind to time or assess for awkwardness.

"I need you to promise me something."

"If I start making promises, I'm not trusting God for a perfect surgery that saves you and keeps your mind intact, Maureen." I refused to look at her for a moment, and she ignored me.

"Promise me you'll go all the way back to the source. And forgive Richard. But forgive Jake first. That's important too. Promise." The passion collected into a whisper. "I didn't mean to pressure you, but if I have an appointment in Heaven, I have to know you'll stop relying on symptom relief before I go."

Maureen gestured outside. All the joy and laughter. My loving husband. My gorgeous children. A fulfilling career where I made an impact on people and the world. In themselves, they were all the worth a woman should need, according to some. But by then, after all the pain that still reared its head despite them, I knew Maureen was right. Because if I had been using them to cover up the wounds of yesterday, they were like Tylenol for Maureen's headaches. Jesus was my comfort, my only source of healing. Just as always.

I only feared that my "symptom relief" would lose all meaning if I handed it all over to Jesus and chose to deal with the source instead.

"This isn't fair." I fought my own tears with a distorted face and didn't respond to her heartfelt request. "It should be me. God made a mistake. Why would He even threaten to take *you?*"

"I knew you'd say that. Which is why I told you about the training wheels. God doesn't make mistakes. We're all better for every life-changing nail He allows to be in the road. And maybe years ago, I was your counselor and helped you through some stuff. But God help me, I don't *care* how you feel about yourself right now. Right now, I *need* you. I'm telling everyone as soon as they come inside. I'll really need your strength, Paige. They'll take it hard. I didn't even know how to tell my *sons* without you." We stood shoulder to shoulder, not speaking. I only listened to the sound of our sniffles and the muffled contrast of joy and laughter from outside for a few minutes.

"When is the surgery?" I finally allowed.

"David says I'm tempting fate, but I told him I want to take long as possible to get everything in order. I want to make it as easy as possible for you to take over at church and with the family and everything if that's the turn this takes. So, I'm scheduled three weeks out. Still not an extraordinarily long possible remainder of my life, but a blessing, nonetheless. Most people don't get to plan for these things."

"You'll be fine. Stop saying you won't. Dave will be in the surgery, right?" I hated that I both recognized and experienced the first stage of grief.

Maureen, who had conquered her own denial, nodded to comfort me. Then smiled. "First order of business: you all have to wear dark purple to my funeral. Black is a little overdone. Everyone looks so good in purple, and none of you wear it enough. Such a classy color."

Unsure of how I survived the last day after Maureen summoned the rest of the family to tell them the news over dessert, I was in my office again. Counseling, as if I was worthy or able. I was almost relieved when Dillon and Angela arrived, in tears, for their final premarital session, which was not at all their purpose for needing a counselor. And after we prayed and I assured them both that God's will is perfect, they had only one determined plea of a sentence to offer me.

"Can you make it happen?"

Chapter 45

Smile

The click of heels from the front door stopped mid-foyer for an appreciative whistle.

"Paige Catherine Henley, are you sure you gave birth a month ago? You look *amazing!*" Maureen inquired of my deep red dress in her usual attitude.

"That is *exactly* what I said," Mark said, approaching the two of us from the darkened corner by the maintenance closet. He was in a full tuxedo with a red vest that made my heart skip several beats at every glance. But before Maureen could ask of his extremely unusual getup, Dave appeared with Lane. They were both in tuxes. Lane in a red vest. Dave in gray. Heather was pretending to be timid on Lane's arm in a red dress that matched mine.

I heard my oldest two children arrive on cue, holding the hands of my father. Mia was in a tiny red dress and Robbie was in a little tuxedo.

"You guys look great! Why is everyone dressed so fancy?" Maureen finally asked with her smile. Though she was no doubt fully aware.

The truth became readily apparent when a young man with his mother's caramel eyes appeared in a tux with a vest of pure white. Secured in one hand was Tucker, a miniature boy in a miniature tux. And draped over the other arm, a garment bag with a dress in deep purple that Maureen picked out just after the engagement.

"Honestly Mom, you'd think as a wedding coordinator, you'd know the standard attire for the mother of the groom. Jeans are in no way appropriate for the occasion. Angela would be livid if she knew what you were wearing." At Dillon's humorous rant, Maureen gasped. She took the dress from him and stepped back to admire her dashing eldest son on his wedding day. Then, of course, she fought it.

"Angela wanted a *summer* wedding!" This, she said directly to me, to the laughter of all as I shrugged defensively.

Dillon responded, and echoed the eye glisten of his mother. "Not as much as she wanted *you* at our wedding."

Maureen went for the scandal. "She's not pregnant, is she?" We all laughed, and Dillon turned bright red in an instant.

"That would be quite the scientific feat." He said in an innocent smile. Then he flashed his mother the purity ring his uncle gave him close to a decade before in almost the very spot he was standing.

"What are you gonna do with that awful thing?" Mark remembered, winking at me but trying to retain the redness in his nephew's face.

Dillon turned to his not-so-little brother with a head tilt. And Lane, knowing exactly his lot for the next few years, first slowly whistled his arm from its union with Heather's. And then he took a humorous bolt for the hall after looking around at all of us with all his charm intact. Dillon ran after him. And the two young boys turned young men wrestled as if they were lacking both years and tuxes. Maureen would normally scold them for something like that. But the past week, she had taken in much more than she'd released. She smiled with deep appreciation for her sons' rambunctious actions. Dave was, therefore, forced to stop them. Maureen turned to me.

"If this is a wedding, we are missing some important people. Guests? Pastor? Um. . .Bride?" She inquired calmly, not seeming to worry about anything anymore. The inquiry was a cue for the church janitor to enter the sanctuary and illuminate it. Even I had been humbled when one announcement had brought in family and friends and faithful churchgoers from all over town. Pastor Dad and Ruth then stood outside the door. One with a Bible in his hands, ready to make official a marriage. The other, a smile on her face, ready to send us all down the aisle.

Maureen gasped at the bustling sanctuary. Which morphed into a sigh. And a multitude of tears for which she only found relief in Dave's arms.

I took to governing. "Angela is waiting for you in the Bride Room. She and Dill haven't seen each other. But she wants to see you before we start. You can go on and change in there. Your shoes are there and—"

"You did this in a week?" She interrupted me as Dave finished hugging her.

"Eight days, but who's counting? It all fell into place. People kept donating services and supplies and their time. You came with us willingly yesterday to get mani-pedi's and were totally clueless. God knew you'd have been angry to have gnarly nails today. God was actually in *all* of this." I gave her blatant truth.

But before it fully entered the foyer, I was within a tearful, deep hug like she'd never given me. A severe and painful gratitude. A gratitude that remained as she watched her son commit his life to the love of his youth. Not one eye was dry as Dillon turned during the ring exchange, to his best man/brother, handing him a weathered purity ring with a few words.

"Grow into it. Grow fond of it. Then grow out of it." Mark nodded proudly at the sentiment. And then the busting-at-the-seams sanctuary burst into laughter when Lane put the ring on his finger only after a dramatic sigh.

I sat with my beloved sister at the reception as we watched two newlyweds dance in a recreation room filled with red flecks of confetti.

Maureen turned momentarily to meet my gaze. "I owe you big-time. I'm glad there's not a chance I'll miss this."

I chuckled. "Owe *me*? I'm still in *your* debt, Mrs. Shrink."

"Well, I suppose." She joked. "And I bet my Dillon was pretty excited to shave nine months off his sentence. Gosh, that's enough time for a baby, isn't it? Dillon is already such a good father. I'm *so* proud."

My eyes filled with tears suddenly after we laughed. They all thought we were a pair of boring old moms. "This surgery... *has* to work out. I can't do this without you. You're our matriarch. I don't know how to corral all these guys by myself."

She laughed. And it was beautiful. Glorious, as always, even though it was but a wheeze of a whisper through her tears. Her eyes squinted and her head tossed back.

"Really? Because it *looks* like you got them all into tuxes and at a perfectly organized and executed wedding without me. I'm officially not worried about the way things will be run here at church when I'm gone. Maybe someday, you'll see what I see." She sniffled.

"Maybe someday."

"And if you ever—" She stopped, almost not wanting to say what she wanted to say. "If you ever need to talk, Ruth is a good listener. She's way more than just a lady behind a desk. She *loves* you. I know you know that, and you're so kind to her, but you mean a lot to her, Paige. More than I can ever convey."

"Even though I ruined her chair?" We chuckled. Maureen got back on course.

"The hospital is treating this like the true risk it is. Which only seems to be working to my advantage. I get to do whatever I want. They said I can even sit in the NICU and hold Darian before they do all my pre-op work."

"I hear you and Dave spend your lunch hour there every day."

"I've been found out." She smiled with pain. And whispered out some intensity of truth. "Robbie is so handsome and brilliant. And your Amelia. She's precious. Heart of gold. They are all the best parts of both of you. But Darian... he's *special*, Paige. Always trust him, okay? He's special."

"Why do you say that?" I asked, wondering her method.

"You're already a great counselor." She smiled. "My methods would only ruin you now."

"Thank you," I told her, "for taking off those training wheels."

She nodded, and chuckled a little. "There's a cute guy over there that is dying to dance with you. He's been ogling at you for an hour." Maureen gestured to Mark, who was across the room with our fathers, and winked in my direction once I looked at him.

Inside my favorite place on a dance floor out of Maureen's view, I sobbed, knowing I may not get a chance later. And then when we were both watching her spin with Robbie and Mia with her crooked smile of a laugh, I asked something I'd always wondered.

"I just love her smile. One of the first things I noticed about her. Has she always smiled like that?"

"Not always." Mark sighed. Sniffled. "You *earn* a smile like that."

"Life has given her a lot of reasons *not* to smile. So how do you 'earn' a smile?" I scoffed.

"From smiling anyway." He shrugged within our dancing embrace. I fell in love with his explanation.

"Well, whatever it is, it's beautiful, isn't it?"

"Yeah." He was as broken as me, but would never use even severe grief as a reason to distance me. So, he used what he knew best as comfort. "Yours is ten times as beautiful."

Chapter 46

News

News, when expected, is still news. A warning the ball may fly must still be followed by a catch. A positive pregnancy test is still followed distantly by the pain of labor and childbirth. Likewise, death. When one knows it is coming, the vibration of a loss is still devastatingly felt, echoing out until the ripple has mellowed. My heart, in full ripple, was far too alone when the news came.

Maureen's aneurysm ruptured as they wheeled her from the NICU to her surgery. We were signing final release paperwork for Darian and had stayed behind, having wished her well in the surgery. They opened her up, as planned, to attempt to save her. But there was nothing they could do. The best part of her was a vegetable.

I was alone with Mark and the newly released Darian outside the room, freshly sugared coffee in my free hand. The steadiest, sweetest love song of a bedside manner was all but wasted when it stopped at me. But I understood fully the delivery when the deliverer heard himself say it, and collapsed into my husband's arms.

My husband, needing to be the hero amid his own reception of news, flicked his head in the direction I'd least like to go. The direction from which newlyweds and their fourteen-year-old brother flowed with haste at the sound of their father's tears. I passed them, and the hallway with the fish tank, where my father had led Robbie, Mia, and Tucker. Knowing the reason for my uselessly dried tears, he stopped the children from intercepting me and took the baby from my arms. All so that I could enter a dimly lit chapel. Carrying the weight of news I would have preferred to die than to grant the sixty-year-old man in the pew.

All news is news. But news itself, after sixty years, I assume, is but a customary wait. Even without warning, he had caught many balls, welcomed many children, and accepted many deaths. But this one was far from customary. Yet he knew, when I took the space of pew beside him, the reason for my visit.

"How bad?" He whispered through a sigh.

"No brain activity. But they haven't pulled the plug yet. They want to stitch her up and give us a chance to. . ."

He nodded when my lack of will to deliver it proved much more powedful than the news I didn't know how to deliver.

As the Dad he had become to me since the day I met him in that very spot, I took his strong hand in mine, leaning onto his shoulder for the support neither of us wanted to need. And he became someone far removed from himself. He didn't allow tears, for my sake, I think. But he allowed something that was the hardest and best news I'd ever heard.

"*'Naked I came from my mother's womb. And naked shall I return there. The Lord gave, and the Lord has taken away.'*..." If I didn't know better, I often would have mistaken my pastor for the very source of faith. His jaw quivered. So, I finished the verse from the book of Job for him.

"*'Blessed be the name of the Lord.'*" This appeared to be at least ointment on an amputation for us both. My father-in-law squeezed my hand and nodded. And after a silence, void of tears my heart could not accept, I spoke again.

"Jesus wept."

After my pastor's compliance to my request, he stayed to seek comfort in arms that none of us could see, but we all relied upon. When I turned the corner and found the family overtaking a waiting room, I realized one monumental task. I had no time to mourn. Because I was a matriarch. All that I could not be all at once, just as my sister was. But just as she, I knew the Source of my strength.

The keys hit the dresser after putting sleeping children in their beds at 2:00 a.m.. My husband sat on the side of the bed as I placed the tiny infant in the bassinet in our bedroom. Mark buried his head in his hands, not even possessing the spiritual strength to untie his shoes or cry the tears he'd never fully released.

"She's gone." Like he was trying to convince himself. "She was *laughing* this morning. How can she just be gone?"

But the words didn't come to me like I begged them to in my spirit. I had nothing to offer him by way of strength or words. So, sniffling, I first removed his shoes. Then he seemed startled when I stood between his knees at the edge of the bed. And in a gesture that didn't fit the grief, I found myself kissing him.

"Paige," he mellowed, eyes still closed.

But I shushed him since I didn't have words. I counseled him in a way that had roots in my past, but had since been sanctified with his help. Mark moved seamlessly from ecstasy to something I'd never seen. Everything he'd concealed to be strength for his family suddenly burst forth in rivers and sobs and oceans from his eyes. He lay his head on my chest and the tears flowed across my skin for a half hour. What should have been demeaning of his pride and uncomfortable for me made me feel like I finally did something right. Especially when the stillness occurred after the tears and Mark whispered,

"Thank you."

"I just didn't know what to say, is all."

He sat up on an elbow, looking at me with the cleansed puffy redness of his eyes.

"Yes, you did. You always do."

After a grueling couple of weeks, we sat in the comfort of Pastor Dad's home. Not dressed in black. But in Maureen's favorite color, deep purple, as she'd requested a few weeks before. "*Such a classy color.*" We complied with honor.

Robbie laughed with Mia and Tucker, the three playing "Ring around the Rosies" right in front of us in the family room.

Randomly, after "falling down," Mia had a request, "Daddy, can I have a kitten?"

"Of course, Princess." Mark's common response to anything his daughter requested. I sighed, hating cats. But already owning one as of that moment.

Pastor Dad winced at the loving exchange. Then I chuckled, out of place. I explained to my troubled husband. "When I said goodbye, first, I made her a promise she'd been begging me to make. But the last thing I told her was that she better tell your mom good things about me. The last thing I need is a mother-in-law to haunt me. She would have laughed at that."

Maureen had spent her last moments in a vegetative coma, and took the things we whispered in her ears to Heaven with her the moment her life support was removed—at her prior request in such circumstances.

The rest of the room allowed some dull laughter. Mark joined in. "I told her to hug mom, of course. To kiss my babies. And I asked if I could have her room. I used to ask her that all the time when we were kids."

More laughter, where there should have been tears. Not-so-mini Romeo spoke next. "I told her to send me a sign when it was time for me to get married. A HUGE one."

We teased him through chuckles. Then Pastor Dad revealed his last words to his daughter. "I told her not to spend *all* of eternity asking the Lord about the mysteries of the universe. Because eventually, the rest of us will want a chance, too."

We knew her and loved her, and appreciated the truth in Pastor Dad's request of her. In laughter, we turned next to Dave, who declared in a smile that what he said was "private."

Then we turned to Dillon, holding his wife of just a month's hand. He and Angela exchanged a look, and she gave him a smile probably only he understood. He nodded, then cleared his throat a little.

"I told her that I was enjoying being a dad." We hummed and nodded, knowing how deeply Dillon cared for Tucker, his new stepson, adoption pending. Then Dillon continued, unexpectedly. "And I told her that I was experiencing a strange juxtaposition of joy and sorrow. Because while she was in surgery, I found out I'm also going to be a *father*." We all sat stunned a moment, reading Dillon and Angela.

Dillon received Dave's sense of sincerity, and the revelation as a joke would have been far beyond his personhood. And as she tucked some shoulder-length dreadlocks behind her ear, Angela bit her lip with a smile we all understood. Thus, with laughter and congratulations, we began our journey to healing with a bit of news worth healing for.

"I miss you." I hold tighter to her hand. "I wish you could see all the kids. They're so big. And you have a granddaughter that's named after you. Olivia Maureen. Dave calls her Livvy Reen."

"It will only be a moment. It's all only a moment."

"You mean I'm not. . ."

"It's not time for you if that's what you're thinking."

"Well, what has all this been? Why were you there in the woods when I was remembering what happened?"

Her laughter seems to cause the stark whiteness to sparkle as the stream to our right. But I remember that about her life as well.

"I couldn't fix you, Paige. All I could do was lead you to the source."

Chapter 47

Gratitude

"But we always sit in the back," I whined after an already exhausting morning of getting the kids to church and dropping them off in their classes. "You know I don't like change."

Mark chuckled. "Please sit in the front with me this once? You'll be glad you did, I promise."

We sat during the few moments before service began, discussing again the notion of volunteering to teach one of the kids' classes on Sundays. But Mark seemed distracted the whole time. Finally, he gave me a giddy smile that did not fit with anything we were saying.

"What?" I couldn't help but laugh a little.

"Change isn't always bad." He reasoned against what I thought was a dead subject, since we were sitting in the front.

"I like the back. I got *saved* in the back."

"The front is good, too. You can watch Pastor Dad sweat if he forgot a page of his notes. And Lane might even wink at you during worship."

I chuckled, knowing the excuses were a humorous vamp. "Why are we sitting in the front row, Boss?"

And then he did something random. He smiled. And he pointed up while still looking at me. I raised an eyebrow. He pleaded with his eyes and a head tilt. I tried to focus toward the ceiling, hoping he wasn't about to say "made you look." But before I worried about embarrassment, I saw something up on top of one of the black metal rafters. Something small and blue and in the shape of a shoe.

"What *is* that?"

"Don't kill me, but I was up there the other day because my old A/C guy retired, and there was a hole in one of those ducts that needed fixed."

I gasped. "Boss! You were up *there?*" Perhaps thirty or forty feet up.

He ignored my worry. "And I saw that. Those horrible things we practically had to pry off your feet. So, I guess you're right about not liking change. But you haven't worn flip-flops in over a decade."

I gasped again. That time because I remembered. Mark had bought me shoes when we'd first fallen in love all those years ago. He'd thrown my flip-flops. We'd never found the second one until today. He smiled at my gasp and stare.

"You still love me like you did that day?" I nudged his shoulder and asked the awful, wifely question.

He gave a husbandly grumble. "You're kidding, right?"

"Just humor me," I prodded.

"That day," He chuckled at the memory. "I thought I was gonna *die* when you let me touch your bare feet. Life was so simple then."

"Yeah. . ." He was avoiding the question quite effectively.

He snickered, "*Now*, I tend to avoid your bare feet-cicles. And we've been through *hell* together on numerous occasions."

"But do you *love* me like you did that day?" I led the cue for us to look again to the flip-flop and our past.

He chuckled then spoke with sincerity. "I don't love you *anything* like I did that day."

"Uh!" I was a little hurt until he finished.

"That's not fair. You can't even compare the two, Cinderella." He whined.

"Apples and oranges?" He wasn't making sense.

He sighed. "Back then, it was like an apple, sure. A nice perfect *green* apple. Now it's an apple *orchard*. Trees and apples everywhere. So complicated that you can't even see them all at once. Bad apples, good apples. Lots of work has gone into it. Lots of fruit has come out of it. It's actually weird sometimes that I have to use the same three words to express my love that I did then. Because they're not even close to the same thing at all."

I whispered a laugh, overwhelmed by him. We were still looking up. And his arm came around to squeeze me by the shoulder.

He sighed. "Reen would have analyzed the snot out of that."

"Yeah." I nearly whispered before the lights dimmed my wayward flip-flop back into a memory, and the worship band began to play.

A few songs and winks later, Pastor Dad took the stage. My own dad, the night owl, yawned his way into the row with us as the sanctuary relit.

"The front row, eh? Change is good, I suppose."

Mark and I smiled at each other and watched Pastor Dad adjust his microphone headset.

"Yesterday, I was at a coffee shop with my grandson. He's a grown man now. The father of my *great*-grandkids, if you can believe that. Dillon is a pastor and has been working with our youth for a few years." Here, the members of the youth ministry present in the church cheered over their beloved pastor, as teenagers do. Pastor Dad smirked, then continued. "Over coffee, my grandson asked me a very serious question. He wanted to know how a pastor knows when his time is up in the ministry. God felt that answer should be *demonstrated* promptly." Wait, I thought. He wasn't thinking of stepping down, was he? I turned to Mark, who was thinking the same thing in the shrug he offered me. A number came on the screen to indicate that the children's ministry was having trouble with a child. Last week, our three-year-old Darian had been having trouble getting along with his little cousin, Olivia. I looked at the number and was relieved when I need not "rescue" him from the incessant bossiness Olivia acquired from both Angela and Dillon.

"A young man that recognized me walked by our table at that moment and asked if you have to believe in Jesus to go to Heaven. This individual wanted to know if believing in a 'higher power,' coupled with good morals, is enough to earn one's way into Heaven. I could understand the confusion. See, this young man was with a friend who called himself a Christian but was a product of a sinful culture, abusing the gift of grace." My father-in-law seemed sorrowful. A new sorrow, deeper than his constant state after Maureen's grand exit. He had a box on the stage, though he was not usually fond of props. And a stool where there was normally an emptiness.

"I told that 'good' man that no matter how good he thought he was, he was a scumbag who needed a Savior." Here, the room chuckled. "We are born sinners. But Christ died for sinners. And until we accept His blood as a ransom for our sin, we are *slaves* to that sin. A slave who acts like a free man is still a slave. Your 'good' will never set you free. Then I turned to the 'Christian' and asked him: 'Why would a free man act like a slave?' I told him that grace may be free for him. But it came at a price for God."

My father-in-law removed a deep purple five-inch heeled shoe from the box on the stage. He placed the shoe on the stool in front of the hushed crowd. I looked away to fight the returning emotion.

Suddenly, a photograph appeared on the screen. It was a full-body shot by the stairs in the foyer. Maureen and Pastor Dad were laughing. When the two of them would laugh together, the whole church would know. The music created by the rustic timbre of the pastor and the cynical joy of the counselor was something barely rivaled by even Lane's singing. To see it was glorious. Maureen's head in the photo was fully back, and her eyes were squinted tight. Pastor Dad had his hands grasping his knees to steady his joy. The two would part ways to their offices in smiles to the click of heels, not knowing how sweet that moment would be years later in a photo I'd taken "just because." Pastor Robert continued his sermon, if that's what it was.

"There is nothing in this life that is worse than losing a child. My daughter's name was Maureen. She was thirty-eight when God took her home. If you knew her, you knew that she fit more life into those thirty-eight years than many of us manage to stretch into ninety. She died a grandmother. A psychologist. She had imprinted a healing touch on countless lives. But that did not make her passing any easier for me. By then, I had lost my wife after twenty short years of marriage. Difficult, to say the least. I had to become a single father for two strong-willed children. Before that, I'd lost two loving parents. That was difficult, as well. I've also watched my son endure the loss of his sister. He'll never be the same.

Unfortunately, all of us will have to endure the loss of a loved one in this life.

"But to bury your own child is vastly more challenging. It is against the very laws of nature. We are simply not built for it. My wife and I buried a baby girl once. She never left the hospital alive. But I found peace about our little Angela. Since then, I've seen generations of miracle babies restored to me like Job saw restoration. But the cost of Maureen's death is not something I will *ever* see restored." Mark grabbed my hand, squeezing it. Feeling helpless for his still-grieving father.

"I told those men, both of them, that '*God* so loved the world that He gave His *only* begotten son. So that whoever believes in Him will not perish but have everlasting life.' I told them that if my *daughter's* life had been the price for eternal redemption for anyone that believed, and I met two men—one who rejected her existence or sacrifice and another who accepted it, only to be a slave to what she'd died to defeat? Hell. Would be the *nicest* thing I could do. I told them they were bought at a price. They should have a little *gratitude.*" The pastor was speaking with a passion and fervor like I'd never seen. He was fighting tears in his voice. The room remained painfully silent.

"I looked up the meaning of Maureen's name the other day when I saw this picture and wanted to remember. I found a few meanings. I remember the one Amelia and I had loved was 'wished for child.' Because we were told we'd never have her. Another meaning is 'rebellion,' which she spent her adult life proving, if you knew her. But the most common meaning of my little girl's name? Is *bitter.* Wished for in birth. Rebellious in life. And when she left, she helped me answer the question I was presented by her firstborn son.

"Those men left that coffee shop disgusted at my talk of fire and brimstones. I expect they will both remain in their slavery. Dillon, my grandson, was devastated, wanting to save them both from that slavery. He asked me which one I thought was worse off. The moral unbeliever or the unrepentant believer? I laughed and told him: 'I don't care anymore.' I am so bitter with ungrateful, careless sin that if

God smote them both with a single blow, I wouldn't give it a second thought. The blood of Christ is perfect and powerful! I have seen it turn a harlot into a saint. A patient of grace into a healer. A selfish child into a mature servant of God. Anything less tells me you've no inkling of the price of that precious blood! I'm too bitter to understand why God continues to love you and save you when you reject or take advantage of His sacrifice as a father. HE. GAVE. HIS. ONLY. SON. Show some *gratitude!*" Here, Pastor Dad was yelling. Pointing. Reddening in his face. And throwing Maureen's shoe back into the box with fervor. Then, he simmered.

"As of tomorrow morning, God has put this fellowship into the hands of someone who aches for every soul in this room. I am old and bitter. So God and I have appointed my grandson, Dillon Little, as Senior Pastor of this fellowship. He is very young. But that just gives him many more years before he, too, feels the bitterness. Pastor Dillon, please come forward and prove yourself."

To our shock, Dillon took the stage in a room with not one closed mouth. His grandfather prayed over him with love and grace and then joined us in the front row, forbidding any questions we had for him. Dillon gave a compelling message about love, based in First Corinthians, for the remainder of the service.

In the afternoon, I was still in shock. I was cleaning, as I did when I wished to not think. Then my daughter's beloved cat came in through the cat door, scattering leaves and mud onto the kitchen floor. I resolved to cover the cat door once and for all.

"Rob- Mi- Dari- Copper! You stupid cat! Now I have to sweep the whole kitchen again!" I could never remember the correct name when flustered.

"Mommy, don't say stupid. It's mean." The three-year-old Darian's words are much more powerful than the wind that blew all the leaves inside.

"Sorry, baby. You're right." I detached the dustpan from the broom and started cleaning again.

"Where is my sister? I'm gonna go find her." Darian bolted around the corner and up the stairs. I giggled and continued to sweep the kitchen.

As I bent over to fill the dustpan with dreadful wet leaves, I heard a man's affectionate whistle behind me. I rose to see my husband leaning against the wall, enjoying whatever it was he thought he saw while I cleaned.

"I always loved watching that part. You should come clean the church with me again sometime." Mark's smile was still beautiful, even in the deepened sadness Maureen still supplied from her grave. The shock from his father's retirement.

I reached past the still handsome man to toss the contents of the dustpan. He leaned his head down to steal a kiss as I laughed. Then we heard two very different sounds that were equally chilling. A large thud against the floor upstairs that shook the living room's ceiling fan. We startled, then flew to the top of the stairs at the second sound—our daughter screaming.

The sight in Mia's room was no less horrific than my heart expected. Darian was passed out on the floor next to Mia's bed. His head was bleeding profusely. Mark stopped me when I tried to run to him, and somehow quickly shooed us both out the bedroom door.

"What happened, Mia?!" I grabbed the six-year-old by her shoulders, and I imagine my eyes were wild at the question.

"He just went up on my bed to get my teddy. He tried to step down, but he fell asleep."

"Well, get your coats. We are going to the hospital. Robbie!" Mark grabbed a towel from the hall closet and used it to try to stop Darian's bleeding. He was holding the tiny child in his arms. Darian was completely and unshakably unconscious. I could not rouse him all the way to the hospital.

I was in a fog as the nurses ushered us back immediately to a room in the ER They began working on him right away, and only some shell of myself heard Mark on the phone with Dave. How was Mark so calm?

Dave arrived just as I heard Darian whimper. I sighed in relief, then realized that even though he was awake, he could still be far from okay. I heard Dave shouting to get him in to scan his head STAT. Another doctor ordered blood work. Mark told me to take care of the kids in the waiting room. I looked at him as if he just grew a tail. Why would he ask me to leave my Darian?

I assume God watched over my children until I realized my father-in-law was sitting beside me, beside myself in the waiting room.

"Hi, Pastor Dad. I didn't see you there."

"It's alright. I've been where you are. It's a tough thing. You should've heard Maureen the day Lane broke his arm. She was in hysterics."

"I can't even think. And Darian is probably fine. How are you still alive after *losing* Maureen?"

"Alive is relative." He nodded, eyes glistening.

"So, Dillon, huh? He's a kid. You think he can handle it?" I quickly changed the subject.

"God thinks he can. Thank you for not criticizing my choice to step down."

I laughed a little through the tears that lay stubbornly within my eyes. "Pastor Dad, 'bitter' and I met and became pals a long time ago. I get it."

Finally, Darian was stabilized and we were led to his room. My father-in-law and children entered the room before me. I saw that my dad was approaching, and waited outside the window of the room for him. He hugged me warmly with words of comfort. Suddenly I looked into his deep and weathered green eyes with a memory or two.

"It must have been terrifying, Daddy. How did you do this?"

He was confused a moment until I watched the memory of a girl in the woods and of a teenager on the stairs flash across his mind.

"Which time?"

"*Any* of them. I've put you through so much." My voice trembled.

"Sweet Pea, when you experience real fear like walking in the door from work and finding your baby girl all crumpled at the bottom of the stairs, that's when you realize how powerless you are. I hate the way it had to be. But it certainly taught me to put it all in more capable hands, that's for sure."

I banished the tears for my children's sake, then hugged my dad again. We entered to see Mark and Dr. David Little examining the tiny boy.

"Uncle Dave, that light hurts my eyes!"

"Well, you bumped your head pretty good. I'm making sure you are okay."

Mark came and calmed me in silence while I stood, unable to look at the doctor who was stitching Darian's wound.

"Aunt Maureen is sooo nice. She kissed my head and it felt better." Darian said this to Dave, who promptly dropped the penlight he was using to check Darian's pupils.

"Darian, when did you see Aunt Maureen?" Mark tried to ease Dave's obvious distress.

"I was sleeping. Can I have candy, Uncle Dave? She said you'd give me candy if I said please."

The room was silent until Dave cleared his throat. "Sure, buddy. I'll get right on that." Dave left the room as if it was on fire. I saw tears forming as he whizzed past.

Mark, our fathers, and I all stared blankly at one another. Pastor Dad spoke wisdom.

"I think if Maureen was going to show up it would be to make sure Darian got some candy."

My down-to-earth self spoke otherwise. "Could have been a memory. Remember when he was born, and Maureen talked him into breathing? She told me she said something about candy then."

"You just have it all figured out." Mark sighed, both teasing and scolding.

After my eye roll and the hurried knock of a doctor, the door opened, and a smile came to my face. The petite woman with a graying ponytail entered, looked at Darian, and sighed in relief.

"Oh, good. I was on a call down here and worried a little when I heard your name. I had to check on the miracle baby to be sure he was alright." Dr. Moreno's lovely accent was always welcome.

"Dave thinks he'll be fine," I assured her. Then inquired. "Is it normal for you to be on call together?"

"No, actually. I was surprised to see him. I assumed *you* called him here." Eva crossed her arms, uncomfortable.

"I called him." Mark supplied. "But he was already here with another patient."

"Oh. Well, specialists get rotated through, and we usually don't get scheduled together. Until tonight, he has traded with someone else if we were scheduled together, just in case we both had a call at the same time. It must have slipped his mind to check the schedule this time." Eva explained.

"After fifteen years of avoiding you? Yeah, sounds like scatterbrained Dave." Mark sarcasm-ed the anomaly, then winked at the doctor.

"I agree. Odd behavior. In any case, I am glad to hear that Dr. Little was able to give a good report for your son." Dr. Moreno smiled and slinked from the room with a wave to Darian once Dave returned with suckers for each of my children.

"These are from your aunt." He said, glancing twice at the OBGYN taking her leave, probably wondering why she dropped in. Wondering fully, actually, as he watched her walk down the hall, nearly getting caught up in the door in the process. Mark and I, never willing to outgrow the gossip, looked to one another with knowing smiles before Darian spoke.

"Aunt Maureen? But she's in Heaven. Do they have candy in Heaven?" Darian had no recollection of talking about Maureen. And thus, she faded again, as quickly as she'd resurfaced.

Another doctor entered with some other startling news. Darian had passed out from low blood sugar. Besides stitches from catching the corner of Mia's nightstand, his head was fine. But he was diagnosed with Type 1 diabetes. I had to give him shots twice a day until he was able to do it himself. Worse, he was born with the disease. And since his birth, his eyesight had been affected. I, of course, scolded myself, knowing all these things happened because Darian was born so early.

392 | Rebekah Tyne McKamie

I was in a dim room with my three-year-old a week later. He was having trouble identifying simple pictures, as usual. I was bitter toward the preschool teacher that had been telling us he was developmentally delayed. He just couldn't *see.*

Finally, the eye doctor reached a certain setting and Darian looked right at me.

"Mommy! You are sooo beautiful!" The eye doctor nodded and I laughed, knowing my baby's life had been renewed.

I remember something I never understood. "Darian is special. Like you said. What I can't explain is why?"

Always poetic in her actions and intentions while alive, this peaceful version of Maureen has now taken on the persona in speech, as she never did in life.

"No wisdom in all of my learning
That the greatest becomes the least
No profit in all of my earning
As the power that dwells within peace."

It soothes me like a balm, these words. But my mind does not comprehend.

"I don't understand."

"Darian helps you understand the way you are loved."

"Why can't I wake up? If I'm not dead, why am I here with you now?"

"Because Mark is resting. You will panic if you wake up alone."

"Darian? Please, I need to know if Darian is alright."

She betrays me with her silence. The face I have not the capacity to read.

Chapter 48

Psalm

My phone startled into the silent Saturday morning. I only heard it after my husband nudged me with a gentle hand on the small of my back. The ringtone was the default, and I didn't recognize the number, but answered the phone anyway. I nearly detected someone breathing, but hung up after receiving no response from three hellos.

The clock told me it was 7:30 a.m. Since I could never go to sleep again after being awakened, I began to rise.

"Where you going, Cinderella?" My groggy husband pulled me close.

"To make pancakes. Unless you want me to stay. Your choice." I melted into his embrace.

"You're gonna make me choose?" He smiled, eyes still closed.

We heard a door open in the hall, and then a knock at our bedroom door.

"Pancakes." We determined with a laugh. I opened the door to a little boy in glasses.

"Is it Sunday yet?"

"No, buddy. Your birthday is tomorrow. But guess what? It's party day! Let's get your insulin since you're up."

I descended the stairs to the kitchen and prepared a syringe from the fridge. I muttered under my breath a familiar prayer.

"Lord. Give me the strength to keep my son healthy. And give him wisdom to know I love him. Amen."

I tapped the syringe and then squirted out a bit over the sink. When I turned around, Darian had produced an alcohol swab and cotton ball. He looked up at me with tousled blond hair and Mark's dimples.

We sat on the couch, and Darian lifted his pajama shirt. I cleaned the area with a swab while Darian pinched the minuscule bit of fat he had on his belly. He squinted his eyes tightly under his glasses while I did this.

"Relax, Dare Bear. Psalm 23. You first."

"'The Lord is my Shepherd. I shall not want. He makes me to lie down in green pastures. He leads me beside the still waters. He restores my soul. He leads me in the paths of righteousness for His name's sake.'" Darian had finally relaxed his eyes. I loved the sweet and articulate canter of his little voice.

At this, I sneaked the needle past my inhibitions and let it slide into his little tummy. But just as every day when I completed the necessity, my eyes filled with tears. Darian knew it was my turn.

"'Yea, though I walk through the valley of the shadow of death, I will fear no evil. For You are with me. Your rod and Your staff, they comfort me.'" We both breathed a sigh of relief as Darian held a cotton ball over the injection site.

"You prepare a table before me in the presence of my enemies. You anoint my head with oil. My cup runs over." This from the yawning voice of my husband, who looked at me from the stairs, wondering where his pancakes of compromise were.

I rose to greet him as we all recited the next line, "'Surely goodness and mercy shall follow me all the days of my life.'"

"'And I will dwell in the house of the Lord forever.'" This was from a ten-year-old redhead who spoke with my counselor's conviction. Smiled with our green eyes, holding tight to the innocence of a red split-French-braid. But moving down the stairs with poise and charm. She was a source of both joy and fear in our lives. A call to trust.

"There's my princess!" Mark exclaimed. He was likely seeing the toddler version of her through his Daddy eyes. He embraced her and kissed her forehead, never willing to let her go astray.

"Morning, Mia. Help me make breakfast?" I giggled at the way she rubbed her Daddy's kiss off.

"Only if it's pancakes." She smiled, bearing much hope.

"What else is there?" I hugged my only daughter. I held onto her for dear life, as my mother never did for me.

"You wanna wake the bear now, or after breakfast is ready?" I winced at Mark, who rolled his eyes.

"Is next week an option?" He scratched the graying hair that covered his dimples. "I'll start now and see what happens."

Just as I was flipping the first batch of pancakes, my phone rang. My sociable daughter answered. She said hello three times and then hung up.

"Who was that?"

"I dunno. It wasn't anyone's name. And I didn't know the number."

I picked up the phone to check the log. It was the same number as before. I assumed a pocket dialer and shrugged it off.

Robbie made it to the table when most of us were on our second helping. He grumbled a hello in the voice that was changing. I marveled at his resemblance to his father. At twelve, he was approaching six feet quickly. I had to look up at him to discipline him. Naturally, he was as strong-willed as his father, too. I was determined to keep his innocence intact, though it had proven difficult. Twelve was an age that terrified me. Again, a call to trust in God.

"Good Morning, Robbie. Sleep well?" I asked cheerily.

A deep and groggy reply. "Whatever."

I rolled my eyes at Mark as I began to clear the dishes. Mark, seeing my powerlessness at the disrespect, took matters into the hand that tapped the back of Robbie's black hair. Robbie cried out more disrespect, and Mark needed only look at him to end it.

"Yes, ma'am. Thanks for breakfast." Still a mumble, but a much cheerier one.

I spent the morning readying the house for a party. Darian had few friends that were not family. But that did not bother me. It simply gave me an excuse to tease my nephews and love on the kids, since the church had gotten so big we could hardly spend two minutes at a time together there.

Dave, however, usually found himself on soul-clearing journeys whenever a potential family gathering neared. He would spend an evening with us here and there, but felt the tangible absence of his wife more deeply than any of us combined. Dillon had a demanding calling and a family of his own, and Lane lived at home, but was a college student with his own hectic schedule. But even if that hadn't been the case, Maureen, not the boys, had been the glue between us and Dave. We could usually expect he would not attend parties, especially as of late. I suspected he'd either slipped into a deeper depression or there was a scandal involved. With Dave, it was hard to say.

Midday, I received another call as I was looking frantically for the bags of decorations I'd purchased. The same unfamiliar number.

"Hello?" No response. I was sure I heard a breath this time. "Who is this?" The line went dead on the other end.

Mark heard. "Give me the phone the next time, okay?"

"I can handle it, Boss. It's probably some kid or something." I gasped suddenly, a palm to my head.

"What?" Mark inquired with a tinge of jumpiness over the phone calls.

"I left *all* the decorations at church. I got them on my lunch yesterday and never brought them home after work. They're in my office." As I was speaking, I was procuring Vinny's worn-out keys. I grabbed my coat, knowing we were expecting an unexpected September snowstorm. "Be back soon."

A kiss and a flight out the door took me first into my office at church for bags of decorations and then almost out the front doors of the church. That was before I was startled by a lone guitar on the stage through a propped sanctuary door in a nearly empty church. I smiled and redirected my steps for my favorite version of my favorite song, sung by my favorite singer.

"What can wash away my sins?. . Nothing but the blood of Jesus."

The joy I find in little boys is that they never really grow up. A grown man still finds happiness in weapons of war, fast cars, and the form of a woman, just as he did at birth. A warrior first staged battle scenes in his living room as a boy, and Velma was not the first car my favorite man had ever toyed with. They go through stages of change and self-discovery like Robbie in those days. But they all eventually come back to who they started out as when they'd been untouched by the world.

My feet were taking me to the wild but beautiful singing voice of a boy-turned-man. The voice with a rumble like his father's. But weathered joy, like his mother's. The voice that has led us all to choir concerts throughout the years, and him, to lead worship at church. As I drew nearer, I heard another familiar singing voice. A lovely likeness of her sister and my friend, Emma. Heather had grown into a rustic sort of feminine. She'd rather wear boots than heels and feathers tied in her wild waves than the flowers I'd tried to adorn them with on Emma's wedding day. Skirts alluded her. But never beauty.

Both singers were juniors in college, attending for music, as well they should. My heart told me that in the fullness of their harmony. They were practicing for worship services they had to do alone while the rest of the team was on a mission trip that weekend. Lane had stayed behind for Darian's birthday. Heather had stayed behind for Lane. I sneaked in and listened from a chair behind a pillar. I saw them in full view, listening to the heartfelt hymn, but they could not see me.

Lane and I were as close as we were the first day we met. He looked just like his father but got along much better with his uncle. Therefore, when he lost his mother at fourteen, we all but inherited another son. For this closeness, I often asked Lane to play or sing for me. But he always refused, even though he was willing to do it for thousands of strangers. The only way to get a private concert was to sneak in as he practiced.

I fully enjoyed the song until I saw Lane's eyes straying to his companion. Then after a few moments of distracted rehearsing, Lane stopped singing and playing all at once. Heather had been engulfed in the song, just as I, and was startled that her accompaniment had ceased. Her eyes opened, and she looked at Lane.

"Did I miss that harmony again?" Heather looked inward, still focused on rehearsal and shuffling something on the music stand in front of her. Then she sang, to herself, the harmony line she'd just sung, to clarify it. I sighed, knowing Lane wasn't concerned about harmony.

"Naw." Lane smiled. Cleared his throat and made some silly attempt at smoothing his wild curls. "It was perfect. Gave me chills, Feather."

See, the trouble with boys is the same as their joy. They are who they are, from birth until death. As a boy, he'd been as spry and flirtatious as a kitten, but had grown into his lion's heart. We had once called him "mini Romeo." And that lion's heart had grown, and belonged wholly to two entities. Jesus. And Heather McHardy. They admitted their feelings years ago, though neither wore more than a purity ring on that stage.

So, Heather giggled at the look on her boyfriend's face. Because she couldn't control it. No one could. Neither could she control the way he turned to her and walked around the guitar amp between them.

"Lane," she warned with a smile and her raspy voice as she took a step back.

"What? I just wanna kiss you." Both women in the large room recognized the vast difference between the definition of the word "just" and Lane's intentions.

"I want to practice. We have six hours before Saturday night service, and your cousin's party is in between." Heather was being chased in slow motion across the stage by a laid-back but determined young man. She was trying not to giggle.

For some reason, my Aunt hat fell aside and the counselor hat reported during the exchange. And I was immensely curious at what I was about to witness. The twenty-one-year-olds were inseparable best friends for years before finally claiming a label when they attended prom together. Almost two-and-a-half years before. They were ingrained in each other's hearts and lives. Long enough for a nickname to earn a nickname. Presently, Heather stopped running and sighed. Lane stopped two feet from her to justify his request.

"There's a guitar between us, what do you think I'm gonna do, Feath?" His tone, and word choice almost justified the world to *me*. And I wasn't desperately in *eros* with him.

Heather took a step and I watched as Lane leaned in and pecked her once on the lips, hands still steadying the guitar strapped across him. Something I'd seen them do many times, though this was the first time on the stage. Maureen would have flipped if she'd seen as many kisses as I, but I knew that Lane's *eros* was steadied by the Holy Spirit, despite his lions. As innocent as the kiss looked, it lingered in Lane from head to toe as Heather walked back to the mic to refocus. And my heart pounded as I watched the lion emerge. I nearly gasped as I lowered in my chair even more.

Lane turned and played the guitar as he walked. I knew exactly what he was doing. Heather's only mistake was in the half smile she gave him when she asked if they were starting from where he was playing. He nodded. But Lane had been playing guitar most of his life and was probably unaware of what or where he was playing. The only thing more deeply ingrained in him than Jesus or music was his current distraction. My jaw dropped all at once when Lane's guitar stopped playing and was flipped to his back, and Heather was pulled against him fully. The kiss took even my breath away. It would have been tender if it wasn't so terrifying. It only ended when Lane's intoxicated hand tested the limits of the sanctuary, and Heather pushed him away in tears.

"Lane, if you keep doing that, I will call a break, I swear. I love you, but we have to stop. I don't like where this is going."

"A *break*, Feath?" Lane was wounded and trying to shake what couldn't be shaken. He gave a frustrated sigh. "I *love* you."

"If you loved me, you'd stop leading us places we can't go." Heather began gathering her things, abandoning the rehearsal effort.

"What do you think I'm gonna do in the sanctuary?"

"The guitar. The sanctuary. Why can't you rely on yourself? That would save us at your house when your dad is out of town." She said as Lane set his guitar down.

He shushed her and looked around for discretion's sake but missed sight of me still. "I'm sorry. I'm just a *guy*, Feath. And you're my girl. This is harder than you think."

Heather nodded. "I'm sorry. I just don't know if I have many more no's in me, baby."

Lane and Heather embraced. Lane then smoothed the feather in Feather's hair with a little smile. A full-blown fight started and concluded within a few moments. But nothing had been solved. And with both the aunt and counselor hats upon me, I intervened.

Maureen always taught me never to ask questions I didn't know the answers to. Always to assume the best, but to love and encourage in spite of the worst. Though usually well aware of the answers, I was much more of a pessimist than Maureen, and simply expected the worst, knowing I'd more than the understanding required to love someone through it.

I stood and let them see me walk up the aisle, fully expecting them to do exactly what they did—panic, wondering what I heard and saw. I reseated myself in the second row and patted two chairs in front of me. They complied, though terrified. Sitting side by side, but turning to face me. Heather's face was tear-streaked.

Maureen always had half the session calculated in her head before it ever started, and would often start at *that* point when talking with someone to prove she already knew what was going on. But I found that there was so much to be learned in the way a concern was presented, and always started with an open-ended question instead of presenting them with the truth. I started with a sigh. A clicking tongue.

"What's up, guys?"

"You *know* what's up, Aunt Paige," Lane mumbled, embarrassed and defeated.

"Why does abstinence make us fight more than the people we know who aren't?" Heather, I saw, was willing to unleash the whole pent-up fountain at once. "And why can't these two years until school is over go faster so we can stop fighting about this? This is way too hard. I feel like we're trapped, and we'll never make it."

Lane took Heather's hand with compassion, allowing her to share her heart. A mark of a good husband.

I tried not to smile at the song and dance I'd heard and lived a hundred times. I simply cleared my throat and spoke the truth. But not in my words. I used words they could not contest. "'But if they cannot exercise self-control, they should marry. For it is better to marry than to burn with passion.' That's in First Corinthians. 7:9, I think. Not to be the voice of conviction, but that was quite a passionate kiss, mini Romeo. According to the Bible, you need to marry that girl before things get carried away. And then they can get carried away to your heart's content." I elicited a smile from the young couple. A bitter laugh.

"I wish," Lane shook his head in frustration. "Two more years of school. I want to have my degree so I can support Feather and the ten kids we want to have. When I'm done, I'll be a worship pastor."

Heather warmed my heart with her giggle as Lane winked at her and kissed her hand. Even as I sought the correct collection of words in my heart, they were chatting about ten or twelve baby names they'd chosen. I cleared my throat.

"Life is messy and unpredictable. You can't possibly sit here and tell me every college degree you'll go after or every job you'll ever have. Who you'll lose in the next five years. The ways your kids will break your heart. Life is fickle. But *love* doesn't work that way. Especially not in marriage. We don't know what God has coming for us, even tomorrow. But in marriage we at least know *with whom*."

"It's not like we can just get married. We have to finish school. We both live at home. We're poor as dirt." He chuckled.

"And what if it's for the wrong reasons?" She fretted. "We're struggling with abstinence. Should we really get married just because of that?"

I smirked. "Heather, that is destroying you two. It's making you lose sight of how wonderful you are together. Lane, who was there for you when we lost your mom?"

"Everybody. I'm really grateful for how amazing everybody was." Lane laughed once. Then looked to Heather. "But I don't know what I'd have done without you, Feath. We were kids, and it was way too much to ask my friend to handle."

"You didn't ask," Heather whispered. "Lane, I'm with you through everything."

My phone rang. And what should have been a conventional ring tone had been changed to the voice of my husband for a couple years by that point. But a full cello suite would not be as beautiful. *Dr. Henley. Answer your phone. Your man is calling.*

Heather giggled. Mark's pride in my newest prefix had not dwindled. But he was the only person I allowed to use my "proper" title. I was first God's servant. Then Mark's wife. Then a mother to three incredible children. None of that required a doctorate. I earned that so I could do my job better. And to make my own former shrink proud.

"Hey, Boss."

"Um, party? Decorations? Did you find someone to fix? That's not in the definition of 'hurry.'" Mark, even annoyed, was blissfully jovial in tone.

"Right." I'd almost forgotten my primary mission. "Be there in a few. Love you."

"Love you. Hurry! Bye."

I smiled and hung up the phone. I stood and addressed the young couple one last time.

"Think of it from this perspective. The whole point in your life is to glorify God. You two do that *beautifully* well by worshipping on this stage together. But if you mess up this purity thing, Dillon will have you two off the worship team in a hot minute, and you'll have failed on two counts. Get married, and the same guy will *encourage* you to go and enjoy one another. God will be glorified by the same act that would break His heart today."

The young couple agreed, hanging on my every word.

"Thanks, Aunt Paige. We'll see you at the party. Sorry if we kept you from home," Lane apologized.

"It's fine. Monday 3:30? My office. You can let me know when the wedding is."

"Yuck!" Grimaced Heather. "Do I have to? I hate weddings! I was my sister's flower girl, and she was so into the whole big day and white dress. And even at five, I couldn't wait to get those horrible flowers out of my hair!"

"You were six." I laughed at the memory of the tomboy as they went over in their minds their insane schedules and finally nodded at the slim opening I knew they usually spent in the foyer talking.

Before I re-entered my front door, I heard the always early Pastor Dillon and his family. More accurately, I heard the ever-rambunctious Olivia, who had found her favorite cousin Darian. Tucker had found his idol, Mia, who was eager to show him her latest painting. I saw that my dad and Pastor Dad had also arrived together, dressed in the gear of two retirees. Collared shirts and golf hats included. Last week it was shooting gear. On my heels, Lane and Heather arrived, wisely choosing not to remain at the church alone.

Together, we hung the decorations. The pizza arrived, and the party time came. We celebrated the birth of a miracle together. And I mourned in my heart for his namesake, who was never given the privilege of this life. Halfway through the party, I forgot my mourning when I heard Olivia exclaim at the top of her shrill voice that one of her favorite people had arrived.

"Papa Dave!"

Dave lifted her and swung her around. Glad he decided to join us. To hug and kiss the closest likeness of Maureen on earth. "Livvy Reen," He affectionately called her. I smiled at him from across the room.

Unfortunately, the head of neurology received a call on the less preferred cell phone just an hour after arriving. Dave caught my eye on the way out. He asked since I was nearby.

"Would it be alright if I called you sometime this week? I wanted to run something by you."

I nodded and then smiled at the still compact life. Always Mom and wife. Always sister and daughter. Always counselor. Always needed. But largely on my own, I was reminded as they all played in the fickle September snow. The children caught the flakes on their tongues. Lane and Dillon gathered as much from the patio table as they could to lovingly hurl at Angela and Heather. Mark stood with crossed arms and our fathers, slowing down, becoming them. And I stood inside the sliding glass door. Alone in my watching.

Our guests departed around the time Mark and Robbie left to clean and patrol the Saturday night service. Since only church staff was in our midst, it seemed a mass exodus, in which I did not participate on Saturday nights—my only day off. I received another call from the mysterious number, glad Mark was not home to traumatize some kid with threats. I let the call go to voice mail for the first time. Until Mark returned, my phone awakened every few minutes to tell me I had a voice mail. Something inside me felt sick, and I didn't want to check it if he wasn't around.

The rest of the evening was a blur of begging a redhead and a nearly seven-year-old to get to bed. Robbie went to bed without question when he and his father returned close to 11:00 p.m. And before we realized it, we ended the day where we began it. Mark and I were whispering into the reverence of the night as he caressed, with weathered fingertips, my fading three-leaf clover of a past. Alone for the first time since we'd chosen pancakes.

"Ten bucks says they're married by Christmas," Mark spoke of Lane and Heather.

"Lane is way more impulsive than that, Boss. And she doesn't want a wedding. I'll give them a month, tops."

"You're on!" We took the bet with a kiss. We both snickered but knew the situation deserved more depth than laughter.

"All in a day's work, I guess." I sighed, jealous of Maureen's upgrade from a fallen world. "I really miss her on days like this."

"Me too. But God wouldn't have taken her if He didn't think we could handle it." I saw my phone flash to the lock screen for two seconds, as it had been doing for hours. "You gonna check that? It's driving me crazy."

"Oh, yeah. It's from that number. I wanted you to listen with me, so you can punish the culprit." I joked.

I played the voice mail, hoping it was just a hang-up. I turned on speakerphone as Mark and I lay on our stomachs, eyes straining for the bright cell phone. What I heard confirmed the sickness to my stomach in a profound and terrifying manner.

"I've reached who? Doctor? Paige. . .Henley?" At first, Mark laughed at the obviously intoxicated slur. But I recognized the voice, and laughter was the closest opposite of what I felt like doing. "Henley. Hhhhhenley." Much more than a hint of liquor. "Your voice is so sexy, baby. Even if you have a stupid last name. I've been thinking about that red hair of yours all day. Mmmmm. Does that little girl that answered your phone have red hair too? I bet she's as beautiful as you. Too bad I keep my promises, huh? I always kept my promises to you, Paige. Always. You better hope your husband isn't that pansy Mark Henley I knew in high school. Oh, I miss you, Paige. . ." after two more minutes of listening to the second most terrible voice in my history, I could no longer contain the terror. My emotion manifested itself as a full sprint to the toilet and a relief that I skipped the second slice of pizza that day.

Mark was on my heels and encouraged me to vomit all I needed to as he held my hair. There were advantages to being the wife of a jaded janitor. I finished, and the tears came anyway.

"Was that him? I'll track him down and *kill* him, Paige."

"Mark, our babies are not losing their Daddy to prison because he lost control. You'd be just like him." I was sobbing into the echo of a toilet.

"I know. . ."

"He talked to our baby, Mark. Our Mia. I wanna die right now. He promised he'd—" I flushed and slinked to the floor across from the toilet, Mark still rubbing my shoulder.

"I'm an idiot for not telling you," he confessed.

"Telling me what?"

"I. . .well, you. . .got a notice in the mail last week about Jake getting out. Back when he got sentenced, the judge said you'd be involved in the appeals process, but I guess they just decided to release him after the minimum. No appeal necessary. I didn't tell you because I knew you'd react like this. I didn't think you had anything to worry about. I didn't think he'd. . .I'm an idiot, okay?"

"Thanks for the warnin," I said with bitter nastiness. "I could have been thinking about what to do if—"

"I thought the actual 'if' would be better to deal with than having you worry if 'if' would happen."

"Okay, what now?" I was fighting away the tears, trying to focus on a solution.

"We call the police in the morning." Mark decided.

"On a Sunday? On Darian's birthday? We'd have to go down and give a statement, and—"

"Right, Monday then. First thing."

I nodded.

But Monday was a day, a staircase, and a few gunshots too late.

Suddenly having a sense that there is an end, a change, I make a case I've always wanted to.

"I disagree, Maureen. You should know that. I never agreed with you that my whole life was just symptom relief."

"Nothing is ever 'just' anything." Maureen agrees.

"Mark and the kids, the family. They are blessings all on their own."

"Grace." Maureen smiles. "There is no better counselor."

"Exactly." I nod. "I can forgive. Not just because it'll fix me. But because I have to extend the same grace I've been extended."

"Nothing is ever 'just' anything," Maureen repeats. Then changes the subject. "You are so beautiful. Take care of our boys, and if anyone offers to help in whatever way they are able, give them only grace." Maureen's voice changes again. And then I am alone in the light. Warm and comforted and fearless in the light.

I hear the beep again and then a voice. I do not recognize the voice except that my heart is moved. I close my eyes to draw me nearer to the voice in spirit. A voice that beckons me. A voice that commands with admiration and pleading. A voice I remember now that I'm madly in love with. I respond to its gentle command and open my eyes.

Chapter 49

Forgive

Panels that house fluorescent light come into focus as I hear the most vehement sigh of relief in all my history. The sigh is followed by sobs that this particular grown man has rarely made me privy to. I try to say his name, but my vocal cords refuse. I don't know why he's crying so. My head is splitting, and there is a horribly incessant beep nearby.

"Don't talk, Paige. You're on a ventilator. I'll get someone to take it out." Mark uses an intercom button to call for a nurse. Then he stares into my eyes as if he's never seen something so remarkable. "I don't even know if you recognize me. They said you could have a lot of brain damage. You had swelling, and they induced a coma. You slept a long time, Cinderella. Maybe I should start calling you 'Sleeping Beauty.'"

I reply to this by finding his hand with mine and squeezing with all my might, which turns out to be not so much. He understands, which brings another sigh and more tears.

"They thought. . .But I knew you were there. I *knew* it." He kisses my hand over and over, and then I bring it to his face to comfort him. He probably thinks it's odd, but I know I've received a lot more comfort than he has recently.

Shortly after this, I bring my hand up to my own head, wrapped in gauze. I realize that I'm not able to move my left shoulder, and touch it, as well, only to be met with pain.

"Don't worry. It will heal. They didn't know if you could see and they said you wouldn't remember what happened. I hope you don't," Mark is flooding me with information. I know he's doing his own preliminary evaluation of my mind. The real neurologist happens to be our brother-in-law, who enters the room with a nurse as Mark is talking.

Dave looks at me to see the fond recognition in my eyes. "Well, Mark. It looks like husband trumps doctor this time. Let's get that tube out to be sure." I gag as the nurse that accompanies Dave pulls a tube from my throat. She hands me water before I can speak. I take a large drink and wonder how long it's been since I've done so.

Mark scoots his chair over to let Dave sit on my hospital bed next to me. There is an out-of-place bounce in Dave's step and a smile that my being awake does not fully cover. His mood reminds me of watching him lift Maureen into an embrace a million Valentine's Days ago. I marvel until he shines a painful light in my eyes and starts to ask me a series of questions. "Okay, what is your full name?"

"Paige Catherine Henley." My throat is raw, and it is almost excruciating to talk. But because of the look of wonder on Mark's face, I've never been happier to do it.

Dave gestures to Mark, "His name?"

"Mark Ernesto Henley. My husband." Though the word does him no justice, Mark smiles at it, nodding.

"Excellent. Fifty-two minus sixteen?"

I laugh. "You know I don't 'math.' I saw her, Dave. She looks beautiful."

"You might not want to tell your neurologist you are seeing ghosts after a three-day coma." Dave winces momentarily but remains professional.

"She said it would only be a moment." At this vague memory of a dream, Dave falters.

"How did you know that? I need you to focus. You sustained some serious injuries. Do you remember under what circumstances?"

"How did I know what?" I ignore his interrogation.

"I've never told anyone the last thing I said to her. That was it. That it's all only a moment and we'd be together soon. Didn't realize how relative that was at the time." Dave is now distracting himself by poking each of my fingers and toes with a pen until I react.

"Interesting," I speak as the psychologist I've become, and give Dave a look that convinces him.

"Every time one of you gets a head injury, she shows up. Anyone got a two-by-four handy? What else did she say?" Now he's curious. And I suddenly have a revelation in a smile, inferring and translating a message.

"She alluded to the fact that I should be okay with it if you move on. Isn't that what you wanted to run by me when you had to leave the party?" I smile and draw out the name dramatically. "Eva?"

"What about her?" Dave tries to pretend to not understand. But there is something hidden in the way he says 'her.' More than a substitute for a colleague's name. More like the way Dillon might refer to Angela's hair. Or Lane to Heather's singing voice. Or Mark to my tattoo. And my husband tucks his lips and remains silent, though he sees that I've heard the anomaly.

"I'm pretty sure Maureen wouldn't mind. I mean, I'm sure you still love her. So do I. Agape is funny like that. But *eros* is a bit easier when the woman has a pulse. I'm pretty sure you'd agree that for the past several years, Dr. Moreno has been aging quite well?"

"Quite well, indeed." Dave chuckles. Conceding far too easily. And Mark laughs too. Which tells me I slept through something.

"Why are you so smiley and happy, Dave?" Though I'm feeling a bit loopy and finding no reason not to smile.

"You are such a shrink!" Mark can hardly contain his joy.

"But before you continue in my session, minion of my late wife, I need to see what memories you've retained. Long-term memory seems intact, but I want to see if we hit a snag somewhere." Dave tries quickly to regain his professionalism.

"Sorry. Go on. I'll be good."

Dave clears his throat. "Do you remember why you're here?"

I close my eyes a moment to recall a memory, then open my eyes and strain them against the sun that streams inside. My mind is blank, just before a flood of terror returns in only seconds. I gasp.

"Darian! Where is my Darian?!" I become frantic, searching the sterile room for signs of my son. This, because my last memory is how he collapsed helplessly onto the stairs.

"I hoped you wouldn't remember." Mark seems crushed at the thought, and his gaze drops to the floor in his defeat.

"I need to know. Please. Maureen wouldn't tell me. She wouldn't. . .Mark, please just tell me." I begin to cry, and my breath leaves me as if I haven't used my own breath in days.

Mark shushes me, and Dave stands back from me in disbelief. Then his mind formulates another question, "Did you see Darian too? While you were comatose?"

"No," I remember, "But I feel like I heard his voice. But it looked like Maureen. Strange dream. . .And that beeping!"

"Well, that seems right." Mark smiles as he says this.

"Why does that seem right?"

The door opens, and Mia and Robbie see me and immediately shed away all customary preteen inhibitions. They jump onto my bed with mountains of hugs and kisses. They are both talking at once about how they came and talked to me. I remember the strange voices of Maureen and my father in the woods. These things are now explained. I am now aware that Darian must have been here too.

"You got found!" I see Darian run to me—a sling on this left shoulder, just like mine. My dad is right behind him. "I knew you weren't too lost. I prayed, and God told me you were just lost. But you got found! And we match, see?"

I hold tight to him, sobbing into his tiny shoulder. In my ear, I hear whispered by my husband, "He doesn't remember, don't worry."

Now I'm sharing an ice cream cone with my family and even a timid version of Eva Moreno. All of them, save Lane and Heather, arrive to see me awake. My two dads are tearing up as I tell them about my dream. But my memories return in short uncomfortable bursts, and I interrupt myself.

"Lane and Heather! I was supposed to meet with them. Are they okay? And you were going to call me, Dave. Gosh, I'm not doing any good in this bed, am I?" I fret, frustrated.

"You think she's ready, Dr. Dave? 'Neurologically'?" Mark mocks.

"I think she can handle it," Dave says before retrieving a tablet from Eva's hands with a curiously loving smile. He fiddles with it, and I allow the words.

"Wow, what is going *on* between you two? And could you stop screaming about it? I mean, please tell me. With words." I demand, and they all laugh.

Dave chuckles. "Patience, junior Shrink."

Dave continues to tap at the screen, Eva rising to help him, while Mark speaks.

"This all made us think, you know. Lane said you mentioned life is fickle and love is the most important thing. When they told us you may or may not wake up or remember us or be yourself, it refocused us. And we wanted you, if you did wake up, to know we take your counsel to heart." Mark prefaces what I assume is a video that Dave hands me on his tablet.

I smile when I see Lane and Heather halfway through singing the same song they sang the other day at church before I spoke with them. Everyone is singing along, worshipping together in this very room. I had *heard* them singing it in a dream.

What can make me whole again? Nothing but the blood of Jesus.

I see I am hooked up to all manner of tubes. But they seem joyous regardless. After the song is over and I'm already in tears over the private concert I've always been refused, I realize that Eva is holding the camera when she says, "I have the video going. You ready?" To Dillon, I see, when he reacts by standing.

Lane sighs and sets his guitar aside. He and Heather stand. And when the young couple joins hands, I gasp. I watch in flowing tears as Dillon performs a short little wedding ceremony. When the couple kisses, the room erupts in joy, both in life and on video. They sign their license, then, just as they are about to bolt out the door, Dave stops his son with a word. "Wait."

I begin to comment on my wonder of the ever-impulsive Lane as I watch his eyes roll on screen.

"You owe me ten bucks. Which I owe Maureen. Seven years almost to the day. . ." I smile at my husband. But he doesn't owe me a cent. The last ten dollars anyone in the family exchanged was placed in Maureen's hands by her father just before we put her in the ground. We make bets now just to remember her.

"Shhh, keep watching." Mark whispers. I watch again, and the room around me is in a forced sort of hush. The video jostles around a bit as Robbie takes the tablet from Eva.

Eva appears on the screen in a lovely little pink dress. And when Pastor Dad stands and Dave and Eva join hands, I am not the only person to gasp. The whole videoed room erupts in disbelief, and the live version laughs at the hindsight of the video. I am in bewildered shock as I watch Pastor Dad perform a marriage ceremony between his son-in-law and "the other woman." But the ceremony does not distance Dave from the family. No. I watch as a hundred versions of "It's about time" are tossed around on video. And Eva becomes one of us.

The video ends just after my Robbie turns the device around, giving the camera a dramatic face of confusion. Dave takes the tablet from me. And Eva approaches, showing me a sparkle on a hand that had never thought it possible.

"This was yesterday?" I confirm.

"Yeah," Mark mumbles.

"I don't know if I'm okay with this." I laugh, scolding Dave and Eva.

"Paige," Mark begs against what he perceives as insensitive.

"Boss, they got married and went to *work* the next day. White coats and everything." I shake my head. They chuckle in relief.

"I'm sorry we didn't tell you," she starts. But I interrupt her with a hug.

"How long have you two been dating behind our backs?" I tap her still timid arm and look up at the proud and relieved Dave.

"That's a tough question," Dave answers. "Eva helped me *survive* work after. . ."

"But I was only a friend." Eva translates when Dave falters a little. "Dr. Little was mourning his wife. You must understand that I respected that line. I was in a bad place all those years ago when I ignored that line. I am grateful for Maureen's forgiveness."

"Then I stopped sabotaging the schedule, and we started being on call at the same time, and there is always an OB patient in the ER So, whenever I was called in, we would talk." David goes on.

"Then it was phone conversations. And then coffee. Supper." Dr. Moreno bites her lip. "We started to try out every restaurant in town."

"And then Eva wanted to see this show, and I took her."

"Oh, off-Broadway?" I ask.

Dave clears his throat. "*On* Broadway. In New York. We had separate rooms and everything, don't worry. We did every time we traveled. We were still just friends."

I gasp. "All that time, I thought you were going alone." Then smile. "How is that not dating, Dave?"

Eva answers, "It honestly wasn't. We enjoyed each other's company. When not at work, we were alone. Being together was. . ."

"Almost exactly the point in marriage?" I giggle.

Dave chuckles. "Right. So, this has been going on for a couple of years. We coordinate our vacation time and just go somewhere together. It's been healing for me. Then the other day, when this happened with you, we were all reeling, Paige. It hit us all that we were doing things you'd advise us against. I saw clearly that I wasn't being fair to Eva. She's been my best friend, but I was keeping her at a distance, thinking Maureen would smite me if I fell in love with my mistress again."

"But she's always loved you, Dave." I wink at Eva's coy smile. "And you've loved her for a few years, too. Whether or not you admitted it."

"I was taking what I could get and giving what he'd take. Like always." Eva sighs. "Traveling with him as friends has been wonderful."

"But the other day, I went to Eva and told her that I canceled our second room for the next trip. Bought this ring instead." Dave smirked. "And yesterday we crashed Lane's wedding."

"Dr. Little!" Eva scolds, already very much his wife. Then she turns to me. "Lane was aware. He was happy. He's been calling me Dr. Mom for days."

"And begging me to marry her for *years*. He's known about all the trips and everything. But to answer your question, we *weren't* dating. Last night was the first time we had a meal together as something other than friends. In twenty years, at least." Dave reaches over and squeezes Eva's hand. Nearly in tears. It is soul-cleansing to see him smile like this.

Almost on cue, I hear what sounds like the breathless laughter of two singers barreling into the room. Lane, setting Heather down from his back, the two caught in some red-faced funny we all missed. They can't even squeak the repeat of the punch line to each other, and almost forget they've entered a room busting at the seams with people and a relative reawakened. But I need not to have heard the symptom of the laughter to know its source. Years and questions and anxiety lifted from their shoulders, leaving them twenty times lighter than any worries that may arise. In case I might start to think I'm experiencing it alone, Mark kisses my hand and winks at me.

Fully grown Romeo finally comes to, and turns to me. "Aunt Paige! You woke up!"

"So did you, I'm told." I can't help but share in Lane's rampant smiles. "In which case, what are you two doing *here*? You guys are *all* breaking the rules."

Heather drops to her knees at Darian's side, giving him a teddy bear with glasses. Telling him she's glad they are cousins, and she hopes he gets better soon. *"So precious. I Love that girl."* The words of a past encounter echo in my soul.

"Where else would we be?" Lane laughs, confused.

"Somewhere far away with your phones off?" Dillon teases. Sounding like some mix between Pastor Dad and Dave.

"And miss *this* call?" Lane punches Dillon's arm, having inherited Dave's stature over Dillon. "Seriously, though. We're too poor for a honeymoon right now. Just *life* together is plenty for us. I'm sure you know this, but you were right,

Aunt Paige. Now to find a place to live other than in my childhood bedroom at my dad's house."

Dave delivers a similar shoulder punch to his younger son.

"Ow, Dad! What?" Lane asks, annoyed.

"*Poor?* Come on, your college fund, which I've been filling most of your life, covers the schooling. Maybe you don't have cash to spare after that, but I'm your dad. You know I can and *will* send you to any corner of the world with your bride, Lane. Come on." Dave is hurt, I can tell. Always at odds with his son.

"For real?"

"Yes! For real." Dave chuckles. Then Dave looks to Eva, who nods. "Also, Lane, the house. Mom chose that house and everything in it. She's everywhere. She even paid the thing off with her life insurance, which is why I can't bring myself to sell it. But I also can't bring myself to live in it as of yesterday. I'm moving in with Eva. The house is yours, Lane."

"Dad, we live in a five thousand square foot custom home in a gated community." Lane crosses his arms. Overwhelmed.

"*You* do. I live in a townhome with a view a mile from this hospital. You'll need a place you can raise the dozen kids you two want on the salary of a worship leader." Dave smirks.

"Dr. Little, that's like *extremely* generous." Heather starts. "Are you sure?"

"Positive. And you should call me Dad or Dave or something, Heather." Dave chuckles.

I giggle. "So, Dave? You two are *only* forty five. Are there more nieces and nephews in my future?"

Eva smirks. "If God wills it."

Dave rolls his eyes, smiling at his new wife. "She means yes. Probably through adoption. We've visited a few countries in the past few years that put that on our hearts as individuals. Now we're together, so we want to do it. Possibly one of our own, also. Eva has always wanted children of her own and has spent decades helping people become parents. One way or another, I'm making it happen for her."

Dillon laughs a little. "My children would have uncles and aunts younger than them."

"I worry that I messed up the first batch, especially the past few years, so. . ." Dave begins.

"Shut up, Dad. You did fine." Lane laughs and embraces his father in severe gratitude, which I haven't seen in years.

Then Lane embraces me, thanking me for good counsel.

"Oh, Robbie!" He exclaims, rising and searching through all his pockets frantically. Lane's new wife watches his distress a moment, then giggles as she places something in his hand. His smile lingers a moment, then he remembers his mission and turns to my son in confidence, holding up a scratched, scuffed, tried, and true piece of silver jewelry. I'm blessed my ears are close to the heart to heart and the explanation of something I always thought I understood.

"My mom gave this to your dad when he was about your age. They had lost their mom, and she wanted to remind him that no matter how hard life is or who we lose, we need to remember to grow in Christ. My mom was pregnant with my brother then, out of wedlock. But she had a good godly man, even without purity. Us guys, we make mistakes. But we are the only thing God can use to make men of God.

"This isn't *just* a purity ring. When he put this on, your dad made a promise to God that he'd allow God to move in his life and *grow* him into being a man of God. He messed up sometimes, Robbie. But he became a man of God. Next, he promised he would grow *fond* of God's Word and His promises. So that they were more comfortable and natural than sin. And then he promised he'd one day get married and teach his son to do the same thing. But when your parents got married, Dr. Mom over here told them you'd never get to be born. So, your dad gave this to Dillon. Who gave it to me. And now it's yours to grow into. Obviously, even though we've been passing it around when we get married, you have to continue to grow long after you grow out of purity and become a husband. Being a man of God is a *huge* responsibility, Rob. And there seriously aren't enough of us. There are bad dudes that do bad things. But I'm entrusting *this* responsibility to you. Grow into it. Grow fond of it. Then grow out of it. *None* of that is easy."

Robbie, looking into the unleashed lions of eyes that are his mentor, sets aside disrespect and humor, as are his normal way. He has changed in these few days and asks a question. "But is it worth it?"

Lane gets a half smile on his face, glancing at Heather. "There's nothing else that *is*."

Heather, Eva, Angela, Mia and Olivia are all chatting and giggling away in the corner, generations of women admiring Heather's new ring. Heather and Eva, who had become a mother and daughter all at once, giggling about the wedding they shared. But Robbie only looks at them a moment. What he sees as he slides the slightly too big ring onto his future wedding finger is the way his own father kisses my head despite years, pain, and all the things he's lost.

After a while, most of the family leaves so I can recoup. But more importantly, Mark asked both of our dads to stay while he reveals to me the business with which my soul is truly concerned.

"They ruled it a suicide to make my life and their paperwork easier. But in reality, he only pulled the trigger because *I* did. A reflex. They were telling me I did the right thing. That he was a monster. But I'm still not sure how I'll get over taking someone's life. I don't think we're ever meant to hate someone that much." Mark carries with him the most profound sorrow I've seen in him as he says this.

"You won't get over it, Boss." I whisper, turn to him, touch his face. "And you shouldn't." My throat is sore from the intubation, but my spirit has been seeking Mark's counsel for days. And though I know he was well aware of God's presence, I don't know whose counsel *he* sought. I choose to take my counseling cue from the demeanor of our elders. Silence is often the best type of counsel.

After a time I use to consider deeply a question I don't know why I'm asking, I inhale. Unsure of the tone of my own voice as it will escape, and unsure of its reception, I trust the still small voice that instructs me.

"What are they doing with Jake? With his remains? I read his mom's obituary a few years ago while he was in prison. He didn't have anyone else." A scratchy tone.

"No one has come to claim the remains yet. He's already scheduled to be cremated for a state-funded burial. Potter's field." Mark has the information at the ready, which I hadn't expected. "I already asked."

The combination of physical pain, emotional devastation, and pain meds make my next question come out with streaking tears. "Can we—?"

"I thought you'd ask. Darian doesn't remember or at least doesn't understand what happened. But he says he had a dream about you. He only told me because he was asking why you said something to a strange man he didn't know."

"And what's that?"

"He told me you *forgave* him. And told him about Jesus." Mark seems within a revelation.

I nod, using the tissues Pastor Dad hands me. My multitude of tears and sore throat will not allow more than the nod.

"Dr. Henley, you amaze me. You move people, change lives, even when you are asleep. Even if you hadn't pulled through, Darian's last memory of you would have been *forgiveness*. Yes. We can *absolutely* bury Jake. I know you *need* to. And so do I." My husband and favorite human kisses my hand once again, happy I'm alive. Which makes two of us.

"I know a place, Sweet Pea. A good spot for him." My father pipes in. My pastor seemingly understands, evident in his solemn nod.

"Dee, it's not your fault. You've raised her the best you could."

"So why is she acting out? And my husband just says to let her be. And he's wonderful, don't get me wrong. But he doesn't understand why I'm desperate enough to seek counsel."

"Thirteen is a tough year. My Robbie is about that age. The Holy Spirit will move in her, Dee. The way *He* wants to. Just keep praying."

"Paige, is this my punishment for being so awful to you all those years ago? It's just my luck I'd get paired with you for counseling."

"Dee, we were kids. We both made a lot of mistakes back then. At least your heart was in the right place. You've been forgiven, Dee. It's not a punishment. However, you do get another chance to get it right. Don't waste that on anything but grace."

After the sense of coming full circle this Friday afternoon, I walk into the foyer to meet my family. It is weeks after my release from the hospital. Velma, Mark decided, was the only fitting vehicle to transport us to the mountains. To my father's cabin, where we will bury Jake.

I manage to withhold from the situation my emotion, since my children are present. Robbie and Mia understand how I could have known another man besides their father. Darian retains his innocence, and I do not see a need to destroy it. As is fitting for a funeral, the skies open up with a light mountain rain. Sweet against our noses and adding to the music of the nearby stream.

Much of the church staff is present in support of my family and myself. But one in particular remembers my fated flight across the parking lot so many years ago. Ruth Silverman, who still stands at the information booth day after day, warmly greeting me with a face I still feel like I've always known.

My father-in-law speaks a few words. I do not. Jake had rattled like stones in my soul for far too many years. And today I release them by burying ashes in dust. Forgiving him fully. Feeling free.

And yet a part of me wishes Maureen was alive so I could keep my promise. She had promised me, should I ever forgive Jake, the full name of that man who'd stolen my innocence at the age of twelve, just a mile from where my feet are planted now. If she ever knew it, it died with her.

Jake is lowered by my own hands. My own muddied black pants and heels. He is buried, and we congregate in the tiny solemnity of my father's cabin. Hot cocoa in the making from his wood burning stove. Mark and I sit against a wall, our children around us, forming a circle the children fill with laughter and peace.

Suddenly Dave approaches, and reaches into his inside coat pocket. He crouches to my level and hands me an envelope.

"What's this?" I assume it is another 'head case' he's referring to me from the hospital. Until he speaks cryptically.

"I made her a promise. I bet she thought I'd forget. But I didn't. She told me to give this to you. But only when—well, you'll see." Dave stands again and begins to walk away.

"Where's Eva?" I ask before he gets away from me.

"She's on her way. She was feeling a little under the weather today." Dave winks, then puts a finger to his lips at my gasp. Then he walks off, stopping to say something to Ruth before he exits the cabin.

My family inquires of the letter in various maturity levels and tones. Mark sends the children off to help their grandpa with hot cocoa and then scoots closer to me so he can read what Dave has written.

The front of the envelope says: *From Maureen to Paige, when the time comes.* In doctor's chicken scratch. I open it slowly, and there are two sheets of paper. Both, I quickly see, contain the calligraphic handwriting of the classiest and most put together of women. Years ago, I'd have thought nothing of it when she handed me a draft to approve or a card to sign. But today, I'm immediately brought to tears just at the handwriting. And I know she would never have written something meaningless.

"Paige,

If you are reading this, two things have happened. I am in Heaven, walking with Jesus. And either my David left this to you in his will, or you have finally decided to take my advice and forgive Jake. How does it feel? Free? Almost, right? Because you know that you could feel freer if you could forgive someone else, too.

Well, don't hate me. But years ago, when you told me the details and I told you I'd find him? I did. I was pretty proud that I found him with just 'To My Beloved Richie' in a compass to go on. I swear, I only broke a couple laws to do it. When I did, it blew me away. I didn't believe it for a while. And then I confirmed it. I hope that you are still young and that you can have this information before you regret never knowing. On the next page is the name of the man that hurt you when you were twelve. Do what you will with that information. But you know my suggestion.

I'm gone. But I know you, still. I bet you are a great wife, still married to that crazy brother of mine. A great mother to those three babies. And I know that you didn't leave my boys without the nagging and loving voice of a woman to help guide them.

You are better than I could have ever been. Simply because you'd never admit it. I love you. It'll only be a moment, so don't spend it missing me. It's all only a moment.

Your sister. Your friend. Your counselor. Your apprentice.
Maureen (Mrs. Shrink)"

I spend the next few moments in the deepest of tears I've cried today. I look up to see that Ruth is approaching, and try to pull myself together in time for her to arrive. Then I realize I still have another paper to read. And my heart lurches as my Spirit moves to my fingers, forcing me to turn to it.

"His name is Richard Silverman. He was married once for ten years. Then he got divorced. And now he is deceased. He took his own life about an hour after he hurt you. He left what

little he had, including a cabin near your dad's, to his ex-wife.
Her name is Ruth."

I look up into her face and lose myself completely. I remember the pain. The panic. The fear of that cabin. And then I remember peace. Solace. The wholeness I've always shared in the foyer with Ruth. And I wonder, how could she have been married to such a cruel man? And had she ever known about me?

She does the best she can in consideration of her age to lower herself to my level and sit with my husband and me. Mark is also speechless with tears. Ruth simply stretches out her hand.

"Walk with me?"

I muster a nod and I think Mark tells me he'll be along shortly. But I'm not concerned with Mark. Or my children or either of our fathers. As Maureen had told me, at this moment, all I want to do is follow a woman where I know she'll take me. The place I never thought I'd want so ardently to return.

We walk arm in arm in the night to the music of the stream beside us, the leaves half damp half crunching beneath us. I contain my tears after a time. And I pray for courage. Instead, I receive the still, hollow and familiar voice through the darkness.

"I was young. Seventeen when I married him. That was my excuse for a lot of years. When I was young, he was charming. Passionate. Devilishly handsome. I thought he was perfect. But in the years since Richard, I've learned never to trust those things on their own. Charm is fleeting. Passion can turn to anger. And looks blend into the mundane things of life after enough years. But still I never found someone I loved quite as much. He didn't show me like he should, and he certainly had his flaws, but I do think he loved me."

I've always loved the careful tone and cadence of Ruth's voice. The way it carries itself inside my heart as a welcome guest.

"I was married to him for ten years. I knew him for a month before we ran off together against the will of my parents. For that month, he was perfect. Then I discovered he was mentally ill and hated his medication. And for ten years he found an excuse every day to hurt me in some way. I'd, in turn, come up with excuses to hate myself. Lies to tell people to protect Richard. I protected him those ten years. Even after I endured three miscarriages at his hands. I never had children because of him. And I tried so hard to tell him about Jesus. Tell him God could give him direction. But he didn't think God could speak to him because of all the wrong he'd done. On our tenth anniversary, I gave him that compass with that inscription. It wasn't from me, Paige. I wanted him to know that he was loved by God. That same day, I left him and never looked back."

I nod in silence, remembering Jake so much more clearly. And I stop, my heart startling when we reach a clearing. And there, in plain sight from the stream, is a tiny cabin. My memories had placed it much further into the woods. Into the darkness. Ruth allows my heart's hesitation with her silent stillness. And then we take a few steps. And I nearly step into a hole, treacherous now from erosion, I'd also placed much further into the woods. The hole that broke my ankle. As if it had all occurred last week.

I look to Ruth to apologize for stopping again. But when I see her tears, I know there is no need. Her tears make me want to heal her. And thus, they make me stronger. Strong enough to walk with her, even to the door of the little cabin. Here, she stops and speaks.

"Twenty-five years after the divorce, I got a call that Richard had died. He'd left me the cabin he'd been living in for the past ten years. I had no ties to it. So, I came up here to see it right away. I still own it. Keep it up. Visit every now and again, remembering that month when he loved me so well. Please, won't you come in with me?"

I gasp at the thought. But trust Ruth with my whole heart. She knows my every secret as well as the foyer at church. She watched me fall in love. Get married. She watched babies grow inside me. And she's watched me raise them thus far. Any memory, no matter how painful, is easily forsaken by the trust of a sister in Christ. I nod and let her lead me inside.

The cabin is just how I remember it. And it is just the opposite. The worn sofa by the door. The faint smell of cigarettes. The table where Richard had placed a gun to face me so I didn't run. Instead of that gun is a single glittery shoe. I'd thrown away its mate decades ago. And instead of the fire crackling beneath the stone mantel, I see that a simple brass urn is atop it. I stand near the door, unwilling to venture further.

Ruth moves to a desk not included in my memories that is against the far wall. She opens the drawer and returns to me, handing me an envelope.

"This is what I found when I came here the very first time." She is fighting tears, and so am I, when I take the envelope and open it. A letter, wrinkled and tearing at the folded seams. Written quickly. I read it, not hesitating long enough, I decide. But not until after I know why.

"Ruthie,

She is twelve. Just twelve. Lovely red hair. I gave her that compass to find her way home, because it never worked for me. I ruined her life, just like I ruined yours. But because you are better than my best days in our first month, I need you to take care of her. Find her and look after her. Don't let her hate herself because of me. Tell her God loves her, if you ever get the chance. Just like you told me. I broke His heart today. But Ruthie, I loved Him. Please tell that sweet girl that the last thing I ever was. . .was sorry.

Richie."

Though my vision is dim with the tears and the one light bulb illuminating the cabin, I look into the envelope and find a lock of my own hair I never knew I was missing. I'd carried him with me. But he'd carried me with him, as well. I fall to my knees in tears, and Ruth speaks.

"I worked at a drug store around this time. For about five years total. I figured finding this little girl would be like finding a needle in a world of haystacks. So, I promised God that I would dedicate my life to praying for the very next redheaded girl of the correct age that came into that drugstore, because I didn't know what else to do. It took two years, can you believe that? To find a girl the right age. And as it turns out, the girl I began to pray for needed my prayers.

"She came in with a lot of different boys. Buying things she shouldn't have had knowledge of at her age. So, I prayed. After a few years, this girl started coming in alone. Leaving a very nasty looking blond boy in the car smoking. She would buy the kind of things I used to buy when I was married to Richard. Lie the same lies. So, I knew she was making the same excuses to hate herself. The day she came in for a pregnancy test, I knew that prayer was not enough. I had to speak. I had to tell her that she had Someone that loved her far better than any boy."

"You told me God loved me. Ruth, that was the first time I'd ever heard that. I didn't know that was *you*." I sob once.

Then my tears cease in the realization of who Ruth was. Why she's always seemed familiar to me. But I'd never asked, knowing if she knew me before I knew Jesus, she probably knew much more than even I would admit. Now, as my suspicions are confirmed, I am in awe of God's power even before Ruth gives me an increasingly profound reason for it.

"It broke my heart when you didn't believe me. So, I quit my job. Told God I was done praying for you, because you were just some coincidental red headed teenager anyway. Pastor Robert paid me to do the volunteer work I'd always been doing at church. But to do it full-time, like I do now. I got my eyes fixed and changed my hair. I felt free, Paige. But God certainly made it clear that I wasn't. You came running in that church, like you were running right back into my keeping. So, I was obedient again. And prayed for you.

"I loved you like my own child. I'd pray for outlandish things. That you'd marry the man of your dreams and he'd never hurt you and that he'd give you beautiful children. That you'd reach out and help other people like us. All the things I'd never gotten to do myself. Then one day I looked over at your little table and saw that compass I'd given my Richie. The one he said he'd given to *you*. I saw that God is good. For sending me the right girl to pray for. So, I kept praying. But you were so broken. And I wasn't sure if you'd ever forgive yourself. Ever stop hating.

"Then one day Maureen told me they were going to give you a job. When you met Mark, it was the most beautiful thing I'd ever seen. But God didn't stop at beautiful. I watched Mark grow up, Paige. He is still, to this day, the kindest man I've ever known. He'd never looked twice at a girl. Then after just a short time working with you, everyone in the church would know when you left for the day. Mark would practically fall to his knees and tell the person nearest him that he was going to marry you. Usually, that person was me. God was so faithful to the prayers I'd prayed to have someone treasure you the way Mark does.

"The day Maureen discovered that it was my Richard who hurt you, she was determined to convince you to forgive him. Which was something else I'd been praying for since long before we ever met."

"Ruth," I stop her. Astounded, overwhelmed by the revelations. But more than anything, grateful for the power and mercy and glory of my Father in Heaven. "Thank you for prayers. I bet that's all I had sometimes. You are incredible. And I can never thank you enough."

I stand, finally receiving the courage I'd asked God for on the walk over. I walk to the edge of the same sofa I remember in cold sweats and anesthesia induced dreams. I bend to my knees, my elbows on the sofa. I read Richard's suicide note again. And then I speak.

"Richard. Richie. God's *beloved.* I've blamed you my whole life for all the pain I caused myself and everyone around me. But that isn't fair. We both deserved eternal death. Life is only of Jesus Christ, our Savior. I think you knew that. But even if you didn't, I *forgive* you."

I sob with Ruth for just long enough to feel the burden lift. And finally feel light enough to breathe on my own. How, I wonder, have I breathed for the past twenty-two years?

My heart lurches. "Ruth, I'm so sorry. Mark threw the compass into the ocean during our honeymoon. If I'd known, I'd have returned it instead."

Ruth sighs. "Oh, Paige. Mark needed to drown that compass more than I ever needed it back. Did you ever think that you weren't the only one who needed to forgive Richard for what he did? You were Mark's *bride*. Half of his own flesh, Paige. It was like Richard violated *him*, too. I'm surprised it only took until your honeymoon to forgive him."

I sniffle. Hating that I hated for so long. Then I smile. "Well, that's Mark for you."

We walk out of the cabin, and are greeted by three men. My father, my beloved pastor and my husband. My husband offers my favorite place as comfort. His arms. Unexpectedly, Pastor Dad clears his throat.

"Paige, have you ever been baptized?"

"No. Baptism is a public symbol of submission to God. I guess I always knew I was holding back something." I smile. "Why?"

"Well, it's not a requirement to enter the Kingdom of Heaven. It is, however, quite a nice illustration of how Jesus's blood *washes* our sins away. I love baptisms." Pastor Dad explains.

"Right." I nod, and see that everyone is smiling at me. "What?"

I hear more rustling in the trees and see that Dillon and Angela are arriving with the children. All of them. And that Lane is walking hand in hand with his new wife, with a guitar strapped to his back. Dave and Eva follow; also hand in hand. They are all members of some loop that I've yet to realize. I know just what it is when I look at their hands. I see a towel in Robbie's hands. A little bag I use for overnight conferences over Mia's shoulder. And I see that Dillon, *Pastor* Dillon has brought a Bible.

"What do you say, Cinderella?"

I look up into the eyes that have granted me love, peace and unconditional acceptance. And I marvel that even Mark can only ever be a distant echo of God's affection for me. I have forgiven, because He first forgave me. I want to be immersed in icy water. Because He washed me with something far costlier.

My hair, still drying this evening, drapes over my shoulders, cascades down my back until it meets the sheet beneath my folded legs. I take in the silence of the night, wondering how the peace I've merely tasted in my life now finds me fully in the most ordinary of places. In darkness, even.

"Lord, kiss Darian for Paige and me. And comfort my wife as she cries for him. Amen." Even the cello is an intrusion into the peace. He speaks to our nightly ritual. Something we've done our whole marriage. The symptom relief his arms have always provided. But my heart now floats above those things, released from their chains. Cured at the source. And now able to enjoy them all as the abundant blessings they are.

I smile, because I want my most beloved companion to know it too. "Why would I do that? He's in the next room."

Mark sits up almost in a start. But our years and our fusion do not require the words. He only smiles and pretends he hasn't been praying for the effects of the cure for well over a decade. Surrendered a compass to the ocean, and tested the outer limits of his patience.

"Well then go kiss him yourself." He playfully hits me with a stray accent pillow at the end of the bed. I comply as I giggle.

I leave a crack in Darian's door and see that my children are still choosing to bunk in the same room even weeks after the traumatic event when I was in the hospital. I step over the charming and now appreciative young man who had held the family together when they thought they'd lose me. His new purity ring creates a glimmer, even in the darkness. I stroke once the crimson innocence of my daughter's hair that I'll fight for until my death. Then I join the tiny seven-year-old on the twin size bed, collapsing his yellow comforter under the weight of my arm. I thank God for Darian. Not as symptom relief or because he's every definition of a miracle baby, or even because the bullet from my past spared all but the shoulder that will heal beautifully. Just for him. For who he is. And who he'll become. As if nothing ever happened before today.

The tears come, not from anguish. But from gratitude. From the new depths of love I've found outside my cage. Darian stirs.

"Mommy? Are you sad? Don't be sad, Mommy. I love you and Jesus does too," He mumbles, eyes still shut tight. Wisdom leaking even from the clutches of sleep.

"I know, baby." I sniffle. Stroke the stark blond hair. And smile. "I'm not sad anymore."

His name means "upholder of the good." And that's why he is special. The world may shake him. Hurt him. Try to destroy him. But they can never take his truth, humility, his love for what is good. This, on its own, is beautiful. But Maureen had known that he got it straight from me. I'd never lost it, because who can lose what is in the hands of Christ from the start? Goodness is only possible through Christ. And through Christ, grace covers anything else. I close my eyes to sever the tear, and hold tight to what God gave me that I least deserved. Innocence. In a world set to destroy it.

There are things, I now know, that should never be said aloud. Suddenly I understand my source of pain. Maureen had never lacked words, unless it was with willful intent. As I'd removed my shoes to step to the water's edge I'd realized that she had wanted me to forgive Jake so I'd want to forgive Richard. And Richard? So I could finally forgive myself, the way that Christ did long ago.

The water was frigid. But I was almost unaware as Pastor Dad, Pastor Dillon, my father, and Mark all lowered me into the stream. Baptizing me in the name of the Father, the Son and the Holy Spirit, as Lane played my favorite song.

Oh precious is the flow that makes me white as snow.
No other fount I know
Nothing but the blood of Jesus

Counsel is not meant for just words. It cares with eyes I never knew were looking. It hides in a sanctified kiss. Softens in a child's smile. It is in the silence. In an unseasonal snowfall. In brokenness, even. Or in a stream in the woods when hope is most desolate. The stream has haunted my dreams for decades. The sound and constant clarity had been ever present in my worst of memories. I had strayed from it. Found my way back to it alone, or so I thought for many years.

But as I'd opened my wetted eyes to the gentle falling of September snow, I'd known that the stream had never *haunted* me at all. Unless the Holy Spirit haunts the soul. Ever present. Ever loving. Ever Good.

Acknowledgments

Disclaimer (Updated 2026): A traumatic moment or season can change a person, even causing them to be broken and remade. God is faithful to teach us a new song, but we cannot carry many of the old tunes with us. This book was written "before" one of those moments, and these acknowledgments reflect that version of me. However, in reverence for the way that God uses our *whole* journey to shape us, and because even reading them to modify them is simply too painful for me today, I left them intact.

...

First, I want to thank my Kickstarter backers! I told you I was releasing a new book. Sight unseen, you got behind it. Your support meant so much to me that you'll find your name listed here:

Carol Otto
Greg and Ann Kaumeyer
Charlotte Kaumeyer
Melissa Rocha
Ryan and Diana Hutson
Thor and Gail Kaumeyer

I'd also like to thank:

To the babies God gave me that keep growing and growing. I met myself when I met you. I can never begin to deserve you. Thanks for putting up with an imperfect mommy.

My R.J. We've been through a lot of seasons, haven't we? We were practically children when we started out. If someone told me then all the trials we'd face together, I'd have run for the hills. . .with you, of course. Because looking back, I'm grateful for every single one. There's only you.

Rocky Mountain Calvary. My place of worship for many years. Sometimes a writer can invent a mood or an atmosphere. Sometimes they can only begin to describe one. There are too many names and faces and memories and gestures to mention here. But when I walk in your doors, I sigh in relief as if I'm home. Thank you, thank you, thank you.

Niki. For the gorgeous painting, all your encouragement, and your radiant, refreshing innocence.

Melanie. For closing the laptop that summer day in my garage and seeking a tissue. For believing in me.

Emily, Kaitlyn, Brandy, Melanie, Kathleen, Lesley, and many others. My sisters. I wanted a sister my whole life, but instead of giving me one through my parents, God delivered them through marriage and through friendship. Even if we haven't spoken for a time or don't speak as a general rule, if you read this book, you might begin to understand how I love you.

My brothers. You, on the other hand, I got through our parents. For being ridiculously annoying, ugly, stupid faced, finky boys. And for somehow becoming godly men, husbands, and fathers. Thanks.

Dad/Papa. For making lemonade out of lemons, or any other version of that saying you prefer. You are so loved and admired.

Daddy. For pushing too hard. For being too soft. For silly, sarcastic and strict. For showing me the Way.

Brenda. When I was writing this story, I never thought I'd be taking a minute to *thank* you in it. Let's be honest. I would never have had the perspective to write a story about the completeness of God's forgiveness if it hadn't been for you. That is, of course, bittersweet. But that doesn't matter, does it? We are both forgiven by the same Savior. I love you immensely.

Momma. I got a strange assignment my sophomore year of college. I was instructed to ask someone something I'd always wanted to ask them. Reluctantly, and at the last possible minute before the assignment was due, I asked you something. Your answer stayed with me. A few months later, I started this novel. It took quite a few years and divine courage to bloom and grow. But you planted the seed. I love you so, so much and appreciate all you do and who you are. This one is for you.

To the Source of all comfort and the Conqueror of all sin. Lord, these words were worship and healing and strength for me, when I had to walk a tough road my soul didn't understand. I can't wait to spend eternity thanking You and praising You for Your goodness and Your love. There is no greater Counselor.

"In Him we have redemption through His blood the forgiveness of sins, according to the riches of His grace." Ephesians 1:7

To the Forgiven:

This was a tough one to write, and I've spent the last few years trying to convince God that I shouldn't publish it. We can see Who won that battle…

To My Beloved Richie, originally titled "Good Counsel," was my first novel, which I started just after I got married while I was longing for a child. I wrote a page. I'd never written anything longer than a college paper at the time. I took a long break from it when I realized I needed a mother's perspective to finish it. Something that is, indeed, hard-earned and valuable. But if you followed the rules and began at the beginning of this book, you know that this novel didn't spring *only* from the joys and hardships of being a young mom.

When I was pregnant with my third child, I walked through the most difficult time in my life. It was my first encounter with the wickedness of humanity. I, along with those I love most, had been willfully betrayed, and I struggled with forgiveness. The pain eventually channeled into music and writing, and to a Word document I'd written a page of years before. But forgiveness was certainly not a theme in early versions of this story. I couldn't write about that then, because I was angry and unwilling to forgive. Many have said I had the "right" to be angry, and for a time, I said it too.

God prodded me daily to forgive, but I was terrified that I'd be giving up the only thing that proved I was the righteous one in the situation. Because I was. I'd done nothing wrong. But everything in Scripture told me otherwise. Therefore, I submitted to His will and laid down my anger and bitterness before Him. That day, I breathed more deeply and saw more clearly than ever in my life until that point. I saw my own self-righteousness. I saw that the stories of evil in this fallen world were not just stories, and I wanted to reach back in time to change the ones I saw from the outside. That day, I understood the heart of my Redeemer afresh.

Paige's story is everyone's story. The events and relationships in her life can be taken as symbols for the ways we are loved by God, despite our demons.

We are *all* sinners and deserve to die. Yet God saw us at our most broken, and sent his son to save us. Like a pastor finding us in a chapel we didn't deserve to be in.

Jesus Christ, God in human flesh, came to teach us the unconventional Way of His love. Not only did He counsel us, he took our punishment with His own blood. Then He left His work with us sinners—healing a broken world. Like a broken sinner in need of counseling taking over for her counselor after her death.

But He didn't leave us alone. He continually ministers to us through the Holy Spirit. Once covered in Jesus's blood, we are completely absolved. God considers us to be blameless, just as a husband views his beloved bride. Fighting for her honor, even when her sins haunt her and the world tells him the notion is insane. He sanctifies us, makes us holy. Otherwise He could not dwell within us.

It wasn't free or easy. Someone had to die. Someone suffered for our forgiveness. But still we are freely forgiven if we take up residence in Christ.

You are, therefore, never too far from His grace, because in reality, we all are. It is *nothing* for the Light of the world to reach into the darkness to rescue a hurting child.

You are His *Beloved*. You can be redeemed. You can be counseled. You can be healed. There is no sin or shame that is beyond His reach.

Come to Jesus. Wash in His blood. The price has been paid.

Until we meet again,

Rebekah Tyne McKamie

Keep in touch!

Website: http://www.rebekahtynemckamie.com

Facebook: www.facebook.com/rebekahtyne

TikTok: @rebekahtyneauthor

Instagram: @ rebekahspelledlikethebible

Painting by Niki Wyneken